EVERYONE IS CHAR[...]

Betina Krahn

PRAISE FOR . . .

The Book of the Seven Delights

"An abundance of dastardly villains . . . keeps things edgy, while an ancient Greek sex manual adds spice to Krahn's lively romp. Look for her trademark wit, her appealing characters, and a delightful dose of the exotic, just for good measure."
—*Library Journal*

"Betina Krahn's newest release is a reader's seventh heaven . . . If you can buy only one book this summer, choose *The Book of the Seven Delights* by Betina Krahn."
—*A Romance Review*

"Readers who treasure strong female protagonists starring in historical romantic suspense thrillers will take immense delight in Betina Krahn's fabulous late Victorian tale."
—*The Best Reviews*

"Krahn's latest wonderfully creative historical is itself a treasure: an irresistible blend of impeccably crafted characters, an adventure-rich plot set in North Africa, and wickedly dry humor."
—*Booklist* (starred review)

"Krahn's written a book as fast-paced as an Indiana Jones adventure . . . and as sexy and witty as anything she has ever written. This is a book you won't put down and one you'll delight in rereading."
—*Romantic Times BOOKclub* (Top Pick)

The Marriage Test

"With *The Marriage Test*, Krahn has perfected her unique recipe for highly amusing historical romances as she deftly brings together two perfectly-matched protagonists to create a delectable romance most readers will find impossible to resist."
—*Booklist* (starred review)

continued . . .

"The golden pies and savory pasties that Krahn lovingly describes will make even the pickiest eater salivate . . . [A] delicious romance." —*Publishers Weekly*

"Krahn gives the adage 'the way to a man's heart is through his stomach' a whole new meaning in this utterly enchanting, heartwarming keeper. With her unique talent for blending humor, poignancy, and unforgettable characters, Krahn sets a sumptuous banquet for readers to devour with relish. This book will whet your appetite for more of her smart and sexy romances." —*Romantic Times*

"Betina Krahn has done it again. *The Marriage Test*'s plot left me speechless. A weak stomach and delicious food are at the hub of the story . . . You'll feel the heat of the kitchen and smell the exotic spices . . . You're in for a feast." —*Rendezvous*

"Krahn has outdone herself in this funny, sexy, medieval romance, which nicely concludes her Convent of the Brides of Virtue trilogy and will keep readers smiling—and hungry—until the end . . . Whimsical [and] witty." —*Library Journal*

The Wife Test

"[A] witty, rollicking romance . . . Krahn's amusing follow-up to *The Husband Test* quickly blossoms into a bright, exciting adventure." —*Publishers Weekly*

"An absorbing read. Add in Ms. Krahn's unique and witty humor and, once again, she scores a winner with the Convent of the Brides of Virtue series." —*The Best Reviews*

"A delightful romp of a read that delivers joyous wit and comic action." —*BookPage*

"Betina Krahn never disappoints her readers. Her plots are always exciting and unusual. Her characters are always fresh and unique. I thought she couldn't improve on the first book of this series but she has. *The Wife Test* is delightful. This is a 'Don't miss it.'" —*Rendezvous*

and other novels of
Betina Krahn

"Packs the romance punch that fans have come to expect from this bestselling novelist . . . smart, romantic . . . sure to delight readers." —*Milwaukee Journal Sentinel*

"Genuinely funny Elizabethan sexual puns, a strong but believable heroine, and an absorbing story of forbidden love make this an enjoyable read." —*Booklist*

"Spectacular . . . a wonderful reading experience." —*BookBrowser*

"A very amusing medieval romance . . . The story line is humorous, descriptive, and downright entertaining as the lead couple squabbles over everything, including love. Bestselling Betina Krahn shows her incredible skills with this top-rate tale." —*Midwest Book Review*

"Merry, heart-charming . . . Betina Krahn is a treasure among historical writers, and *The Husband Test* is a story to savor." —*BookPage*

"Wonderfully romantic . . . brilliantly written and a joy to read . . . humorous, witty, and original . . . Betina Krahn is talented and gifted. Her writing is superb . . . perfectly charming." —*The Literary Times*

The Book of True Desires

BETINA KRAHN

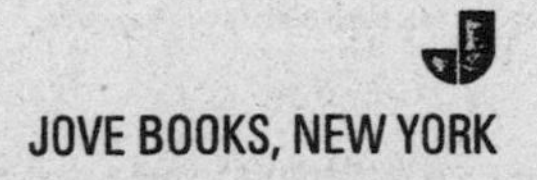
JOVE BOOKS, NEW YORK

THE BERKLEY PUBLISHING GROUP
Published by the Penguin Group
Penguin Group (USA) Inc.
375 Hudson Street, New York, New York 10014, USA
Penguin Group (Canada), 90 Eglinton Avenue East, Suite 700, Toronto, Ontario M4P 2Y3, Canada
(a division of Pearson Penguin Canada Inc.)
Penguin Books Ltd., 80 Strand, London WC2R 0RL, England
Penguin Group Ireland, 25 St. Stephen's Green, Dublin 2, Ireland (a division of Penguin Books Ltd.)
Penguin Group (Australia), 250 Camberwell Road, Camberwell, Victoria 3124, Australia
(a division of Pearson Australia Group Pty. Ltd.)
Penguin Books India Pvt. Ltd., 11 Community Centre, Panchsheel Park, New Delhi—110 017, India
Penguin Group (NZ), Cnr. Airborne and Rosedale Roads, Albany, Auckland 1310, New Zealand
(a division of Pearson New Zealand Ltd.)
Penguin Books (South Africa) (Pty.) Ltd., 24 Sturdee Avenue, Rosebank, Johannesburg 2196, South Africa

Penguin Books Ltd., Registered Offices: 80 Strand, London WC2R 0RL, England

THE BOOK OF TRUE DESIRES

A Jove Book / published by arrangement with the author

PRINTING HISTORY
Jove mass-market edition / September 2006

Cover design by Richard Hasselberger.
Cover illustration by Danny O'Leary.
Handlettering by Iskra Johnson.
Text design by Kristin del Rosario.

For information, address: The Berkley Publishing Group,
a division of Penguin Group (USA) Inc.,
375 Hudson Street, New York, New York 10014.

ISBN: 0-515-14170-4

JOVE®
Jove Books are published by The Berkley Publishing Group,
a division of Penguin Group (USA) Inc.,
375 Hudson Street, New York, New York 10014.
JOVE is a registered trademark of Penguin Group (USA) Inc.
The "J" design is a trademark belonging to Penguin Group (USA) Inc.

PRINTED IN THE UNITED STATES OF AMERICA

10 9 8 7 6 5 4 3 2 1

For Ruth Cohen,
mentor, agent, and friend
through all the stages of my career.
With love.

One

January 1898
Tampa, Florida

The old boys tucked into rocking chairs on the veranda of the exclusive Tampa Bay Hotel inhaled some of their gin-and-tonics as she walked by. Coughing ensued. Nurses hovered. Spectacles were donned.

She was tall enough to be called statuesque, with extravagant curves barely contained by a tailored silk dress with a square neckline that bared enough to make the viewer wish it bared even more. She moved effortlessly down the colonnade, seeming to float above the polished floorboards while she collected the attention of every eye not yet clouded by cataracts and every libido not yet surrendered to age or infirmity.

She seemed to have escaped from Charles Dana Gibson's sketchbook, and it was little wonder. Her bountiful chestnut hair was a single pin away from falling into glorious dishabille . . . her long-waisted gown emphasized the provocative S curve at the small of her back . . . the creamy perfection of her skin was enhanced by a dark ribbon bearing a cameo at her throat. Gibson's celebrated talents could only have captured her in two dimensions and it was as clear as the winter sky that she was all but bursting the bounds of *three*.

When she neared the end of the veranda she slowed, glanced from the corner of her eye at the row of aging robber barons she had just passed, and then paused by a table on which a chessboard was spread between Samuel P. "Hardacre" Blackburn and his long-time rival J. P. "Cash" Morgan. She positioned herself at Samuel P.'s side and scrutinized the chessboard with a gaze as cool and clear as Baltic amber.

"Do you mind?" she asked Hardacre, gesturing to the game board.

"Be my guest." He waved permission and leaned back in his chair.

Nothing on the veranda stirred—not breeze nor wheeze—as she took up his play and moved three chess pieces in as many turns before straightening.

"Checkmate."

Cash Morgan stared at the board in disbelief and Hardacre chuckled and leaned forward to study her victory and then to raise his scrutiny to her. To his surprise, she returned his inspection, her vivid eyes roaming him with a thoroughness that would have been an outrage coming from any other woman.

Clearly, she had come to conquer.

"You play well, madam."

"Well enough, it would seem," she responded with a lilt. He tossed the lap blanket aside and grabbed his cane to rise, but she waved him to keep his seat and gave him a potent smile.

"Care to give me a game yourself, Mr. Blackburn?"

All around him Hardacre heard gasps. Nurses down the way lurched to feel for pulses. He glanced at his fellow moguls from the corner of his eye and was gratified to see they were impressed by her interest in him.

She had indeed come to conquer.

And he was going to let her.

For now.

"I would be honored, madam," he said. "If my esteemed opponent will—oh, just get the hell up, Cash, and give the gal your seat."

She was soon perched on the edge of Cash's vacated rocker, studying Hardacre even as she studied the chessboard. As they played, her hand movements were like a ballet; quick, sure, and oddly entrancing. Hardacre had difficulty keeping his mind on the game. It took her only nine moves to bring him to the same ignominious conclusion: "Checkmate."

His face reddened as he looked up.

"Anything else I can do for you?" he asked with a hint of pique.

"As a matter of fact, there is. You can join me for dinner tonight. Seven o'clock. In the dining room."

He sat for a moment, unsettled by her consummate self-assurance. He glanced down the row of old men. She had chosen him. How could he refuse?

"Be pleased to do so,"—he nodded gravely—"Miss? Mrs.?"

"Miss. O'Keefe."

"Until seven, Miss O'Keefe."

Having gotten what she came for, she rose and made her way at the same unhurried pace back down the veranda into the Great Hall of the hotel. As she passed the row of rocking chairs, sunlight filtering through the gingerbread carvings on the veranda arches ignited fires in her hair and set her cinnabar-colored silk shimmering like hot Northern Lights.

No pale, society-grade bit of femininity there, Hardacre Blackburn thought to himself. This was one for the ages. Magnificent. A full-blooded, one-of-a-kind, knows-her-own-mind, lives-on-her-own-terms *woman*.

The instant she disappeared from sight, the old boys around him cackled and crowed.

"Ain't set eyes on a female that frisky since Lillie Langtry," toothless old Sledge Hammermill declared.

"Watch yer wallet, Hardacre. You can bet *she* is," Cash Morgan advised, still stinging from his defeat at her hands.

"Try the milk before you buy the cow, Hardacre," crusty old Bottomline Vanderbilt called before a fit of coughing overtook him.

Hardacre ignored their comments as he hobbled down the veranda with a smugness undiminished by the pain in his gout-ridden foot. He still possessed a remnant of the robust figure he had enjoyed for most of his seventy-two years. He had a full head of white hair, brows like steel wool, a ruddy complexion, and a pair of flinty gray eyes that were as apt to throw sparks as the blast furnaces of Pennsylvania where his considerable fortune had been made. The faces of the old boys registered a grudging admiration for his unexpected good fortune.

That admiration, tinged as it was with jealousy, made the ordeal of walking all the way to his suite almost bearable for him. As he moved through the Great Hall and entered the motorized elevator, he kept recalling that luxurious chestnut hair, that alabaster skin, and those eyes like lucid amber.

As spectacular as the young woman was and as flattered as he was to be the recipient of her invitation, he knew there was more to it. A good bit more. And damned if he wasn't going to enjoy finding out what it was.

"Goodnight!" he roared as he burst through the doors to his suite on the fourth floor, minutes later.

A tall, cutaway-clad form carrying a handful of suspenders appeared in the doorway between the parlor and the bed chamber.

"Yes?"

The old man took in the Brit's stiff back and flared nostrils. Damned limey still refused to call him "sir."

"Draw me a soak. And lay out my best evening clothes." He tossed his cane on the settee and rubbed his hands together before easing down onto the upholstery beside the walking stick. "I'm having dinner tonight with the most beautiful woman on the goddammed continent."

Goodnight took in the news, then turned on his heel to retreat to the bathing chamber, muttering.

"Poor creature. Must have the worst eyesight on the continent, as well."

Cordelia O'Keefe sailed into the parlor of her suite, closed the double doors behind her, and leaned back on them with a sigh of pleasure so sensual it was almost indecent. She had felt the old boys' stares, their desperate boredom, and their hunger for energy and vitality. That long, sad line of creeping decrepitude . . . if she were a different kind of woman . . .

"Cordie?" a voice called from the bedroom. "Is that you?"

"Yes."

"You're back already?" A striking older woman with auburn hair that was graying at her temples hurried from the adjoining room. She took Cordelia by the hands and pulled her toward the settee. "You saw him? Talked to him?"

Cordelia was too excited to sit. "He accepted my invitation. Proving he is part human, after all."

"About that much," Hedda O'Keefe said, indicating the very tip of her smallest finger. "Don't forget for a minute who and what he is, Cordie."

Cordelia was busy recalling the curiosity, skepticism, and anticipation that had scrolled across the old fellow's face as she spoke with him. In that brief exchange, her grandfather had become shockingly human to her. There was an energy about him, even in his seventies and riddled with gout, that she hadn't expected. And those piercing gray eyes . . . sharp as a surgeon's scalpel . . . hard as the alloy steel they'd helped launch into the world industrial market. She'd have to watch her every move with him, gauge her timing perfectly, leave nothing to chance.

"And?" Hedda prompted.

"We didn't exactly talk. I beat him in a game of chess and issued the invitation."

"God knows what he must think." Hedda studied her for a moment, interpreting her flushed cheeks and hint of distraction as symptoms of a deeper, more complex reaction. "You know, it's not too late to reconsider."

"Absolutely not. We've come too far and spent entirely too much." Seeing the genuine worry in her aunt's eyes, she softened. "Besides, what's the alternative? Haven't you had enough of sitting on riverbanks watching our supplies tumble downstream without us because we can't afford extra hands? Or of fleeing desert Kasbahs after our money is stolen and tasting nothing but sand for days afterward? Remember what it was like guarding my back with a gun while I dealt cards for traveling money in an 'infidel tavern'?"

Hedda rubbed at the memory of cold steel that lingered in her fingers. "But there are other deep pockets, Cordie. Some in this very hotel . . . on that very veranda . . ."

"It has to be *his* pockets," Cordelia declared with a fierce expression that wrenched a sigh from her aunt. "Did you send the menu to the dining room?"

Hedda nodded. "And the order to the wine steward. And I've made sure your gown was pressed and laid out your best silk petticoats."

Cordelia strolled over to the table set before a pair of long windows flanked by plantation shutters. On it lay a large granite slab inscribed with exotic carvings. Anticipating the lighting conditions after the sun went down, she moved a triple candelabra from the sideboard to stand beside the large, flat stone. Candlelight would make the viewing more dramatic. She ran her fingers over the carved figures of hieroglyphics that would soon cast a spell over Samuel P. Blackburn as they had over her.

"After we eat, I'll bring him to see it. *Then* we'll talk."

Two

"Good evening." Cordelia extended a graceful hand, drawing Samuel P. "Hardacre" Blackburn across the grand dining room to her side.

The large, ornately appointed dining room was full to capacity, in part because of the popularity of the Tampa Bay Hotel with well-to-do northerners escaping winter, but also because of what had happened on the veranda earlier. Word had spread among the guests, and all wanted to see what would happen between Hardacre and the beauty.

She had positioned herself in front of their table, knowing the candles behind her would frame her hair and green watered silk in flattering light. Her mother had taught her long ago that her appearance was an asset, not an identity. And assets were meant to be used.

"Miss O'Keefe." One of Samuel P.'s woolly eyebrows rose to acknowledge Hedda's presence as he leaned heavily on his cane.

"May I present my aunt, Hedda O'Keefe." As he took in the name, she watched again for any spark of recognition. There was none. "Mr. Blackburn gave me a spirited game of chess this afternoon."

"She trounced me," he said, taking Hedda's offered hand.

"She trounces everyone," Hedda said with a smile and gracious nod.

As soon as they were seated, Cordelia nodded to the waiter to begin serving the aperitifs and appetizers she had already selected. He settled back in his chair, surveying the hand-printed menu lying across his plate, then turned to her with a frown.

"You've got me here. And you're about to feed me wine and red meat that will settle on my foot like a ball-peen hammer. You'd best spell it out for me, missy."

She studied him a moment, determined to proceed at her own pace, and waved to the white-coated server to continue.

"I'm an explorer, Mr. Blackburn. I've traveled considerably and published accounts of my adventures in various journals and magazines."

"Boston. O'Keefe." He shifted back in his chair with a frown. "*Irish*."

"Half," she said with an arch look, which caused him to glance between her and her aunt and think better of whatever comment he was about to make.

"And just where have you been that's worth payin' hard-earned money to read about?" He curled his nose at the salad—citrus laced greenery—on his plate.

"I've concentrated on exploring places few others—male or female—have gone. I've rafted down the Colorado River just after the spring thaw, when the river's still running full and wild. I've packed and canoed the length of the Grand Canyon, climbed a volcano in Hawaii, and trekked across the Moroccan desert on a camel. I've dined with sultans and Hawaiian princesses and Indian chiefs. I've wagered with riverboat card sharps, Kentucky horse breeders, and Barbary pirates . . . and *won*." She studied his half-narrowed gaze and answered the question she sensed would be coming next. "And I've said 'no' to five marriage proposals."

"Only five?" He barked a laugh that surprised even him. "Damned young bucks. Got no guts at all, these days."

"In all fairness"—she gave him a wry smile—"I did those intrepid gentlemen a favor by refusing. I've yet to meet a man who would put up for very long with a wife who has a head full of ideas, a penchant for digging up secrets, and a yen to see what's over the next mountain. I know I'm something of a handful." She glanced apologetically at her aunt, who wryly shook her head, and waited until she had Samuel P.'s full attention to add, "Not unlike yourself, sir."

"*Heh.*" The old boy huffed what passed for a laugh, then sipped his wine. "It's a rare woman who knows her own faults."

"And a rarer man," she responded, savoring the flash of surprise in his face as he looked up. Mindful of the many pairs of eyes watching them, she gave him her most lavish smile. "Care for more wine, Mr. Blackburn?"

Through dinner courses the conversation centered politely on the questions about her background, her education, and which magazines had published her accounts of her travels. He had apparently heard of *Harper's Bazaar*, *McCall's*, and *Vanity Fair*. An expectant silence descended as the dessert and coffee were served, and none did more than touch the strawberry consort the chef had labored long to produce. With an irritable glance at the nearby tables, where people were prolonging already fashionably late dinners to watch them, Samuel P. laid his napkin aside and leaned toward her.

"So. Tell me how much you want and what you want it for." He seemed pleased to have surprised her with his bluntness. "You didn't think I knew it was about money? Missy"—he leaned back in his chair and tucked his thumbs into the exposed armholes of his vest—"with a man like me, it's always about money. That's the only language I speak."

Cordelia took a breath and boldly met his searching stare.

"Fine. Some months ago, I was in Charleston for a while and won a wager of sorts. The loser, it happened, was short of funds."

"Aren't they always," Samuel P. muttered.

"Being an enterprising fellow, my debtor offered to settle his obligation to me with something he claimed to be worth many times what he owed."

"You had more sense than to take it, of course," Samuel P. declared.

"I didn't take it without examining it first. The contents of the crate that settled his debt to me are right now on a table in my suite."

"What is it?"

She leaned forward and lowered her voice, drawing him to match both.

"A stone slab archaeologists call a *stela*, engraved with hieroglyphics."

"Scratching on a rock." He sat back, looking disappointed.

"I've spent considerable time and energy trying to determine what the engravings say. I've consulted two of the country's leading Egyptologists, who were very excited to see the rubbing I made of the stone."

"Rubbing?" He scowled, searching her visually.

"It's a transfer process used to make an exact copy of the relief on a stone carving. You take thin paper, like onion skin, and place it over the carvings, then lightly rub the surface of the paper with charcoal. The blacking outlines the ridges and misses the valleys, giving an exact rendering of the carved figures."

"And you made one of these 'rubbings'?" He squinted harder at her.

She nodded, unable to tell if he was truly interested or merely waiting to deliver another skewering remark.

"Keeping the stone safely stored, I shared the rubbings with Everett Bitters at Harvard, and with Thomas Stephenson, curator of the Egyptian collection of the Metropolitan Museum. They were unified in the opinion that the origin was Egypt and that one of the figures on the stela—strangely—refers to a king who was not an Egyptian at all."

"Yeah? Who was he?" His hand tightened on the edge of the table as he battled a rising interest in her story.

She leaned closer, both eager for and dreading his response.

"King Solomon."

He gave a harsh hoot of laughter that caused heads to turn their way.

"The one from the Bible? You don't really believe that?"

"I do. And so will you when you've seen it with your own two eyes. Come with me."

Minutes later, they stood in Cordelia's suite, looking down at the candlelit stone slab that bore a message in hieroglyphs carved by long-dead scribes. She watched his face as he studied the stone, felt the edges, and gradually extended his examination to the carvings themselves. She could almost see wheels turning in his mind as he explored the worn figures with time-gnarled fingers.

"Interesting, isn't it?" She probed for a reaction as she came to stand by him. "According to Dr. Bitters, these particular bird images are generally associated with royalty. These other symbols around it delineate which king or pharaoh is meant. But what is even more remarkable is that reference to this king is always accompanied by another group of symbols." She waited for him to look up before going on. "Symbols that represent wealth—specifically, riches from the earth." She braced and took a deep breath. "My experts tell me this stone is very likely the key to the location of the source of the riches that once belonged to King Solomon himself."

He apparently understood more than she realized.

"King Solomon's Mines," he concluded. His eyes moved over a mental tally sheet, adding one and one and coming up with: "And you want to go search for this lost treasure, these King Solomon's Mines."

"I do," she said earnestly. "And I want you to sponsor the expedition."

It didn't take long for her to get an answer.

"You expect me to lay out thousands—hell, tens of thousands of dollars—so you can go gallivanting all over the world—"

"Just Africa, actually," she inserted.

"Fine, all over Africa"—he amended his complaint with a sardonic tone—"looking for treasure from a fairy tale."

"I am proposing a scientific expedition to uncover a legendary source of treasure. And I'm giving you a chance to sponsor a history-making venture."

"Well, I'm saying *no*. You're beautiful. You're smart. And you put on about as good a hustle as any I've seen . . . poppin' the old boys' eyes out . . . beatin' me at chess . . . invitin' me to dinner. But the answer's *no*." He drew himself up straight, a glint of satisfaction in his eye. "I didn't get to where I am by throwin' money after every damned fool idea some huckster threw at me."

"I'm no more a huckster than you are, Mr. Blackburn," she said, clamping down on her rising anger, using it to energize instead of undermine her response. The stubborn old goat was forcing her to put all of her cards on the table before she was ready, and she couldn't help resenting him for it. "I might even be tempted to say that we're cut from the same cloth," she continued, honing the edge in her voice. "But it would be more accurate to say that I'm cut from *your* cloth, Mr. Blackburn. Flesh of your flesh. Bone of your bone. Because I happen to be *your granddaughter*."

She had actually managed to surprise him. He scowled, then glared, then grew agitated, a little apoplectic, and finally angry.

"Now you've gone too damned far!" he roared, jabbing his cane at her.

"Or not far enough." She shoved the walking stick aside and stalked closer, pushing her face toward his. "I hadn't intended to tell you—at least not this way—but my birth name is Cordelia O'Keefe *Blackburn*. My father was

Thomas Blackburn, whom you disowned upon his marriage to my mother, Maureen O'Keefe." She looked him up and down, letting her assessment of him show in her eyes. "Those names must mean something to you even if mine doesn't."

The old man backed away and stood gasping like a fish out of water, his face reddening and his arms twitching at his sides. Then suddenly he stopped dead, holding his breath, staring at her face . . . scrutinizing, measuring every feature, examining every nuance of texture, shape, and color. He closed his eyes for a minute, gathering himself. When he opened them, they were filled with tangled memories and emotions.

"Boston born and raised," she said. "My mother helped to develop the Boston Public Library. For all practical purposes, I grew up there, among the books and the people who used and valued them. It was her connections at Harvard and Vassar that helped me get into college when we had no funds for it. And it was her access to the country's top scholars and researchers that inspired my curiosity and love of adventure."

"H–how do I know you're telling the truth?" he asked, a tremor in his voice betraying a suspicion that she was doing just that.

She went to the writing desk for a leather folio and handed it to him.

"It's here. Read it for yourself. My birth certificate. Letters my father wrote to you that you returned to him *unopened*. Copies of the magazines containing my articles. If you need more than that, I'm sure you have the means and resources to find it for yourself."

He squeezed the folio as if he could make it cry the truth and glared at her, the tumult in his soul visible in his eyes.

"I'll investigate every detail . . . go through it with a fine-toothed comb. And if I find you're lying—"

"You'll do what? Disinherit me?" Her eyes heated. "I believe you've already done that. I'm not asking for a fortune, Mr. Blackburn. I'm asking for backing in a venture that, while risky, could yield you a thousand percent return. I doubt you've had an offer like this in years."

He fell back one step, and then another. After a moment, he whirled and thumped out the door, slamming it behind him.

The sound echoed in the breathless silence of the parlor. Hedda came to put her arms around Cordelia's still-braced shoulders.

"Well. That went well," Cordelia said with the half of her voice that wasn't being squeezed by emotion.

"Are you all right?" Hedda rubbed Cordelia's shoulder as she watched her struggle with her emotions. When there was no response, she answered the question for herself and moved on. "What do you think he'll do?"

Cordelia felt a prickle at the corners of her eyes. She'd seen in the old man's face that he'd been truly shaken by her revelations. There was a weakness, after all, in the steel-plate armor around the old boy's soul. Family. He'd thought he freed himself from all connections, purged himself from the demands of family and feeling years ago. And now, in his twilight years, she'd barged into his life . . . demanding that he reckon with her . . . claiming him and challenging him to claim her . . . if he dared.

Yes, it was about the money. And exploration. And establishing herself as an explorer to be reckoned with. But it was also about a great deal more.

"He took the papers with him," she said, patting Hedda's hand on her upper arm. "My guess is, he'll read them." She took a deep breath. "And he'll be back."

Three

Hartford Goodnight heard his employer blow through the main door of the Presidential Suite like a typhoon run aground and inserted a bookmark into his page and closed the book. As a stream of invective burst through the bedroom door, he rolled off the old boy's bed and hastily smoothed the bedclothes behind him.

When he entered the parlor, Blackburn was stalking furiously back and forth, staring at a leather folio lying on the floor as if it had fangs and rattles. Goodnight frowned. Anything that could rouse such trepidation in Samuel P. Blackburn had to be potent indeed.

"Get me a bourbon," the old man ordered without looking up.

"Well, well. In the mood for a little pain, are we?" Goodnight headed for the liquor cabinet that Blackburn insisted on carrying everywhere with him even though he was strictly prohibited from imbibing. "I take it dinner with your 'beauty' didn't quite live up to your expectations."

"I don't pay you to give me lip," the old man snarled.

"No you don't. I throw that in for free," Goodnight said,

refraining from mentioning the fact that the old man didn't pay him at all. That it was he, in fact, who was paying the old man. With his presence and service.

He came to stand beside his employer, holding a tray containing half a glass of bourbon, and staring down at the folio on the floor.

"Dare I hope it's venomous?"

The old man looked up at him and the glass of certain pain he was holding. There was something unsettling in those aged eyes, something unprecedented, something that almost made him regret his jibe.

The old man snatched the glass from the tray and barreled over to a stuffed chair, where he sat holding the liquor and gazing into it. After a long moment, he aimed a curt hand at the door, indicating he wanted to be alone.

Goodnight stood for a moment, watching the old man, torn between an intrinsic concern for the pain of others and righteous pleasure at the old devil's discomfort. Still . . .

With a soft huff, he shoved the leather ottoman over to the old man and bent to lift the gouty foot onto the stool without touching the extra-sensitive toes. Then, caught hard in the grip of conflicting urges, he retrieved the folio and placed it on the table at the old man's elbow.

There was no thanks—there never was—but there was also no sneer or cutting reminder of his servile status. There was nothing in the old man's stare. Nothing at all.

With a frown, Goodnight backed to the door and exited for his own room in the economy section of the hotel. The sight of the old man slumped in the chair, gripping a bourbon he dared not drink and looking grimly at that leather folio, stayed with him as he stretched out, diagonally, on his too-short bed. He'd give another full year on his cursed "indenture" to find out what was in that folder.

The banging on the door the next morning was loud enough to rattle the teacups on the room service tray between Cordelia and Aunt Hedda. They sat at the parlor table in their dressing gowns, sipping coffee and reading the newspaper and the day's schedule of events at the hotel.

"Open up," came a voice that sent a shiver through Cordelia's shoulders. Hardacre Blackburn had returned—she glanced at the clock over the mantle, eight o'clock—even earlier than expected. Shooting to her feet, she quickly began tying together the front of her dressing gown. Hedda, who never left her room with a ribbon undone, headed straight for the door.

"About bloody time." Samuel P. barged past Hedda into the room, his hoary head swiveling as he searched for Cordelia. He was wearing rumpled evening clothes from last night, and his chin was hazed with stubble. He halted for a moment to take in her long hair and the feminine flounces on her dressing gown. "Humph." Then he headed for the stela, which Cordelia and Hedda had moved to the top of the nearby sideboard.

Strong morning light bathed the surface, illuminating the engravings and setting small flecks of mineral in the granite shining. Cordelia met him there, hoping his early morning return was a sign he was on the brink of a decision.

"Am I to assume you've reconsidered my proposal, Mr. Blackburn?"

He shifted, leaning more heavily on his cane to relieve his bandaged foot.

"The only thing you should assume, missy, is that I'm no fool. You made me an offer. I've got a counteroffer." Inside his scowl she could see a glint of excitement that brought her instantly to the edge of her guard.

"This is not a negotiation." She drew herself up straighter.

"*Everything's* a negotiation. The sooner you learn that, the better off you'll be." His one narrowed eye made him look like a pirate, reminding her that despite his aged and sagging frame, he was in fact a cutthroat at heart.

"Now, as I see it," he continued, "you want me to give you a hunk of money to go chargin' off on a treasure hunt.

My guess—your odds of success are fifty-fifty. You find it or you don't. Assumin' it's there . . . it might or might not be . . . that takes the odds to four-to-one against. Don't much like them odds."

"I've provided affidavits on the opinions of eminent scholars—"

"Yeah, yeah. So much palaver." He waved her protest away. "I never put stock in 'experts,' missy. If they're so damned smart, why ain't they *rich*?" He shuffled closer, eyeing her. "Then there's *you*. How do I know you got the grit for treasure hunting? Hell, how do I know you won't melt like a sugar cube the minute the temperature reaches ninety?"

"I've led expeditions before." Her teeth began to ache from clenching her jaw. "I provided you copies of magazines with published accounts."

"Accounts you wrote. For all I know, you made it all up."

"I was there." Hedda stepped in, furious, and pointed at herself. "I lived through it with her. If you have questions, Blackburn, you ask *me*."

Blackburn blinked at Hedda's defense of her.

"I may just do that," he said. "But not before I've laid down a counteroffer." He turned again to Cordelia. "Seeing's as how you may be my seed—an' worth somethin' after all—I've decided to give you a chance to prove yourself. I have somethin' that needs findin' a bit closer to home. Here's the deal: You do a little somethin' for me first. And if you find what I want an' bring back the goods, I'll set you up with everything you need to hunt for old Solomon's mines."

It was Cordelia's turn to recoil in surprise. When anticipating the old man's possible responses to her proposal, she'd never imagined such a thing.

"You want me to *find* something for you?" she said.

"Solve another little puzzle, so to speak. I've got a piece of it and am hankerin' to have the rest. Shouldn't take too long." He looked her up and down. "For a 'professional' like you." He apparently couldn't resist a smirk. "It ain't like old Solomon's mines might get up and move while you're gone."

"You want me to find something for you in order to prove myself worthy of your investment?" she demanded, not knowing whether to smack him before she threw him out or just throw him out. "I gave you a dozen references—"

"Don't want references." His lip curled. "I want the Gift of the Jaguar."

Anger and frustration fought for expression inside her. She had done the research and planning . . . spread her qualifications and experience out before him . . . and he was requiring she prove herself to him on his terms. It was exactly what she'd spent her whole life avoiding: being dictated to by a man with an inflated sense of his own importance.

"I'm not a step-and-fetch-it. Nor am I for hire. I plan my own expeditions. *I* decide where to go and what risks are worth taking."

"You do everything but *fund* your expeditions, missy." He gave her a crafty look. "Well, I've got the funds, and I'm offerin' you a chance to prove yourself and make a tidy profit to boot. I'd be willing to split fifty-fifty with you. Then maybe you could fund your own damned expeditions from now on."

"Fifty-fifty. On an unknown expedition to an unknown place to search for some unknown—"

" 'The Gift of the Jaguar,' " he reiterated. "It's Maya Indian. South Mexico and the Caribbean. There's stones and a legend that says the spirit of the jaguar gave a gift to mankind . . . a great and terrible gift. The old Mayans gave offerings to the jaguar to thank him. Treasure. Centuries of it. All piled up." He shrugged. "Of course, it may just be poppycock." He pinned her with a glance. "But it's *your* kind of poppycock. What do you say? Interested?"

"Stones?" She twitched involuntarily. Was he parodying her offer?

"Not th' actual stones. That'd be what you're lookin' for . . . them and the treasure sacrificed to 'em."

"Then what evidence do you have that this 'Gift of the Jaguar' exists?"

"I got a 'rubbing.' "

The words were like a slap in the face. He *was* making fun of her proposal. The deranged old coot.

"You expect me to believe you have a rubbing of ancient Mayan stones, when last night you'd never even *heard* of one?"

"I never said I didn't know what it was. You were so all-fired bent on explainin' it to me that I let you."

"You *let* me?" She stiffened and pointed toward the door. "I'll thank you to take your sad little parody, and—"

"Don't believe me?" He grabbed her by the wrist and dragged her toward the door. "Come up to my rooms and I'll show you."

Startled by his grasp and strength, she floundered until her feet began to move. She tossed a mute glance of alarm at Hedda as she was pulled along, and Hedda hurried after them.

Four

The old boy dragged her through a set of ornate double doors into a grandly furnished salon, where a man in a black cutaway sat with his feet propped up on an ottoman, reading a well-worn copy of what appeared to be *Harper's Bazaar*. He looked startled by their entrance and sat straighter, his eyes widening on Cordelia. Lowering the magazine, he removed his feet from the stool and stood up, unfolding like a large crow about to take flight.

"Where the hell's my steamer trunk?" Samuel P. demanded of the crow while heading for the bedroom, taking Cordelia along. "The one with my papers."

"This is an outrage." Cordelia kept looking back to make certain Hedda was with her. "If you don't release me, sir, I shall have to resort to force."

"Aim for the bandaged foot," the crow advised with a frosty British air as he strode behind them into the bedroom. "It's especially sensitive."

Cordelia gaped at the man as she was pulled along, registering dark hair, intense gray eyes, and the cut and quality of a servant's uniform. Annoyed by the momentary snag in her attention, she turned back to Samuel P.

"There it is." He pointed at a trunk standing on end in the corner, half hidden by a massive mahogany wardrobe. "Keys."

The crow stepped around her and held out a ring of keys to the old man. "Don't just stand there, dammit! Drag it out here and unlock it."

In moments, they were looking into a trunk overflowing with papers, books, ledgers, rolled-up canvases and broadsides, and the odd faded tassel, jade carving, and silver hip flask. Memorabilia, no doubt.

The old man sorted through several of the rolls, selecting one wrapped in chamois skin, then hobbled over to the bed, pulling Cordelia along with him.

She watched as he unrolled with trembling hands what appeared to be a parchment that was frayed at the edges, thin enough to be almost translucent, and covered with a haze of black and gray. The scroll contained three long pieces nested together, each bearing words and figures. As more of the parchment was revealed, it became clear that the figures were in fact rubbings of large, grainy, block-like images.

Her frown melted. If this was a hoax, it was a darned good one. Where would someone, even someone with Samuel P.'s resources, be able to come up with such an elaborate fake in less than twelve hours? She crossed her arms, determined not to let her curiosity draw her into the old man's sway.

"You expect me to believe you just happen to have the secret to a Mayan treasure with you in your luggage?"

"Oh, I've taken in a passel of stuff as collateral, over th' years. Some of it pretty odd. Racehorses, stone quarries, pushcarts, magicians' tricks, canal boats, pipe organs, hansom cabs—"

"The odd arm and spare leg," the crow tossed in as he closed and locked the trunk. Samuel P. shot him a glare that didn't ruffle a single feather.

"Some got redeemed, some didn't." The old man tapped his temple with a look that would have made a rattlesnake forget to rattle. "Got th' inventory right here. Never know when you'll get a chance to turn bad collateral into profit."

"A pity he never took in a spare *foot*," the crow said, leaning on the trunk.

She looked over her shoulder at that sizeable bit of baggage, thinking of the documents, books, and odd personal objects she had mistaken for memories. Collateral. From desperate people. When she looked up, her gaze caught on the crow's sardonic expression. He patted the trunk's worn brass bindings.

"Makes one wonder what he feeds the flock of 'first-born' he has in here."

"Don't you have some socks to sort?" Samuel P. snapped at him.

The crow merely smiled, straightened, and strolled over to lean a shoulder against the bedpost. He was easily the rudest manservant on the planet.

Her gaze lingered a moment. He was also very, very—

Reddening slightly at her distraction, she turned back to the bed and the rubbings that held the key to a deal with the old man. She studied them for a minute, then picked one up and examined the texture and weight of the parchment. When she carried it to the window, Samuel P. and Hedda followed and peered over her shoulder.

In the strong morning light it was easy to see they were genuine rubbings; the prominent grain of the figures could only have been achieved on actual stone. They also seemed to have been nested together for some time; the figures were worn from being repeatedly rolled and stored, and charcoal dust from the two bottom rubbings had transferred to the backs of the documents on top.

"I need a magnifying glass," she said to Samuel P., who passed her demand on to the servant. Moments later, with the reading glass in hand, she scrutinized selected spots on the parchment and made "tsk"-ing sounds.

"Well?" Hedda stared anxiously between Cordelia and the figures.

"Very fine parchment." Cordelia fingered the frayed

edge. "Delicate, but meant to last. I can't imagine anyone using such a thing to make rubbings these days." She looked at Samuel P. "How old is this? Did the owner tell you?"

He allowed a hint of pleasure to creep into his canny face.

"Said it come from a monastery in Madrid. Made by priests who came over to the new world with th' '*conquee-sta-dors*.'"

"As many as three hundred years, then." With something akin to reverence, she rolled out each of the long rectangular pieces and asked Hedda and Samuel P. to hold the ends. Looking at them side by side, she saw that they were rows of blocks roughly ten inches on a side. One block in the middle of one row was slightly larger and one side of each row was straighter and cleaner than the other side. She paced the side of the bed, studying the figures, making a mental note of motifs that matched and elements that were repeated.

Suddenly she felt as if someone had turned on an electrical light in her. "Come on—into the other room—where there's more space."

She laid out the parchment strips on the rug at right angles, smooth sides inward, forming a U shape, and stood back to study them. They didn't seem right, so she knelt and turned them the opposite way, smacking old Samuel P.'s pant leg to make him move his foot.

"I'd have bet a fiver he wouldn't have her on her knees in twenty-four hours," the crow intoned, heading for a distant chair with a hand full of magazines.

The pieces seemed to fit together better in one configuration. The larger stone in the middle of one row began to look as if it might have functioned as a keystone. She repositioned the rows and examined the results. Her eyes were drawn again and again to that larger block: a stylized head of some sort of cat. A jaguar?

A shiver went up her spine.

There was no guarantee it was a complete rendering of

a complete object, but on first analysis, the pieces seemed to form an arch or a doorway. A portal to history's secrets. A passage into the unknown. An adventure beckoning.

"Any idea of what it might be?" Hedda asked from a nearby chair.

She groaned silently at finding herself on her knees in the middle of the old man's floor, in her dressing gown. Her breath was coming fast, her heart was hammering, and she was on the verge of losing track of everything but the mystery spread out around her.

Excitement, dammit. Not too smart.

She looked up to find the old boy's eyes aglow. He knew that he'd just set a hook in her. Well, she might be on the line, but she wasn't giving up without a fight. Sitting back on her heels, she affected an air of detachment.

"It could be anything. A roster of tax obligations. A signpost to the local fish market." Her eyes narrowed in defiance of her own enthusiasm. "The decoration on a ladies' privy."

There was a choking cough from the crow's direction.

"Or"—Samuel P. stumped closer—"th' stones that mark the place where riches were sacrificed to the Jaguar Spirit."

"Hard to say." She pushed to her feet and dusted charcoal from her hands. "It would be foolhardy to undertake such a mission with no hint of where the originals are and no clue where to start looking."

The old man evaluated both her and her statement, no doubt reading between the lines, looking for loopholes. And she had left him plenty. She hadn't actually declined the opportunity. She hadn't said it was impossible. She hadn't said she wouldn't do it. She had just said it would be foolhardy to proceed without more information.

His eyes narrowed and features sharpened as he stepped closer.

Her jaw clamped as she met his intense gaze and refused to give an inch.

It was down to final bargaining.

"And?" he demanded.

"I won't do this without Arturo Valiente. He is a renowned professor of antiquities in Mexico City, conversant with the native cultures and history in the region. He has made some headway in translating the Mayan alphabet and calendar. He would have to authenticate the rubbings and identify the region where stories of the 'Jaguar Spirit' are most prevalent before I take the first step on a search for your 'stones.'" She tucked her arms across her front and gave him a withering look. "But what are the odds you would actually send for him and pay him a consulting fee? He's an *expert*."

The old man studied her for a minute, assessing the strength of the resolve in her eyes, the set of her jaw, and the angles of her shoulders.

"Behold the proverbial peas." The crow's very British disdain lapped around them. "One would think it would get a bit cramped in that pod."

That comment caused her to glance toward where the crow had retreated. He was sitting with one leg thrown insolently over the chair arm, perusing a magazine. The heat of her stare caused him to look up, with a half smile that made her palm itch for contact.

When she looked back at Samuel P., the old man's gaze went from her to his insufferable servant and back again. His eyes narrowed.

"All right," he said, shocking her with his abrupt acceptance. He couldn't be agreeing this easily to her demand. "A professor to 'read' the stones. I'll give you that. But I don't give nothin' without gettin' somethin' in return." Brace yourself, she thought. But then he surprised her again. "I get to send along my own representative—to 'authenticate' your finds. Otherwise, how do I know you won't just haul back a bag of rocks and say that was all there was?"

"Because that's what you would do?" she charged. "How do you know a bag of rocks isn't all there is to find? There are no guarantees. If my 'payment' is contingent on my bringing back a hoard of gold and jewels, say so now. And the deal is off."

She folded her arms, realizing with mild discomfort that her stance indeed mirrored the old man's and that her determination matched his stubbornness to a T. They very well might be two peas in the cursed butler's pod, but she wouldn't let that influence her decision. It surely wouldn't sway the old man's.

"Agreed." He signaled the end of the stalemate by straightening and rubbing his chin. "You find the stones and learn what the Gift of the Jaguar is. And you bring back whatever valuables you find along the way. My observer will tell me if you've done all you could to find it and have brought back the truth. You take my observer or the deal is off."

That was it. The make-or-break terms were out on the table.

She took a step back to study the rubbings. Weeks in the tropical heat. Terrible food. Mosquitos by the millions. Cutting and hacking her way through jungle no man—or woman—had set foot in before. She really must be a little off—her very veins were itching at the prospect.

"I run the expedition," she declared, turning back to Samuel P. "I hire the bearers and guides. I decide what trails we follow. And I set the pace. Your observer is just that—an observer—subject to the rules I establish. Are we clear on that?"

In retrospect, Samuel P.'s smile should have given her pause. It was genuine delight. Unalloyed with suspicion or subterfuge. What was it about the deal, she should have asked herself, that would give the old boy such undiluted pleasure?

"Clear as glass, missy." He stuck out his knotty right hand. "I believe we've got ourselves a deal."

She met his hand with hers, giving him a firm and businesslike shake.

With a hoot of a laugh, he turned to the crow and ordered brandy all around.

"At this hour of the morning?" The servant shrugged, levered himself up out of the chair, and headed for the liquor cabinet. "It's *your* foot."

The crow brought three glasses back on a tray and the old boy sent him back for another glass. He returned with the fourth glass and set about pouring and serving—until it came to that last full glass.

"Go on," Samuel P. ordered the servant. "Pick it up." When the crow looked wary, he chuckled. The sound wasn't at all reassuring. "You'll need a few stiff drinks where you're going."

"And where is that?" the crow asked, reaching for the glass, regarding with equal suspicion its contents and the news that would accompany them.

"On an expedition. To Mexico." The old boy fixed a look on Cordelia. "As my appointed representative."

She hadn't yet taken the first sip of brandy. When she strangled, it was on her own juices. She coughed and gasped and coughed again, her eyes watering.

"What?" she croaked.

"Here, missy. Meet your new travelin' companion," Samuel P. declared, waving sharply at the stunned servant. "Hartford Ignatius Goodnight. Presser of pants. Tender of gout. Folder of socks. Without a doubt, the worst butler in the history of 'butling.' "

"*I am not.*"

"You must be joking." Her fingers turned white on the glass tumbler.

"Not a bit. Goodnight here . . . he's th' one I choose to send along. The way he's kept an eye on me, I reckon he'll be the perfect man to keep an eye on you." He cast a jaded smile in the butler's direction. "Plus, it'll do 'im good to get out and get a little fresh air."

"You devious old codswallop—" Goodnight began, his chest broadening as it puffed with indignation.

"This is not a Sunday outing!" She slammed her brandy down, untasted, on a nearby table. "This will be a difficult and dangerous expedition into wild, unexplored territory.

There won't be time for"—she shot the manservant a disparaging look—"folding socks and crocheting tea cozies."

The full outrage of it descended on her. His *butler*! Then she looked between the crow and his employer, seeing with fresh eyes the tension and antipathy that lay beneath the servant's barbs. It struck her that old Samuel P. was pawning off one of his problems on her!

"No," she declared furiously. "I won't take him. Name someone else. Anyone else." She skewered the adder-tongued butler with a glare. "I'm not taking *him*."

"You agreed to a deal, missy." Samuel P.'s mask of humor evaporated, baring the steely sinew of the impervious character he'd spent a lifetime building. "And you don't renege on a deal with Hardacre Blackburn without payin' for it, kin or no kin. The deal said I could send someone with you to make sure you search proper and bring back what you find. The deal didn't say you got to okay who I send." He flicked a finger toward the red-faced Goodnight. "He's goin'." Then he turned his steely glare back to her. "Get used to it."

Three times she opened her mouth to break their verbal contract. And three times she closed it. Her face was on fire, her hands were shaking, and she couldn't bring herself to look at Hedda, who had warned her repeatedly about the old man's unscrupulous nature. He'd had decades to perfect the art of the devious deal. What had made her think she could come out on top in a match with him? She had asked for it, she realized, and he'd given it to her.

When she looked up she caught the butler's spiteful expression.

" 'She who sups with the devil,' " he quoted, " 'had best use a long spoon.' "

"Is that so?" She raked him with a look savage enough to leave furrows. "Well, I've got another pithy little nugget for you: 'It makes the devil laugh to see the biter *bitten*.' "

As she sailed out the door and down the hall, laughter lapped at her back. The old man's pure unadulterated glee.

Five

Hartford Goodnight's face burned as he watched the old man set the brandy aside untouched and shuffle over to the chair with the ottoman.

"What in bloody hell do you think you're doing?" he demanded.

"Wheelin' and dealin'." The old man paused for an instant before lowering himself into the seat with a grunt of discomfort. "Like always."

"I am not going on a treasure hunt captained by a woman," he said, propping his hands on his waist in a way that emphasized the breadth of his chest. "Especially *that* woman."

"What's wrong with 'that' woman?" The old boy scowled, studying him. "She's a feast for th' eyes and she very well may be my own flesh an' blood."

"Exactly."

Blackburn continued studying him, letting him wait for a reaction to his comment.

"She'll do it or she won't," he finally said. "Either way, I want you there."

"Absolutely not. I'm not the stew-in-sweat and gnaw-on-hardtack sort."

"Don't underestimate yourself." Blackburn's chuckle had a nasty edge. "I figure you'll be right at home in the jungle—with th' snakes and blowflies and heathens who shoot poison darts."

Goodnight's face tightened in spite of his attempt to rein in his emotions.

"See here—I was hired to be your—"

"You weren't *hired* to be anything. You were taken. As collateral."

"As your *butler*."

"As anything I damned well see fit to make you!" The old man's eyes narrowed ominously. "Check th' contract, Goodnight. It doesn't say what work you have to do, only that you have to work. For me."

As quickly as it had come, the old man's intensity subsided and genial wickedness spread over his gnome-like face again. Before Goodnight could exit, his employer gave an unprecedented order.

"Pull up a chair an' sit down."

He stared at the old man in disbelief. This was hardly get-cozy-with-the-indentured-help time.

"Sorry." He turned sharply toward the bedroom. "I have socks to sort."

"*You have a decision to make.*"

The old man's words struck Goodnight right between the shoulder blades. Dead on center. The ground under his feet tilted and he felt himself sliding inexorably toward another boondoggle. He knew better than to stay, but he couldn't seem to make his feet carry him out of the room. Glancing over his shoulder, he couldn't stop himself from uttering those fateful words.

"What decision?"

The old man didn't blink.

"Whether or not to accept the deal I'm about to offer you."

"I wouldn't make another deal with you if my life depended on it."

"The hell you wouldn't."

Goodnight exasperated himself by walking back to the old man, who—true to form—had a worrisome gleam in his eye.

"All right. What are you talking about?"

"A little agreement on the side. Between you and me."

"Regarding?"

"A chance to pay off your debt early."

His heart actually skipped a beat.

Hope.

Dammit.

He should know better. Samuel P. Blackburn would never voluntarily reduce or forgive a legitimate debt. The old cod had far too much fun applying the torments of servitude to a well-born, highly educated limey to end his service early. At least, not without exacting an even greater cost. Something *worse* than months of misery in the steaming jungles of Mexico. He shuddered. But some perverse, curiosity-ridden, pain-inured part of him had to hear it. He sank onto a stuffed chair and tossed his leg defiantly over the arm.

"I'm listening."

"On this 'treasure hunt,' you'll be travelin' places folks don't usually go, you'll be seein' things your usual snake oil salesman won't ever see."

"Not if I can help it," he said grimly.

"You can't help it. But while you're out in the jungle, if you happened to come across some plant or root or some native hoo-doo useful for curin' gout . . . bring it back to me and I'll call your debt paid."

Goodnight refused to give voice to the scream clawing its way up the back of his throat. He had landed in the old man's clutches courtesy of the unholy fine print of a business contract that—if his efforts had succeeded and his "proven" pharmaceuticals company had fulfilled its promise—might have yielded genuine help for gout and other diseases. Now the old boy was exiling him to the jungle and promising him freedom if he happened to stumble upon a cure while scrambling to survive!

He wrestled with the urge to throw this "opportunity" back in the old boy's face; he couldn't rid himself of the stubborn clutch of hope on his chest.

He would be going places where everything was fresh and unexplored. There would be untold numbers of new species . . . the bark, sap, flowers, and roots of trees and herbs not yet cataloged . . . insects, birds, amphibians, and reptiles . . . secretions and venoms . . . eggs and webs and hives and nests. It could be a treasure trove of undiscovered medicinals. And one find on the order of a salicylic acid, belladonna, or even tea tree oil was all it would take to satisfy his debt and make his fortune at the same time. His heart pounded.

"Let me get this straight. I bring back a treatment for gout and you'll tear up the mortgage on my soul? We'll be finished, you and me?"

"You want it in writin'?" the old man demanded.

"Hell, yes. And I want it spelled out in print that I and I alone will have the right to exploit, produce, and sell all cures I bring back. Including your damned gout reliever."

Blackburn rubbed his stubbled chin, looking like a pensive old turtle.

"Done." He barked his decision. "You can have the rights to whatever you bring back. As long as I get the gout cure *first* and *free*."

Goodnight rose and turned a jaundiced eye on the hand the old man extended to him.

"I'll wait until I see it in writing. Meanwhile, I believe I have some socks to sort."

"If I send a telegram to Professor Valiente straightaway, I should be able to get a response within a day or so," Cordelia said to herself as much as to Hedda while she hurried around her bedroom filling her arms with garments draped over furnishings. "Maybe he'll agree to meet us somewhere to look at the—"

"What in blazes do you think you're doing?" Hedda said from the doorway.

"I am not taking that *man* with me," she said emphatically. "A butler! And you heard the way he talked to his employer. He's arrogant. Insufferable. Probably never set foot outside a place with running water and indoor plumbing. If we pack fast, wait until dark, and go down the back stairs—"

"We'll be leaving without the rubbings and the money to pay for the expedition?" Hedda crossed her arms, looking patient in the extreme. "And we'll be right back where we started—out of money and out of options."

She stopped in the midst of throwing garments into her open trunk. Damn. Her chest was heaving and her face was on fire. Where was her head, letting the old man get the best of her like that? Worse still, she'd been so intent on making an exit that she forgot to pick up the blasted parchment.

"I won't take him. It's bad enough that I have to go at all." It had been more than two full decades since she threw a tantrum, but right now it would have been so satisfying to scream and stomp. "I won't!"

"Well, if it's any consolation," Hedda said, recalling the butler's shock, "he's probably no more keen to go than you are to take him."

Cordelia halted in the midst of tossing a hairbrush into her train case. She looked at her aunt with a flash of inspiration.

"Aunt Hedda, you're a genius."

"I am?"

"He's not crazy about the idea. What would it take to make him refuse to go?" She thought of the butler's air of superiority and fastidious appearance. "If I apply myself, I might be able to find a way to help him make that very decision."

• • •

Girded with stays, a silk-shot challis day dress, and an impeccable Gibson coif, Cordelia headed upstairs to the Presidential Suite two hours later. She was carrying several folded papers in her hands and a sense of mission on her shoulders. As she knocked on the door, she prayed the old man would be sunning himself on the veranda with the rest of the old lizards. It was the blasted butler she needed to see.

The door swung open and she felt a small surge of satisfaction at the way her target's eyes widened. Good. She had the element of surprise.

"Mr. Blackburn isn't in . . . at the moment."

"I didn't come to see him. I came to pick up the parchments so Aunt Hedda can make copies of the figures. We have a great deal to do and precious little time to do it." She planted a hand on her waist and watched his gaze follow it. "Well? Are you going to let me in?"

"I–I suppose." His jaw snapped tight and he backed hastily away, as if afraid breathing the same air might somehow contaminate him. Did he treat the entire female sex with such disdain or did he reserve it just for her?

He disappeared into the bedroom and returned presently with the chamois-wrapped scrolls, holding them out to her at arm's length.

"Here."

"There," she responded, thrusting the papers she carried into his hands as she took the drawings from him.

"What is this?" He turned the packet over and over, regarding it warily.

"A list of equipment you'll need, along with the rules you must agree to before we board the ship."

"Ship? No one said anything about a ship." He looked a bit unsettled.

"How else do you expect to get to southern Mexico? Walk?" She stored away his dismay at the idea of crossing water and motioned for him to open the lists. Wary but clearly curious, he complied.

"One pair of sturdy riding boots or Wellingtons," he read aloud.

"Double soled and fang-proof," she clarified. "Snakes are everywhere."

"Two sets of Jaegers—good God." He looked up with an imperious scowl. "I've never worn woolen underwear in my life."

"Then this is your chance," she said with taunting brightness. "The wool wicks away moisture and keeps you cooler in the tropical heat." He looked as if he might object, but gave the paper a straightening snap and went back to reading.

"*Twelve* pairs of woolen socks?"

"Imperative to keep the feet dry. Nasty foot diseases under every rock."

"I'll be careful not to disturb any rocks," he said. "Two pair of *goatskin* breeches?" Another incredulous look.

"Slightly heavier than deerskin, but impervious to thorns and stickers." She gave him her most patronizing smile. "You'll thank me."

He gave her a look that said "over my dead body."

"Pith helmet?"

"With insect netting," she added, pointing over the edge of the paper.

"Khaki shirts. A sidearm and bullets. A dozen—what the devil are bandanas?"

"Large cloths, like handkerchiefs, only more colorful. For wiping sweat." She dragged her gaze over his pale English form, then pointed at the list. "Make that two dozen."

His half-audible growl was music to her ears.

"A large umbrella. A machete. What in blazes is a *machete*?"

"A broad, eighteen-inch blade sharpened on one side. You never know when you may need to chop something."

"I can see, traveling with you, how true that would be." He returned to the list and saw something that made his jaw drop. "Surgeon's steels, needles, and silk? Quinine, iodine, and sulfur powder?"

"As I said," she responded, "you never know when you may need to *chop* something." His pupils contracted to pinpoints.

"You don't honestly expect me to drag all of this along into some jungle?"

"You won't set foot along on my expedition unless you do."

He turned partly away and fidgeted with the papers, wrestling with something inside him. She felt an anticipatory swell of triumph . . . that deflated an instant later when he turned back and fixed her with a suspicious gaze. She braced internally, watching him take her measure, realizing the argument was about to get personal.

"This, Miss Blackburn"—he waved the papers at her—"is a pack of codswallop. You cannot expect me to believe that *you* wear goatskin breeches."

All she could think, for one interminable moment, was that he towered a full head above her. As he stepped closer, his shoulders completely filled her vision. A trill of surprisingly not unpleasant shock went through her.

"The name is O'Keefe."

"You claim to be his granddaughter," he charged.

"I go by my mother's name—thank you very much—and I don't give a rat's rear what you 'believe.'" She raised her chin to a combative level. "I always wear goatskin breeches on expedition and they've saved my hide a number of times. All it takes is one encounter with a prickly pear cactus, some sharp volcanic pumice, a thornberry grove, or a desert scorpion to make you a believer."

"And I suppose when you're out trekking about the globe you tote a gun around on your hip and wear khaki shirts?" His gaze dropped boldly to her bosom. "I happen to know, Miss *O'Keefe*, that khaki is only produced for military issue. They don't make khaki shirts for women."

"Of course they don't," she snapped, resisting an overpowering urge to cross her arms over her breasts. "I wear men's shirts."

Men's shirts. The words echoed in Hart Goodnight's head and—alarmingly—in his blood. She wore men's shirts. He was rocked to the very roots of his British-bred propriety.

Disturbing visions of her wrapped in *his* shirt—perfectly pressed, medium starch—flooded his mental machinery and all but shorted it out. He sucked in a breath, caught between dueling images of her properly corseted and gowned and her wearing a half-buttoned shirt that bared naked skin in abundance. What the hell was happening to him?

"You think I'm a fraud," she charged, seizing his gaze in hers and hauling it upward. Her eyes were the color of wildflower honey.

"A woman like you could never survive out in the wilderness." He swallowed hard, struggling to reassert control over his reeling thoughts.

"A woman like me? And just what sort of woman is that, Mr. Goodwin?" she said, deliberately misconstruing his name.

Soft, beautiful, elegant, breathtaking, clever, devious, terrifying . . . answers that clogged his throat, every one unspeakable. Some mad and reckless impulse made him reach out to grab her hand and wrestle it, palm up, to a standstill between them. After a moment, he thought of a plausible explanation for doing so.

"See that?" he demanded, staring at her skin. "Soft as a baby's bottom."

"Gloves, Mr. Goodall." She jerked her hand away and used it to bat the edge of the papers in his other hand. "Goatskin. Also on the list. They prevent blisters and calluses from forming when one repeatedly wields canoe paddles, hammers, axes, or machetes. And yes, I have wielded all of those at one time or other on my journeys." Before he could react, she grabbed his free hand and turned it palm up to give it the same inspection. With the same result.

"No calluses. Sorting socks isn't particularly strenuous. I'm not at all sure a man like you could survive out in the wilderness, Mr. Goodenough."

Her smile made him think of a cat with cream on its whiskers.

"You're a *woman*, Miss O'Keefe," was the only retort he could manage.

"I know," she said with sardonic wistfulness. "But I've made peace with it. The question you must ask yourself, Mr. Goodacre, is whether *you* can."

She edged closer. He could feel her skirts pressed against his lower legs. He could also feel her hot amber eyes searing a path into his ill-equipped pride.

"Can you bear to place yourself in my hands? I assure you they're not as soft as they may seem." She presented both of her hands to him, palms up, and he felt his knees weaken as he looked at them. The skin of his belly went taut and began to ache in a very disturbing way. "Can you take orders from me and stay out of the way and try not to get yourself killed? In short, can I trust you, Mr. Goodbody?"

An inch or two was all that separated them. Desperate as he was to get away, his body was busy obeying a physics-defying gravity exerted by hers . . . edging closer . . . and closer still . . .

The suite door swung open with a thump and he lurched back with a swallowed gasp. Hardacre Blackburn charged through the doorway, his face a mask of pain. At the sight of them, the old man's eyes focused on their proximity, hasty movements, and flushed faces. A wicked smile crept over him.

"I just came to pick up the rubbings. To make copies," she explained, snatching up the chamois skin roll from the floor by her feet, where it had fallen. She looked toward Goodnight without looking at him. "Get started, Goodbody. You've got only two or three days to collect your 'kit.' "

With a nod at the old man she strode out the open door with her chin up and her bustle swaying. Both men stood watching until she was out of sight. It took a minute for Goodnight to come to his senses and close the door. When he turned back, he found the old man's eyes crinkled at the edges.

"Good*body*. Heh, heh. Watch yerself, boy. She has better men than you for breakfast."

The old man hobbled into the bedroom, and Hart strode over to the writing desk and picked up a handful of magazines.

"Goodnight," he muttered, transferring his glare from the dog-eared publications to the door. "The name is *Good-night*."

Six

Clearly, her attempt to suggest to the butler that he was ill-suited to adventure and life in the rough hadn't worked, Cordelia thought as she watched him stride across the lobby of the grand hotel wearing knee-high boots into which he'd tucked his satin-striped trousers. In the day since their confrontation in Blackburn's suite, he'd managed to obtain a formidable pair of footwear, have it double-soled, and begin to wear it in defiant combination with his broadcloth vest and tailcoat. Some men didn't respond well to hints of their inadequacy.

But there was more than one way to de-fur the proverbial feline. If the negative approach didn't work, she would try the positive, play to his strengths—persuade him that the trip would be a waste of his valuable time, that he should direct his energy instead toward pursuing his true desires. The main drawback seemed to be that such a plan presumed that Hartford Goodnight actually had desires—she stared at the trousers tucked into those boots—besides a bizarre inclination to give the world a guffaw or two at his expense.

Tall, bloodless, and British. What would such a man *want*?

A messenger was referred from the main reception desk to the lounge where she sat. "Miss O'Keefe," he called. "Telegram for Miss Cordelia O'Keefe."

She waved to identify herself and beckoned him over.

Tearing into the yellow envelope, she learned that Professor Arturo Valiente was not at his home university in Mexico City, but at the University of Havana consulting on some translations. She asked the messenger to wait while she penned a cable to Dr. Valiente in Havana, had the fellow charge the cost of sending the telegram to Samuel P., and gave him a tip. Afterward, as she sat studying the news with some dejection, wondering how much of a delay this development would cost them, a shadow fell across the yellow telegram.

"*Tsk, tsk,*" came a frosty voice. "Your professor isn't home?"

She turned and looked up to find Goodnight silhouetted against the brightness of a nearby window, reading over her shoulder.

"Excellent news, actually," she said, rising to escape the feeling of him all around her. "It means we won't have to go to Mexico City to get his opinion and translation of our documents. Havana is on our way to southern Mexico."

"Havana." He crossed his arms over his chest and scowled. "You do know there's a revolution going on down there?"

"In the countryside."

"With the occasional spillover of murder and mayhem into Havana."

"Oh?" She busied herself folding the telegram and tucking it into the Spanish phrase book she'd been studying. "Where did you hear such a thing?"

"A clever new invention called a 'newspaper.'"

"Don't tell me you—" She halted, realizing she'd just waded hip deep into an opportunity. "Well, if Havana is embroiled in the conflict, too, we may have difficulty entering or leaving the city." She paused for effect, giving the impression she was troubled by the thought. "Two women traveling together might pass more easily. You know, your employer didn't say you had to accompany us every step of the way. You could meet us in Veracruz or Campeche once we learn where to begin our search."

"Generous of you."

"I can't blame you for not wanting to go." She ignored his sarcasm and tightening expression. "I'm not exactly looking forward to the trip myself . . . not with rioting in the city." She stepped back, hoping to make a quick exit. "Astute of you, Goodrich, to pick up on that."

"Goodnight," he said with clipped diction. "The name is Good*night*."

"Right. Good-night." She couldn't resist a glance at his footgear. "Nice boots, by the way."

As she turned away, he grabbed her elbow and held her for a moment.

"I'm going with you."

Her hope he might prove reasonable or at least persuadable shriveled under the heat of his glare.

"Look." She lowered her voice and reversed her resistance to the grip on her elbow, leaning toward him. "You don't want to go any more than I want you to go. Surely we can come to some sort of accommodation here."

"Are you suggesting I abandon my duty, Miss O'Keefe?"

"Are you open to such a suggestion?"

"Certainly not."

"Damn."

How that word escaped her mouth she would never know, but it was a cat that clearly wasn't going back into the bag. She straightened, fighting the heat blooming in her face.

"Why? Why aren't you open to a reasonable, misery-relieving solution for us both?"

"You're even more like him than I thought." He raised his chin to look down that long, superior British nose of his. "It never occurs to you that one might actually conduct one's self according to a code, that one might answer to a power higher than self-interest."

"You're a *butler*, for heaven's sake. And you're about to charge off into steaming jungles to face God-knows-what in search of God-knows-what for an employer for whom the description 'miserable and manipulative' would be downright charitable." The strong light from the window behind him made it difficult to see his expression. "What is it you want, Goodwin? Why would you insist on going where you're not comfortable, not needed, and not wanted?"

His nostrils flared. He looked as if he were holding something highly unpleasant between his clenched jaws.

She stepped to one side to see his expression better, and it struck her.

"Because you have no choice."

Abruptly, he turned on his heel and strode off toward the servants' stairs at the far end of the hotel's main corridor. She watched his big boots pounding the polished floor and narrowed her eyes.

"Well, well, well. A butler with *secrets*."

"We now know our first port of call," she said to Hedda the next morning, brandishing the telegram containing the professor's reply. Hedda looked up from checking the details of her sketches against the original rubbings laid out on the table in their suite.

"Havana?" Hedda's eyes lit. "I've always wanted to see Havana. They say the air is filled with sweat and sugar by day and rum and music by night."

Cordelia leveled a patient look on her aunt.

"*They* also said lava never came that far down the volcano's sides."

Hedda thought about that, then surrendered her fond imaginings with a sigh. "True."

Cordelia suffered a twinge of discomfort as she watched her aunt dutifully setting aside her dreams to pour over every line and bit of shading in the sketches she was making. For all her practicality and sensible approach to life, Hedda was a devout romantic at heart. She, on the other hand—unconventional female and seeker of the exotic experience—was an unflinching realist. She bit the inside of her lip, feeling that the mismatch was probably harder on her aunt than on her.

"But then 'they' were right about spitting camels and the sunrise over Mauna Loa," she said, a bit too brightly, causing Hedda to look up with surprise. "So, 'rum and music' it is. Now, where is that steamship schedule?"

A quarter of an hour later, she knocked on the door to the old man's suite and was greeted by the butler, who had added a pith helmet complete with bug net to his ensemble. With a doggedly superior sniff, he stepped back from the door and barked to his employer: "It's for you." Then he disappeared into the bedroom with the stack of khaki shirts he was holding.

Samuel P. sat in an overstuffed chair with his bandaged foot propped up and his lap full of ledgers and papers. He waved her over.

"What?" he demanded.

"The professor has agreed to meet with us and to try to decipher the rubbings," she announced, struggling to rid herself of the image of that pith helmet. "We leave for Havana tomorrow."

The old man thought that over and nodded. "And?"

"Before I can arrange passage, we need to finalize the financing."

At the mention of money, Samuel P.'s expression grew more intent.

"That's all taken care of."

"It is?" Cordelia was understandably puzzled. "So you've—what? Decided to draft a letter of credit?"

"Gave the money to Goodnight. Three thousand cash an' a letter of credit good at any bank near a telegraph pole."

"You gave the money to the butler?" She glanced at the

bedroom door, then back at Hardacre with a gripping urge for mayhem. The miserable old—was there never any relief from his manipulations? "This is *my* expedition."

"And *my* money. He's my representative, so he holds the cash."

"We agreed I would run the expedition as I see fit: destination, schedule, pace, hiring, and purchasing."

"Nothin' was said about who held the money, missy." His mouth was a fierce flat line for a moment. "It's Goodnight or nobody."

"You don't think I'm capable of handling money?"

"Ain't about that," he said, leaning forward with the help of the chair arm. "If he's got th' cash"—his eyes narrowed—"ye can't just stash him somewheres an' go on without 'im."

Heat exploded through her upper quarter, sizzling the underside of her skin. Did the old man somehow read minds? Or had the butler blabbed about her attempts to dissuade him from going? Whatever caused his suspicions, she refused to be convicted for an impulse she had yet to act upon.

"I would never stoop to such a thing," she said fiercely.

"You wouldn't? I sure as hell would. If it never crossed your mind, missy, you either ain't as smart as I thought, or you ain't thought this business through." The old man chortled as he watched her struggle with the conundrum he'd just posed. When she whirled and headed for the door, he called out: "It's business, woman. Just business!"

The door slammed hard enough to vibrate the wall. Goodnight came stalking out of the bedroom to look at the still humming door.

"Off in another pique, are we? What was it this time?"

"You know females," Samuel P. declared with a snort. Then he looked over Goodnight's bizarre mix of apparel. "Or mebee you don't." He scowled. "See here, boy, you keep a tight fist on that purse o' mine. She'll figure fifteen ways from Sunday to part you from it and leave you chokin' in 'er dust. If a man ain't got the purse strings, old son, he's got nothin'."

An expedition leader who didn't hold the purse strings, Cordelia muttered to herself on the way to the steamship office at the Port of Tampa, didn't have control of the expedition. Now, not only was she stuck dragging the butler along as she fought her way through equatorial jungles, she was stuck applying to him for funds to cover the expense of doing so! By forcing her to take the butler and to have to squeeze every penny out of him, Samuel P. was maintaining control by proxy. And he would do so as long as he had access to them.

They couldn't leave for Havana quickly enough.

This greedy and unrelenting control was what her father had battled from the moment he announced to the old man that he intended to marry Maureen O'Keefe. Hardacre had sneered, bullied, berated, and threatened them until they finally married without his consent. Then in a fit of anger, he disowned his only child and to her knowledge, never set eyes on him again. The old man had not even bothered to respond to her mother's letter informing him of his son's death.

An intense stab of loss caught her by surprise, taking her breath. Her beloved father, who died when she was seven, had been a bright, rational, and caring soul—the very antithesis of his pitiless and grasping father. Her parents had deserved better than being disdained, demeaned, and disowned, and she had come to require a reckoning of the old man . . . an admission of wrong, an acknowledgment of regret . . . a reinstatement of their memory in the old man's strongbox of a heart. Her eyes burned at the corners. She was going to have all of that and more before she was finished with him.

See if she didn't.

Seven

The Plant Line's SS *Olivette*, a long, single-stack freighter, was scheduled to depart Tampa for Key West and Havana the next night at 9:30. Built with a dozen comfortably furnished cabins topside and a passenger salon and dining room, the Plant Line's flagship was the most comfortable vessel plying the passenger trade in the entire gulf . . . or so the ticket agent had insisted while booking their passage. After charming, wheedling, and finagling passage on the busy steamer, Cordelia then had to insist that her "bursar" would pay for the tickets when they boarded.

Well past sunset, Cordelia and Hedda arrived at the pier where the *Olivette* was berthed and found Goodnight standing by the lantern-lit gangway, still wearing his butler's tails and boots and holding a leather-bound journal tucked between his chest and crossed arms. He scowled as they stepped out of the carriage and began directing the longshoremen to unload the mountain of baggage from their carriage and wagon.

"Traveling light, I see," he said as they headed for the gangway.

"It would be a good bit lighter if we weren't forced to carry so much dead weight along with us," she said pointedly.

His jaw muscle flexed and he reached for his fountain pen to make a notation in his journal.

"What are you doing?" She detoured to see what he was writing, but he slammed the volume shut before she could get a glimpse.

"Recording. As required. Every dot and tittle."

"See here, Goodnap." She leaned close enough to scorch his eyebrows. "This is my expedition and if anyone publishes an account of it, it will be *me*."

"You needn't worry I'll attempt to steal your literary thunder," he said with a hint of disdain. "This is a strictly private accounting, required by my employer. And while we're on the subject of accounting—"

"Indeed . . . while you're pinching every penny and scribbling reports to your master"—she opened her leather satchel and thrust a several-page document into his hands—"you may as well take charge of our equipment and supplies. It will be your job to see that everything arrives with us wherever we go."

He looked at it in dismay.

"My assignment is—"

"To pull your weight as a member of this expedition." She looked him up and down, not bothering to hide her doubts about his ability to do so. "I suggest, if you find that prospect too daunting, you march yourself back down the pier and tell your master to find me another watchdog."

She picked up her other bag intending to join her aunt on the gangway, then turned back for one last salvo.

"Oh, and don't forget to pay the ship's bursar for our passage."

Goodnight watched, steaming quietly, as she greeted the ships' officers with a dazzling smile and the poor wretches beamed as if she were the Queen of Everything and had just knighted them.

Dear God. He had been a heartbeat away from handing

over all the money to her and she wouldn't be civil long enough to permit it. Much as he wanted to spite the old man, he had to admit that the old cod was probably right about who held the money. If he gave up that bit of power, even voluntarily, he would be nothing more than an overworked dogsbody for the rest of the expedition. *If* she didn't just bolt off into the jungle and abandon him first.

Crates being carried aboard by longshoremen intervened in his sight and he refocused on them with annoyance, then anxiety. Crates?

Following a pitched internal battle, he bolted up the gangway after the dock workers to find out where they were stowing the expedition's equipment.

January 21, Day 1

Passage for three to Havana: $75.00, U.S., he wrote in his ledger later, by the light of a deck lantern overlooking the cargo hold. *Four large crates. Two small ones. Two steamer trunks. Per the handwritten inventory.* Then he allowed himself something of an aside. *Infernal female. Barks orders like a training sergeant. God knows what she has packed into those crates. Looks to be half of civilization. She'd better have budgeted money for pack animals—I am not carting a thimble collection and tea service for twelve through the bloody jungle on my back!!!*

Goodnight didn't join the other passengers in watching their departure from the top deck, nor did he appear the next morning for breakfast. Cordelia banged on his cabin door that afternoon, and it took some time for him to answer. When he did, he looked gray in some places and green in others, and the smell coming from his cabin left no doubt that he was battling seasickness. Her fears that he would have difficulty keeping up on the expedition became a dread certainty; the man simply was not constituted for adventure.

She offered some tips on combating the illness, which he took with the grace of a baited bear.

"Unless you have quantities of liquor or laudanum on you . . . no thanks."

She left him to stew in his misery.

The minute the engines stopped at the Key West pier, his door flew open and he came roaring out in stocking feet, a rumpled vest, and trousers savagely crimped from being tucked into boots. Under their disbelieving stares, he dragged himself hand-over-hand down the gangway and onto the pier.

"What would make a man so determined to be so miserable?" Cordelia said, watching him charge toward the nearest tavern.

Hedda shook her head. "How much do you suppose old Hardacre is paying him, anyway?"

When they left Key West for Havana, he dragged himself up the gangway reeking of alcohol and barricaded himself once again in his cabin. He didn't emerge until the next morning when they slowed to take aboard the pilot who would steer them into Havana Harbor. As the ship's motion smoothed in the bay's waters, he emerged barefoot, wearing the same crumpled shirt and tortured trousers, clasping his boots to his chest as if afraid they might escape.

"A pity Mr. Darwin isn't around to see this," she said to Hedda as he passed them on the passenger deck. "Evolution in reverse. Another week at sea and his knuckles would be dragging the ground."

He looked over his shoulder with a bleary indignation that said he'd heard and stalked down the steps to the main deck to stare at the approaching dock.

A squad of armed Spanish soldiers waiting on the quay beside the *Olivette*'s berth caught her gaze. She joined the captain as he stood on the upper deck watching their progress toward the dock.

"Is something wrong?" She nodded to the welcome awaiting them.

"Nothing more than usual," he said, indicating the log book and ship's manifest he was holding. "The government's touchy these days. They'll be searching our cargo and passengers to make sure we're not transporting guns or potential revolutionaries."

"Guns?" She searched the grim expressions of the soldiers and officials lined up to meet their ship. Her gaze went uneasily to the cargo bay where their equipment was stowed. "I thought you said the city was calm."

"As calm as government soldiers on every corner can make it," he said with a rueful smile. "Now, if you will excuse me . . ." He headed for the stairs and began shouting orders to the dock workers waiting ashore to receive mooring lines and prepare the gangway.

Soldiers and customs officials swarmed up the gangway and boarded the ship. The head bureaucrat presented himself to the captain and demanded in a mixture of English and Spanish to see the ship's manifest, to inspect all cargo being offloaded, and to personally interview all disembarking passengers. The captain nodded stoically and motioned to the steward to fetch the passengers.

The customs inspector spotted the expedition crates being hoisted out of the hold, and pointed at them, barking orders that they be stacked on the deck for inspection. Cordelia saw Goodnight, who had managed to don both boots, searching through his precious ledger and coming up with a handful of papers that looked alarmingly familiar. Her knees went weak as she watched him head for the inspector with the inventory of their equipment.

She flew down the steps and across the deck to intercept him, but he had already entered the inspector's sights.

The inspector gasped when she planted herself before him with her most winning smile. Blinking, he straightened to his full height.

"Senora. I did not realize there were ladies among the passengers."

"Senorita," she said with a tilt of her head. "My aunt and I boarded at Tampa. Those are ours." She swept a hand toward the stack of crates.

"I have this quite under control," Goodnight declared, attempting to offer the papers for inspection, only to have Cordelia step into his path and seize them.

"This won't be necessary," she declared with forced pleasantry.

"I insist." He refused to relinquish the papers. "This is my assigned duty, and I intend to 'pull my weight' on the expedition."

"This isn't the time." Her tone flattened as she pulled harder. "We don't want to burden the inspector with unnecessary paperwork."

"I'm certain the inspector"—he clipped every word—"is quite accustomed to the monotony of paperwork."

"In which case, he'd probably rather open the crates and have a look." She gave a final, fierce yank and claimed the papers, which she tucked behind her as she turned to the inspector and batted her eyes. "After all, *anything* can be written on paper. It's what's in the crates that counts, is it not?"

She reached for a pry bar one of the soldiers held and smiled. Dazzlingly.

The inspector accepted the tool from her and smiled back. Dazzled.

The official handed off the manifest to his assistant, ordering him to see to the rest of the cargo and passengers.

She waved aside his apologies and insisted he open one of the large crates to verify that they were filled with expedition equipment, and to retrieve a small package, which she presented to him with a smile potent enough to melt the buckles on his suspenders.

With relief, later, she watched him recall the soldiers and his assistant from the cargo hold and order them back down the gangway. He handed the captain back the ship's now-approved manifest, then kissed the women's hands and strode down the dock with a box under his arm and a self-important swagger.

"What in infernal blazes was that all about?" Goodnight confronted her the minute the inspector was out of sight. "You assign me to see to the baggage, and when I try to do so you swoop down and rip the inventory out of my hands!"

She motioned for him to keep his voice down.

"The captain said they were looking for guns and ammunition."

"So?"

She paged through the inventory and held it up, pointing to the guns listed at the bottom of one sheet. It was gratifying to see the color drain from his face.

"You bloody well might have told me," he snapped. "What would you have done if he hadn't taken your little bribe?"

"It wasn't a bribe, it was—"

"Never had such an easy inspection before, miss!" The captain's voice intruded as he strode past. When she looked up, he tipped his hat to her. "We should have you aboard every trip."

After the captain passed, she tried to stuff the crumpled inventory into Goodnight's hands again. "Here."

"You took it back—you can keep it." He leaned closer, his eyes suddenly hot and turbulent. "And do the explaining if we get stopped and searched again. You're better at fluttering your eyelashes than I am."

She found herself poised at the edge of a massive whirlpool of tensions and emotions, startled by the strength of her desire to step deeper into it and let it sweep her along. His gray gaze . . . now almost silver . . . molten . . . swirling . . .

"Don't think I don't know what you're doing," he said, in a rumble that vibrated her fingertips. "You think if you make it difficult enough, I'll fold and slink away. Well, you're wrong, O'Keefe. I'm here to stay."

After a few steps away he halted and looked back, his anger replaced by his customary sardonic air.

"So, what was in the package you gave him? In case you come down with a touch of malaria and I need to bribe a custom's official . . ."

January 23, Day 3

Arrived Havana Harbor, nine o'clock, a.m. Greeted by customs official—who should be sacked for abandonment of duty. One blasted smile from HER and the poor devil lost higher brain function. Practically drooled down his vest.

Confronted her afterward, demanding to know what sort of "bribe" she'd given him. It wasn't a bribe, she said; it was a teacup. Gold rimmed. A gift for his wife. Dammit—I knew she was packing china!!!

The transfer to the hotel went smoothly, owing largely to the fact that Hedda and Cordelia had long since worked out a system for handling such operations. That, and the fact that she assigned the aromatic Goodnight to ride on the baggage wagon and make certain all of their things arrived.

On the way they passed through a warren of warehouses and into the city proper, where soldiers patrolled the street corners and people moved along the narrow thoroughfares at an unhurried pace. As they entered the center of the old city, the streets broadened and they encountered sun-drenched plazas clogged with carts and people and alive with the sounds of trade being conducted.

Havana was unlike any place Cordelia had seen before. The stuccoed brick of the houses and shops was painted a lush pallet of tropical colors, and every building, however modest, possessed an upstairs balcony bounded by handsome ironwork. The long plantation shutters that bracketed every door and window, thrown open to admit the morning sun, released a tantalizing melange of spicy smells on the morning air. Bougainville and jasmine ran rampant over doorways and up trellises. Vibrant hibiscus in a rainbow of hues flanked the aged fountains that occupied places of honor in the busy plazas.

The Hotel San Miguel, recommended by the captain, turned out to be a small but charming inn with a stunning view of the old fort and lighthouse at the entrance of Havana Harbor. Cordelia negotiated the cost of their rooms and breakfasts in phrase-book Spanish, then turned to her bursar with a prim smile.

"Pay the gentleman, Goodskin."

He handed the hotel manager a twenty-dollar gold piece and a handful of American silver, then seeing her pointed stare, followed it to the porters. Reluctantly, he fished a few dimes out of his pocket for them.

"Are we quite finished playing Lady Spendthrift?" he demanded archly.

"For now." She turned her attention to the placid, sunlit street outside. "Thank Heaven we made it through the swarms of bloodthirsty revolutionaries in the streets." She leaned in his direction with a glint in her eye. "Be sure to bring your sidearm with you when we head to the university, Goodruff. Hordes of free-thinking students can be so unpredictable."

He watched her swaying up the stairs with an infuriating little smile and reached for his journal.

The narrow streets of Havana were coming to life again in the late afternoon as they left the hotel on foot, bound for the university. The smell of coffee wafted from the open-air cafés they passed and pushcarts laden with saffron-scented rice, spicy pork, and sweets redolent of hot sugar and cinnamon spread a feast for the senses. The pling of guitars and thump of handmade drums on street corners provided lively accompaniment for people emerging into a post-siesta round of work, late-day commerce, and socializing.

But as Cordelia and Hedda, trailed by Goodnight, made their way past bookshops and cantinas of the sort found near universities everywhere, they noted there were more soldiers in this part of the city and that the patrols seemed more vigilant and heavily armed. Here, people lowered their heads or averted their eyes as they passed the soldiers, as if afraid a direct glance might be taken as a challenge.

Cordelia pulled the mantilla she had adopted closer about her face and glanced at Hedda, who read her look and copied her precaution. Then she looked back at Goodnight and her stomach clenched. He was striding along in boots, a khaki shirt, and breeches, over which he had donned that absurd tailcoat again, looking disastrously tall and foreign and oblivious to the potential threat only yards away. She slowed to allow him to catch up.

"Try slouching a bit, will you?" she hissed. "You're drawing attention."

"Well, excuse me"—he stretched a defiant bit taller—"but my height is not exactly within my control."

"You stick out like a sore thumb. If the soldiers stop you and find you're carrying a pistol, they'll arrest you."

"A pistol?" He gave a "tsk." "It so happens, I'm not carrying a gun."

The news, delivered in his customary tight-jawed tones, rasped her last intact nerve. It was all she could do to keep from punching him.

"Then it's a good thing I am."

Eight

Hart stood immobilized, watching her head for the stone arch visible at the end of the street, grappling with the twin realizations that she had been serious in her suggestion that he carry a loaded firearm in the streets and that she was actually carrying one herself, somewhere on her person. He had difficulty swallowing. As if she weren't already dangerous enough.

His mind went inescapably to the question of where she was carrying it. Her purse? Her pocket? Under her petticoats? Strapped to her . . .

God Almighty.

That was quite enough of that.

Straightening his shoulders despite her warnings, he headed after the women and caught up as they passed through a pair of great stone pillars hung with iron gates. The inscription carved into the stone arch spanning the opening read *Universidad De La Habana*. The square beyond the pillars was bounded by architecturally distinctive buildings that seemed to bear out the arch's claim.

He watched Cordelia pause to survey the plaza, then head for a group of students gathered in front of a busy cantina. With her Spanish phrase book, effortless American beauty, and devastating Irish smile, she was soon surrounded by eager young males from several countries vying to provide her with directions to the Departamento de la Antiquedades . . . as well as libation, private tutoring, and a range of other "educational" experiences.

She didn't need a pistol, he thought irritably, he needed a brickbat.

His overpowering impulse to reach through the crowd and snatch her out by the hair of the head appalled him. He told himself it grew out of his conviction of the superiority of his male judgment and an outraged sense of propriety. At least, he hoped it did. Any other explanation would mean he was responding to her as a man to a woman, and he did not intend to give Blackburn's unpredictable progeny that sort of edge with him.

When she declined all offers that didn't involve directions and struck off to continue the search, he released the breath he'd been holding.

As a part of the renowned School of the Humanities, Antiquedades was housed in one of the more prominent buildings on the plaza. Once they were inside, it was only a matter of inquiring in the department offices to learn that Arturo Valiente had been assigned offices and a work space on the lower level.

They found him pouring over documents at a long, brightly lit worktable in a cavernous shelf-lined room. He looked up with surprise as they entered, and his magnifying glass and his jaw both lowered. His expression warmed and he said something in Spanish that set Cordelia scrambling for her phrase book. Seeing her searching for a proper response, he rose and shifted immediately to English.

"May I assist?" His voice was a deep baritone and his English, though deeply accented, was perfectly understandable. "You are lost?"

"Professor Arturo Valiente, of the University of Mexico?" she asked, and the man nodded.

"What do you know—he does exist," Hart muttered.

"I am Cordelia O'Keefe." She stepped forward to extend a hand to the professor across the table. "You were kind enough to agree to look at some rubbings of Mayan stones for me."

"O'Keefe?" He blinked. "*You* are the 'yanqui' O'-Keefe?"

"I am."

Valiente hurried around the table, banging into the corner of it in his eagerness to take her hands in his.

He was slightly shorter than O'Keefe, who admittedly was tall for a woman. He had the black hair and dark eyes common to Latin types and the flashy white teeth and reckless grin common to lothario types. His age was hard to guess—silver at the temples, fifty at least—but his solid frame and quick movements made him seem younger. He wore well-tailored trousers, handmade Italian shoes, and a shirt embellished with white-on-white silk embroidery.

Expensive clothes for an academic. Hart hadn't spent eighteen months as a tycoon's butler without learning to read a man's clothing. He knew at a glance that Valiente didn't furnish his wardrobe on a professor's stipend.

"Welcome Senorita O'Keefe." Valiente admired her with an openness that skirted the bounds of decency. "Is rare to meet so *lovely* a colleague."

"I take it you were expecting a man."

"Forgive me, senorita. I am very, very pleased to be wrong."

The bounder kissed each of her hands and didn't release them until she turned to make introductions. "Allow me to introduce my aunt, Miss Hedda O'Keefe, the artist and recorder for our expedition." Then she thought to include him with an offhanded wave. "And, of course, that is Goodnight."

The professor stared at him, taking in his odd pairing of garments and trying to make sense of her dismissive introduction.

"Would it be possible to show you our sketches now,

Professor?" She plunged emphatically into the reason for her visit. "We know you're busy, and we don't wish to take you from your work for long."

"But of course." Valiente hurried to clear his worktable and arrange lighting for viewing the drawings.

Hart bristled at the look of disapproval she shot him. It inflicted a sting to his pride that took him by surprise. He had thought himself beyond caring about other peoples' opinions; a year and a half in domestic service to Hardacre Blackburn had inured him to humiliation and invisibility. In spite of himself, he looked down at his rumpled tailcoat. What began as a show of defiance and a demonstration of his indifference to others' opinion had just taken on the unpleasant odor of a joke past its prime. Goodnight the butler would have dismissed it with a stroke of sarcasm and remained above it all. Goodnight the scholar, the chemist, the son of a respected family felt perfectly skewered by it.

The professor hovered around Cordelia as she laid out the sketches in rows down the long table, and Hart watched him staring at her narrow waist, flame-kissed hair, and graceful movements. When she turned to invite the professor to inspect the drawings, he was so close they almost bumped noses.

Blushing, she glanced at Hart and he experienced a brief but vivid memory of being exactly where the professor was now, in close proximity to her glowing eyes and voluptuous curves. An unwelcome surge of heat boiled up in him, making him fiercely aware of the mantle of servitude he wore. This—*this* was what he hated most about her, he realized, ripping the coat from his shoulders and tossing it aside. She reminded him he was a *man*.

It took only a question or two from Cordelia to elicit from the professor a short lecture on the representation of nature in the language and culture of the Mayans. After a few minutes extemporizing on familiar symbols and elements in their imagery, he turned to the topic of writing.

"Initially, the scholars think each block or pictograph represents a unit of meaning, a word. But some—like myself—believe that the glyphs are made of symbols that are combined again and again to make new meanings. Diego de Landa's alphabet—it makes too many problems in translating other writings. No one uses it now. But the German mathematician, Ernst Forstemann, he discovers the key to the Mayan number system in the Dresden Codex, which helps us understand a great deal more.

"Clever Mayans." He tapped the side of his head. "One of only two cultures in history who make a number to be 'zero.' Forstemann uses his 'number key' to unlock the secret of their calendar. The Mayans mark events with carving and writing that show dates. Now we can read these dates.

"But scholar Alfred Maudslay"—he wagged a finger—"he is most important to we students of the ancients. I use his magnificent photos and drawings myself, in my work. They help me to make elements of an improved alphabet."

"So, you think these blocks are a form of writing?" Cordelia asked, trying to steer him back to the sketches.

"No doubt of it." He reached for the closest drawing. "But like other languages, a symbol here has many meanings. Here, you see this dots and bars?" He pointed to tiny balls and what looked like stick bundles at the side of the drawing he held. "Wherever these are, you know you look at numbers. And this figure that looks like an eye, this is always a zero."

Cordelia began to reconsider her decision to withhold the story Samuel P. had given them concerning the rubbings. She and Hedda had decided to say nothing of it, so as not to influence the professor's evaluation. They needed his best scholarship and full objectivity if they were to learn what the rubbings truly represented. The temptation to tell him what they suspected was overwhelming.

"Sketches are drawn to what—scale?" he asked.

"One to one," Hedda supplied. "They are the exact size of the rubbings."

"Is big tablature, blocks nearly a foot on each side," he mused, moving methodically along the table with his hand outstretched, as if sweeping it along a line of print he was reading.

Goodnight, standing behind Hedda, watched for a time and then suddenly leaned over the table.

"I say, Valiente, is that a school ring or a family signet?"

The professor roused from contemplation to glance at the ring on his hand.

"Family. Valiente is venerable name in España and also Mexico."

"Ah. *Family.*" Goodnight's knowing look puzzled Valiente and annoyed Cordelia. "That explains the shoes."

Fortunately for him there was nothing suitable for throwing within Cordelia's reach. What was he doing—making personal remarks to the man who held the key to their expedition? She smiled, then touched the professor's sleeve to distract him from Goodnight's hostility.

"In the original the blocks are attached and form three columns," she said.

"Order is critical to learn the meaning," he said earnestly.

"I numbered each of the sketches." Hedda pointed to the numbers on the corners. "So we would know exactly how each block fits with the others."

With Cordelia and Hedda helping to match the numbers, it wasn't long before the sketches lay in the same three columns found on the originals. With the blocks now aligned, it was easy to see that one stood out as different: the block with the head of the cat.

"What is here?" He grabbed a lamp and held it closer to the drawing. "A cat, yes? But with such"—he muttered a moment in Spanish—"deepness and realness. Elaborate carving work for this period."

"And what period would that be?" Goodnight asked from the opposite side of the table. "Jurassic? Devonian? Paleolithic, perhaps?"

Cordelia *so* longed to give her "observer" a swift kick.

"*Classical* period," the professor said, catching the sarcasm but gallantly rising above it. "Mayans' first and longest time of building is called 'Classical.' In this time, religion, myths, and culture all come to full flower." He ran his finger over what seemed to be smudges on the drawing. "Spots? Are these spots true?"

He bent to inspect them closer as Hedda assured him they were.

"This is the panther the old people and today people call the *jaguar*." Excitement rose in his eyes. "Where do you get these rubbings?"

"From a collector in the States, who asked that we investigate them."

"Does this 'collector' say how he comes by them?"

"Only that he took them as collateral on a debt not repaid," she answered.

Valiente thought a moment, frowning, then walked up and down the table tracing lines of connection between blocks. After a while, he rubbed his eyes, arched his back, and sat down on his stool to gather his thoughts.

"Well?" Cordelia prompted, wringing her hands with tension.

"This cat . . . he is certainly a jaguar. Your drawing is very fine, senorita." He shot a smile at Hedda, who blushed.

"We know there are groups—sects—in Mayan times which are devoted to the Spirit of the Jaguar," he continued. "They worship the great cat for his strength and smart cunning and long life. They believe he lives from the creation of the world, a spirit who has helped humankind since its infancy. Warriors in these villages, when they do great deeds in battles, they are called 'Knight of the Jaguar.'

"It is told that this spirit of the big cat is wise in all things. And noble of heart. He sees the short, hard lives of people, and he decides to give them a gift to comfort them in their days."

"A gift from—the cat spirit," Cordelia murmured, catching herself.

"Exactly." Valiente's face lighted. "The Gift of the Jaguar."

"Can you tell what the blocks says about this 'jaguar spirit'?"

He shrugged. "It takes some study yet. These 'jaguar people' are known by the writing and stories of others—no sites are found. But there are places to explore, many treasures not yet found. A whole world sleeps beneath the sands of Mexico, waiting to be uncovered."

He went to Cordelia and took her hands in his.

"You go to search for these stones, senorita?"

"Yes. It is our task to find them."

"Then I go with you." He drew her hand to his chest above his heart. "My soul does not rest until I know their secret."

Nine

"You cannot honestly be thinking of taking him along," Goodnight said to her in a forceful whisper, later, as they trailed the professor and Hedda through the darkened streets. After another hour of studying the drawings and demonstrating on a map the various locations where stories of the jaguar people had been encountered, the professor had insisted on taking them to dinner at one of his favorite *cocinas*. They had to accept.

"Why wouldn't I?" she answered in an even more furious whisper. "He knows the languages." She enumerated the professor's assets on her fingers. "He knows the country. He knows Mayan culture and can recite the entire catalog of recent discoveries. I'd be mad *not* to take him."

"He's . . . he's . . ."

"What?" She halted on the cobbled street and jammed her fists on her waist. "Too knowledgeable? Too helpful? Too qualified?"

That stopped him. Briefly.

"Too eager," he blurted out after a pause. "He's too bloody eager."

She narrowed her eyes, refusing to admit to him that

that bothered her, too. But they needed the professor's help, and she would be deviled if she let a butler tell her what to do on *her* expedition.

"Considering how reluctant the rest of us are to be here," she said, moving again, "his enthusiasm should provide a much needed bit of balance."

The restaurant was a bright and noisy place on the point of an intersection between busy streets. Floor-length shutters between the pillars on the two main sides were thrown open to draw the night air, and light spilled into the street in puddles that bathed small tables erected outside to accommodate the overflow of patrons. Inside, the walls bore colorful hangings, and the tables were covered with bright cloths and lit with candles that gave the place an exotic golden glow.

The professor was greeted half a dozen times before they made it to the table the owner cleared for them. His acquaintances ran the gamut from university scholars to government bureaucrats, from merchants and community leaders to students and waiters. At each stop he introduced the women as American explorers, pointedly ignoring the British contingent. They even ran into a fellow American, a short, robust ship's captain from New York, named Johnny O'Brien.

After a lengthy and bewildering recitation of the menu in Spanish, the professor took it upon himself to order for them. They were soon served tall, fragrant glasses of the city's best sangria, a mixture of wine, fruit, and sugar that was pure ambrosia. Goodnight watched Cordelia sipping it and glowered; she narrowed her eyes at him and took several emphatic gulps.

Through the meal the professor regaled them with stories of adventures in the wilds of southern Mexico, British Honduras, and Guatemala. As the food arrived and the pitcher of sangria was refilled, his tales grew wilder and more outlandish. And the music began.

Tables at one end of the dining area were taken down, clearing an expanse of floor for dancing. The music of the guitars, drums, maracas, and brass rose steadily, with infectious rhythms unlike anything Cordelia had heard before. The music demanded movement, even if it was only tapping toes or drumming fingers on a tabletop. The professor invited Cordelia and then Hedda to take the floor with him, and Goodnight looked outraged and shook his head. As if they didn't have sense to decline on their own. Cordelia refused to look at him again.

Just as the noise and atmosphere began to overheat, there was an abrupt change in tempo and the professor and most of the men present roared approval.

"What is it?" Cordelia leaned toward their host. "What's happening?"

"Feel that?" The professor undulated his shoulders in time to the beat. "Is a new dance from Argentina . . . called tango." The next moment, he was pulling her to her feet, bent on ushering her onto the dance floor.

"Really, O'Keefe." Goodnight shot to his big, heavily shod feet as she passed. "This is most irregular."

As the professor drew her into a dance pose at arm's length, her need to defy her watchdog's disapproval far outweighed her worry about what the professor had in mind. She embraced the dramatic but oddly natural rhythm and was soon moving in steps not unlike the social dances she knew. As she mastered what seemed to be a fundamental step, the professor pulled her into a sort of promenade that ended with her whirling back and forth at his direction. As the dance progressed, their lower halves drew steadily closer. And closer still. So close, in fact, that their legs brushed and even entwined at times. Mildly alarmed, she considered leaving the floor. But one look at the outrage that awaited her at their table made her decide to see it through.

Suddenly the professor brought her body fully against his and guided her leg into a dramatic extension that pressed her into a startling proximity with his, mimicking a far more intimate dance between a man and a woman.

• • •

"Good God." Hart gripped the edge of the table to keep from bounding onto the dance floor to pull them apart.

"Most . . . unusual," Hedda said in a constricted voice.

"Unusual?" He sounded a little choked himself. "If they were spaniels, we'd be throwing buckets of water on them!"

"Cordie is a remarkable dancer," Hedda's voice shrank to a squeak. "More than one gentleman has fallen in love with her on a dance floor."

"Believe me," he said, "Valiente isn't falling into anything half that noble."

"Oh, my! That was extraordinary!" Cordelia was breathless and fanning herself with her hands when they returned to the table. Goodnight pushed up from the table and turned on her with his eyes hot and shoulders oddly swollen.

"I'd like a word with you, if you don't mind."

Before she had a chance to object, he seized her upper arm and escorted her toward the arches that formed a colonnade along the rear of the restaurant. Reluctant to make a scene, she allowed herself to be pulled to the far corner of the corridor. There he released her but planted an arm against the wall in front of her to bar an escape.

"What the devil's gotten into you?" she demanded.

"Me?" He nearly strangled on the word. "What's gotten into *you*—making a spectacle of yourself out there? There are mating rituals in Borneo less explicit than that. May I remind you that you're in a foreign country, you're on a mission, and the man whose shirt you just steam pressed with your . . . *body* . . . has just attached himself to our expedition to Mexico."

"I'm in Rome—I'm doing as the Romans do," she said irritably. "Or don't they teach that little nugget of wisdom in butling school?"

"I wouldn't know. I didn't attend 'butling school.'

Where I went, we were encouraged to develop more rational and coherent standards."

"And where was that, Goodnight? Where do they teach condescension, snap judgments, and insulting references to other people's shoes?"

"*Oxford.*" It came out in a burst, as if it had been building in him for days, weeks, months. Even he seemed surprised by the force of it; he visibly reined the rest of his reaction. "Though to be fair, I never saw 'shoes' mentioned on a single exam there. That bit I learned from your grandfather."

"You? Oxford?" She had difficulty mating the two concepts at first. Then she realized that in a moment of raw pride he had handed her the key to his secrets. Her ire was seriously undercut. "What did you study there?"

"Chemistry," he declared, looking like he had to struggle to keep from saying more, "which is irrelevant." He straightened and she could actually see his sardonic detachment sliding back into place. "What is important here is how you expect to maintain control of the expedition if you behave like an accommodating tavern wench around the professor."

"A *tavern* wench?" She sucked a sharp breath. One minute he was almost human and the next—

A thunderous crash and a boom burst from the dining room. The music died in a discordant bleat that was replaced by shouts and screams and sounds of furniture being overturned and dishes shattering. Shock galvanized them. Together they headed for the arches, where they were turned back by frantic waiters and patrons escaping back through the colonnade toward the kitchens.

"What's happening?" Hart demanded of them as he pulled Cordelia out of the way. The only word he recognized was "soldados."

"Soldiers?" Had they somehow wandered into the middle of the rebellion spreading across the country? Cordelia's first concern was for her aunt. "Hedda!"

She fought her way up the passage to the nearest arch.

From there she could see some people in the dining room scrambling for the exits, while those less fortunate were pressed against walls while a squad of khaki-clad soldiers tore apart the restaurant.

It took a minute to locate Hedda and the professor. They were inching their way toward an opening on the far side of the dining room. Hedda's blanched face peered past the professor's shoulder at the arch where Cordelia and Goodnight had disappeared. Desperate to signal her aunt, she waved until Hedda spotted her in the shadows.

Her heart sank as she realized the khaki-filled distance between them was impassable. The professor turned to follow Hedda's gaze, then nodded to her and gave a faint jerk of his head toward the window.

"You can't reach her," Goodnight's whisper came near her ear. "He'll find a way to get her out safely. Come on."

The minute she turned to object, one of the soldiers spotted the professor's attention to the arches and followed his gaze to Cordelia. He raised his gun, shouting, "Yanqis—Americanos!"

"Now!" Goodnight barked, pivoting and lurching back down the passage, dragging her along.

They burst into the kitchen and ran smack into a pair of soldiers who had paused in the midst of the invasion to fill their bellies with the restaurant's excellent fare. The rifles they had propped against the table beside them clattered to the floor, and food flew as they went diving for their guns. Cordelia and Goodnight were most of the way to the door before the soldiers' greasy fingers found secure holds on the weapons. Crouching and dodging among the outraged cooks and terrified waiters and dishwashers, they cleared the door just as a shot was fired.

Behind them they could hear a voice booming orders and there were no more gunshots. They reached the main street and began to run, spurred by the sound of boots pounding the hard-packed dirt of the alley and then the brick of the street. They had no idea where they were or in what direction they were moving, but at least there was moonlight enough for them to keep their footing on the uneven paving.

They raced down one street and then another before Hart spotted a niche in a high stuccoed wall. He pulled her into it, only to find it already occupied by a young couple doing what young couples everywhere did on moonlit nights. A furious stream of Spanish set them scrambling back with a "Dammit!" and a frantic "So sorry!"

Hearing the sound of running closing in on them, Cordelia pulled Hart along with her into a nearby alley, narrowly avoiding two soldiers barreling down the street with rifles ready, clearly searching for them.

"What do they want with us?" she whispered as they pressed their backs against the wall. "We didn't do anything."

"We're foreigners. We make easy targets."

"Especially you." She gave him a scowl. "I told you to slouch."

Slipping from doorway to loggia to public fountain and then to other doorways, they made their way through an area that included mostly residences and shops before hearing raised voices that seemed to be moving quickly through the streets. Unwilling to take a chance, Hart spotted a set of steps leading up a hill and headed for it, looking for an opening. There was a stone wall supporting the lower half—

"Aaaaayyy!"

They found themselves nose to nose with an overheated caballero wearing a shirt half off his sweaty shoulders and a murderous glare. A girl's tousled head and fierce black eyes appeared around his shoulder. "*Vayase!*" she hissed before she got a look at them. Her response afterward wasn't much better: "*Yanqui estupido! Vaya Ud. a paseo!*"

"God Almighty!" Goodnight, incensed, glanced over his shoulder as they darted down the street and ducked into a recessed doorway. "Don't these people have homes to go to? Do they have to do their 'begetting' in the streets?"

Pressed against a wall, she closed her eyes for a moment, trying to catch her breath. When she opened her eyes Goodnight was staring at her, breathing hard, his light eyes reflecting the moonlight coming from behind her. For a moment she was caught speechless, her mental functions occupied with calculations of the distance from her waist to his hands, from her breasts to his chest, from her lips to—

Voices approaching kicked her higher faculties back into operation and she glanced at the street, then at him in alarm. He grabbed her by the waist and pulled her over against the door, covering her with his body so that only her skirts could be seen from the street.

"Gun," he said in a whisper so low she couldn't tell at first if he said it or she thought it. "Where is your pistol?"

She was too busy trying to breathe and swallow to reply.

"Your purse?" He continued in a hoarse whisper, "A pocket?" He ran his hands down the sides of her waist. "This is not a good time to tell me you don't really carry one."

Her body began to tremble and her breaths came short and quick. He was suddenly above her and all around her, surrounding her with his heat and invading her thoughts with a low, provocative whisper that slid along her nerves like thick, hot syrup. She couldn't tell whether she was reacting to the danger or to him. All she knew was that every part of her body was aching for contact with his and that at the moment—there in the dark Cuban night, with danger dogging their footsteps—all she could think about was what his lips would feel like against hers.

His head lowered.

"What are you doing?" she said against his mouth.

"I'm in Cuba," he said, without the slightest trace of irony. "I'm doing as the Cubans do." And he claimed her mouth.

Soft . . . his lips were soft on hers and his arms felt hard and very male as they clamped around her. Every irritation he had generated in her drowned instantly in the flood of pleasure that took its place. She rose onto her toes and wrapped her arms around him, pulling him closer, spreading her hands across his back. Strong, she realized with mild surprise; he was lean but well muscled.

Nothing in her experience with gentlemen of good breeding and respectful attentions had prepared her for the shock of being kissed passionately by a surly butler in a dark doorway while hiding from armed soldiers—and feeling the ground fall away from under her feet. She was buoyant, floating, drinking in the wine-scented heat of him, opening her mouth to his sensual probing, relishing the taste of him and the feel of his hard body against hers.

At the edge of her consciousness she heard laughter—male laughter—and what sounded like desultory comments in Spanish. It registered briefly that the soldiers had spotted them in the shadows and paused long enough to ogle what they were doing. After a moment, the laughter faded, but it was some time before the intensity of their kiss began to fade and the realization that the danger had passed ended it.

When they drew apart she was panting, feeling like she'd run a race for her very life. She looked up into his face, his angular, silver-eyed masterpiece of a visage, and felt her feet slam back down onto the pavement.

"Are they gone?" she managed, desperate to fill the silence looming between them.

"God, I hope so," he said, taking a step backward, and then a second one. His eyes looked huge and startled, his surprisingly muscular arms were now limp at his sides. "I don't think I could take much more of that."

She watched him turn away and stumble to the edge of the alcove to look up and down the street. She blinked, wiped her mouth, and tried desperately to take a deep breath to clear her head. His words rumbled through her, banging on her pride as if it were a bass drum.

He couldn't take much more of kissing her? It was that bad?

A moment later the absurdity of the conclusion struck her.

So it was that bad, was it?

With the heat of her burning face hidden by the shadows, she pulled her dignity and self-possession back into place. Then she strode to the corner where Goodnight was taking a deep breath or two himself.

With a hostile gleam in her eye she stepped in front of him, hiked her skirts above her knee, and propped her stocking-clad leg against the corner of the building, blocking his way. Under his widening eyes, she removed a small revolver from the holster strapped to her thigh and inspected the chambers.

As she lowered her leg and her skirts fell back into place, she heard him suck two partial breaths in quick succession.

"You'd better stay behind me," she ordered, giving him an incendiary glance while stroking the gun's trigger with her finger. "Oh, and in case you get shot," she said with vengeful earnestness, "you better tell me where you keep our money."

January 24, Day 4

Bathing water for three: $2.00. Afternoon tea: $1.50. Dinner: ?

Found the university. Entire place could use a coat of paint. Found Arturo Valiente. More like a waiter than a professor, the way he dishes it up. Wretch pointed out there was a cat head in the drawings—DO SAY—then announced he was coming along to look for it. Tried in vain to get O'Keefe to see what a bad idea that is. He took us to a restaurant, fed us stuff that turned my mouth inside out, and introduced us to a Yank on the government's enemy list.

Place was raided by government soldiers. Had to take to the streets.

Blasted woman really does carry a firearm—strapped to her thigh! Just yanked up her skirts and hauled the damned thing out!! I nearly had a heart attack. God help me—every time I close my eyes for the next month I'm going to see her naked leg.

Note: Look for St.-John's-Wort in local apothecary. Maybe salt peter.

Ten

Despite the uproar that accompanied Cordelia and Goodnight's escape, the young officer in charge of the search had managed to prevent any more of the patrons from slipping away. His men slammed the great shutters closed just as the professor and Hedda were about to bolt through them. The pair was stuck with the other unlucky diners, under the scrutiny of a swaggering lieutenant who was determined to make his raid profitable.

"What do they want?" Hedda whispered to the professor.

"They look for rebels," Valiente declared, watching the officer's behavior and gauging his influence in the chain of command by his crude tactics. When the officer struck a brash student and ordered him taken to the palace of El Capitan General for questioning, the professor began to clap slowly.

"Bravo," he said with a mix of superiority and disdain.

"Who the hell are you?" The officer stalked over, unholstering his pistol.

"One who agrees a firm hand must be taken with certain *classes*, if one is to make them respect authority." He raked the officer with a pointed look.

Hedda held her breath.

"Name?" the officer barked.

"Professor Arturo Valiente of the University of Havana *and* the University of Madrid." Mention of the Spanish capital registered with the officer.

"And her?" The lieutenant waved his pistol toward Hedda, who watched the professor's provocative air with growing anxiety.

"I have the honor of entertaining a renowned archaeologist from New York, Miss Hedda O'Keefe. She is come to consult with me at the university."

"New York?" The lieutenant's eyes narrowed. "Americano, eh?" He stalked over to Hedda, who managed not to cower. "What do you know of your countryman, O'Brien? Did you see him here tonight?"

Hedda looked to Valiente for both guidance and translation, for she recognized the name and recalled meeting the captain earlier in the evening. Valiente's emphatic neutrality as he translated warned her to say nothing.

"Please tell the officer that I am sorry, but I cannot be of help," she addressed both the professor and the officer. "I know no one by that name."

Valiente translated, adding for his part, "Now, if you will be so good as to release us, I must escort Miss O'Keefe to her hotel."

The lieutenant, green as he was, had watched the professor and Hedda during the translation and detected more than words passing between them.

"No, I think she must stay." He looked Hedda over with ominous interest. "Perhaps I can help her remember more."

Valiente stepped in front of her, his shoulders braced and his chin up.

"You will let us go now," he said, his voice full of restrained anger, "or you will find yourself in very large trouble, *chiquillo*."

It was a calculated insult and it had a predictable effect. The lieutenant stuck his gun in the professor's face, and the professor boldly slapped it away.

"I demand to be taken to the governor."

Minutes later, Hedda and the professor were tossed into the back of a commandeered wagon and hauled through the darkened streets to the palace of El Capitan General. But the leader of Cuba's Spain-supplied military was dining at the governor's palace with a contingent of dignitaries from the mother country. The professor made such a point of his outrage that the lieutenant, on advice from his anxious superior, took them to the governor's palace after all.

"Not to fear, senorita," Valiente said, taking her cold hands as they rode through the moonlit night. "We do nothing wrong. The governor does not wish to insult America by detaining her innocent citizens."

"Why are they looking for that man?" she asked, shivering with tension.

"O'Brien? He runs the blockade to bring guns and supplies to the rebels. They cannot catch him. It embarrasses the government." He leaned closer to whisper, "He is a great hero among the people."

"He was there tonight, at the restaurant," she whispered back, on the verge of reminding him it was he who had introduced them.

"Surely not. The rascal would never be so bold as to appear in a such a public place." The twinkle in his eyes gave her a very different kind of shiver.

She didn't know whether to be troubled or reassured by the professor's intrigue.

Soon they arrived at the governor's residence and were bustled through a warren of corridors and increasingly elegant rooms to the governor's study. When they were admitted and the governor greeted Valiente with a handshake and a smile, the lieutenant paled visibly.

"It is clearly a misunderstanding," the professor declared magnanimously. "The lieutenant is eager to perform his duty. I am eager to protect my colleague, Senorita O'Keefe." There he changed to English and introduced her as an explorer and archaeologist from New York University, who had brought him a marvelous Mayan piece to work on. It was unsettling how quickly and deftly the professor wove truth and half-truth into a tapestry of convenience.

"Mayan? Truly?" One of the governor's guests—a tall, severe-looking man in an exquisite Spanish-cut suit—spoke up in English. "I myself have something of an interest in Mayan culture."

He was introduced by the governor as Don Alejandro Castille, head of one of Spain's foremost banking families. He insisted Hedda take his seat and sent the governor's servant for some sherry to steady her nerves.

"A dreadful incident. I pray this will not mar your opinion of our dear Cuba," Castille said, stubbing out his cigar and waving the others to do the same.

"Your excellency's graciousness," Hedda said looking from him to their host, "has already more than made up for the fright."

The governor smiled and nodded at her gratitude, but it was Castille who continued the conversation. Clearly, he was a man of considerable power.

"How long have you studied Mayan culture, Miss O'Keefe?" he asked.

"Not long, actually," she said, praying the truth of her statement would balance the lie that had prompted the question. "My specialty is in . . . other areas. But my niece and I recently came into possession of a rubbing that is quite promising. Knowing Professor Valiente to be the foremost scholar in this area, we came to consult with him."

"A rubbing?" Castille settled on the arm of the stuffed chair across from her, swirling his brandy and attending to its bouquet. "On what sort of stones?"

"Very interesting ones," Hedda responded, glancing at the professor, who was busy accepting a glass of brandy. "They seem to speak of an old legend about a Mayan spirit that dwelt in a cat."

Castille, whose mouth seemed to be permanently compressed into a thin line, sat a bit straighter and produced a genuine smile.

"What legend? This interests me, you see, because my family owns much land in southern Mexico and I grew up hearing stories of the ancient ones."

"I believe it concerns something called the Gift of the Jaguar," she said. The professor cleared his throat and she glanced at his oddly impassive face. "But our work is preliminary. Perhaps in six months we will know more."

"The story of 'the Gift from the Jaguar Spirit'? Indeed, I have heard of it. How interesting. And you, Professor?" Castille turned to him with sharpened interest. "Do you think these 'jaguar' rubbings are authentic?"

The professor sipped his brandy before replying.

"I have confidence that our work together produces a valuable step toward knowing and understanding the ancient Mayans."

Soon Castille paid their host the usual compliments for the lovely evening and insisted on seeing the professor and Hedda home in his carriage. He kissed Hedda's hand before the professor helped her down from the carriage at the Hotel San Miguel. When Valiente climbed back aboard Castille's coach, the powerful Spaniard fixed him with a rapier-sharp gaze.

"We must talk, Professor. About some stones and a large, spotted cat."

Cordelia welcomed her aunt with a frantic hug in the lobby of the San Miguel and listened anxiously to Hedda's account of her adventure. Outwardly she appreciated her aunt's spirit and composure, but inwardly she was appalled by the danger Hedda had faced. Whatever the circumstances in their adventures, Cordelia had always been there to deflect the worst and emphasize the best.

The night was two-thirds gone before they had calmed enough to go to bed. Even then, Cordelia lay staring up into a moonlit haze of mosquito netting, going over and over the events of the day. The despair she had felt seeing Hedda's ashen face across the restaurant came circling back again and again. She couldn't help feeling she had let her beloved aunt down. It gave her an uneasy feeling as she considered what might lie ahead in the jungles of Mexico.

But as bad as such thoughts made her feel, they were preferable to remembering the rest of the evening, especially her response to the butler in that darkened doorway. Never in all her experience with fawning, infatuated, and just plain amorous men had she experienced anything as pleasurable as that kiss. Two kisses, actually. In quick succession. That was how she knew he was lying when he behaved as if he had found it distasteful. No man subjected himself to a second kiss if the first one was truly disgusting. He had found it just as pleasurable as she had, which left her somewhat bewildered. How could she be stirred to such passion by someone she found so irritating?

Socks, she told herself, squeezing her eyes shut. Whenever she was tempted to think of that kiss, she would just think of him sorting socks. She scowled, turned her pillow to try to find a cooler spot, and ran smack into the memory of him saying "Oxford" and "chemistry."

Who—or what—was Hartford Goodnight, anyway?

The morning was almost spent before she dragged herself from bed and sent an invitation to the professor to join them at the hotel. She expected that they would spend the rest of the day pouring over the original scrolls, trying to find in them some hint of the stones' location. Thus, when she answered the knock on her door she was startled to find another man standing just outside her room.

This man was moderately tall, slender to the point of gauntness, with dark hair and Moorish eyes that matched the exotic cut of his white linen suit.

"Senorita O'Keefe?" he said, in an expressionless way that made it seem his lips hadn't moved. "The *other* Senorita O'Keefe."

His dark elegance made her recall Hedda's description

of the wealthy Spanish gentleman who had befriended her last evening.

"I am Don Alejandro Castille." He made a curt bow. "I had the great fortune to meet your aunt and Professor Valiente last night."

"She isn't here just now," Cordelia said, thinking that he must look less sallow and dyspeptic by candlelight. Hedda had described him as dark and dashing. "She had some shopping to do." She turned toward the writing desk to fetch paper and pen. "Perhaps you would like to leave a note."

"No need, senorita. I was actually hoping to meet *you*." He took advantage of her movement away from the door to step inside. "I understand from the professor that *you* are actually the leader of this expedition."

"That is true," she responded, turning back, unsettled by the way he strolled into and around the parlor of the suite, looking over the furnishings as if pronouncing Final Judgment—*this one stays, that one burns.*

"I visited the university this morning," he said, pausing to examine the papers and documents, including passports, spread on the desk. She was on the verge of expressing outrage at his presumption when he broke it off and turned to her. "But I missed our friend Valiente. I thought perhaps he might be here."

"I expect him, at any moment," she said, having to work to keep her instinctive dislike of the man from pushing her to a rash response. "Why do you wish to see me, senor?"

He looked her up and down, letting his gaze linger too long on her curves but clearly taking her measure in other ways as well.

"I have come as something of an envoy for my country." He pulled out a chair from the table beneath the window and sat down without an invitation, gesturing for her to be seated as well. Bristling at his presumption, she remained emphatically on her feet. He tilted his head, studying her and her refusal, then smiled broadly enough to show startlingly large, tobacco-yellowed eyeteeth.

"Spain—as you are no doubt aware—has a long history of cultural involvement with Mexico," he said, toying with the brim of his Panama hat. "Since the days of the original explorers, many precious relics and artifacts have been taken back to Spain for safekeeping in our monasteries and libraries."

The way he emphasized the word "safekeeping" sent a quiver of anxiety through her. She ran mentally ahead with his revelations, anticipating where he might be headed, tensing at what her intuition told her.

"Last night, when your aunt spoke of 'the Gift of the Jaguar,' my heart leaped in my breast." He spread a long-fingered hand over his chest. "I have not only heard this story, I have heard of these very stones that speak of the jaguar's gift. You see, rubbings made on just such stones were stolen from the library of a famous monastery in Madrid."

Eleven

"Stolen?" Cordelia steadied herself on the back of a nearby chair. "How dreadful."

"My uncle, a bishop of the church, contacted me to ask for help in finding and returning them to the monastery. Being a good nephew and a loyal Catholic, I agreed to contact my acquaintances in the world of antiquities to locate them."

"Theft of antiquities is a serious charge, senor," she said tautly.

"I am not here to accuse, senorita. Last night, your aunt said you have come to Havana to consult with Valiente on stone rubbings that speak of 'the Gift of the Jaguar.' There can hardly be two sets of stone rubbings dealing with so obscure a legend."

"I assure you, the rubbings I brought the professor are not stolen." She set her jaw. How like Hardacre to stick her with less than lawful antiquities just to see if she could squirm out of the situation!

"I understand your reluctance to admit that your work may involve illegal materials." His eyes narrowed. "May I ask how you acquired these scrolls?"

"They were entrusted to us by an American collector who has held them for quite some time. Samuel Blackburn of Blackburn-Allegheny Steel."

Castille searched her visually, seeming to digest that news.

"I have never heard of this 'Blackburn Steel' person." He drummed his fingers on the table, clearly calculating his next move. "It may be that he did not know they were stolen. It does not matter, senorita. The whole unfortunate situation can be easily resolved if you produce the scrolls for me to examine."

A chill ran up her spine. Whatever he saw in the scrolls, she sensed he would declare them to be the ones he sought and try to confiscate them.

"I am certain our scrolls are not the ones you seek."

"And I am equally certain"—he sat sharply forward, his face almost predatory—"that they are. These precious scrolls belong to the library of the Monastery of St. Montelado. And they must be returned."

Her mouth dried and her hands grew icy.

"How do I know that you truly represent a bishop or a monastery? How do I know that you are who you claim to be?" She stepped back sharply as he rose from the chair and regretted it when she saw a glint of pleasure in his eyes.

"In the interest of justice, I will ignore the insult to myself and my friend the governor of Cuba." His face heated, his lean features growing sharper and more predatory. "I shall say instead that my uncle, Ramon de Castille, Bishop of Sienna, is well known throughout Spain, Cuba, and even Mexico. I must warn you: if you do not cooperate, I will have no choice but to take stronger measures." That yellow-fanged smile appeared again. "If I take this unfortunate matter to my friend the governor, he will have no choice but to declare you and your aunt thieves and enemies of the Spanish people. He will confiscate the stolen scrolls, and you will lose both your work and the compensation you might have had from me. Perhaps you will even lose your freedom."

"I must ask you leave, senor."

She strode to the door and threw it open, finding two beefy men with coarse faces and hardened eyes filling the threshold. She fell back a step. Clearly, Castille had come prepared to take the scrolls by whatever means necessary.

"Allow me to introduce Senor Blanc and Senor Yago. They, too, are loyal Spaniards," Castille said with an edge of amusement. "And loyal churchmen."

"This is an outrage." She glanced at the door to the adjoining room, thinking of her gun in the nightstand by her bed. "I will go to the governor myself and ask him to investigate the matter."

"The scrolls, senorita." He dropped his increasingly strained pretense of civility. "Give them to me now, and there will be no harm to yourself or your possessions."

When she didn't move or speak, he flicked his wrist and brought the thugs into the room to begin searching.

"Stop—leave that alone!" She tried to intervene when they began overturning furniture, but they were huge and determined. She turned on her heel and headed instead for the nightstand by her bed. Before she reached it, beefy hands seized her and all but lifted her off her feet. Her tension exploded into an anger-fueled cry.

"Let me go—how dare you? Put me down!" She bucked and twisted against their grip, trying to break free, then tried going limp and dropping to the floor to loosen their hold. Unfortunately, the pair were no strangers to that maneuver and quickly hauled her back up between them to face Castille.

"You won't get away with this," she said furiously.

"You are very much mistaken, senorita." Castille headed for the open steamer trunks along the far wall of the room and began pulling out drawers, looking in and behind them, dumping both contents and drawers on the floor. "You could have saved yourself this distress by doing as I asked."

He ripped out a handful of hanging clothes and threw them on the floor with a smirk that transformed into a snarl as he continued from trunk to bureau to trunk, finding nothing. Barking orders for one of the thugs to hold her while the other helped him search, he began to take apart everything in the room. Soon mattresses were overturned and gutted, pillows were slit, and the remaining luggage all opened and emptied. Still there was no sign of the prize he sought.

Simmering, Castille stalked over to shove his face into hers.

"*Where are my scrolls?*"

"I'll never give them up." She met his fury without quailing.

"Shall we test that statement, senorita?" He raked a hand down the side of her face, then clamped it hard around her throat. "No doubt Blanc and Yago could think of ways to make you regret you ever thought it."

Her scream was an instinctive reaction to his tightening grasp, but once it began, she threw heart into it and began to fight with everything in her. Castille muttered a curse when her foot connected with his shin. He released her throat only to draw back his hand and smack her so hard across the face that she saw stars. Her knees buckled.

From somewhere outside that disorienting blaze of light and pain came a familiar voice.

"Just like you to have a party and not invite me."

For a moment everything but the spinning of her head stopped.

Goodnight.

Something slammed down on the thug holding her, knocking him over and sending her glancing off the bedstead to the floor, where she lay for a minute gasping for breath. The sound of cracking—wood or bone, she couldn't be sure—split the air and she looked up to see a dark blur and what seemed to be a parlor chair connecting with everything still upright in the room.

She felt hands on her, groping, searching for purchase,

and she kicked and jabbed with her elbows to keep them from getting a grip on her. When a hand slid over her mouth, she bit down with all the force she could muster. The resulting howl, at such close range, nearly burst her eardrum.

But for the moment she was free and grabbed the empty bed frame to pull herself along toward the nightstand. Sounds of scuffling, groans and curses, and the thudding impact of fist against flesh and bone seemed to come from everywhere. In the distance she could hear orders being snarled in Spanish and then the sound of feet, running. She reached the nightstand and found the drawer overturned on the floor. Through the goose feathers and tangle of bed-clothes she felt a shaft of steel and seized it—just as one of the thugs grabbed her ankles and started to pull her back across the floor.

She coughed, choking on the down and feathers, but managed to seat the handle of the pistol in her palm and swing it up in time to meet Yago's eyes. Still on her back, she held the pistol with both hands and growled, "Get back!"

He glanced toward the door and eased back onto his knees, lifting his hands at his sides as he struggled to his feet. She sat up and rolled onto her knees as the first step in getting back to her feet.

Yago shouted at his partner, then spun around and ran off through the adjoining room. Blanc caught sight of his partner escaping and the next instant was struggling to free himself and do the same.

A moment later, the room was still except for the feathers floating slowly back to the floor and the fading sound of footsteps. She blinked, steadying herself against the footboard, and realized it was Goodnight's widened eyes she was seeing at the other end of her pistol.

Goodnight. She'd never been so happy to see someone in her life.

"What in hell was that about?" Goodnight stalked over to her, panting and running his hands back through his disheveled hair. "Who was that?" He pushed the barrel of her gun to one side, glowering. "What did they want?"

She looked around the wrecked bedroom with disbelief, struggling to recover her voice.

"R–Rubbings." The throbbing in her face caused her disjointed self-possession to snap back into place. "Castille . . . the man Hedda and the professor met last night . . . he demanded I turn the rubbings over to him . . . said they were stolen from some monastery in Madrid. When I told him to leave, he threatened me and—and—"

"Carried out his threat." He looked around the bedroom, then took her by the shoulders and steered her into the comparative order of the other room. There he righted a chair by the window, pushed her down onto it, and peeled her fingers from the gun. Setting it on the table, he turned her head to get a better look at her face. With a wince, he plucked a number of feathers from her hair and dress, then gave a long-suffering sigh and headed for the door.

"Stay. I'll be right back."

As minutes ticked by, she reached for the gun again and cradled it on her lap. When he returned carrying a black leather satchel, she raised the pistol. With an impatient hiss, he again pried the gun from her fingers.

"What is this obsession you have with firearms?"

"They even the odds." Her *t*'s were sounding more like *d*'s; her lips were swelling. "If I'd had it on me, they coun't 'ave made dis mess."

"Something of a relief, actually, to know you don't wear it around the clock," he said with a sniff as he opened his bag. "I had visions of being shot for an intruder while going for a constitutional in the middle of the night."

She gave him a dark look and peered over the top of the satchel. It was filled with a jumble of instruments, boxes, paper packets, and variegated glass bottles—looked like an apothecary's attic.

"Hold still," he ordered. Using a gauze square saturated with a gold liquid that smelled like turpentine gone bad, he cleaned the blood from the corner of her split lip. It stung like the dickens.

"Owwww!" She drew back and scowled. "What is that stuff?"

"Listerine. Antibacterial agent. Relatively new."

" 'Anti' what?"

"Bacteria." He gave a quiet huff. "*Germs*—I assume you've heard of those. This liquid kills the *germs* that cause sepsis. Keeps wounds from becoming infected."

She stared at him, at a loss for how to respond.

"What? I suppose you'd rather have Hunt's Lightning Oil or that cursed Radam's Mibrobe Killer." He glowered. "May as well pour whiskey on it—that's all the old quacksalvers put in their damnable snake oil."

"Back-terria?" she muttered. "He's on a first name basis with *germs*?"

"I don't think you'll need stitches." He ignored her comment. "Since we don't have any ice, you'll have to make do with a bit of witch hazel. I'll give you some acetylsalicylic acid for the pain and inflamation."

She blinked. For a second time in the last hour, reality was taking a very disorienting bend. When he reached into his bag again, she grabbed his wrist.

"Who *are* you?" she demanded.

He looked pointedly at her hand, waiting for her to remove it. She didn't.

"Hartford Goodnight, remember?" He exhaled a long, tortured breath. "Presser of pants and sock folder extraordinaire."

"Who went to Oxford," she declared, studying him. "And studied chemistry. Is that how you know about germs?" He tried to take his arm back but she wouldn't let him. After a brief tug of war, he relented.

"My acquaintance with germs came from a stint in medical school. It's a theory of illness quite in vogue: bacteria and other microscopic organisms—known to laymen as germs—cause most sickness."

"Medical sch—" She pounced on the admission, the

pain in her head taking second place in her awareness. "You're a doctor?"

"No. Not officially. In my last year of medical training, I switched to chemistry." He twisted his hand again, and she released it.

"How did you get from Oxford to being Samuel P.'s butler?" For some reason, the sight of Goodnight leaning on top of that trunk in Samuel P.'s bedroom and talking about the "firstborns" the old man had taken as collateral popped into her mind. And suddenly she knew.

"You owe him." Her eyes widened. "You're working off a debt!"

He reddened and busied himself pouring witch hazel into some gauze.

"That's it, isn't it? You lost a bet and you're working it off."

He put the cloth against her injured lip and brought her hand up to hold it in place. Then he pulled out a tin of white powder and a sheet of paper, folding the latter to make a dose packet for her.

"What was the bet?" The ache of curiosity was suddenly much more acute than the pain in her lips.

"Mix this with a cup of lukewarm water and drink it quickly. It will taste vile, but it will relieve the pain you are in or soon will be experiencing."

"Tell me." She stood up as he handed her the packet and repacked his bag of medicines. "I'll get it out of you sooner or later."

"*Later* is better for me," he said, turning to go.

She stepped into his path and when he tried to move around her, she grabbed his sleeve to slow him down. He froze. Her hand closed around the strong, sinewy arm beneath that khaki, and she was broadsided by the memory of it clamped around her last night.

Her gaze slid up his chest. Hard, cleanly muscled. His shirt had pulled partway from his belt during the fight. Khaki shirt. Khaki trousers. This was the first time she had seen him without his butler's tailcoat. Wait—last night in the restaurant, in the streets as they ran, in that doorway—he hadn't been wearing it then either. Somewhere along the way he'd removed it.

There was a bruise forming on his cheekbone and around the outer edge of his reddened left eye. That blur she had seen when he first entered the bedroom now replayed in her head, growing clearer. It was Goodnight.

He had fought? Goodnight the surly, superior, irritating, Oxford-educated *butler* had fought a street tough to a standstill? It seemed incredible, but there he was, sporting a manly souvenir as proof. She took the gauze from her face and placed it on his. He flinched as she touched his injury but made no move to avoid the contact.

Student, doctor, chemist, butler—he had more facets than a chandelier. And she was seized by a fervent need to know about every one of them. She stepped closer and looked up into his eyes.

It was all there for her to see—all the aspects and experiences of him, his heartfelt hopes, lousy luck, and unhealed wounds . . . wit, pride, and desperation—the entire depth and breadth of his interior landscape was visible in those expressive quicksilver eyes. Gone were the usual layers of finely honed sarcasm and superiority. For that brief, remarkable moment he was just Hartford Goodnight, ungodly complicated, chagrined by his circumstances, and clearly more than he seemed. It was a potent and compelling combination.

Stunned, she pulled her gaze from his. The last thing she needed was to be enthralled by a man who was likely to wind up a crocodile's dinner before the month was out. But, in spite of herself, she reached up to touch his bruised face and let her fingertips drift over his cheeks to his lips.

His head began to lower.

Twelve

"Merciful Heavens!" Hedda's gasp sent them reeling apart.

"What is happen here?" the professor said, standing by Hedda just inside the doorway. Their eyes widened on Cordelia's face and feather-littered dress, then went to Goodnight's swelling eye and the overturned chairs and settee.

"Cordie? What's happened to you?" Hedda rushed forward to insert herself between Cordelia and the glowering Goodnight. "How *dare* you?"

"It wasn't him." Cordelia came to her senses and intercepted her aunt. "It was that Castille wretch you met last night. At least that's who he said he was."

"Alejandro Castille?" the professor said in shock. "He comes here?"

"He demanded to see our scrolls and when I wouldn't let him, he said they were stolen from a monastery in Spain. When I refused to give them to him, he and his men started to search. I tried to stop them, but he"—she put her hand to her injured face—"he hit me."

"*Madre de Dios*," the professor gasped, looking to

Hedda in horror, then back at Cordelia. "Castille does such a thing?"

She glanced at Goodnight, who had begun righting the furniture, once again the sardonic servant/watchdog. If it hadn't been for him—

"He must be the one who visits my offices." The professor hurried to help him tip the settee back onto its bottom and then ushered Cordelia and Hedda to seats on it. "When I arrive this morning, my workroom is destructed. It happens early this morning, I know . . . because I go to my workroom last night to get the sketches, and everything is fine. Oh." He remembered the portfolio under his arm and handed it to Cordelia. "He does not find these, so he comes here."

"Why would he do such a thing?" Hedda asked.

"Last night, after we take you to the hotel, he asks many questions about the scrolls. I am thinking he is curious. He says he is a collector of antiquities. When I tell him we are just beginning to study, he says he has interest in our work and makes me promise to tell him of the progress." He looked around with wide eyes. "I–I never think that he wants the rubbings for himself."

"Why would he want them so badly?" Cordelia asked, touching her aching face. "He can't read them. He said they were stolen and he wanted to return them to the church. But, if that were true, why didn't he just report us to the Spanish authorities?"

"He didn't want them involved," Hedda concluded, paling. "Perhaps his actions aren't as noble as he wants it to seem."

"Now that his 'private' efforts have failed"—Cordelia looked to the professor—"will he go to the government?"

Mention of officialdom caused the professor fresh alarm.

"Aiieee—his friend the governor." He shot Hedda a worried look. "The Castille family is well known and has much power. If he goes to the palace—" He drew himself up straight, his eyes darting quickly over images that only he could see. He pulled out a handkerchief and dabbed his face. "We must leave for Mexico right away. Today. We must not be in Havana after the sun goes down."

The minute the professor left, Goodnight turned on Cordelia in disbelief.

"You cannot be serious about letting that bounder find us passage on a ship. Have you completely forgotten the debacle of last night? The man turned a simple bit of dinner into an international incident and damn near got us arrested!"

"That wasn't his fault." She headed for the bedroom, intent on salvaging and repacking her personal belongings.

"No?" He followed and paused just inside the door. "It was his shady connections that brought the law down on us."

"And it may be those same connections that save our hides. He said he knows a captain that may be willing to take us on, no questions asked."

"Exactly my point. You should be asking plenty of questions. What ship? Is it seaworthy? Is the captain experienced and trustworthy?"

She stared at him for a moment in disbelief.

"What do you expect me to do? Waltz down to the docks and politely ask to see each captain's credentials? We can't book passage aboard a regular ship. If Castille goes to the governor, the docks are the first place they'll look for us." She braced to combat her own uneasiness as much as the skepticism in his face.

"Go pack, Goodnight. We're leaving in two hours."

Determination—his and hers—crackled like static electricity between them. When he turned on his heel and strode out, she nearly staggered with relief.

On the way to returning drawers to her trunk, she was stopped in her tracks by Hedda's searching look.

"What?" she said, hating the heat blooming in her face.

"Something happened between you two, didn't it?" Hedda said.

"Between me and Goodnight?" She forced a laugh.

"Really, Hedda. The man's annoying as the devil's toothache. And he's a *butler*."

Just after sunset, a force of government soldiers burst into the Hotel San Miguel, emptying the rooms and herding the guests into the lobby for questioning. The manager's protest netted him a crack on the head from a rifle butt and some individual attention from a tall, sallow-faced Spaniard whose elegant dress and refined air belied a ready appetite for gritty techniques of persuasion.

"Where are the Americanos?" Alejandro Castille demanded, backing the rotund manager against the wall of the lobby in full view of the man's two wide-eyed daughters, who worked in the hotel. "You were to send word immediately if they tried to leave."

"I would have, D–Don Castille, I swear. I did not know they were gone until you came and did not find them."

"Did I not tell you what would happen if you failed me?"

"B-but—j-just this morning they paid for another two days." His voice rose. "And—and they did not ask for the key to the storeroom for their crates!"

"Crates?" Castille drew back with a silent snarl to assess this new information. A motion from his tobacco-stained fingers and his henchmen, Yago and Blanc, peeled the manager from the wall. "Show me."

Moments later, they stood in the alley behind the hotel, staring at a broken padlock on a pair of heavy wooden doors that led down steps into the hotel's cellar. Castille shot a murderous glare from the lock to the manager, then hauled open one of the doors with his own hands and led the others down the steps into the cave-like chamber beneath the hotel.

It smelled dank and sour and was black as pitch. The manager begged to be allowed to light a lantern. As soon as yellow kerosene light bloomed around them, Castille's thugs seized him again to enforce their master's demand to know where the crates were kept. The doughy little manager pointed with a shaking finger to a bare space at the far end.

Castille turned away from the sight of the empty floor in a fury.

"Why didn't you tell me they had other baggage?" He slammed a fist into the manager's nose. "How many? How many crates did you hide for them?"

"F–four large," the manager gasped out, his eyes swimming, unable to focus. "T–two smaller."

Castille ground his bruised knuckles into the palm of his other hand, chewing on the intensity of the discomfort. He took a deep breath and narrowed his basilisk-black eyes as he thought of his quarry's options.

"A Spanish man escorting two American beauties . . . with much baggage . . . headed for Mexico . . . they should prove fairly memorable. And they have to find a ship on short notice." He looked back over his shoulder at Yago and Blanc. "Go to the harbor. Ask around for any ship leaving sooner than usual for Mexico. Check the private ships as well as the line steamers."

As his men charged up the steps, Castille gripped the back of the manager's neck, digging his fingers in and smiling at the way the hotel man flinched. Increasing the pressure, he forced the manager up the steps.

"You have disappointed me, senor. And I do not like to be disappointed." As they headed for the side entrance of the hotel, Castille thought of the man's doe-eyed daughters, huddled in the lobby with the rest of the staff and guests. "But I am a generous man." He gave a humorless laugh. "I believe I will allow your pretty little daughters to make it up to me."

Silhouetted against the setting sun, a mule-drawn hay wagon and a donkey cart loaded with crates of produce wended their way along Cuba's rocky northern shore, west of Havana. They were ordinary farm vehicles, two among many that headed daily for the coastal town of Puerto Esperanza, the small port that served as the primary market for the province's produce. At the reins of the wagon was a sleepy fellow in a wide-brimmed hat, and driving the crude cart was an old woman bent by time and covered with a coarsely woven shawl. At a casual glance, no one would suspect that their humble appearance hid a wealth of contraband and their lethargic pace concealed a daring escape.

Cordelia sat with her shoulders hunched on the wooden plank that passed for a driver's seat on the cart. Her head and shoulders were itching from the shawl—hopefully it wasn't anything worse than fleas—and her rear was going numb from fourteen hours of bone-jarring travel and jostling. She was covered with a haze of dust from the road, and whenever the breeze changed, she was overwhelmed by the smell of musty hay and flats of onions, plantains, and overripe tomatoes stacked on the cart to cover their baggage. She had insisted on driving one of the vehicles, even offered to wear men's clothes. The professor looked her up and down and declared that no man with a single good eye would mistake her for male. She was forced to don a sad wool skirt and the enormous, itchy shawl, and was told to look aged and tired. The tired part came all too easily, now. Uncomfortable as it was, her fate was better than poor Hedda's; her aunt had been consigned to the bed of the cart, tucked between trunks and beneath the vegetables, rattled tooth from bone and subjected to choking dust and a constant smell of fading produce.

The most worrisome part was the fact that Goodnight—clearly too tall and British-looking to pass for a Cuban farmer—was trailing along behind them. Somewhere. Trying not to look connected to them in any way. He'd balked at hiding in the wagon, only to be assigned a donkey laden with cages of squawking chickens, stuffed into clothes too small and a hat too large, smeared with dirt, and ordered to walk stooped. If stopped, he was to keep his head down, say "si, si," and offer his inquisitor a chicken—all of which, Cordelia had observed irritably, would tax his personal capabilities to the limit.

Stuck on that wobbling, jolting seat for an entire day, she found her mind circling endlessly around questions of where they were headed and how she was going to keep Goodnight and the expedition under her control. Their first task, once they were safely underway at sea, was to study the rubbings for clues about where to begin their search. There had to be something in the message of the rubbings that pointed to where the stones were. If they didn't find a clue right away, she feared Goodnight would make her life miserable.

Some distance ahead, she spotted a line of horses and what appeared to be men on foot. It took a minute to register that the thin, dark lines jutting into the air above them were rifles. *Soldiers.*

The wagon ahead of her, driven by the professor, slowed, turned sharply, and headed down a slope that gave Cordelia heart palpitations. Breaking her own rule of silence, she shouted at him. He turned and beckoned while bracing to stay on the wagon. Soldiers. He had seen them and was taking evasive action.

With her heart in her throat, she slapped the reins against the donkey's rump and called "*¡Anda!*" as the professor had. It took some urging, but the animal finally made the turn she insisted on and the cart bounced and hopped over several rocks, swaying wildly. It was all she could do to hold on as she and the weight of the cart pushed the donkey toward the edge of an even more precipitous slope. Panicked by the force behind him, the donkey took off at a run, scrambling wildly down the steeper part of the slope with the cart careening along behind it.

She dropped the reins and held on for dear life, feeling the steamer trunks sliding forward on the cart bed and praying Hedda wasn't being crushed. The wheels banging against rocks jarred the flats of produce behind her loose. The ropes holding the cargo groaned and the next minute she was pummeled from behind by small melons that ricocheted onto the rocks below and smashed.

The donkey made a frantic twist to the left that carried them around a wicked drop, and the cart rolled over the last obstacle and landed on the shoreline sand with a thump. Hedda's scream was muffled by the cargo and the thunk of the cart itself.

Once on level ground, Cordelia sat for a moment trying to get her breath, then called to Hedda to see if she was hurt. Her tousled aunt threw back the tarp and squeezed up between baskets and stacks of wooden boxes to peer over the front of the cart. She stared in horror at the rocky slope they'd just descended.

"Sweet Mother Mary! That's the last time I let you drive," she said hoarsely, crossing herself. "What happened? Where are we?"

"Soldiers," Cordelia said quietly, gathering up the reins. "On the road. Stay down a little longer."

Hedda slid back down beneath the tarp and Cordelia looked over the donkey, who seemed to be taking his brush with disaster in stride. She was able to coax him several hundred yards down the beach, to where the professor was stopping his wagon beside some large rocks.

"We camp here," the professor said, approaching the cart and keeping his voice low. "Many farmers camp here on the way to market."

At his suggestion, she pulled the cart behind some rock pillars that sheltered it from the road, leaving only the larger wagon visible. She lifted the tarp and told Hedda it was safe to climb out.

After climbing down herself and pausing to help her aunt, she planted her hands in the small of her back and arched over them, stretching her spine, feeling relieved to be both standing and still. She closed her eyes for a moment and turned her face into the gentle breeze.

The air was fresh and salty, and when she opened her eyes, the sea in the pre-moon darkness winked like black satin and the surf frothed like a border of lace. In the distance she could see campfires blooming on the beach, confirming the professor's claim about the beach being a common campsite. She strolled over to the professor, who stood on the sand near a place where hunks of half-burned wood and old coals were mixed with the sand, evidence of previous campfires.

"We wait for boat here," he said, producing a binocular telescope to scan the horizon. "We keep watch. They come tonight."

"If they come at all," Goodnight muttered with a strangely nasal tone from close range. Startled, Cordelia turned around. There he stood in his ragged clothes and peasant sandals, looking tired, irritable, and skeptical that those conditions would improve any time soon. With a defiant expression, he tied his chicken-bearing donkey to the back of the cart and stalked off down the beach.

At Hedda's look of alarm, Cordelia went after him.

"What do you think you're doing?" she demanded, catching up with him.

"Looking for firewood." He picked up a piece of driftwood and scouted the sand for others. "I've got to have a cup of tea."

"You're going to build a campfire to *cook*?"

"Fires, it happens, are one of my specialties. Here—" He thrust some wood into her arms. "Carry these back."

"And if someone sees us?" she said irritably.

He turned on her with eyes flashing hot silver light.

"Then we'll just have to pretend it's Havana again," he said in low, resonant tones that called up alarming associations in her. "And run like hell."

He handed her another piece of driftwood before the sting made itself felt.

She wheeled and trudged back through the soft sand to their campsite, where she refused to look at him as he started a fire. He used hay from the cart as tinder, then some slats from a broken produce flat, and soon had a respectable flame going. She found his competence at fire building both unexpected and annoying. And she liked it even less when he pulled out his journal to record what could only be described as their dismal lack of progress.

January 25, Day 5

Hotel rooms, two nights in advance, NOT USED: $23.00 U.S. Gratuities for hotel staff: $6.00 U.S. Wagon and cart rental (with animals): $37.00. Whole damnable flock of chickens: $17.00. Peppers, onions, and all manner of odiferous vegetable material: $24.50 U.S. Tool to break padlock on basement door (rental): $2.00.

Chased out of Havana by a chum of the governor. Churlish bastard smacked O'Keefe around and tried to appropriate the scrolls. Something-or-other Castille. Nasty piece of work.

Forced to flee with a stubborn-arsed donkey and two dozen chickens who shat their cages in unison the minute we left town. Smell was horrific. Sinuses swollen closed. Five bloody hours dragging two arses (mine and donkey's) along impossible roads with nothing but scraps of leather tied to my feet. Now camped on a damp beach...waiting for some boat that is probably a figment of Valiente's imagination. Am exhausted...smell like the bottom of a cat box...have sand in this damned woolen underwear...and just learned there's no water for tea.

Will be homicidal by dawn.

No jury in the world would convict me.

Thirteen

They took turns standing watch. It was well into the night and the others were dozing around the dying embers of the fire when the professor spotted something on the horizon, grabbed two kerosene lanterns from the wagon, and climbed to the top of one of the rock stacks nearby. As he waved the lights back and forth, a sizeable boat emerged from the inky horizon, steaming right for them.

Relief broke over Cordelia as she watched several men jump from the longboat that came ashore and greet the professor. In short order, they began removing cargo from the wagons and settling it in the launch. The chickens and produce, it turned out, were more than camouflage; they were intended to sweeten the price of passage and build good will among the ship's crew. At the professor's insistence, Hedda climbed into the boat with them and was ferried out to the waiting steamer. All went smoothly until the boat returned and was loaded a second time.

Shouts and shots rang out from the road above them, galvanizing the sailors. Government soldiers materialized out of the darkness above them and began closing in on all sides. It was chaos for a moment as bullets careened off the rocks around them and the men shoved the professor into the boat and began to row. Pulling Goodnight to safety behind the wagon, watching bullets peppering the water near the longboat, Cordelia reached under her skirt for her pistol and began to return fire.

"This," she shouted at Goodnight, who was staring at her in disbelief, "is why I'm so keen on guns!"

After reloading, she was up again, pointing her gun over the side of the wagon and squeezing off shots at the soldiers. But there was an endless stream of uniform-clad bodies hurtling over the dunes toward them; they were far outnumbered. A glance over her shoulder at the ship told her the longboat wasn't coming back. The cargo was gone and the professor and Hedda were both safe aboard; the captain would be mad not to weigh anchor and steam off without them. She looked at the soldiers creeping ever closer to their position, then at Goodnight, whose face was hot and ruddy. She stared at him, met his eyes, wishing . . . Shaking her head to clear it, she peered over the edge of the wagon again. She would make every bullet count, but before long they'd be overrun and—

A great boom roared from the ship, followed by a billow of smoke and a screaming whine that ended in an explosion beside the donkey cart. Sand and rock became deadly missiles and flying water obscured the scene momentarily. The government charge reversed as soldiers went scrambling for cover. The shock of it took two seconds to fade.

"They've got a *gun*!" she shouted at Goodnight, grabbing the front of his shirt and shaking it. "*A big one!*"

"Gun, hell—they've got *artillery*!" he shouted as another missile screamed over their heads, aiming for the beach behind them.

Thinking quickly, she unbuttoned her skirt, pushed it down her hips, and kicked it aside. Underneath, she wore a pair of khaki breeches, tall boots, and a holster slung low on her hips. When she looked up, he was staring at her, stunned.

"Come on!" She jammed her gun into her holster and dragged him headlong with her into the surf. They were waist deep before she released him.

"You better be able to swim!" she called, diving in.

"Not . . . especially well."

A bullet smacked the water nearby, and he groaned and plunged into the water after her. Fear for one's life, it seemed, had the capacity to turn mediocrity of skill into stellar performance. Despite being fully dressed—Cordelia doubly burdened with substantial boots and concern for the slower Goodnight—both managed to make the quarter-mile swim to the longboat that hadn't yet been raised.

They climbed into the launch, finally out of range of fire from the shore, and were hauled up to the ship's deck and swung aboard to a cheer from the crew and a frantic welcome from Hedda and the professor.

Cordelia was exhausted and cold and a little nauseous from the seawater she'd swallowed, but one look back at the still-smoking shore and she knew it had been their only chance to get to the ship. She turned to congratulate Goodnight on their success, and found him on his hands and knees, coughing up saltwater.

When she was helped out onto the deck by some crewmen, a short, stocky fellow with lively eyes and a magnificent handle-bar moustache appeared before her, holding out his hand. It took a minute to realize she'd seen him before.

"Welcome aboard, Miss O'Keefe," he said in blessedly American tones. "I'm Cap'n Johnny O'Brien. I should apologize for gettin' you caught in the fireworks. Those bastards have been after us for months."

"They weren't after *us*?" Cordelia asked, swiping water from her face.

"I remember you." Goodnight rolled out of the longboat and came face to face with O'Brien. "You're that Yank they were searching for at the—" He turned on the professor. "You got us passage with a *wanted* captain on a *hunted* ship?"

The professor's answer was eclipsed by a resounding boom from what sounded like a far-off cannon. There was an instantly familiar whine growing louder and a trail of smoke arcing across the sky. The crew ducked and braced until the shell exploded in the water, well to starboard. O'Brien was quickly up and barking orders and the big gun on the foredeck was being primed, even as the ship wheeled about. Hedda dragged Cordelia toward steps leading below, but not before she spotted a ship on the horizon and saw the flash and smoke from another gun blast.

The last thing she heard was O'Brien's laughter.

"Let's get outta here, boys!"

January 26, Day 6

Contribution to boat captain's fund for needy revolutionaries: $1,000.00 U.S. Nine bottles Irish whiskey: $36.00 (a bargain at twice the price).

Attacked by government soldiers. Nearly got ear shot off by O'Keefe when she returned fire. Damned beach blown up by ship-to-shore artillery! Had to swim for it. O'Keefe climbed onto boat dripping wet. Sweet Jesus. Wasn't an eyeball left in a socket.

She really does wear breeches. Got legs like a damned racehorse. Smooth. Muscular. Could crack a man's spine like a walnut. And the upper half... can't bear to think about what I saw beneath that wet shirt. What kind of family lets a woman go gallivanting off into the wilderness wearing nothing but a man's shirt?

Bunking with Valiente, who snores like a water buffalo.

Wonder how many men she's shot.

Wonder how many men she's NOT shot.

The next morning, Cordelia awakened in her own nightgown, face down on a bed that was swaying gently. She pushed up and looked around, not quite willing to trust the normalcy of the sunlit cabin around her. At her feet was another bunk, neatly made up, and familiar steamer trunks stood open in the space between.

"What do you know?" she said through a scratchy throat. "We survived."

She stripped her nightgown, washed in the fresh water someone had thoughtfully provided, and pulled on a dark woolen skirt over some dry breeches, her old boots, and a khaki shirt. She debated strapping on her gun, but decided it would need a good cleaning and a protective coat of oil after being dragged through saltwater, and left it lying on her bunk. Tying her hair back with a ribbon, she stepped out into a short, narrow passage. At the end of it, she found Hedda and the professor sitting at a long wooden table in what appeared to be a common room. They offered her a cup of strong coffee and a bowl of oatmeal littered with raisins. She wouldn't have said minutes before that she was hungry, but she consumed it with groan of satisfaction and felt considerably better afterward.

"Goodnight?" she asked, wrapping her hands around the crockery mug.

"We share a cabin," the professor said. "He is not moved from the bunk."

"He's not much of a sailor," she said grimly. Then she fixed Valiente with a dark look. "Whatever possessed you to book us passage with an outlaw captain?"

"He is an old friend. I know he wishes to make money and has a fast boat. And"—the professor shrugged—"no one else will take us. We are outlaws, too."

"Lovely," she said with a wince. "How much are we paying him?"

"One thousand dollars U.S." said a familiar voice from the door. They all turned with surprise to see Goodnight ducking into the common room. "The paper portion of which was on my person and is now drying all over our locked cabin. Highway robbery. Or should I say 'high seas' robbery?"

"You're up." Cordelia sniffed in his direction. "And sober."

"A condition that can and will be remedied," he said irritably. "But not before the captain gets his money. He is holding my liquor until he gets payment."

"Smart man," she said with a vengeful smile.

"Well." The captain's face appeared in the doorway. "Ye can't make it this long in the revolution business without learnin' a trick or two." He stepped into the dining room to refill his cup from the coffee urn.

"We outran the Spaniards, I take it," she said to him.

"Oh, they're still comin'," O'Brien said, pouring a fresh cup and pressing it into Goodnight's hands. "But it's the *Cuba Espanola*. She tops out at eight knots. They'll soon break it off and head home. You'd best settle back and enjoy the ride."

Hedda shoved a bowl of oatmeal into Goodnight's hands and he groaned and tried to give it back. Cordelia stepped in, saying it would help with the seasickness, and for a moment they stood eye to eye and will to will.

O'Brien looked from Goodnight's black eye to Cordelia's damaged lip and back. "That must have been some fight." He chuckled. "Who won?"

With a growl, Goodnight exited the commons.

An hour later, the affable captain was more concerned as he stood on the watch deck outside the wheel room, scanning the distant ship with his telescope. He lowered it and frowned.

"What's wrong?" Cordelia asked. She and Hedda had

been strolling the upper deck when they saw the captain studying their pursuers, and climbed the steps to join him.

"We're widening the gap. They should have given up by now," he said. When she gestured to his telescope, he handed it to her. "I know this captain, Don Luis Pou. He knows his boat and he's not usually this much of a hard-tail."

It took a while for her to focus the instrument properly. On the deck of the Spanish gunboat she made out several dark-clad figures and one in white, who seemed to be wearing a Panama hat. She jerked her eye from the sight.

"How would he—" She feared she already knew the answer. "I think it's Alejandro Castille." She handed the telescope back to O'Brien. "On the bridge of the ship. See if you think the one in white is wearing a Panama hat."

"Ye've got a good eye, Miss O'Keefe. Must be the Irish in ye." The captain's smile tightened as he lowered his glass. "Who is he—this Castille—and how does he rate commandeerin' a 200-ton Spanish gunboat?"

"A very good question." She studied the distant, indistinct outline of the Spanish ship. "But a better one is *why* he would do it."

That afternoon, Cordelia, Hedda, and the professor took over the dining table in the common room to unroll and study the original scrolls. They had to find out what was in the stone figures that made them so desirable to Castille. He had already ransacked, threatened, and assaulted in pursuit of them, and now called on his most powerful political connections—Cuba's military—for aid. But when the professor saw the originals, he sighed and said they were so magnificent, he could almost understand Castille's desire for them based on just their beauty.

With Hedda as recorder and the professor describing the possible meanings of each block, they began to wade through the translation. Starting at the top of the first column and reading downward, the professor found calendar references that indicated "time before time"—ancient indeed. These dates were linked to a figure that was unmistakably a cat head in profile. It was the Creator Spirit in its jaguar form, the professor said. There was a sunburst and what seemed to be flames shooting from it onto adjacent blocks. Fire was the medium of creation, the professor declared. According to Mayan belief, all of the ancient elements passed through the flame of the sun and were set down on earth still burning.

"Which of course explains why three-fourths of the planet is covered by water," Goodnight said, causing them all to look up. He stood in the doorway with his arms crossed, looking rumpled and disagreeable. "Soggy from putting out all of those fires."

Cordelia gave a sniff in his direction and recoiled. The captain had apparently returned his supply of whiskey.

"Why don't you retire to your cabin?" she suggested pointedly.

"What—and miss all of these erudite musings? For your information, Goodnights are very big on scholarly conjecture. We're whizzes at puzzles."

"If you get sick, you're leaving." She shoved an empty bowl from the sideboard at him, then turned back. "Where were we?"

"These." Valiente tapped one of the blocks partway down the column. "Clearly trees. Four great trees hold up the sky at the four corners of the earth. This is in their creation story. The next block says that animals were then created. Then came bees and all manner of birds. Then boars, monkeys, and crocodiles."

"Are you sure that's a boar?" Goodnight leaned over the figures, squinting. "Looks like a fellow I knew at Oxford. Prinny Lewis. A right porker, ol' Prinny."

"*Really.*" Cordelia inserted herself between him and the rubbings. "We're trying to *learn* something here."

"Trying to learn if this is all a waste of time?" he asked archly.

"Whatever we learn about the stones and the Gift of the Jaguar will be reported back and we'll have done our job." She turned emphatically back to the table. "Continue, Professor."

"Then a great snake appeared." He drew his finger along a banded groove that seemed to run through several blocks. The snake's head was ringed with what looked like feathers, and out of its open mouth came a human face. "This image—people coming from mouths of snakes—appears many places in Mayan art."

"Awful idea." Hedda shivered.

"This great snake is Quetzalcoatl, the feathered serpent, a major god found all over Mexico. Very powerful. He helps in creation." The professor focused again on the snake's head and read: "Numbers of humans are born. Small. Weak." He pointed to small bent-looking figures repeated many times in one block beside much larger animals. "No claws or teeth with which to hunt."

"Which only means the Mayans never met the likes of O'Keefe here," Goodnight said looking her over. "She has teeth. And isn't afraid to use them."

She bared her teeth in a warning smile.

"Humans have few days and lives full of trouble," Valiente said, oblivious to the tension around him. "There are no old men in their villages."

"The old women probably ate them," Goodnight muttered.

"Jaguar Spirit is moved by the wailing and sad hearts of humans. He gives mankind a gift. The gift is so great that humans flourish and their cities grow. They dig in the earth. See this *hacha*—what you call axe?"

"It looks more like a maddox or hoe." Hedda paused in her note taking. "Picks are for breaking ground and hoes are for tilling it."

"Si—yes! Tools. Humans make the earth to bloom like a garden." He came to the three-dimensional head of the jaguar on the second scroll and studied it. "His spirit is very pleased. The people make gifts to him."

The professor turned his attention to the blocks flanking

the unusually realistic cat. Cordelia went to his side to share his view and asked what he saw.

"It says 'come' or 'enter.'" His eyes widened. "I think it invites the people. You see? These small ones enter the mouth of the jaguar."

"They bring gifts to the Jaguar Spirit?"

"It must be. *Madre Dulce!* Do you see it?" He was suddenly beside himself with excitement. "These stones may be the source of the legend itself!"

Fourteen

Cordelia stood for a moment absorbing the professor's idea, letting the possibilities assemble in her mind. The stones might be the source of the legend in more ways than one. They might have been part of the place where the legend—

"Quickly—" She grabbed the scrolls from the table and pushed back benches and stools to make enough room to lay them out on the floor. Soon she was looking at the three-sided portal that she had proposed the first time she laid eyes on the scrolls. "These stones may have originally adorned a doorway or the entrance to a temple." She pointed to the arc of the stones. "They could make up a figurative jaguar's mouth, through which people passed to make their offerings."

The professor sank down on the bench behind him with a plop. He thought about it for a while and slowly began to smile. Dropping to his knees by the rubbing, he took out his magnifying glass to look again at the stone where the little humans were depicted entering the jaguar's mouth.

"It could be," he said with tempered excitement. "These stones could indeed be the doorway to the temple where the jaguar keeps his treasure!"

Cordelia hugged Hedda and the professor, then staggered to a stop and stared down at the three-sided opening, more convinced by the moment that it was the entrance to the storehouse of a great treasure. It would be the find of the century!

Find being the operative word. If they could only *find* it.

Her excitement deflated. There were still dozens of questions to answer.

"What were the stones part of? Does it still exist? If it does, where is it? And how do we find it?"

She joined the professor on the floor; he was studying the other side of the arch. There was another great snake, without the feathers this time. At his mouth was a small school of fish. At his tail were what the professor had identified as flames. Above that were mountains that seemed to be on fire. It didn't seem to either continue or complement the creation story displayed on the other side.

"Perhaps it tells a different legend," Hedda suggested, looking on.

"There is a legend that says the serpent, he also gives gifts to humans," the professor said. "He gives writing and knowledge of the stars and seasons. But his gift is not so great as the jaguar's. He grows jealous and causes mischief."

"Did he burn things?" Cordelia asked, pointing to the burning mountains.

"I do not ever read this . . . that the serpent makes the world burn." He sat back on his heels, studying the great, winding snake and mountains in flames.

"Could that be a volcano?" Hedda said, glancing at Cordelia.

"Possibly. Or maybe a 'forked tongue' of lightning setting the forest on fire," Cordelia ventured with a smile for Hedda. "Professor, are you quite sure those figures represent fire?"

"Oh, yes. Fire is shown many places. Well known in translation." He gave Hedda a hopeful look. "There are one or two volcanoes in the south."

Goodnight, who had planted himself on a bench to

watch them unfold the layered meanings of the images, spoke up.

"There are other possibilities, you know. It could be that the mountains aren't burning at all. Maybe they're just ordinary mountains glimpsed through a ceremonial fire." He raised his eyebrows. "Maybe it's just a matter of perspective."

"Don't be ridiculous. These were primitive people," Cordelia declared. "They didn't have 'perspective.' And they were clearly into representational art. Flames mean fire and snakes mean snakes—the crawl-on-the-ground kind."

"You're thinking so literally, that you can't see the forest for the 'burning' trees," he charged. "What if that snake image *does* represent something else? Something like a river. Rivers twist and turn. And from a hilltop one might look like a big, moving snake." He rose from his seat and planted himself in the middle of the arch, staring down at the undulating snake and the burning mountains by its tail. "What if the mountains are not just floating up there by the tail or meant to show the snake caused problems? What if they're meant to show something's location in relation to the snake. What if the snake represents a river flowing from those mountains?" He drew a path along the snake's back with his finger, then tapped its head. "And what if the mouth of the snake—shown open beside a school of fish, by the by—is really the mouth of a river that leads to the sea?" He straightened.

Cordelia looked up at his adamant "Colossus" pose, astride the puzzle of their enterprise, and felt a sudden and inexplicable heat rising through her, drying her throat. He was so smug. So sure of himself. So . . . so completely . . . infuriatingly . . .

Socks flashed into her mind. Piles of socks. Mountains of socks.

Intent on proving him wrong, she focused on the drawings and was annoyed to find she was seeing them with reoriented vision. Expelling a heavy breath, she stepped into the arch determined to debunk his theory. But what she saw caused her heart to beat faster. From above, it did look like the snake could be a river. If it were, could it be part of a map of the place they'd been talking about?

She looked up at Goodnight, who was concentrating on the drawings around his feet. His hair was sticking up here and there, and his black eye was turning a spectacular shade of green around the edges. But his profile presented an arresting line and the jut of his lower lip was nothing short of absorbing. Leave it to him to come up with something entirely unique.

And contrary to everyone else's opinion.

When she pulled her gaze away, his profile came with it and for some reason she thought again of him and chemistry. His proposal smacked more of science than contentiousness. Maybe it was just a matter of perspective, and they'd needed a fresh approach to see the truth under their noses.

"We could at least see if there is a river that matches that shape." She finally was able to speak. "How many rivers can there be flowing out of the mountains to the sea? What we need is a map—several maps—to compare to our snake." Unknowingly, she proposed the best possible test of his theory: "If we find a river that fits, then we'll look for mountains near the head of the river. Who knows? Maybe the right river will start near a volcano somewhere."

It didn't take much to persuade Captain O'Brien to share his maps of the Mexican coast with them. Unfortunately, they were navigational charts that emphasized underwater topography and coastal irregularities rather than inland features. They needed land maps, Cordelia said, plying him with her most Irish smile. Did he know anyone with reliable maps of southern Mexico and the Gulf?

As it happened, he did, and that was how they decided their first destination in Mexico would be Campeche, a busy port on the western side of the Yucatán that had been home to ancient pyramid builders, conquistadors, pirates, and revolutionaries, and was now the base of entrepreneurs making fortunes from the timber of the region.

It took more than twenty-four hours of hard steaming to reach Campeche, where everyone seemed to know Johnny "Dynamite" O'Brien. During their post-siesta meal in a quaint, saffron-scented cantina, the owner and other patrons were eager to retell the story of how the captain had acquired his nickname: carrying explosives to the canal builders in Panama when no one else would. And they were told that he had been a friend and admirer of Jose Marti, one of the first leaders and greatest martyrs of the Cuba Libre movement. Clearly, many in Campeche sympathized with the Cuban revolutionaries and welcomed O'Brien because of his support for them.

By the time he led them to the mapmaker he declared to be the best south of the Mason-Dixon Line, Cordelia was feeling much better about their course and looking forward to discovering whatever truths the stones had to tell.

Mapmaker Gonzales's shop was down a side street, near the old wall of the once-fortified city, and seemed unimpressive from the outside. But once inside the modest doors, they descended to the shop floor and found themselves in a cavernous chamber lined with shelves and bins overflowing with rolled maps and charts. In the middle of the place were several chart tables, some piled with stacks of freshly printed maps and others cleared for working. In the back, through a broad stone arch, they could see a printing room ringed with drying racks and a number of workers cleaning the day's ink from presses.

"O'Brien," the mapmaker started when he looked up from the magnifying glass he was using to inspect an old bit of parchment. Ruiz Gonzales was a thin, pallid man with bilious eyes that bulged above a pair of spectacles perched near the tip of his nose. He stepped around the counter and offered the captain his hand.

"A long time since your last visit. What brings you to

Campeche? More dynamite?" His chuckle seemed a bit humorless.

"Something even more dangerous. Women." O'Brien grinned and gestured to Cordelia and Hedda. "May I present the Misses O'Keefe. Friends of mine."

Gonzales greeted Cordelia and Hedda with a half bow as introductions were made. He took the hand the professor extended, looking impressed, then acknowledged the aloof-looking Goodnight with a neutral nod.

"I've told my friends that if any chart man in Mexico has th' maps they want, it'll be you. And I'm hopin' you'll not be makin' a liar out of me."

"Si, Capitan. I do my best." He waved a hand at the shelves and bins stuffed to overflowing with charts. "I have many maps. What is it your fine friends seek?"

"We're looking for a river." Cordelia unfolded a sketch Hedda had made of the curves of the snake. "It's shaped like this. We believe it to be in one of the southern provinces of Mexico."

He scowled and studied the drawing, spreading it on the table before him.

"This is the whole river?" he asked, rubbing his chin. "What is the scale?"

Cordelia grimaced at encountering yet another unknown. "We're not sure. We may have to look at all of the rivers, state by state."

"That will take a very long time, senorita." He gave a phlegmy laugh that ended in a cough. "There are forty rivers in Veracruz alone."

"Forty? In one state?" Cordelia's dismay as she looked around the vast map library turned slowly to determination. "Then we'd best get started. Perhaps you could provide materials for Hedda to make copies of this drawing for each of us. That way we could each take a few maps. That might speed things along."

As the daylight waned, lamps were lighted and the search of the selected maps continued all over the main floor of the mapmaker's shop. Some of the maps were old and hand drawn, others were newer and printed on heavy chart paper. All of them were written in Spanish and most contained handmade corrections—which sometimes made it difficult to tell the definite shape of a river. But with the four of them and the captain and mapmaker Gonzales all searching, they had a good chance of finding it. If it existed.

After three unproductive hours, Hedda and Goodnight independently came up with a possibility that turned out to be the very same river. Cordelia, the professor, the captain, and Gonzales crowded around to see both maps, and all agreed it was an amazingly clear match. The fact that two separate cartographers had drawn it with the same exact set of curves lent credibility to both renderings.

"But it's not an entire river," Hedda said, looking up at the others. "It's just a large piece of a river in the state of Veracruz."

"The head of it is nowhere near a volcano," Cordelia observed. "And the mouth isn't in the sea, it's in a marshy delta that lies north and west of the city of Veracruz."

"Still, it is a true match for the sn—um—curves," the professor said. "And it does lead into mountains."

"Nothing else has come even close to matching it?" she looked from one face to another. Each person shook his or her head or shrugged. "That's it then. Our idea led to this one possibility."

The question she did not ask, the question she and she alone had to answer was whether or not they should bet all of their time and resources on that one possibility. It was times like this that she wished she had someone to talk it over with, someone whose experience and judgment . . . She glanced up and found herself looking into Goodnight's eyes, which tightened as if probing her intentions. Turning emphatically to Hedda, she saw in her aunt's face a trust born of shared experiences, but no help for her decision.

One possibility was all they had?

Well—she drew a fortifying breath—one was all they needed.

"We'd like to purchase these two maps, senor," she said

to Gonzales. And she could have sworn she heard a groan from Goodnight's corner.

Gonzales watched O'Brien and his "friends" leave the shop with the two maps they had found, and his yellowed eyes narrowed. He hadn't managed to get them to reveal the source or significance of the wriggling line they had tried to match with a river. But he was fairly certain O'Brien wouldn't be involved unless it were important to the revolutionary forces of Cuba.

Ordering his apprentices to lock up after him, he donned a hat and slipped through the darkened streets to the alley behind the city's telegraph office. He knocked on a door peeling paint and marked with the hand-painted admonition *No Entry*. After a minute the door opened, and a pair of dark eyes appeared in the narrow gap.

"Let me in," Gonzales snapped.

"We are closed, senor."

"Not for this you're not. Open up." The door swung wide enough to admit him and he stepped into a windowless storeroom stuffed with crates, boxes, and bags, and furnished with a bed and a small table. "Where is your master?"

"Upstairs, senor," the clerk said nervously, leading Gonzales through the main telegraph office, where the sending and receiving keys lay silent, and up a set of stairs to a comfortably furnished apartment on the floor above. The manager of the office looked up from his dinner and raised his eyebrows in question.

"I have to send a telegram, Mendez," he said.

"So urgent that it cannot wait until I finish my dinner?" the telegraph agent asked. Then, reading Gonzales's tension, he pushed back from the table.

"O'Brien is here, in Campeche," Gonzales said, "with some Americanos."

"Damned meddling yanqui," Mendez's face darkened and he rose.

"I could not get him to reveal what they are doing here, but I must send word to Havana, alert them that O'Brien is here and a shipment of guns and supplies for the rebels may be headed their way."

Mendez nodded and put an arm around the mapmaker's thin shoulders, ushering him toward the stairs and the equipment waiting below.

"You are a credit to our cause, Gonzales. What would Spain do without loyal sons like you to be her eyes and ears in these far-flung possessions?"

Fifteen

A day and a half after locating maps that contained the curves of the snake, O'Brien's ship steamed past the port of Veracruz and up the Gulf Coast toward a fishing village called Tecolutla. The upper part of the nearby river and the lower part of one of its tributaries had matched the profile of the snake inscribed on the blocks of the arch. According to the professor, the area was known for its fishing, plentiful fruit, and the production of vanilla. And not far to the south was the mysterious El Tajin, site of the Pyramid of the Niches, which had been known for more than a hundred years but not truly explored.

It was also, Cordelia learned as they dropped anchor some distance from shore, the site of a broad, golden beach that went on for miles and required transporting them and their equipment ashore in longboats. Fortunately, the trip from ship to shore was less frantic than the one that marked their departure from Cuba, and they got a warm welcome from the local fishermen and townspeople who hurried from the village to investigate their arrival.

Upon landing, Cordelia declined eager offers to escort them into Tecolutla itself, drawing puzzled looks from

Goodnight and the professor. She declared that they needed to set up their tents and spend a night or so getting the feel of their equipment. O'Brien and his men obligingly helped maneuver their crates to the spot she chose at the edge of the trees, then headed into town with some of the local men to purchase rum and supplies. A number of townsfolk decided to remain behind to watch what the newcomers would do.

Cordelia surprised them all by pulling a pry bar from her trunk and beginning to open the crates to see what had survived the transfers they had made. The glass chimneys of two of the lanterns had cracked, and one of the rubberized tarpaulins for collecting water had melted and stuck together in the heat, but the rest of their equipment seemed intact. She immediately assigned Goodnight and the professor to raise one canvas tent, while she and Hedda erected another. They would share sleeping quarters, she explained, so they could keep the work of setting up camp to a minimum. After scanning the cloud-spotted sky for hints of rain, she decided to erect a third of their four tents and use it to protect their equipment and supplies.

While Goodnight and the professor struggled with their shelter, she and Hedda made quick work of raising both their sleeping tent and the one intended for storage, then turned to emptying the crates and carrying their equipment and supplies into the tent. As the afternoon waned, she glimpsed some of the locals watching the way Goodnight and the professor were struggling with their tent.

"Trouble, gentlemen?" She strolled over to offer assistance. Goodnight sprang up like a bent sapling to confront her.

"It's defective—damned perverse hank of canvas—it's made wrong."

"I suppose one might conclude that, trying to erect it on its side."

Startled, he looked from the ungainly structure he was working on to the two properly raised tents. He tilted his head and finally made sense of the shelter's intended shape.

"Damned bodger—I told him it went the other way 'round." He stalked back to the professor, who protested huffily that he'd never had to erect his own tent on an expedition before and refused to be held responsible for botching a task that was entirely beneath him.

She left them to argue it out under the scrutiny of a group of incredulous local youths and headed to the equipment tent to help Hedda unpack. An hour later, the professor, looking hot and exasperated, came to say he was heading into the town to search for guides and suggested that Hedda's presence might elicit a more favorable reaction from the townspeople.

"I should probably go with him." Hedda quickly smoothed her hair and checked her blouse for smudges of dirt.

"On the way, would you please ask Goodnight to collect wood for a fire?" Cordelia asked. "We ought to try cooking dinner tonight."

Hedda sighed at the prospect.

"It's getting late. How about if we look for some food to bring back with us, and start cooking tomorrow?"

Cordelia was surprised; her aunt had always enjoyed cooking over an open campfire. But she nodded and watched Hedda and the professor set off down the beach before turning back to her work.

Daylight hours flew by and the sun was setting when Goodnight's sardonic voice came from over her shoulder as she knelt on the sand in a circle of cellulose packing material.

"Thank God the teacups made it," he said.

She looked up to find him staring with male disdain at the piece of flowered earthenware she held.

"Yes. Thank heaven." She stuffed it back into the crumpled paper and pasteboard box that had protected it thus far. "Otherwise, we might not have anything for gifts or to barter for supplies and information."

"That's why you brought china cups along? For bartering?"

"Well, it wasn't for tea parties in the jungle," she replied dryly. "You didn't honestly think . . ." But, from the look on his face, he had.

Her eyes narrowed. It was time to disabuse him of his all-too-familiar notions about her. There came a time in all of her associations with men that she had to do so, and this seemed as opportune a moment as any. She got to her feet, flushed from annoyance and determination.

"In the agrarian cultures we are likely to encounter, sharing food and drink has special significance, as does the sharing of ceremonial vessels. Teacups are as close to ceremonial as we can get without being sacrilegious. Presenting village elders with them is a way of sharing a part of our culture and ensuring good will." She propped her hands on her waist. "More effective and *respectful* than cheap tin mirrors and strings of colored beads, don't you think?"

"I suppose that makes sense," he said with a disconcerted edge.

"And that surprises you, does it? That I actually make sense."

He paused long enough to bat away the buzzing of his better sense.

"Frankly, yes."

"And just what about me makes you think I lack intelligence, foresight, and common sense?" She stepped closer and caused him to take a step back, kicking cellulose from underfoot in the process.

"I've never thought you lack intelligence, O'Keefe."

"Just foresight and common sense?" She took another step.

"I didn't say that." The dart of his eyes toward the open beach said he wished there was more of it between them. "It's just that . . . you're a woman."

"I thought we covered that point."

"In a hotel suite in Tampa," he said, his gaze going pointedly past the graceful palms that rimmed the beach to the dense inland forest that awaited.

"Oh. And now that we're on the brink of the real test,

you're not so certain. What makes you think I'm a fainter? Have I been helpless?"

"No."

"Cowardly?"

"No."

"Indecisive?"

"Hardly."

"Overconfident?"

"Not . . . especially."

With each word she had advanced a bit more, backing him steadily toward a palm tree behind him.

"Say it, Goodnight. Say what it is that really bothers you."

"Women are . . . often . . . unreliable."

"We are, are we?" There was a thought worth exploring further: some woman or women had left Hartford Goodnight, enigma extraordinaire, in the lurch. "We don't keep our word or commitments? Don't hold up our end? Quit in the middle of things?"

"Generally speaking."

"Well, speak specifically. We're not talking about women in general or the other women you've known, we're talking about *me*. When have I been unreliable? When we ran through the streets of Havana with soldiers after us? When I refused to give Castille the scrolls? When I held off the government soldiers on the beach with a gun, or pulled you into the water and helped you swim a quarter mile to the ship?"

He reddened more with each example she cited.

"Well, n–no."

"So, I'm not unreliable. Then what's your problem with me?"

"You're . . . too . . ."

"Yes?" She made a winding motion, ordering him to dredge it up.

Backed into a corner, he was forced to finally say it.

"*Beautiful.*"

She paused for a moment, having finally gotten the response she expected, but wishing he hadn't made it sound like a hanging offense. She could see in his face that her appearance was not an obstacle easily overcome.

"By whose standards?" she demanded.

It was a question she had asked a number of times, one for which she had never received an honest answer. Astonishment, chagrin at their own thoughts, or fear of giving her too much power had always kept men silent. Until now.

Goodnight's initial surprise melted into embarrassment and then confusion at her response. He turned a becoming shade of crimson. She'd left him only one way to escape this conversation with a shred of pride; he had to be as honest with her as she was with him. It took him a moment to finally meet her eyes.

"Mine."

That desperate bit of candor set her back on her heels. Briefly.

"So, you're disagreeable and uncooperative because you've decided—by some inexplicable measure—that I am beautiful." She edged closer. One deep inhalation by either of them would bring their bodies together. "How can the difference of a tiny fraction of an inch on a feature or an extra dash of pigment here or there keep me from being a decent, capable human being? Do you have any idea how absurd that is?"

Instead of trying to escape, he squared his shoulders.

"Unfortunately, I do."

She swallowed hard. She'd never gotten this far with a man before.

Hart swallowed hard. He'd never gotten in this deep with a woman before. Never been this honest or felt this damned naked. There she stood—with her hair a blaze of sunset-flamed chestnut, her eyes pools of dark honey, and her face a Pre-Raphaelite masterpiece—demanding that he confront his own irrational standards. And all he could think about was how good it would feel to pull her against him again and kiss her senseless.

"We're headed for the jungle. My appearance is irrelevant," she declared.

Only to a blind man, he thought. Unfortunately, there weren't any of those in the Tampa Bay Hotel, at the restaurant the other night, in O'Brien's crew, or among those residents of Tecolutla—mostly men and mostly young—who had lingered on the beach to catch a glimpse of her.

"I disagree," he said testily, trying desperately to summon more objective language. "Appreciation of your physical attributes is shared by every man you encounter—including the men of this benighted town—among whom we still have to find guides." He flicked an irritable glance toward the youths on the beach and found them hidden from view by the supply tent. "Their eyes follow you everywhere. And where their eyes lead, their hands will itch to follow." He lowered his gaze to hers. "Sooner or later it will cause problems."

"And you're afraid you'll be called on to defend my honor?" She laughed and took that deep breath that brought her breasts into contact with his ribs. His breath caught and he felt a ripple of heat spreading through him from that point of contact. "Please. I've been dealing with men's roving eyes and itchy hands since I was thirteen years old. I'm fully capable of defending myself against unwanted male attentions. I have done so on numerous occasions and in numerous cultures and situations. Why do you think I learned to shoot so well?"

Her response stunned him. Then embarrassed him. She wasn't exactly a babe in arms; she had undoubtedly encountered as many different approaches, overtures, and propositions as she had encountered men. Suddenly, the threat he had proposed to chasten her turned into a shameful reality that chastened him instead. She was a continual target of male lust. His included.

"Long ago I learned that the way I look is both a blessing and a curse." Her tone grew more serious. "It causes some people to expect too much of me and others too little. Unfortunately, like most men, you seem to have fallen into the latter group. You don't want to admit that I am resourceful and self-reliant and intensely practical. You select bits of me that fit your conception and ignore everything else."

Ignore parts of her? He groaned privately. If only he could.

His gaze slid over her cheeks—perfect skin that even in the fading light bore the blush of ripe apples—and came to rest on her wet-satin lips. She was wrong; he didn't expect too little of her. From the minute he laid eyes on her, he had known that she was more than he could deal with, and time had certainly proven him right. Even now, as he glimpsed in her a strength that dispensed with excuses, accusations, and recriminations, she overwhelmed him.

And yet, there was something else in the depths of those stunning eyes, something unsettling, something that touched and then took hold of him . . .

"So if we look at you too much, we're out of bounds; if we don't see enough, we're equally off the mark. You ask men to walk a very fine line, O'Keefe." His throat constricted. "And most of us have damned big feet."

She glanced toward his boots.

"You certainly do, anyway." Her lashes lowered and her chin raised. He leaned toward her and she met him, molding her body against his. When she spoke, her gaze focused hotly on his mouth. "All I *ask* is the cooperation you would give the leader of any expedition you joined." She grasped his sleeves and he could feel her hands trembling. "Quit thinking of me as a woman first, last, and only." Her voice sank provocatively lower. "Stop equating me to whatever woman it was that left you high and dry—"

"I never said a woman left me—"

"You didn't have to," she said, stretching upward.

Sixteen

There were grave penalties, he thought, for defying the laws of physics. And just now, that strange, compelling gravity that she exerted on him was demanding unconditional obedience. He lowered his head and felt a surge of overwhelming pleasure as their lips met.

Dear God—it *was* one of the wonders of nature. Soft and enveloping and wet and stimulating; he was awash in sensations he'd never experienced, never imagined before. His whole body sprang to life as he slid both arms around her and pulled her harder against him, molding her to him.

Her whimper of pleasure came as a mild shock. She was experiencing the same delicious sensations, the same steamy compulsion for joining. Her mouth opened to him, welcomed him, hungry for contact that produced both satisfaction and deeper hunger. He responded with a growl and ran his hands over her back, searching her shape through her clothes, claiming the curves he'd memorized the first time he saw her and discovering even more; her surprisingly muscular shoulders, her narrow waist, the soft edges of her breasts and the neatly rounded buttocks he'd seen as she stood dripping wet on the ship . . .

His fingers encountered a band of leather beneath her soft woolen skirt and traced in downward to her right side, where it ended in polished steel that had been warmed by her body and felt shockingly sensual there on her hip. His hand slid over the gun and the thigh it was strapped against. Hot, unyielding steel pressed against soft, warm skin.

He moaned against her mouth, and grabbed her buttocks with both hands lifting her against his hardness. Her thighs shifted and suddenly he was cradled against her body's delicious, maddening heat. A shudder of anticipation went through his—

"Ahoy there, Miss O'Keefe!" A familiar voice came from beyond the tent.

He froze and felt the shock of recognition that ran through her as well. It was O'Brien and his men, returning from the local cantinas.

"We'll be headin' back to th' ship now and catchin' th' tide." There was a slight pause. "Where are you?"

It took a moment for her to push away and steady herself on her own two feet. He could see her struggling for self-control, smothering her body's lush response beneath a fierce blanket of calm.

"Here, Captain!" she called out, her voice surprisingly normal. She took a deep breath and hurried around the tent to meet him and his men at the edge of their darkening camp. "So, you're leaving?"

"Just thought I'd best check with you once more about th' arrangements. You all right, miss?"

"Me? Perfectly fine, Captain. Never better." Hart could hear in her voice the change in her posture, that shoulders-back and chin-up stance that said she was fully in control. And he knew as he leaned back against the palm and stared at his own trembling hands that it was a performance, one she had perfected over long years of confronting and dealing with men.

The heat and pressure in his loins began to migrate north and settled in his lower chest as a confusing lump of warmth. He had just experienced the woman inside the woman and would never be able to look at her the same again.

"One month from today," he heard her say. "Right here, on this beach."

"I'll wait three days, but that's all I can give ye. Things are heatin' up. There'll be Spanish patrol boats all over th' Carib lookin' for us."

"Don't worry." He could hear a smile in her voice. "We'll be here."

O'Brien laughed. "I reckon you will. A month, then." The captain tugged the bill of his hat at Cordelia. "Best o' luck to you, miss."

Hart peered around the tent and spotted her standing there, watching O'Brien and his men fade across the beach toward the longboats. She remained there well after they disappeared from sight. Putting her hand to her throat, she turned to find him nearby, staring at her. She couldn't meet his gaze.

"So. Where were we?" She hoisted her chin to a defensive angle. "Oh, yes. This unreliable woman who walked out and left you high and dry."

He turned away and headed for the nearby trees.

"I believe I have a campfire to make."

"Sooner or later I'll get it out of you," she called after him, causing him to pause a moment as he headed for the stack of downed limbs and driftwood he'd gathered.

"Later is better for me."

By the time Hedda and the professor returned from town, Goodnight had a welcoming fire going and Cordelia had finished squaring away the equipment and making up her sleeping cot.

"We brought food," Hedda called. "And it's delicious."

"We also find guides," the professor added as they emerged out of the gloom into the golden glow of the fire.

"Really?" Cordelia sprang to her feet to help Hedda

carry the bundle of food to one of the small crates they were using for a camp table. "Who are they?"

"Two brothers," Hedda declared.

"Itza and Ruz Platano," the professor said, watching Cordelia's reaction. "Others say they spend much time upriver and know the people and the villages."

"Have you talked to them? Did they agree to take us inland?"

"What do they charge?" Goodnight inserted a practical note.

"We do not see them. They are away, harvesting honey from the hives of the vanilla bees. They return tomorrow or the next day."

"Platano?" Goodnight tucked his pen in his journal and set it aside. "That sounds oddly familiar. What are they called again? Itchy and Rouge?"

The professor looked nettled.

"What else was it they said at the cantina?" Hedda asked the professor. "*Muchachos or something Platano*?"

Behind them on the darkened beach, one of the local boys caught the names and relayed them back to his friends with a laugh: "Itza y Ruz—*les muchachos Platano!*" The professor charged to the edge of the tents, roaring threats in Spanish that sent the youths running off down the beach toward town.

"Itchy and Rouge? Who names their children after skin conditions and cosmetics?" Goodnight said, strolling over to investigate the food Hedda and Cordelia were laying out on the crate. "Sound dodgy to me."

The professor took a seat on an empty crate as if it were gilded Louis Quatorze and eyed the freshly baked tortillas, grilled fish, and fruit salsa.

"Sometimes," he declared with great nobility, reaching for a tortilla with a raised pinky, "one must make do."

"Well, I don't care if they have two heads," Cordelia said with an arch glance at Goodnight, "as long as they know the area. And are *reliable*."

January 30, Day 10

Fish and tortillas for four: $2.00 U.S. Bottle of native liquor with WORM in bottom: $1.50 U.S., silver. (Worm said to absorb poisons.) (Will NEVER be desperate enough to drink "tequila.")

Abandoned by ship's captain on the backside of creation. Professor unstable. Aunt pleasant but ineffectual. O'Keefe terrifying and unpredictable. One minute gelding me verbally—the things that woman says to me! The next minute backing me against a tree and kissing me witless.

God help me—all she has to do is look at me with those honey-taffy eyes and I'm reduced to blithering. Damnedest color I've ever seen. Correction: she doesn't so much look at me, as she looks INTO me. I get the feeling she can count the spots on my liver. After a few moments, I can feel her reaching through me, sorting me out, all the way to my toes. My knees go weak and my blood heads for my loins. Something takes me over.

Wonder if she's ever spent time in Barbados or Port au Prince.

If she starts killing chickens and dancing around a fire...

Note: Check with local physico—if there is one—about local cures.

And curses.

Cordelia awoke well after sunrise to the sound of a fire crackling and the smell of bacon frying and tortillas baking. But it was the sound of Spanish from unfamiliar male voices that caused her to throw on clothes and burst from her tent with her boots in her hand. There, she stopped dead.

"What on earth?"

By the fire, tending a skillet and a native baking stone, squatted two shaggy-looking men with broad, sunbaked faces and eyes so dark they were almost black. They were barefoot and wore ragged trousers and shirts from which the sleeves had been ripped. They looked up at her and their toothy smiles faded to looks of awe.

The taller, thinner one sprang up.

The shorter, stockier one joined him, nodding shyly.

They produced artless grins of appreciation. "Hola! Senorita."

"Professor!" She headed for the men's tent. Valiente nearly cracked heads with her as he came barreling out. "Talk to them." She flung a finger in their direction. "Find out who they are and what they're doing here."

A fast exchange of Spanish that was peppered with occasional less familiar sounds resulted in a marked easing of the professor's tension. He turned to Cordelia moments later with a smile.

"These are the two guides they told us about," he said with no little pleasure. "Itza and Ruz Platano. Not only brothers, but twins as well. They say they know both jungle and mountain country and can take us to the ends of the rivers."

"Do they know of the legend of the jaguar?" she asked, eyeing the brothers. "Do they know of people who keep the old ways?"

The professor translated and there were several exchanges and some pointing over their shoulders before he came back to her with heartening news.

"They say they hear stories of people who see the Jaguar Spirit, that he walks these lands. Some people in the villages tell stories."

"Tell them we're looking for stones, an arch of stones

that lead to a temple or holy place dedicated to the Jaguar Spirit."

The brothers shrugged and shook their heads at the professor's words.

"They know of no such place," the professor reported back. "But they say many secrets sleep under the feet of the trees. They agree to help us look for it."

"Then they're hire—"

"Aghhhh!" Goodnight came barreling out of the tent wearing one boot and carrying the other, his hair standing on end, and his face gray with stubble.

"What the hell?" Distracted briefly by the newcomers, he quickly dismissed them and pointed at the tent behind him. "There's a bloody beast of some sort eating the back of the tent!"

After a quick translation, the Platanos apologized profusely and scrambled for the back of the tent to rescue both shelter and culprit.

"And," the professor added happily as he turned back to Cordelia, "they have burros. This means we do not have to buy any."

Goodnight groaned as Itza and Ruz ushered a shockingly fat donkey into the center of the camp, talking alternately to her and the professor, apparently explaining the situation to both of them.

"They are very much sorry for her behavior," the professor relayed to Cordelia and Hedda with a chuckle. "She is—how you say, ummm—pregnant. And she eats everything she sees. But she is their lead burro and they cannot leave her behind. They must be with her when her time comes."

The beast proved the brothers' veracity by ambling over to the stack of fresh tortillas lying on a banana leaf beside the fire and devouring the lot of them. Itza and Ruz pleaded, chided, pulled on her halter, and even whispered in her ear. But the determined burro, Rita, would not be moved until she had finished her breakfast.

With a strangled sound, Goodnight retreated into his tent. The professor took a seat on a nearby crate to stare forlornly at the disappearing flatbread, and Hedda glanced at Cordelia with rueful expression.

"I have a bad feeling about that creature," she said.

"I'll see your bad feeling," Cordelia murmured, watching the brothers assure the professor that they would make more tortillas, "and raise you a full-blown sense of dread."

Since the moment Cordelia had shaken hands with Samuel P., nothing had gone quite as she'd expected. They lurched from one predicament to another, always just one step ahead of calamity. Now they were headed into fierce and unforgiving terrain, guided by a pair of toothy yokels whose surname—according to her phrase book—meant "banana," and who had a bizarre, almost familial attachment to a pregnant burro.

She had to face squarely the possibility that they might not find what they sought. And if they did find it, it might prove to be a huge disappointment, robbed generations ago by locals who turned from the old ways, or not a treasure at all, except in the minds of primitive and superstitious people.

Moments later, her own negative thoughts shocked her. Goodnight must be rubbing off on her! Now that they were about to embark on the arduous part of the journey, she had to brace herself for the work ahead and quit dwelling on the results. What was truly important was that she could look Samuel P. square in the eye when she returned and say she had done everything possible to uncover the truth about the stones and the legend they proclaimed.

Seventeen

It took the better part of the morning to pack the equipment properly, balance the loads on the Platanos' six burros, and prepare to move out. Hedda, who had been through this before, donned her broad-brimmed hat to ward off the sun and patiently rechecked her boots and bags and made certain her gloves and machete were accessible. Goodnight grumbled under his breath and stood with his arms crossed and his legs spread, refusing to recheck anything—a monument to the hidebound aspects of British character. The professor channeled his tension into impromptu lectures on everything from edible fruits of the region to boot care in damp climates, to the telltale signs that marked locations of ancient ruins. Then there were the Platano brothers, who went from burro to burro, talking earnestly, informing their charges of the journey before them and pleading for cooperation. None of which boded well for the path ahead.

Cordelia set her jaw and struck off at the head of the group with the Platano who called himself Itza, which she learned was the name of a fierce group of Maya warriors from the west who conquered other Mayans. Before long, they were skirting the town and winding through pastures and around maize and melon fields, headed for what appeared to be a wall of vegetation.

Entering that thick forest canopy on the narrow cart path was like falling into a deep, green well. The temperature dropped and the air grew thick and heavy with odors of vegetation in various stages of life and decay. It was surprisingly noisy. Birds cawed and chirped; insects buzzed, hissed, and clicked. Monkeys chattered and screeched overhead, and frogs trilled continuously. The sounds seemed to be coming from every side. Even—Cordelia shivered and watched her steps more closely—from underfoot.

But the most amazing thing to her was the fact that many of the plants she knew as common house plants in Boston were abundant and living free here, some growing to the size of trees. Not even her experience in Hawaii had prepared her for the sights of such massive vines, towering cycads, palms of endless variety, gigantic ferns, and bushy flowering plants run amok. Not a single inch was left bare of life. Tucked away in every accessible niche—the crotches of trees, the branches of shrubs, and the coils of thick vines—were flowers with thick, fibrous leaves and pale roots hanging bare. Orchids, the professor announced in answer to her question, after which he spent some time lecturing on the astounding variety of them in the forests of southern Mexico.

She could hardly drink it all in: the spongy carpet of organic matter that cushioned every step, the huge leaves all around—shiny, rubbery, blade-like, or feathery—the sinuous vines and bracts of hanging blossoms, the orchids growing in profusion, and the birds darting and monkeys swinging back and forth sixty to a hundred feet overhead. She found herself lurching along with her head back and her jaw drooping. It was truly another world, and for the moment, the thrill of discovery was just too delicious to bother with appearances.

An hour later, they emerged from the forest into afternoon sun and found themselves trekking along the bank of a broad, silt-laden river flowing sluggishly toward a marshy delta. Goodnight came sprinting up from the rear with a reddened face and a point of contention.

"See that?" He pointed to dugouts and flat-bottomed boats being paddled on the river and to others resting empty on the banks below. "Why the devil couldn't we have taken boats upstream? We would have saved time and energy, and wouldn't have had to deal with these wretched beasts."

One of the burros let out a fierce "eee-haw" in protest.

The professor called to the Platanos, who provided the answer.

"The river, she is a deceiver." Valiente translated in spurts as the brothers talked. "She is gentle and easy here, but she tricks you. She leads you upstream until you are too far to turn back. Then she changes her mind and becomes a raging torrent. She pours over the rocks and dashes boats to pieces. By then you are too far to return, and there are no burros to help you."

"She is a bad woman, our river," Ruz said through the professor. "But she is our woman. And so, we stay close to her when we can."

Goodnight was skeptical.

"That poetic bit of balderdash wouldn't be inspired by the fact they're charging a pretty penny for the use of these cursed burros, would it?"

"Your protest wouldn't be inspired by the fact that you developed a marked aversion to donkeys and chickens on the road from Havana, would it?" Cordelia responded in kind, then turned to the professor. "We have to know if what they say is true. Boats would be a faster way to get upriver."

Valiente took the Platanos aside and from the looks and sound of their interaction, he spared no bid to drama in making them feel the honor of both their families and their ancestors was at stake in their judgment. The men stuck to their story, looking bewildered by Goodnight's hostility and shamed by the professor's challenge of their assessment.

"A few miles. The river, she turns fast and treacherous," the professor reported to Cordelia, then shrugged. "I believe them, senorita. For all their simple ways, they are men of honor."

"Then we'll give them a few miles," she decided, "and we'll see for ourselves."

"Well, that settles that." Cordelia stood looking at a set of rocky obstacles in the river that turned the silty water into a churning mass of dirty white. Though it was clear there was calmer water ahead, there wasn't a single part of the channel that was free of the rocky decline that caused the dangerous rapids. "We would have had to get out and portage around this area." She looked up at Goodnight, who was taking in the sight with more resignation than she expected. "Luckily, we won't have to test how much weight can you carry over your head while climbing the side of a hill."

"Fine." Hart frowned. "We're stuck with the burros. But, I'm telling you: if one of the blasted things bites me, I won't be held responsible."

He reseated his pith helmet on his sweaty hair and stalked back to his appointed position at the rear of the line of burros. As he passed the vaunted Rita, she turned her head to sniff at him, then curled her upper lip and made a judgmental braying sound.

Lovely, Hart said to himself. Not only did he have to put up with O'Keefe's jibes and changeable temperament, he now had to bear the taunts of a prima donna burro who looked like a battleship on stilts and eyed him as if he were a juicy carrot. Ahead of him, he saw O'Keefe and Itza leading the column toward the brush and the jungle beyond. He pulled out one of the bandanas she insisted he bring and swabbed his face and the back of his neck.

The forest canopy provided much-needed shade and relief from the late-afternoon sun. Unfortunately, the light–dark interface drew swarms of gnats that tried to invade his nose on every breath. He found relief by tying his bandana over his nose and mouth. Another use for that ubiquitous scrap of cloth.

It annoyed him that O'Keefe was right about the bandanas. Just like it annoyed him that she captivated their guides, who hadn't been able to take their eyes from her trouser-clad legs and bottom since the trip started. She seemed not to have noticed their bulging eyes and doltish grins. She was too busy consulting their main map and thinking two steps ahead to worry about what others saw or thought. Too busy being competent. Too busy pursuing her mission.

Take a lesson, he chided himself. *You have a mission here, as well. And it's high time you began attending to it.*

As the daylight filtered through the high canopy overhead, he began to scrutinize the area visible from the path for specimens of exotic species of plants he might recognize. There were all manner of ferns and Areca palms, plants that looked like the dieffenbachia of Victorian parlor fame, only larger—much, much larger. And there was a tree with slightly hairy leaves and bright orange clusters of blooms that looked for all the world like Borage, tisanes of which were useful for treating dyspepsia and diarrhea. He fought his way through the undergrowth and was soon investigating the showy tree and its blooms, the nicest examples of which were clearly at the top, nearest the sunlight. He estimated the height and began to climb.

The path they followed narrowed and in some places grew difficult to see. A few days' growth in that climate could obliterate a footpath, unless you know just where to look, which was where Itza and Ruz came in. They knew precisely where to look; they could read the subtlest nuances of the forest. That fluency assured Cordelia they had made the right choice in hiring the odd pair. By the end of the day, they were faced with paths that were all but invisible. The humans had to go first to clear a path for the pack animals and the only way to clear a path was to hack some of the vegetation out of the way.

"You're sure this is the best way to get upstream?" she asked Itza, who looked puzzled until she called back to the professor for a translation of "best way." "Camino mejor?" she asked waving at the dense foliage in their path.

"Si, si. El camino mejor," Itza declared, heading for Rita and pulling his machete from the bag draped across her broad back. Immediately he began to chop the fronds and scrubby branches that grew over the path.

With a huff of resignation, Cordelia went to her own bags and fished out her gloves and her machete. She knew full well how taxing it would be to have to chop their way through undergrowth. She called back to Hedda to pass along the news to the professor, Ruz, and Goodnight that all would be taking turns in the lead until they came to thinner vegetation.

Hedda dutifully passed the word to the professor, who passed it to Ruz and turned to tell Goodnight—who wasn't there. He shrugged, assuming the tall Brit had stepped into the undergrowth to take care of personal business and that he would see what was happening when he came back.

But later, when the professor tired of swinging his blade and called for Goodnight to relieve him, they discovered that Goodnight still wasn't there.

"When did anyone last see him?" Cordelia demanded, looking from Hedda and the Platanos to the professor. All shook their heads.

"I think he goes into brush for . . . relief," the professor said apologetically. "I think no more of it."

"Curse his hide," Cordelia muttered, reaching for her machete with one hand and beckoning to Ruz with the other. "You come with me. Itza, take the rest and go on to that campsite you spoke of near the river. We'll catch up."

She and Ruz retraced their path without speaking. Seeing the way the vegetation had been flattened by their feet and the burros' hooves into an unmistakable trail, she was tempted to simply go on with the others and leave him to catch up on his own. But there was always the possibility that he couldn't follow, that he had fallen or stepped in a hole . . . or been bitten by a snake, spider, or scorpion . . . or walked into a fire ant colony . . .

She glanced at the dense rainforest around them. Beneath the disguise of a lush, green paradise was a savage arena where everything battled for survival. Everything that had legs also had fangs, claws, stingers, or venom of some kind. What would a starchy Oxford chemist know about the dangers of such a place? What if something had happened to him? Anxiety constricted her chest.

She walked faster and began to call out to him.

Almost a mile back down the trail, she thought she heard something and stopped dead, pulling Ruz to a halt as well. Through the normal screech and hum of the jungle around them came the sound of passage, something moving, disturbing foliage. She raised her machete as the bushes to the side of the trail thrashed wildly and parted.

Goodnight broke onto the narrow path, bashing clinging leaves and branches from his clothes. He barked a startled "hey!" at the sight of her standing there with her machete upraised and her face fierce with tension.

"What the bloody hell are you doing?" he demanded, holding up both hands, palms out, and spitting out the twig he was chewing.

"Me? What are *you* doing—out here in the jungle by yourself—sneaking around?" She lowered her blade, her arms weak from a surge of relief.

"I wasn't sneaking around. I was investigating some of the local flora." His hands went protectively to his pockets, which were bulging with all manner of twigs, leaves, flowers, bracts of blooms, and dried pods. He looked like he'd swallowed a packet of seeds and was sprouting. "I must have lost track of time."

"Darn right you lost track of time," she snapped. "And

us, as well. If we hadn't realized you were missing and come back to find you, you'd have been lost out here."

"I wasn't *lost*," he protested. "Just lagging behind."

"Going off on your own—lagging behind—it doesn't matter, it's still unacceptable. We're having to cut our way through this growth. Not only have you not been there to do your share of the work, we had to spend precious time and energy coming back for you. We have a mission, Goodnight, and it takes precedence over"—she snatched a specimen from his shirt pocket, glared at it, and tossed it aside—"picking flowers. Is that *clear*?"

"Perfectly."

"Good." She scowled as she looked him over. "Where's your machete?"

"I didn't think—" He straightened to his full height. "In my haversack."

"You were out here by yourself unarmed?" She exchanged looks with Ruz, who seemed to understand without translation. She thrust her machete at Goodnight, handle first. "Take mine. Get to the front and help clear the way."

He took the blade and stalked irritably up the path to join the others. As he passed the lead burrow, Rita stretched out her neck to sniff after him and nickered softly. Itza laughed and the professor chuckled as he translated.

"She says she likes you, my friend. She thinks you are pretty."

"The feeling," Goodnight muttered, "is *not* mutual."

February 1, Day 12

Two guides: $40.00 U.S. gold. Six mangy burros (rental): $30.00 U.S. and one bottle of Irish whiskey (requisitioned from yours truly). Flour, corn meal, dried beans, salt pork, carrots, onions, peppers, and coffee: $34.00 U.S.

Camped by the Tecolutla River. Bugs everywhere. So noisy I can't sleep. Every beast in the jungle comes out at night to screech, grunt, yip, or howl his arse off. Itchy said noise is from mating. Now strangely aroused by listening.

Hands raw from wielding damnable machete. Can hardly hold pen. Shoulders in knots. Back and feet aching. Took aspirin with whiskey. Must have canceled each other out. Still feel terrible.

Personally cleared two miles of path. O'Keefe probably cleared twenty. Swings a machete like it's a butter knife. George Almighty—she's lethal with that thing. And stamina . . . she never seems to get tired. But at least she sweats. Saw it show as a strike-through on her. Strangely aroused by that, too.

Must be the heat. Bloody wretched heat. All I can think about is . . .

Note: Began collecting specimens. Limited possibilities for testing necessitate using self for guinea pig. Methods: Application to skin and ingestion.

Eighteen

That night, as Cordelia's party camped by the river, the mapmaker Gonzales was receiving a response to his telegram to the Spanish governor of Cuba, in the person of a small, dapper man in a white linen suit and a pristine Panama hat.

"May I help you, senor?" Gonzales studied the man who had entered his shop flanked by two burly men whose flat black eyes bore no trace of light or humanity. Clearly, this was a time for answers, not questions.

"The governor of Cuba is very grateful, Senor Gonzales, for your loyalty to Spain and her emissaries in the colonies. I bring you his personal thanks. And I must add my own to them." He doffed his hat. "Don Alejandro de Castille, of Madrid. Without your message, senor, we would have lost track of the pirate O'Brien. I understand he was here." When Gonzales nodded, the man smiled humorlessly. "Did he happen to have someone with him? A very handsome woman, perhaps?"

"Si. Two women, in fact. And a man they called 'professor.' "

Castille's smile broadened, revealing prominent eyeteeth that lent his face a reined savagery. A wave of uneasiness swept through Gonzales.

"Ah, yes. That old thief, who calls himself Professor Valiente. He has stolen important materials from the Monastery of St. Montelado. Did you know that?"

"How could I, senor?"

Castille removed one of his gloves as he strolled by the shelves and he feathered his fingers over the ends of the rolled maps in the bins.

"He has taken a set of scrolls that are very precious and must be returned." Castille turned on the mapmaker with a wave that dismissed further explanation. "Clearly, O'Brien brought them here for maps. Did you sell them any?"

"Si, senor. Two maps of the same river, in the same region."

"And where is this river?"

"Veracruz. It is called the Tecolutla. There is a village on the Gulf coast by the same name." Eager to get the man out of his shop, he turned to the chart table behind him and selected a rolled map from the stack lying on it. "I found another map of the area, after they left. They had a curve drawn on paper, and looked for a river to match it."

"And this river matched it?"

"Si. I studied this map—it is a better version of the ones I sold them. But I cannot see anything along this river that merits such interest."

Castille traced the lines of the river, seeming to absorb them through his fingertips. It was like watching a snake's tongue searching for food, Gonzales thought with increasing discomfort. This "friend of the governor" was not a man many would call "friend."

"You needn't concern yourself about it, Senor Gonzales." Castille motioned to one of his henchmen to roll the map and take it. "It is in my hands now. I will see that the things he stole are returned to their rightful owner."

He tossed a large gold coin on the map table and with a chilling smile, climbed the stairs to the street.

Gonzales looked at the coin for a moment, then turned away with a shiver, leaving it for his apprentice to collect.

It rained in the night, which was both good and bad. It allowed them to collect fresh water for drinking, but everything was soaking wet when they had to pack up the tents. It seemed to be a good/bad kind of a morning; later Itza and Ruz announced they would reach a village by nightfall—welcome news—but they had to make their way through another day's worth of jungle to get there.

They had to make seven to ten miles with spongy, waterlogged ground underfoot and leaden skies and dripping vegetation overhead. The steamy wetness made the scent of the vegetation—rampant new growth on top of unrelenting decay—all the more pungent and seemed to make the edges of the fronds and leaves sharper as they glanced off collars and shirt sleeves and slid against unprotected skin. Tiny unseen scratches filled with sweat and stung, making the lead position as miserable as it was arduous.

"It's all yours," Cordelia said, offering her machete to Goodnight when he came to relieve her. He raised his own, and she noted wryly that he was wearing the goatskin gloves she had required him to bring.

"I see you're learning," she said, stretching her knotted shoulders as she watched him grasp and hack branches that intruded on the way.

"I'm stubborn, not insane." He glanced at her from the corner of his eye.

"I thought you were just *British*," she said distractedly, focused on the movement of his back muscles beneath his sweat-dampened shirt. She shook her head. "Which explains perfectly your gambling problem."

"I do not have a gambling problem," he said, displaying a surprising array of leg strength and dexterity as he nudged and kicked aside brush.

"Of course you do. It's the English disease. That and blocked bowels."

"Blocked bowels?"

"Haven't you noticed that nine out of ten purgatives on the market are produced by Englishmen?" Once more she lost her concentration to the spell of his strong, sure movements.

"That's ridiculous." He paused to glance back at her.

"Name one that isn't." She joined him, stepping over plants he had purposefully trampled.

"Wampole's—" He frowned and tried another. "Latham's Cathartic—" He stopped again. "Fletcher's . . . Carter's Little Liver . . . a-ha! Cascarets Candy Cathartic!"

"Made by an Englishman named Sterling," she countered.

"Persian Pills."

"Made by Henry Benton. And don't forget Simmons Liver Regulator and Doctor Mintie's English Dandelion Liver and Dyspepsia Pills."

After a satisfying pause, she heard him mutter something that sounded suspiciously like "bullocks."

"How is it you know so much about purgatives, O'-Keefe?" he said over his shoulder as he took another slice at some stubborn branches. "Got a little English in *you*?"

"It so happens that I used to work in a pharmacy when I was girl. At one time I wanted to—" She halted and veered quickly from that territory. "So, this wager you lost with Hardacre, was it business or pleasure? Not that wagering with Samuel P. would ever actually qualify as 'pleasure.'"

"My business is none of your business," he ground out, pushing back a stubborn branch and giving it a chop when it refused to yield.

"So, it *was* business," she concluded. She was making progress. "A doctor-cum-chemist who wagers on business matters with a steel tycoon—it would have to be something weighty and important, right?"

"Feel free to speculate," he muttered irritably.

"Maybe he bet you that something couldn't be done. Or made," she said, thinking of how the old man had turned the tables on her. When Goodnight halted for a minute, refusing to look at her, she came alert. "Is that it?" She seized the possibility. "You were trying to prove something could be done or to invent something?"

The longer he remained silent, the more she sensed she was on the right track and had touched on something highly personal to him. True, it was his business and no concern of hers. But therein lay a major part of the attraction. Seeping through her vague sense of guilt at prying was an overpowering urge to know every detail.

Then it struck her: everything Hardacre did involved *money*.

"Wait. You didn't bet him, you borrowed from him! And he *foreclosed* on you. That was it, wasn't it?"

"Owww—dammit!" He scrambled back suddenly grabbing his arm and then ripping back his sleeve to stare at his flesh in horror.

"What is it?" She rushed to see what had happened.

"Something bit me." He was inspecting his arm as Itza and the professor arrived to see what had happened. "It couldn't have been a snake—I was watching for bloody snakes."

The guide saw the punctures on his forearm and whirled, scanning the ground and nearby brush. A moment later he pounced on a long, dark branch that abruptly coiled and fought as he lifted it for inspection.

"Vine snake," the professor translated as the guide displayed the culprit. "They hang stiff and still . . . pretend to be branches . . . also called 'whip snake.' "

"Are they poisonous?" she asked, her stomach knotting.

"Yes." The professor interpreted Itza's nod and then his hand motion. "Some." They watched Itza slice the snake in half and sling it into the bush.

"What does that mean, 'some'?" She held Goodnight's arm, watching the area around the bite reddening fast. "What do we do?"

"He gets a little sick." After more consultation with Itza, the professor sighed. "It makes a bad sore, but he does not die."

"Is he sure?" Goodnight asked, looking at Itza, who nodded and showed two whitish patches on his left arm—presumably scars from similar bites—and nodded. "Lovely. Just lovely."

Cordelia went back for Goodnight's bag of medicines and helped clean and bandage his arm. He took aspirin to ward off the fever he expected and insisted he felt fine.

But as they pushed on, his eyes darkened and it became increasingly clear he wasn't himself. He ambled along mechanically, staring blankly ahead, unresponsive to their questions, looking as if he were listening to something only he could hear. She suggested they stop and rest until the heat of the day passed, but he refused to sit. His hair was wet and his shirt was drenched with sweat.

When she shot the professor and Ruz worried looks, the guide pulled some leaves from his pocket and offered them to Goodnight, saying that chewing them would help the discomfort in his arm.

To her surprise, Goodnight stuffed them into his mouth. The more he chewed, the more he relaxed and his limbs loosened. Walking with an increasingly eratic gait, he strayed off the path to investigate odd looking plants—sniffing blooms, leaves, bark, and sap, rubbing some parts on his skin, popping other bits into his mouth, and tucking leaves, seeds, and pods into his pockets. She held her breath each time he charged away and exhaled each time he came loping back, looking a little less stable.

"What on earth are you doing?" she demanded, following him, frantic that he might step on a coiled rattlesnake or into a hole and break a leg.

"Did you know," he said slowly, exaggerating each word as if he were playing with the sound of his own voice, "that there are only about ten pharmaceuticals that are proven to work? *Ten.* Yet, how many pills an' elixirs are sold with promises to restore hair or relieve dropsey or cure club feet—to cure everything from common colds, to catarrh, to cancer?"

Fearing he might fall flat on his face at any time, she took his good arm and tried to steady him.

"Just ten? Why don't you come back to the others and tell us all about it? It's not good for you to be out here by yourself."

"Only *ten*. Out of the thousands and th–thousands that make millions and millions for th' snake-oil hawkers. The rest don't do a bloody thing. If you're lucky. If yer not lucky and you get hold of a bad 'medicine' it can make you worse or even kill you."

He paused to gnaw on a particularly gnarled twig, waited a moment, analyzing it's taste or effect, then tossed it aside with a curl of his nose.

"Nobody bothers to test their drugs, see. Jus' brew it an' bottle it up. One dollar, two dollars a bottle. As long as there's enough alcohol in it—"

"Really, Goodnight." She snatched a huge, hairy looking leaf from his hand before he could shove it into his mouth. "You're starting to worry me. You can't just go munching your way through the jungle. Some of this foliage may be poisonous. Come back with me and we'll find you a place to rest until you—"

"Science." He held up an index finger and swayed around it. "Science must lead the way. Test the medicines. Prove they work." He reached out and grabbed a thick, rubbery leaf and, before she could stop him, took a huge bite out of it. After two chomps, he froze, wretched, and frantically began to dig it out of his mouth with both hands. "Ack–k–k— argh–h–h— ugh–h–h—"

"For heaven's sake—" She waited until he'd spit several times to clear his mouth before seizing his hands and pulling him back toward the main party. "I refuse to stand by and watch you make yourself sick."

He allowed her to pull him along, until he spotted something interesting. "Wait, wait—there's something that looks like Hart's Tongue—Wait—" He pulled free and headed straight for the leaves of a long, blade-like fern with hairy, nasty-looking brown curls on stalks above it.

He pulled leaves and sniffed and tasted them, fortunately with better results than his last specimen.

"What are you doing?" She planted herself in front of him, seizing the leaves and trying to wrest them from his grip. "What does any of this have to do with . . . ohhhh. Medicine and chemistry." Her mind flew as she looked up into his unsteady gaze. "You were trying to make medicines?"

There was a long silence before he answered.

"I built a laboratory. To develop *proven* cures."

"So you borrowed money from Samuel P.," she supplied, searching his face and seeing in his glazed eyes a melancholy glint of confirmation. "And did you develop any cures?"

"Not . . . fully."

"So, you didn't make any medicines.

"Not as such."

"Or any money."

His silence as he stood there swaying and looking miserable and bereft was all the confirmation she needed.

This backhanded revelation certainly explained Samuel P's antagonism toward him. His venture smacked of an idealism that was heresy to a devout capitalist like her grandfather. That, paired with his upper-crust British superiority, made Goodnight a perfect target for Hardacre's bootstrap American prejudices.

"Look! Hibiscus!"

He was off and running again.

She wrestled the large red flowers from his hands—though not before he managed to stuff a few in his pockets—and dragged him bodily back to the rest of their party. Ruz gave him another handful of leaves to chew and he gradually slid from his seat on an upraised root to a seat on the moist ground. Soon he was sprawled on his back with his eyes closed and a hint of a smile on his face.

Itza and Ruz shook their heads and, through the professor, registered the opinion that he was better off this way. After redistributing the supply packs to free one of the burros, they lifted him gently and hung him across its back.

They continued on with Goodnight dangling over the burro, oblivious to both his ignominious position and the warmth of Cordelia's gaze on him.

It took a snakebite, heaven knew what mix of exotic herbs and poisons, and some intoxicating leaves the natives chewed to do it, but she finally got the truth out of him. He was a scientist, a researcher, trying to make the world a better place. And he'd had the bad luck or bad judgment to borrow money from her shark of a grandfather. When he couldn't pay, the old man required him to work off the debt.

How callous and shortsighted, taking a man like Goodnight from his work to make him draw baths and press clothes and tend gouty old feet. How dare Samuel P. do such a thing? It exceeded even her worst expectations of him and made her all the more determined to succeed with this expedition.

It struck her, as she watched Goodnight's strong arms sway helplessly, that he felt the same. His strange behavior with the plants was his attempt to find something to take back, a discovery of substance, something to use in making *real* medicine. Something swelled in her chest, making it harder to breathe.

They were more alike than she had guessed. Stubborn, proud, independent—they even had similar goals with regard to her wicked old grandfather. Glancing around to make certain no one could see, she reached out to rifle her fingers through his hair. No wonder she was so attracted to him.

Nineteen

The village, nestled in a sharp bend in the Tecolutla river, was little more than a handful of dwellings surrounded by maize fields carved haphazardly out of the surrounding jungle. Chickens roamed the huts at will and the local children were employed in a continuous patrol to keep the burros and pigs out of the fields. The people recognized the Platanos and welcomed them warmly. Most had seen English-speaking men before, but "yanqui" women were a novelty. They were fascinated by Cordelia's long, burnished hair and amber eyes and by Hedda's split skirts and flower-trimmed sunhat.

As the sun set, long planks were set around a communal campfire in the middle of the village, and the women came by with dishes of various kinds and a fermented drink akin to homemade beer. Cordelia accepted a cup but didn't drink it until the professor assured her it contained enough alcohol to kill anything unhealthy in the water.

In gratitude for their hospitality, Cordelia presented the three elders with teacups and saucers, then pulled out her tin kettle and brewed them some of her favorite breakfast tea. The professor transmitted her suggestion that it was often sweetened with honey, and one of the women fetched a jar of it from her house. Their first sips produced doubtful looks, but after several additions of honey, they began to smile and even ask for seconds.

It was then that Goodnight appeared in the middle of the village, looking for them. He had just awakened in their camp at the edge of the huts and was holding his head as if afraid it might roll off his shoulders. He shuffled into the firelight and froze as he caught a whiff of the tea Cordelia had made.

"Is that what I think it is?" he said, lurching over to her, sniffing.

"These people shared with me; I wanted to share with them."

He glanced at the three scruffy, sunbaked elders sipping tea from dainty flowered cups and nearly choked on his own juices. She gave him a dark look and pulled him down onto the bench beside her. When he was settled, she handed him her cup of tea. He sipped, sighed, and closed his eyes.

"Nectar. Pure nectar." He finished the cup and held it out for more.

The women present tittered at the longing visible in his face. Or perhaps it was his spectacularly long and well-knit body that warmed their eyes and made them grin and nudge each other. Whatever it was, Cordelia found herself wanting to give them a shake and tell them to quit it.

The elders apparently didn't like their wayward gazes either and soon sent them off to secure the children and other livestock for the night.

"We were hoping you could direct us to any stone ruins in this area," Cordelia said to the head elder. The man looked to the professor, who translated.

The fellow didn't know of any ruins, but said, "The hunters say there are hills with doors a day's journey to the south and west."

"Hills with doors?" She frowned.

"They've been chewing too many cocoa leaves," Goodnight muttered, drawing a covert "shhh" from her.

The professor repeated "hills with doors" and widened his eyes so that only she and Goodnight could see. From his reaction this was good news.

The elders were eager to drag out stories that had been passed down through the generations, some of which strained credulity. Several times she had to interrupt or elbow Goodnight to stop him from pointing out how implausible a story was. Then Cordelia asked if they had any stories about jaguars or the Jaguar Spirit and everything fell deathly silent.

Even without translation, they understood the phrase and sensed what she'd asked. One of the three elders abruptly withdrew to his hut. The others waited until he was gone to say that some months back, his son had been killed by a jaguar in the upland forest.

"Near here?" She looked with fresh concern at the darkened jungle visible beyond the edges of the village. "There are jaguars around here?"

"Si," the man informed them through the professor. "Every few years, the Jaguar Spirit—he comes down from the mountains to see what the people do. Sometimes he finds people's hearts weak or finds them doing evil and he must punish them." He leaned closer and jerked a thumb at the hut his neighbor had entered. "His son is a bad boy. A thief and a forcer of women. The jaguar punishes him." Again, he pointed. "He does not wish to hear it, but it is true."

"The jaguar judges humans and metes out punishment?" Goodnight said wryly. "A pity we couldn't take him back to Havana. Better yet, *Tampa*."

"For heaven's sake, Goodnight, watch what you say around these people," she admonished, as they left the center of the village for their tents.

"They can't possibly have known anything I said," he protested.

"They may not know your words, but they read your face," the professor put in scowling. "They know you are not believing of their stories."

"Don't tell me you *do* believe them," Goodnight responded.

"It is enough for me that they believe it," the professor said with a shrug. "My respect for their ways helps to get the informacion we need."

"And what information was that?" Goodnight halted in the middle of their fireless camp. "Beyond the fact that they're superstitious as hell?"

"We learn of the hills with doors, a day's walk to the south and west."

"Hills with doors?" Cordelia was even puzzled by that one.

"A better description of buried ruins I never hear," the professor said with a grin. "Look." He stooped in the moonlight to draw in the dirt. "Over time, the buildings of the old ones"—he drew the outline of a stepped pyramid—"crumble outside and are covered by dirt. The tops grow a blanket of grasses." He drew a curve over the tops of the pyramid steps. "Look like little hills. But on one side, openings of doors are still seen." He drew openings in the side of the drawing. "They look like hills with doors in them. Yes. Truly. These people must see real ruins to describe them so."

Cordelia laughed and threw her arms around Hedda and the professor.

"Hills with doors. Let's just hope when we get there and knock, the Jaguar Spirit answers."

February 2, Day 13

Two days without spending a cent. A bloody miracle.

Snakebit. Not sure how I went to sleep, but woke up in a village. Head and arm hurting like a toothache.

Cocoa leaves—found out that's what they gave me to chew. Felt damned good for a while. Feels lousy now. Can hardly bear to open my eyes. Snakebite getting worse—ripening into huge, nasty sore. Tried everything in my bag. No idea what might neutralize the poison. Just pray Itchy is right and the arm doesn't fall off.

Brighter note: Spotted several species of borage, edible ferns, mother-in-law's tongue, and a strange form of laurel. Arnica and aloe vera everywhere. Cocoa leaves effective, but already known.

Also—O'Keefe got to give away some of her blasted teacups. She kept looking at me strangely. Like I did something to her. Don't remember much after the snake incident. Hope I didn't kiss or grope her while I was out of my head. If I'm going to humiliate myself, I should at least get to remember it.

For the second time in a week, a shore party from a ship anchored nearby entered the fishing village of Tecolutla and took over the town's only cantina. But this second crew, unlike the first, was a volatile mix of Spanish Navy and hired mercenaries—loud, crass, and spoiling for a fight.

Curiously, their leader was a dark, slender man whose dress and manner were as elegant as the men he led were crude. For a time he watched his men overwhelm the tavern, demanding beer and liquor, pawing the serving girls and threatening the patrons who objected to being displaced. Then he had two of his men bring the cantina owner to him. The little man's gaze kept fleeing to a far corner where some of the sailors were harassing one of his daughters.

"Please senor," the owner pleaded. "She is a good girl."

"Undoubtedly," Castille said with a menacing chuckle. "And if you don't cooperate, she will be 'good' to all of them. Was there a ship here recently?"

"Si, senor. A few days ago . . . three . . . four."

"Americanos aboard?"

"Si, senor."

"Where did they go?" Castille sat forward, his eyes as black as obsidian.

"The one they called 'professor,' he asked for guides." His daughter cried out and begged for someone to stop. "To go upriver—please, senor."

"Where upriver?" Castille grabbed the owner's shirt. "Tell me!"

"I do not know, senor, I swear it! Please—"

"How do they travel?" Castille shoved to his feet. "By boat? Overland?"

"I told them of the Platanos—brothers—from a village up the Ataxacal River. I do not know more, senor . . . please . . . my daughter . . ."

"Who in this stinking boil on the ass of creation"—he slashed a look around the cantina—"can take me up the river?" When the girl screamed and owner lunged against the hands restraining him, Castille struck him hard across the face. "Pay attention, dog. I need guides to take me up the river and into the mountains. Who knows the area best?"

The owner covered his bleeding lip with his hands and mumbled something, a name Castille forced him to repeat.

"Hector Varza. He has a farm . . . on the river road . . ."

Castille looked around. "You!" He snagged a young boy crouched near the door, hauling him up by the hair of the head. "You know where this Varza lives?" When the boy nodded, Castille's face became a mask of pure malice. He dragged the boy to the cantina owner and pulled a knife from Yago's belt. Under the boy's frightened gaze, he punctured the skin at the base of the owner's neck several times, circling the man's throat with small gashes, causing the man to cry out and the hard-drinking sailors to call for their employer to cut deeper.

"Run, boy. Fetch Varza. Tell him if he does not come, I will connect these dots . . . and this man and his very accommodating daughter will die." His voice took on a lilt of pleasure. "Do you understand?"

The boy swallowed hard and nodded. The moment he was released he raced out the door, and Castille's henchmen sent up a howl of approval.

The next morning Cordelia and her party headed out just after daylight, on a path that was well worn and relatively dry. The altitude was changing noticeably; they were starting a slow climb that would eventually carry them to the source of the river in the mountains. From the distance they could hear the water rumbling over another set of rapids on its way to the Gulf. Fortunately, the buzz of insects seemed to lessen as they made their way through this drier zone of forest. Every turn, rise, and slope of terrain created a different set of growing conditions that hosted a unique array of flora and fauna. Around every bend, there were new plants to discover, some quite spectacular.

Hart zigzagged back and forth across the path trying desperately to take it all in and still keep the main party in sight. Several times over the day's trek, he went back to his bags and journal to record his discoveries and unload the specimens in his pockets. As he passed Rita, she never failed to nip at his rear and sometimes tried to turn and follow him. Itza and Ruz were baffled by her behavior, but soon began to tease him about his new "sweetheart." Another good reason, he thought, to spend time off by himself, looking for medicinal plants.

Then midday, he discovered a whole grove of small yellow and green orchids that had covered the trunks and branches of a stand of trees, turning it into a serene, lightly scented bower. He went running back to call the others to come and see, and before he realized what he was doing he had O'Keefe by the hand and was pulling her along.

When they reached the orchid grove, he found himself watching her reaction to the orchids more than the flowers themselves. There was an unabashed sense of wonder in the way she touched them and put her face against them, nuzzling the creamy petals, luxuriating in their silky coolness. It was beauty drawn to beauty. When he made himself look away, his gaze ran straight into Hedda's perceptive regard and he smiled nervously, telling himself she couldn't read minds.

They were vanilla flowers, Itza and Ruz declared, and proved it by locating bean-like pods forming on the vines. Hart smelled and tasted the developing pods eagerly, but their bland, starchy taste was a disappointment. The professor chuckled and informed him that the beans had to be harvested, fermented, and aged before they developed their characteristic flavor and aroma.

As they absorbed the tranquil atmosphere, the professor rolled up his sleeves and climbed partway up a tree to pick several of the flowers. With a mischievous smile, he presented them to Hedda. She blushed like a schoolgirl when he put one in her hair.

The old boy was really turning on the charm, Hart thought, surprised by the annoyance it generated in him. Hedda was a handsome, capable, and thoroughly pleasant woman. She deserved better than the flattery of an aging Latin lothario who probably had a wife and ten children at home in Mexico City.

Hart looked at O'Keefe and found her watching the same interaction with a similar surprise. Clearly, she hadn't noticed what was developing right under their noses either. It was reassuring to learn she had at least one ordinary human failing. When she looked up and saw him watching her, she seemed unsettled, and after a moment, struck off through the brush on what appeared to be an old animal trail. Neither Hedda nor the professor seemed to notice her departure, and Itza and Ruz chose that moment to head back to their animals. He stood looking after her for a moment, deciding.

He struck off after her, intending to remind her—as she had been reminding him for days—not to stray from the rest of the group. The moist, spongy ground retained her footprints and out of habit she was bending back branches and fronds that were in her way; it wasn't difficult to track her. It didn't occur to him that he might not be the only one interested in doing so.

When he caught up with her some minutes later, she had come to a stop in a sunlit spot at the bottom of a break in the tree canopy. He could tell by her tense stance and the canting of her head that she was listening, and thought for a moment she had heard him moving up behind her. But he was still some distance back and, oddly, she didn't turn or call out to him.

He stopped, his face heating as his gaze roamed her. He had no idea what he was going to say to her; when he started after her he hadn't exactly had conversation in mind. This was a bad idea. Very bad. If he had an ounce of common sense he would backtrack to the vanilla grove and abandon all ideas and intentions where she was concerned. But standing there in the sunlight, with her hair shot through with fiery strands and her curves warm and beckoning, she was a possibility that he couldn't make himself abandon.

So he stayed and listened, too, imagining he could feel her heart pounding against his, could hear each passionate breath . . .

Wait—he could hear her breathing? Over the last few days he'd gotten used to the constant noise of nature around him. The stark silence in the clearing was so complete—absent even the ever-present hum of insects—that he could indeed hear the raspiness of her breath. She sounded as if she had run a distance and was winded, but he couldn't see her chest moving at all.

It took another minute for him to realize she hadn't stopped randomly, she had halted to look at something in the trees on the far edge of the clearing. He searched the scrubby undergrowth and missed it at first; the color was almost indistinguishable from the brown-edged yellow of the aging vegetation all around. But the shape—*rounded*—and the luster—*glinting in the light*—

A pair of eyes. Golden. With vertical slashes for pupils.

His heart seemed to rise into his throat. He couldn't move, couldn't speak, couldn't swallow. Then he saw the nose, the ears, the open mouth, and the wickedly sharp, meat-tearing teeth.

A cat. Huge. With brown and black spots. Panting.

That was the breathing he heard. Not hers at all.

"Sweet Jesus," he prayed on an indrawn gasp.

It was a jaguar.

The silence was almost deafening as Cordelia stood in that pool of sunlight, staring into a pair of eyes that made the hair on the back of her neck prickle and her flesh shrink inside her clothes.

Cat eyes. Huge. Sizing her up. Probably deciding on condiments.

The spots registered next. And a pair of rounded ears. And huge feet. It was more golden than she expected a jaguar to be. It was probably too much to hope that it was just old and yellowed with age. The beast's mouth was open enough to show a horrifying set of carnivore teeth and a shocking pink tongue. It was breathing heavily, almost panting. Cat's weren't supposed to pant, were they? But then, maybe nobody told the prince of the jungle here. Or maybe he just figured he could get by with bending a few ru—

For God's sake—she tried to rouse her own stunned and floundering responses—*don't just stand there—RUN!*

But her feet wouldn't budge and her mouth had gone dry. She was afraid to make any movements, sudden or otherwise. An old-timer's caution surfaced out of the nuggets of lore she had collected in her travels: "Big cats chase runners. Don't run. Because they also *catch* runners."

So she stood silently, trembling, praying for help and wishing she had heeded her own blasted rule about not venturing off alone. She told herself not to look the jaguar in the eye—she'd heard somewhere that was dangerous. But she soon found herself doing just that: staring helplessly into the creature's tawny gaze and suffering an insane stir of curiosity. What was the beast doing there? Watching her. Flicking its tail. Looking almost . . . relaxed?

She was no expert on jaguar hunting techniques, but this one seemed to be stretched out comfortably on a mat of grass, not bunched, coiled, and ready to spring. It was watching her. Just watching. She imagined it saying: "You were curious about me; I thought I'd have a look at you, too."

In spite of her better sense, she took a half-step sideways.

The beast followed her with its eyes and flicked its tail, but otherwise didn't move.

She took another half step, and then a full one. Still, it only looked.

She glanced over her shoulder, searching wildly for a possible escape route and thought she saw a form, an outline in the vegetation behind her. Her heart leaped at the thought that she might have help in escaping this terrifying situation. She took a step backward and saw the great beast spring to its feet, its eyes sharp and ears forward, alert now. And formidable.

She froze, unable to breathe, unable to feel her heart beat.

Seconds ticked by and the big cat didn't charge. It started, instead, to pace back and forth, looking at her, occasionally raising its nose to sniff in her direction. Regal was the word to describe its carriage and serene air of command. Beautiful and terrifying were equally apt to describe its exquisitely muscled frame and lithe, powerful movements. Finely honed muscles rippled beneath that glorious spotted coat and those eyes. Those *eyes* . . .

It was slowly working its way closer, investigating her, testing her. Would she put up much of a fight? How fast was she?

Why hadn't she at least drawn her gun?

She was as astonished by her lack of defensive behavior as she was by the jaguar's lack of aggression. Sliding her hand down her bare hip, she remembered with horror that she had left it hooked over a pack on one of the burros. It was the first time she hadn't carried it in weeks.

The jaguar halted, facing her, and stared at her with its oblate pupils contracted to slits. How could she possibly protect herself? The big cat was twice her weight, all predator instinct and responsive muscle. It could outrun and outclimb anything in its domain.

They were eye to eye for a long, terrifying moment that she somehow sensed preceded the jaguar's decision about her.

Then abruptly the big cat turned away and, in a blink, melted back into the tangled foliage from which it had emerged.

It was gone? She nearly collapsed from disbelief. It had looked her over, shredded her nerves, and then just left her there?

"What the hell was *that*?" Goodnight's voice startled her.

She jumped with a cry and whirled. He rushed into the clearing with his face dusky and his eyes glowing like molten silver. Before she could stop herself, she ran to him and grabbed his shirt front, hanging on to it for dear life. It was a minute before she could speak.

"D–did you see it?" she finally said. "Th—the jaguar—those teeth and ears—big yellow eyes—did you see what it did?"

"Dear God. I saw and I still can't believe what I saw." He squeezed her upper arms tightly, looking her over. "You're *sure* you're all right?"

"He didn't lay a fang or a claw on me," she said, realizing that chewing and mauling were just two of several stomach-churning possibilities she had faced. Her knees went weak. She wanted to throw her arms around his big body and feel the warmth and safety of his arms wrapped tightly around her.

"Why didn't you just shoot the damned thing?" Goodnight planted a hand between her shoulder blades to propel her back along the path and suddenly realized her hip was bare. His eyes widened and he halted. "Where the hell's your gun?"

"I . . . I think I . . ." she said, mirroring his disbelief.

"You what? Forgot it?" He pulled his hand from her as if she'd scorched it and backed away, emotion swirling in his face. She couldn't tell if he was disappointed, contemptuous, or just plain outraged. He stalked off down the path, stopped, then came stomping back to grab her hand. "Dammit, just when you think you can *rely* on a woman—she starts forgetting her bloody gun!"

An hour later she sat on a fallen tree trunk, clutching a tin cup containing a shot of brandy. They had walked, then run back through the jungle along the path she had forged earlier. By the time they reached the vanilla grove, it was empty, and they headed straight for the jungle road and the rest of their party. Between gasps, she managed to tell the others about her encounter with the jaguar. Itza and Ruz crossed themselves and clamped their hands over Rita's long ears. Hedda threw her arms around her niece, and the professor went straight for the medicinal brandy.

"I've never seen anything like it," Cordelia said, her sense of adventure recovering more quickly than her nerves. "It was magnificent. Jaguars are larger than I thought. At least this one was. And it just stared at me with those big golden eyes." She looked at Goodnight. "It was beautiful, wasn't it?"

"Not the word *I* would use for it." He downed another shot of brandy.

"What do you think it means?" Hedda asked, settling beside her.

Cordelia was unsettled by the question; she had been asking herself that very thing. A jaguar. Looking her over. While she was searching for the Gift of the Jaguar. A chill went through her leaving gooseflesh in its wake, and she prayed no one noticed.

"It means we're definitely in the right area for jaguars, probably for ancient jaguar worship and artifacts. It means that our decision to follow this river was right on target." She struggled to sound more sensible and objective than she felt. "It certainly means we push on. I want to see those 'hills with the doors in them.' I can't help thinking one of those doors will have a carved jaguar head on top."

Determined to put some space between themselves and the jaguar and hoping to make the promised ruins by nightfall, they traveled through the heat of the afternoon, stopping only for water and to distribute some hardtack and jerky from their supplies. Cordelia was once again wearing her revolver on her hip, Hedda had pulled out her own pistol and loaded it, and the professor hauled out and strapped on a long-barreled Colt revolver with ivory handles. Every snap and rustle of vegetation had their trigger fingers twitching.

As the sun set, shadows spread out over the forest and the hunters' trail they followed faded into a tangle of undergrowth. Itza and Ruz, unsettled at the prospect of camping in the deepest part of the jungle, nervously agreed to push on. The ruins couldn't be far now.

Unfortunately, the burros had other ideas. As the light faded, they balked and had to be tugged, coaxed, and bribed. Goodnight finally got the stubborn Rita to move by walking ahead of her. But every time he slowed enough to come within range, she nipped at his rear. Cordelia happened to be looking when Rita finally made contact, sending Goodnight bolting into some bushes. When he climbed back onto the path, she spotted something sticking out of his back pocket and pulled out forgotten twigs and leaves that had been warmed by his body to an alluring, edible aroma.

"She wasn't being fresh." Cordelia laughed, dangling the leaves before the ravenous Rita, who began to nibble them. "She was being hungry." Hedda, the professor, and the Platanos joined her in laughter, relieved to have a lighter moment in what was becoming a dark end to a stressful day.

Quiet descended over the party as they plunged over the final slopes, where recent rains had made footing treacherous. Every member of the party was tensed and trying to pick out sounds of a big predator's movement from the ordinary buzz and rustle in the brush around them. Tension mounted as the vegetation thinned and they glimpsed a haze of moonlight ahead.

The high canopy ended and they emerged into a clearing in which a number of strange, cone-shaped hillocks rose ten to twenty feet and were covered with a rolling blanket of grasses. The mounds exuded the mystery and menace of strange shapes glimpsed in a moonlight graveyard, especially so when Cordelia spotted odd-shaped shadows tucked into the sides of some of them. It struck her that if these were the "hills" the village hunters referred to, then they *were* part of a graveyard—one that held the remains of a civilization.

Lacking both light and energy to begin explorations, they made a fireless camp in the middle of the mounds and agreed to start work the first thing in the morning. It wasn't easy going to sleep in the middle of an eerie ruin that might hold the key to a great mystery, but as they found their beds, exhaustion finally took hold of them, one by one.

Cordelia sprang up some time later in the moonlit glow of her tent with her heart pounding. Without knowing quite why, she reached for the pistol hanging on the corner of her cot and sat with her nerves taut and senses straining. It came again . . . from behind her . . . causing her blood to still in her veins.

A sniffing, snuffling sound. Loud. Animal-like. Only a scrap of canvas away. Her hand tightened on the grip of the pistol as it came again . . . sniff, sniff . . . moving around the tent . . . on her side . . . sniffing . . . then *panting*.

She clamped her free hand over her mouth to stifle her gasp. She glanced over at Hedda, who had turned on her side and was soughing softly, still very much asleep. Waking her—startling her and probably whatever was outside as well—was a bad idea.

She pushed back the mosquito bar and slid her legs over the side of the cot. Fortunately she had gone to sleep in her breeches; all she had to do was pull a shirt over her camisole. Then she reached under her sheet for her boots, giving thanks again for the old guide who had taught her to sleep with her boots on her cot. She had taken two steps toward the flap when she saw a shadow moving on the tent wall to her left. It was low and indistinct, but substantial enough to be solid.

It didn't have to be a jaguar, she tried to tell herself. It *could* be something else.

She slipped outside and turned right, holding her gun in her right hand and cupping both gun and wrist with her left. Her heart was in her throat as she rounded the opposite corner, intending to sneak around the tent and come up behind whatever—

A gun barrel appeared right before her eyes!

"Aghhh!" She jumped back with a cry.

"George Almighty!"

As Goodnight jerked his gun up, he lurched backward and tripped over a tent rope. The rifle landed nearby. As he hit the ground, with his legs tangled in the collapsed rope, he nearly took the tent down with him.

"What are you doing skulking around my tent this time of night?" she demanded in a loud whisper, jabbing the air with her gun.

"Will you point that bloody thing someplace else?" he demanded, still tangled but determined to rise. "My nightmare come true—nearly shot in the middle of the night while coming back from—" He made it to his feet. "*Two* legs. Count 'em." He pointed toward his feet. "One, two. *Not four*."

"I heard something," she declared defensively, still whispering.

"Of course you did. At night this place turns into a bloody lover's lane for the local four-, six-, and eight-legged populations." He brushed himself off.

"It sounded like a large animal. *Sniffing*."

He retrieved his gun and glanced at the ghostly terrain. "It's probably just this place. It's a little unnerving by moonlight. And after what happened—"

"I'm serious, Goodnight. There was definitely sniffing. And panting. The same kind of panting I heard yesterday when—" She was suddenly distracted by the rifle in his hands. "You were—you're holding a gun."

"So it would seem." He looked at it as if it had somehow magically appeared there, but then rearranged his grip, claiming it. "Our benighted guides have guns, and even your *aunt* is packing a firearm. After yesterday, I didn't think it fair that I was the only member of this expedition unarmed."

"You're prowling around in the dark with a rifle?" She choked on the last word. "Talk about nightmares. Do you even know which end to point?"

"I'll have you know, I have more than a passing acquaintance with guns. I am the terror of the grouse population of the Lake District." He raised his nose to look down it at her. "Pheasants quake at the sound of my name."

She erupted in a noise somewhere between a snort and a giggle.

"Laugh if you will, but someday, you may have to depend upon my marksmanship." He raised a lofty finger in blatant parody of himself. "And then I shall have my revenge."

Her giggle became laughter that released something pent up inside her. The next minute she was smiling at him, and he was smiling back. It felt good. Very good.

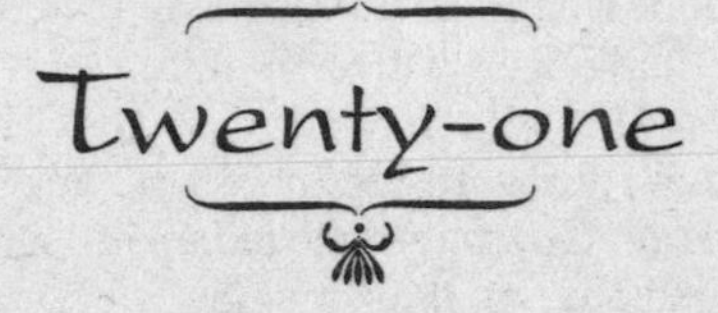

Twenty-one

"I need to check out the rest of the camp," she said. "Are you coming?"

"I suppose someone has to keep you from shooting at moons in the forest."

They walked around the tents, checking, listening. Other than the professor's snoring, all seemed quiet and peaceful—until they got to the area where the burros were grazing. There, a ragged panting sound was coming from the far side of one of the hillocks. Guns cocked and ready, they inched their way around and found Rita standing with her back bowed and her belly contracted into an odd point, panting heavily with each breath.

"Did your 'panting' sound anything like that?" Goodnight scowled.

Suddenly, Rita brayed loudly, sank onto her knees, and rolled over onto her side. They rushed to see what was wrong and Goodnight—muttering to himself—checked her rear quarters and issued a diagnosis.

"She's foaling." He laid his gun against the nearest hillock and went around to the animal's head. "You'd better get the 'banana boys.'"

Minutes later, the Platanos were on their knees beside Rita, one stroking her head and the other checking the progress of her labor. Ruz declared the feet were coming . . . he could see a membrane bubble . . . which burst as a sharp little hoof emerged. But there, all progress stopped.

"Only one leg!" Ruz called to Itza, clearly panicked. "Only one comes!"

Cordelia knew the word for "one" and "leg" wasn't difficult to figure out. Goodnight picked up the same information and grabbed Ruz by the shoulders.

"The other leg is back," he declared. "It needs to be pulled forward with the other one so she can deliver." He made thrusting and grasping motions, then pantomimed pulling. Ruz's eyes became the size of saucers. He began wringing his hands and rattling off a lament to Itza, a few words of which were close enough to English equivalents to let them know Ruz was wishing for a *bruja*, undoubtedly a midwife of some sort.

"Is it serious?" Cordelia asked, pulling Goodnight aside, studying his grim expression.

"In that position, the baby can't fit through the canal. They could both die."

"Surely something can be done," she said, glancing at the cantankerous Rita, feeling an unexpected sympathy for the struggling mother-to-be.

"I tried to tell him—I don't think he is up to doing what has to be done."

"You know about donkey births?" She looked at him in dismay.

"Horses. I've been around a number of foaling horses. Assisted a few." He looked at the brothers who were panicky and yelling at each other, and he began to roll up his sleeves. "I'll need my medicine bag."

A heartbeat later, she was in motion. Soon after, she entered his tent and located the leather bag of medicinals she had seen in Havana. The professor woke up as she exited and lurched from his cot demanding to know what was happening. Grabbing his boots, he followed her to Rita's location.

Soon they were standing by the laboring burro, watching in astonishment as the fastidious British butler inserted a well-lubricated arm into the birth canal and managed to find the other front leg and reposition it. After some sweating, straining, and cursing, he got it to come out alongside its mate. From there, the birth of one furry littlc burro proceeded normally and without further assistance.

Goodnight washed and scrubbed his arm, and sanitized it with Listerine, then sat down beside Cordelia to watch the burro inspect and nuzzle her offspring and see the foal take its first tentative steps. A male, the Platanos declared joyfully, making over their prize jennet and her wobbly infant. Goodnight was much better than a bruja, they said, and he did not charge nearly as much. So they would name the colt "Goodnight" in his honor.

When they weren't looking, the honoree rolled his eyes at Cordelia. A wicked taunt of "remembering forever the sight of him 'up to his elbows in a burro' " died unspoken on her tongue. She smiled instead, and in that moment realized with a shock of intense warmth that she was falling in love with Hartford Goodnight. Totally, hopelessly, delirious—

She choked on that last word.

She was delirious, all right. What was she smiling for? It was a disaster in the making!

She had no money, no home, and no reputation except that of an eccentric adventuress. He had no money, no home, and no reputation except as a failed businessman who was reduced to domestic service. If she survived the harrowing experience of declaring her love for him and he somehow reciprocated her feelings—both highly unlikely—what would they be together but two ambitious people with no money and no prospects?

The chill of reason swept through her heart. Better to stanch such feelings before they became entrenched and were too painful to root out.

"So you helped deliver foals—ones you owned, I assume," she said, probing a subject she knew to be tender. "And you hunted in the lake country." She narrowed her eyes. "Smacks of the 'gentlemanly life' to me."

He wasn't looking at her and didn't see her expression.

"You make a lousy fisherman, O'Keefe." He expelled a measured breath. "My family is well off . . . an estate in the south, a hunting lodge in the north, and a town house in London. They sent their sons to the finest schools, never guessing that we might actually learn something and develop ideas of our own."

"They didn't want you to be a doctor?" she asked, battling her curiosity.

"They resigned themselves to the medical schooling. Medicine was a profession, after all, and a lot of well-bred men 'dabble in careers.' It was the chemistry they found unacceptable. 'Smelly and appallingly industrial' is how they put it."

"But you did it anyway."

He nodded. "At some cost."

"There is always a cost," she said, speaking on several levels. She'd never seen him so cooperative; it sent a quiver of panic through her. "So you got your loan and built your laboratory, and somehow forgot all about making money."

"Money isn't everything," he said, tightly.

"It is when you have bills to pay. Without it you're completely at others' mercy. Or lack thereof," she said with an adamance she soon regretted.

He turned and studied her carefully.

"So." His voice had an edge of triumph. "Who was it that held the note *you* couldn't pay?"

Scrambling for a response to his abominable insight, she pushed to her feet and brushed the dirt from her hands.

"Really, Goodnight." She quoted him: "My business is none of your business."

"So there was someone. Spill it, O'Keefe." Then he quoted her: "I'll get it out of you sooner or later."

Alarmed that he remembered their exchanges so well

and that the fact made her heart beat faster, she turned and headed for her tent.

"Later is better for me."

She felt his gaze on her bottom as she walked away and was chagrined to realize it was a source of guilty pleasure for her.

She had to stop this continual tête-à-tête with him, she thought. She had to get control of herself and the situation. The last thing she needed was having to explain herself to Goodnight, especially now that part of what she had to hide was her susceptibility to him. Clearly, the less he knew about her, the better off—

A sudden movement caught her eye and she halted just outside the entrance of her tent, her senses coming alert in the predawn haze. She looked toward the trees at the edge of the clearing and saw nothing unusual. She was about to dismiss it as the activity of an overtired mind when she saw it again. Something was moving in the grass near the edge of the clearing. She held her breath, watching, searching . . . afraid of what she might see.

And there it was. The line of a back . . . the curve of a tail . . . a swarm of moving spots. And just as she convinced herself it was really there—it was gone.

February 5, Day 16

No expenditures. Am taking off this damnable money belt. For good.

Chaffed and rashy all over. Snakebite is killing me. Looks worse every day. Almost out of aspirin. Could use a bath. We all could. Especially Valiente. Even mosquitos won't come near him.

Villagers pointed us to some ruins. Longest day of my life, getting here.

Caught O'Keefe in the jungle staring down a jaguar. Took years off my life. Damned thing just watched her and sniffed her. She just stood there, preacher-in-the-parlor polite. As curious about it as it was about her. Cool as a cucumber after. The woman doesn't have a nerve in her body. Me, on the other hand—I was hysterical. Had visions of her being pawed and mauled. Made me physically ill. If there was ever a reason to get drunk...

Loaded a rifle from O'Keefe's stores. Not letting it out of my hands for the rest of this cursed ordeal.

Later, I heard sniffing and panting around the tents after we all went to sleep. Felt like somebody stepped on my grave. Could have sworn I saw spots lurking around O'Keefe's tent. Investigated and she nearly shot me—again.

Delivered a burro colt in the dead of night. Now have appalling acquaintance with female burro anatomy. They named the thing after me. My "Jr." has four legs. Should write the parents, they'd be thrilled. In moment of weakness, told O'Keefe about the family. She didn't take it well. Probably a good thing. Less of a chance I'll be pawing or mauling her myself in future.

But dammit—the way she looks at me. Sometimes I see a scared, hungry little girl inside her and want to pull her into my arms—other times there's this wild, brazen Amazon. Other *times, there's a smart, resourceful, witty—*

Dammit. If the woman would just put on some skirts.

Almost forgot: the most amazing array of botanical specimens all around. Vanilla orchids something of a disappointment. No promising medicinals.

Note: Food terrible. Thank God for bananas.

The fruit, not the guides.

The hills did have doors.

The strange, half-buried ruins cast no less a spell by the light of the searing tropical sun. They seemed to huddle under their blanket of earth, waiting for a signal to throw off that mantle of neglect and come to life again. As Cordelia and the others walked around the conical mounds it was clear that the villagers had been accurate in describing them as hills with doors. There were stonework openings tucked under the brow of each; some mere stone niches, others sizeable openings. The professor proposed that these were likely the tops of the taller buildings in the city or complex of structures, and the openings might lead to inner chambers.

They assembled their equipment—lanterns, picks and shovels, rope, and materials for recording their findings—and began to climb, crawl into, and peer into all of the openings they could reach. It soon became clear the smaller mounds were too buried or deteriorated to yield much without major excavation.

Shifting their attention to the three tallest mounds, at one end of the clearing, they chose one and entered. Cordelia insisted on going first, since she was the lightest and could test the floors as she went. At Goodnight's insistence, they tied a rope around her waist so they could rescue her if the surface gave way or she got into trouble.

The first mound was more collapsed inside than she expected and yielded no further opportunities for exploration. The second mound was in better condition, but equally stark, showing chisel marks on some surfaces that indicated things had been removed, but giving no indication of what.

The final and largest mound was their only hope of finding something to guide their search. The sizeable opening was littered by rubble from the crumbling exterior, but inside, the stonework was in better condition. The professor, Hedda, and Goodnight joined Cordelia one at a time in a rectangular room that had collapsed on one end.

If they were indeed standing on the top of a buried pyramid, according to the professor, this would be the temple chamber at the summit and it was unlikely to hold any great revelations. These ruins—he looked around sadly and fingered the now familiar chisel marks—had been stripped of valuables centuries ago. All that remained was a carcass for scholars to pick.

To one side, they found a half-crushed stone table stained and blackened over the years. They might have left then, if Cordelia hadn't tripped on an uneven paving stone and felt it rock under her weight. With some effort they levered that stone aside and discovered steps leading down into the heart of the pyramid. Their spirits rose as they lighted lanterns and began to descend, picking their way past the litter of stray stones and debris from the small animals that had called it home over the years. Spiderwebs draped the passage, which descended into a forbidding gloom and was partially blocked below. It took major effort to roll a large block of fallen stone up the steps and clear the passage.

It was midday before they had could proceed, but what they found at the bottom of the steps was worth the wait and effort. Ducking through a narrow doorway, they entered a chamber decorated with faded but still amazing paintings that echoed elements they recognized from their jaguar arch rubbings.

Near the entrance, their lanterns illuminated a fierce portrayal of a huge snake breathing flames that soon faded to the tops and bottoms of the panels as a decorative motif surrounding a procession of large, ornate human figures, which the professor identified as a succession of kings. Each king carried weapons and was accompanied by hordes of small, stylized figures representing warriors and in some cases conquered royalty and prisoners.

The professor was beside himself with excitement. This was a record, he crowed, of the royalty of the area centuries ago. Hedda sat down immediately on a rectangular stone in the middle of the chamber and began to sketch what they saw. The professor proceeded around the chamber pulling out salient details about the rulers until he came to one that was holding a snake, who from his posture and fierce expression was locked in deadly combat with it. As they fought, the snake's fiery breath flowed down around the ruler's feet to engulf his warriors and the palaces near his feet. Impatiently, Goodnight shone his lantern on the corner ahead and froze.

There, facing that tableau of destruction and chaos, another painting depicted a large human figure with the head of a cat, a huge, spotted chimera of legend, with his claws sunk deep into a massive snake who spit flames. The four of them collected before it and stood in silence, taking in the energy and passion of the portrayal, feeling chilled by the violence it represented.

"The jaguar . . . he fights the fiery serpent . . . he saves the people," the professor whispered, removing his hat and touching the painting with reverence. "This is so magnificent . . . so . . . exquisite . . . so . . ." His voice thickened and for a moment he struggled to conquer his emotions. "Do you see?" he finally was able to say. "It tells the story of the Jaguar Spirit saving mankind!" He grabbed first Cordelia's, then Goodnight's arms, rocking the lanterns, then threaded his arm through Hedda's and whirled her around and around in boyish glee.

But Cordelia hurried past that corner to the final wall of the tableau, where she found a single scene of glory and bounty. Fields of maize and vegetables and orchards filled with fruit bloomed over the earth, and pyramids and cities were a testament to the prosperity of the people. But the rays of light carved across the landscape originated not in the pale, subservient sun, but in the head of the jaguar, who sat on a throne in the mountains above it all.

They stood before it awed. The head of the jaguar in the painting was identical to the carving of the jaguar that dominated the arch in their rubbings. At the ruler's feet lay the dead serpent, stretching out from the throne, across the land, to a mass of blue at the bottom.

"Jesus, Mary, and Joseph," Goodnight breathed. Then he turned to Hedda. "Do you have a copy of the snake curve—from the river?" She produced a copy that he hurried to compare to the conquered reptile. Tracing the smaller curves on the drawing with his finger, he enlarged and transferred them to the larger figure of the snake in the painting. They fit perfectly.

Cordelia stared at the wall panel, then at Goodnight, astounded by his intuitive grasp of the symbols and their correlation to the real world. It would have taken her hours—days—to see what had occurred to him in a second.

"We need a map," she declared, catching Goodnight's eye and holding it. He nodded and she couldn't help the brimming smile that came over her before she broke away and headed for the steps.

Twenty-two

Minutes later, she returned with the maps Gonzales had sold them, on which she had faithfully traced their progress along the river in red pencil. Eerily, the painting on the wall seemed to be a more complete version of the map spread on the floor for study. The city shown as a complex of pyramids on the wall map corresponded with the location of the very ruins they were standing in, and from there they could extrapolate on their map the supposed location of the throne of the Jaguar Spirit. Ringing the mountain retreat of the Creator Spirit were a number of villages, from which people carried offerings toward the jaguar on his throne. The scale was difficult to calculate, but the location of the throne seemed to be only a few days away.

As if Goodnight hadn't been helpful enough, he noticed and commented on the precision and regularity of the rays of light radiating from the jaguar across the landscape. Cordelia stood looking at him for a moment, trying to master the confusion boiling up in her. How did he always manage to discover things no one else would have considered? Did his mind just work so differently? Was he really as rare and exceptional as she was beginning to think?

"Isn't there a way of measuring those angles geometrically to see if they are significant?" She turned to Goodnight, who thought about it and nodded. "These artists seemed to have taken pains to be precise. Perhaps these rays meant to indicate more than just a general location."

Hedda, accompanied by the professor, spent the better part of the day sketching the murals in what they came to call the Hall of Records. Goodnight retreated to camp to do some calculations, and with Cordelia's help to plot a course from their present location toward the mountain throne that dominated the landscape. They consulted with the Platanos, who said they had not been as far as that particular mountain, but that they had been to a village at the base of those mountains and could probably find it again.

Afterward, Cordelia and Goodnight stood together staring at the snowcapped peak that sheltered the answers they sought. Would it be the end of their adventure, or mark the start of something even more fascinating?

"Well, enough of that," Goodnight declared, handing the maps back to her. "I have things to do."

"You do? What?" she demanded, watching him disappear into his tent and emerge a minute later with his journal and what she had learned was his collecting box. "Where are you going?"

"Out." He picked up his rifle and tucked it under his arm.

She watched him striding toward the dense vegetation and found her gaze settling on his taut buttocks and sliding down his long, muscular legs.

"But what if you run into—" She bit her lip and thought of her second jaguar sighting in the wee hours of that morning. She had no doubt about what she had seen, but she had withheld it from the others, knowing they would think she was just overtired and imagining things. The thought of Goodnight out there alone, coming face to face with . . . thinking he might try use that gun . . .

"You're not going without me!" She headed for her tent, grabbed her hat, and went after him.

Some minutes later, she came up behind him as he stood in a lush patch of ferns, and she paused, looking around, trying to see what he was seeing.

"How do you know what you're looking for," she asked. He turned with a scowl, acknowledging her, then turned back to whatever he was contemplating.

"I know," he said tautly.

"Enlighten me. Because from here it looks like you're just roaming around the jungle munching anything that looks interesting."

"I'd rather not discuss it."

"Above my pointy little head, is it?" She watched him reach for a twig, snap it, and sniff it, and tried to keep him from popping it in his mouth. "Stop it! I won't have you using yourself as a guinea pig for whatever plants you think may do something to the body. What if you come across something potent and deadly—something that puts you into a coma? Then where would we be?"

"A coma?" He made a notation in his journal and moved on along the old animal trail. "How do you know about comas?"

"I know a lot of things," she declared, annoyed by his cavalier attitude toward his own safety. "Including some fairly *reliable* medical tidbits."

"Oh? And where did you learn these 'medical tidbits'?" His tone was back to familiar upper-crust condescension.

"From my father. He was a physician." Her voice softened in spite of her. "Who contracted typhoid while combating an outbreak in a small town near us and died in spite of everything my mother and the doctor he went to help could do. I used to spend time in his office, helping with his records, tidying his medicine cabinet, running for help when he needed to set a bone. He let me watch when he did surgeries." A smile tugged the corner of her mouth as a memory worked its way free. "He said that he'd never seen a little girl who appreciated the sight of blood as much as me."

"It's a wise father who knows his own daughter." He looked at her.

"So, I started picking up tidbits. After he died and I was older, I worked in a pharmacy and studied books on medicines and anatomy, thinking that—" His strange expression stopped her, then jolted her back to her senses. What in heaven's name was she doing rattling on about the dark ages?

"Look, are we going to do this or not?" she said, jamming her hands on her waist and glancing irritably at the foliage around them. Spotting some large plants with long phallic-looking bracts, she headed straight for them.

"*We're* not doing anything," he insisted. "This is *my* hunt, *my* project."

"Yeah? Well you may not have the last word on that, Goodbody." She ripped off part of one of the big, striped leaves, rolled it up and took a bite. It was bitter and drew her mouth like alum. She gave it a chomp, then another.

The identity of the plant struck him as she took that bite.

"Stop! Spit it out!" He dropped his equipment and rushed to her, grabbing her jaws and squeezing to make them open, yelling, "Spit it out! Dammit—that's *dumb cane*—spit it out!"

She felt a strange numbness in her mouth, but managed to open it and tried to do as he said. Her mouth felt thick as she tried to clear it of the leaf.

"Don't swallow! Whatever you do, *don't swallow!*" he ordered, tilting her head back to see if they'd gotten all the leaf out. In the process she gasped and inhaled a trickle of saliva and leftover juice that caused her to cough, then to wheeze. "Shit!"

He grabbed her by the hand and started to run with her back toward camp, yelling over his shoulder. "Breathe—just concentrate on breathing."

They crashed through underbrush, ignoring bends in the trail and sliding down one short, muddy slope. Her throat felt strange and her tongue seemed twice its normal size. She felt her lips with her fingers and knew they were swollen, which kicked her into a near panic—that became a full panic when she felt her throat tighten further and tried to tell Goodnight what was happening.

She couldn't utter a sound.

Then suddenly, he stopped dead on the path ahead of her. She crashed into him and pounded his arm trying to get him to turn and see what was happening to her. He kept pushing her around behind him, and she fought free and lurched around him—only to stop dead herself.

On the path in front of them was a jaguar. Standing. Watching. It's yellow eyes shifted from him to her as she came into view. The big cat stood squarely on the path between them and their camp. For the longest minute in the history of time, they were forced to stand there, breathing, steaming, frantic . . . waiting to see what the beast would do.

It turned slightly, took two steps toward Cordelia, and stopped, watching her with a look that would have given Goodnight a chill if he hadn't been panting and sweating like a horse. It was a piercing, knowing look. Worldly. Acquisitive. Claiming. Just short of hunger.

And then, as quickly as it had appeared, it slid away through the underbrush and was gone. Her breathing was constricted, but it wasn't the effect of the dumb cane that made her knees feel rubbery. He pulled her toward him by the shoulders, his eyes filled with anxiety.

"Can you breathe?" he demanded. "Is your throat swelling?"

She nodded, unable to hide her fear.

"Camp's not far away. Can you make it there, or is it getting worse?"

She opened her mouth, but no sound came out. She pointed ahead.

A moment later, they were running across a grassy slope and up toward their camp among the mounds. He shouted for help and the Platanos came running. He sat her down on a camp stool and began to plow through their cooking supplies, pulling out things and tossing them aside. He came up with a tin of English tea and held it up in triumph.

She was incredulous—she was fighting for breath and he was making tea? She jumped to her feet and started flailing her arms and pointing to her throat.

"It's all right—you're going to be all right!" He rushed back to her and grabbed her shoulders forcing her back down onto the stool, looking into her eyes, willing her to listen. "If you were going to die, you'd have done it by now. I'm getting you something to reduce the swelling. Trust me, Cordelia. I can help you. Just trust me."

She was trembling. Her laboring heart felt like it was going to burst from her chest. She was having to work for every breath. But when she looked into his eyes, all she could see was his promise—his capability, his caring. If anyone could help her, he could. She bit her swollen lip and nodded.

A moment later, he was emptying dried tea into a tin basin and pouring water left over from the morning's tea into it. As the leaves softened and uncurled, he began stuffing them into her mouth, telling her to hold them there and to swallow any juice or saliva she produced. Soon her mouth was full of damp tea leaves, and he was kneeling in front of her holding her hands.

"Tea," he said in a level, reassuringly knowledgeable tone, "contains a constrictor. It causes swollen veins to contract and draws excess fluid from tissues. It works just the opposite of the chemical in the dumb cane, which is a 'dilator.' Thus the swelling you're experiencing." He smiled tightly.

"Funny how nature likes to pair opposites. Dilators and constrictors. Purgatives and antidiarrheals. Sedatives and stimulants. Poisons and antidotes." He paused for a minute. "Men and women."

She couldn't help trying to smile. Her lips felt like they would split.

"So, to answer your question, I've studied plants and families of plants that have been used in medicines for thousands of years. I can recognize a lot of them by sight. Plants related to one another often have similar effects." He grinned sheepishly. "So, I'm really looking for long-lost relatives."

He kept talking to her, distracting her as the tea worked, until Hedda and the professor arrived, summoned by the Platanos. Hedda was frantic at the sight of her swollen lips and was astonished by Goodnight's explanation of what had happened. For the next few hours, attention focused on her recovery. Her breathing returned to normal, and the swelling subsided everywhere except her larynx, which remained inoperative and reduced her to using hand signals and writing. She couldn't complain or reply in kind when Goodnight quipped about her being a near-perfect woman now that she was *silent*.

They gathered around the campfire for supper later, and it was only then that Cordelia wrote a note informing the others of the second jaguar sighting.

"Another jaguar?" Hedda looked to Cordelia, who shook her head.

"It looked like the same one," Goodnight spoke up, looking to her. She nodded, agreeing with that opinion. "If I didn't know better, I'd say it was following us." He looked at Cordelia, who appeared unsettled by the prospect.

"It's stalking us? Do jaguars eat people?" Hedda shivered visibly.

"Remember the legend—the jaguar comes down to see the people and judge their hearts." The professor took a drink of his coffee. "Maybe it was deciding about us." He looked to Cordelia. "Or about you."

It wasn't a comforting thought as she sank onto her cot in her tent later: being judged by a big, tawny-eyed beast of the forest.

She tossed and turned replaying in her mind the events of the afternoon and thinking of the threat lurking in the darkness around them. She had taken what precautions she could; a big campfire, everyone armed, a watch posted, and the burros brought between the tents and put on a tie line for the night. The Platanos were taking turns dozing beside the campfire as they watched the animals. But her chagrin over her behavior—Good Lord, she knew better than to eat anything strange in the jungle!—caused her to question her own judgment.

The night went by without an incident, but it was still a relief to all to see the morning light.

February 7, Day 18

Had the scare of my life today. O'-Keefe followed me when I went out to do some collecting. Pestered me and took a bite out of a dieffenbachia—dumb cane!!! I nearly had a stroke. Thank God she didn't swallow more than a trickle—she'd have suffocated before my eyes. Wanted to shake her and kiss her and—and—never been so frantic in my life. Every bone in my body turned to rubber. Thought I was going to puke. Felt like the whole world was tilted up on its corner—on the head of a bloody pin!

Was able to drag her back to camp and pack her mouth with wet tea leaves to get the swelling down. Turns out, she's lost no more than her voice. Damned bloody miracle is what that is. It's got me twisted up in knots. Can't look at her now without feeling gut-shot and oozing inside.

The woman's making me crazy!!!

Also found ruins. Interesting. May not be on wild goose chase after all.

• • •

"You're sure their trail goes inland?" Alejandro Castille demanded of the guide he had extorted into taking him and his men up the Tecolutla River. They stood on the bank of the muddy flow, staring down at boats resting half out of the water. "How do you know they didn't take boats?"

"Because their guides know, as I do," Hector Varza said, keeping his gaze averted to hide the anger simmering in it, "that boats are no good past the next bend. Fast current. Many rapids. They go by foot." He pointed up the path, away from the bank. "See the tracks of the burros for yourself."

Castille followed him, searching the tracks as the guide pointed them out, his hand caressing the butt of the pistol strapped to his thigh.

"They cut away branches," Varza said, holding out a branch that had been hacked recently. "They leave a big trail." He glanced at the surly, heavily armed men who accompanied this man. He thought again of his Helena and their children, being held prisoner by another of this man's thugs to insure his cooperation. "They do not know you are coming."

"We will see that it stays that way," Castille said with a smirk, "until I am ready for them to know." He turned to his men, each of whom led a burro loaded with supplies and gestured forward with the riding crop he carried. "Move out!"

As the lead burro passed, he reached out with the crop and struck it to make it move faster. The animal flinched and brayed. Castille pushed Varza into motion, and the farmer saw blood welling on the rump of his favorite burro.

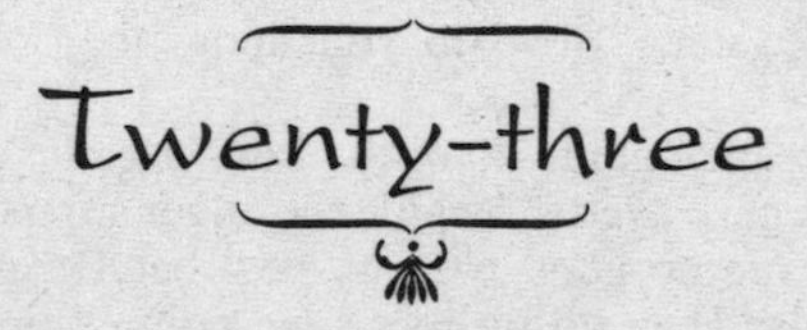

Twenty-three

While Hedda finished making her sketches in the Hall of Records, the rest of the group packed and took care of camp-related chores. The drawings in the ruins had confirmed their direction and given new impetus to their search. They were able to leave before midday.

The terrain, as the Platanos had predicted, grew increasingly hilly. They had to climb awkward slopes at times and cross deep, treacherous ravines lined with moss-slick rocks and springs seeping water. Progress slowed and Itza declared that at this rate, they might have to camp several nights before locating the village they sought.

On the brighter side, Cordelia's voice was beginning to come back. She could whisper now, and that small achievement reassured her that she would recover. But she could hardly bring her self to look at Goodnight, who to his credit hadn't uttered a single taunt about the incident itself. His refusal to take advantage of her impetuous behavior was totally unlike him.

He looked so serious, and when his gaze drifted her way his expression darkened in a way that made her revisit everything she had said to him. She couldn't help thinking that her revelation of reverence for her physician father had somehow put him off. Or worse, made him pity her.

Cursed man. If she lived to be a hundred, she would never figure him out. Not that she intended to be around him for one day longer than necessary.

When they rose on the second morning out, the air was less humid and the heat had moderated. The trees here were both more familiar and more strange: soaring hardwoods towering over beds of ferns, and stands of bamboo growing so thick they had to detour around them.

The change in altitude had brought a corresponding relaxation in attitude; as they left behind the oppressive heat of the jungle, they seemed to be leaving behind its dangers as well. By afternoon, when they spotted a crystal clear stream flowing beneath overhanging trees in a rocky swale, they were all ready for a bath, a good meal, and an uninterrupted siesta.

It felt good to be clean again and have a full stomach. Cordelia saw the others settled comfortably on massive, low-hanging branches and rock outcroppings, and she climbed onto a large flat rock shaded by a large tree. Spreading her wet hair out to dry she fell into a drowsy, pleasant state between waking and dreaming. In that delicious almost-sleep, she recalled a secluded doorway in Havana . . . a palm tree on the beach at Tecolutla . . . the relief she'd felt when the jaguar left and she found herself in *his* arms . . . his eyes as he talked calmly to keep her from panicking after she tasted the dumb cane . . .

Hart watched her spreading her hair out on the rock around her and groaned. What had he done to deserve this punishment? Watching her . . . wanting her . . . knowing that he had nothing to offer . . . knowing that she responded to his kisses as if that didn't matter.

But it did matter. He was virtually indentured to Hardacre for the next five years, and it was his mission to find something on this trip to take back to barter for his freedom. Squeezing his eyes shut, he revisited the array of plant materials he'd encountered. The forests here were chock-full of extraordinary vegetation. If he only had more time . . . more resources . . . more . . .

It was the story of his life. Too much of some things and not enough of others. Too much breeding and wealth, too little choice and encouragement. Too many expectations and restrictions, too few resources and allies.

This recitation of old conflicts didn't solve anything, he told himself, sliding down from the tree branch he occupied. He was here. He had now.

He went quietly to retrieve his collecting box and rifle, then scanned the sides of the stream bed below and the trees along the uplands on either side. Glancing up at the sun, he set off, telling himself he wouldn't be gone very long.

He strode quickly along old animal trails in the multilayered tree canopy, searching the plants, categorizing and dismissing most of them. Orchids were prevalent, though different species than in the lowland jungles, and yellow bellflowers and fragrant vining jasmine replaced the sight of pitcher plants and the more bizarre bromeliads. Aloe and odd bits of cactus were wedged in rocky crevices, bottlebrush trees and what looked like another species of laurel.

The tree canopy was so thick it blotted out much of the sun. He was starting to lose track of time when he saw a flash of red tucked high in a tree and stopped. Even from the ground he could see it was a rare specimen. Epiphytic—air-rooted—undoubtedly an orchid. Dropping his gear and propping his rifle against the tree trunk, he charted a path up the tree and began to climb. The bark was covered in lichens and slippery, but he managed to reach the limb and flatten on it, easing out along the branch. It was just beyond his fingertips when a flash of something below distracted him.

Something gold. And moving. His heart stopped as he watched a sinuous form pad across the ground directly beneath him. From twenty feet up he could see every movement of its shoulder blades, every expansion of ribs caused by its breaths, every variation in its asymmetrical spots.

It was huge. And captivating.

And down there with his gun while he was stuck up a tree.

He held his breath as the jaguar slowed beneath his perch, stretching and sniffing. He was too far from the others to call out for help, and his gun was out of reach. Then the big cat's head swung up and those entrancing golden eyes fixed on him matter-of-factly, without malice, without pity.

Jaguars were panthers. Panthers were terrific climbers. He was in a tree.

He was probably toast.

Or crumpet.

He just hoped he snuffed it proper before the cat headed for his tasty bits.

Just as he was trying desperately to remember which shoulder to touch first when crossing himself, the beast gave his gun a swipe with a huge paw and sent it clattering across tree roots into the underbrush. Then the beast turned to his haversack and gave it a sniff. *Nothing of interest there*, he pleaded silently. *On the other hand, it's a lot more interesting than what's up this tree.*

As if in response, the beast looked straight up, and he could have sworn it curled a lip into a half snarl. He couldn't breathe, couldn't swallow.

The beast turned to stroll down the path, but stopped several feet away, raised its tail, and removed all doubt of its gender as it sprayed a potent blast of urine all over Hart's haversack and the tree trunk beneath him. With the area duly marked, it padded off down the trail with what he fancied was a spring in its step.

It took a full minute after the cat faded from sight before Hart could pry his arms from around the tree limb and inch his way back down the trunk. His legs were rubbery by the time he reached the ground. The area stunk like—well, it stunk. His canvas haversack was a goner. He retrieved his rifle from the brush, pulled his collecting box, journal, and writing materials from the smelly bag and—suddenly realized where the jaguar was headed!

"Shit!" Shouldering the rifle strap and clasping the box in his arms, he stuffed the rest inside his shirt and began to run toward the ravine.

The beast had a head start and was probably already making his approach. Hart slowed as he neared the little valley, trying to minimize the noise of his footfalls and panting, dropped his gear and pulled the rifle from his shoulder.

When he reached the upper edge of the slope above the small ravine, he halted to search the trees visually. Below he could hear the burros stirring and Goodnight Junior braying nervously for his mother. The animals had caught the scent of the predator; he just hoped someone was awake to notice it.

Then he spotted movement on a rock ledge above the bank where Cordelia and the others rested. Crouching, he crept forward, then he dropped to his knees and crawled until he spotted the big cat inching out onto a ledge ten feet above the rock O'Keefe was on, still asleep, vulnerable. Above her, the jaguar looked straight ahead, tensing, gathering. Hart's blood was roaring in his ears as he braced himself on his elbows and sited down the rifle at the jaguar—and froze as he spotted movement that had nothing to do with the big cat.

On the branches of the tree over O'Keefe was a monstrous brown and tan snake with diamond-like markings, a boa constrictor, fifteen feet at least . . . shifting, sliding, lowering its massive coils, preparing to drop. He shifted his gaze back to the cat and realized it wasn't looking down at O'Keefe, but across at the boa. Every muscle in his body contracted. Was it planning on attacking the snake or the woman? Either way, in two seconds O'Keefe was going to have a ton of trouble drop in her lap.

He squared himself, took aim, breathed out, and pulled the trigger. The crack echoed off the rocks and around the valley. The recoil was more than he anticipated and cost him a second's recovery before he could regroup and aim again. The snake was nowhere to be seen and when he swiveled the gun, the ledge where the jaguar had been was empty, too.

An unearthly cat roar blended with Cordelia's scream of surprise, and in a blur she rolled aside and dropped off the rock onto the ground below. A moment later, she saw Goodnight careening down the hillside, shouting and pointing, and scrambled for her gun.

"What was that?" She rasped out as she pointed her pistol toward the low, spine-tingling growls coming from the thrashing brush. "What's happening?"

Running full tilt, he bounded up onto the big rock and just managed to stop himself in order to stare down at the dense vegetation where the snake had fallen and the cat had apparently pursued it.

"Boa," he panted, "in the tree." He pointed to the thick branch above the rock. "Dropping."

"Boa constrictor?" Her astonishment was echoed by Hedda and the professor as they came running. "Then, what is that growling?" She climbed onto the rock and looked down into the trembling bushes. "It sounds like a—"

"Jaguar." He finished for her, then took a deep breath. "There was one up there." He pointed to the ledge above them. "I think it went after the snake."

She looked at him in dismay and then at the underbrush that was still trembling from the passage of whatever had moved beneath it.

"What you shoot?" Ruz said, nudging between them to scan the area.

"I have no earthly idea," he said truthfully.

Quiet descended as the distant thrashing and growling ceased. Even the incessant shriek and caw of birds and the chatter of monkeys stopped. Everything in the forest seemed to be attuned to the passing of a great predator. But if the big cat had gone after great boa and they had battled, which had won?

"Damned eerie." Hart scowled. "A fight between jaguar and snake."

"Especially after what we saw in the ruins," she said, nodding, her still-healing voice giving her words a hushed quality that suited the moment.

They stood listening, with tension raking spidery fingers up their spines. The noise of the forest slowly began to return. Whatever had happened was over.

"¡Mire!" came Itza's voice from behind them. When they looked he was standing in the water, pointing downstream. "¡Toma! Jaguar!"

The question of who won was settled and, thankfully, the victor had decided to celebrate elsewhere.

Ruz thumped his chest with a callused hand. "We find."

"No, really—" Hart's protest fell unheeded as Ruz and Itza headed into the thick vegetation, determined to see the results of such an epic battle firsthand.

He climbed off the rock and loped back up the hill to where he had left his gear. When he returned, Cordelia, Hedda, and the professor were waiting with questions.

He couldn't rest, he explained, and had gone out to look at the local flora. When he returned, he saw the snake and knew there wasn't time to both wake and warn Cordelia. Their expressions ranged toward skeptical. He couldn't blame them for doubting him as they watched him root around inside his shirt for a leaky fountain pen and stray pencils.

O'Keefe avoided his gaze. "It's time we moved on," she said hoarsely. "Let's pack up and be ready to leave when the Platanos get back."

A quarter of an hour later, the brothers came struggling up the stream bed, shouting, splashing, and straining as they carried something. Cordelia and the professor rushed to see what caused the excitement. Hedda, who remained behind with Hart, saw what they were carrying and promptly slid to the ground in a dead faint. Hart caught her and moments later, nearly lost his own lunch.

It was fourteen feet long. Fourteen of Itza's feet, for that was who measured it, heel to toe, when it was stretched out on the bank. The professor estimated its weight at somewhere near a hundred pounds, and Ruz was delighted to demonstrate with his finger where the bullet had gone—through the snake, just behind the head. Hart got woozy watching him demonstrate it again and again, then pantomime the snake's last frantic gasps with the jaguar at his throat. Then the brothers gleefully explored the torn flesh and bite marks inflicted by the jaguar. Their verdict: without Hart's shot to weaken the snake's neck, the jaguar might not have been able to bite and crush the snake before the snake's powerful coils crushed it.

Itza and Ruz grinned toothily and addressed Hart with solemn regard.

"Good omen. You shot. Jaguar fought." The professor translated as Itza cupped and interlocked his hands, demonstrating a strong bond. "You and jaguar *partners.* Now Jaguar Spirit guides you to his home."

Hart reddened and continued waving the smelling salts under Hedda's nose. He couldn't remember aiming the bloody gun. All he could think about was hitting something, anything to keep the thing from attacking O'Keefe.

Then he looked up and saw *her* staring at him with the softest, honey-taffy warmth in her eyes. It was respect. He hoped. He could use a little just now. He was tired of being thought a contrary, priggish, inept British domestic. And even more tired of thinking of himself that way.

Squaring his shoulders, he strolled by her on his way to restow his equipment and lowered his head and voice as he passed.

"You can thank me later."

February 9, Day 20

Bagged first boa today with help of new chum: Gerald Jaguar. A real boost to my standing with O'Keefe. She's quit looking at me like I'm intolerable. Graduated to not looking at me at all. This is what I get for helping to save her life. Why do I bother?

Don't understand women in gen-

eral, but she's a bigger mystery than most. Knows she's beautiful. Quick as a whip. Not at all affected, except when she wants to put it on. Terrifying then. Could have parlayed that lot into a spot in some ducal family tree or a tycoon's—hold up—she already has one.

She has designs on old Hardacre's...what? Money? Prestige? Power? What is she trying to get from him? And what does that have to do with me?

And that business with her father, old Hardacre's disowned son. Turns out he was a physician who believed in helping people. Hardacre apparently has it in for doctors. Legions of fired gout specialists. His son. Me. All the more reason to find a lucrative cure and rub his nose in it.

Well, at least I don't have to worry about O'Keefe kissing me again. I doubt she'll try, now that she knows I'm a crack shot.

Twenty-four

The remote hamlet of Tierra Rica was nothing like the village they had visited on the Tecolutla River. This collection of twenty or so structures was a bizarre mix of primitive thatch-roofed huts made of bamboo and ancient-looking stone buildings that seemed to have emerged from the very hills themselves. The dwellings were nestled among mature trees that had been harvested, here and there, to provide space for animals and human activity. The wooded valley around and beside them was shot through with clear-running streams that irrigated a varied patchwork of crops.

The women tending vegetable patches on the edge of the village saw Cordelia's party coming and dropped their hoes to run back to the village and announce their presence. The entire village turned out to welcome them. The women and young girls gathered to approach Cordelia and Hedda, touching them, stroking their hair and clothes, and giggling at Cordelia's breeches. The men looked over the burros and went straight to Itza and Ruz, demanding to know who they were, why they'd come, and how much they would take to breed their jack to some local jennets.

Through the professor, Cordelia asked to see the *alcalde*, mayor, and the people just looked at them, puzzled. A few more questions revealed that the Spanish system of governance had never reached this far into the hills. They operated on a far older system of rule by *ancianos*, literally "old men." Four old men with weathered faces and hair liberally streaked with white stepped forward to accept the strangers' respect.

The professor, who had traveled to many villages in southern Mexico and understood the protocol, bowed and raised his hands skyward to call down a blessing on the village and these illustrious ancianos. Then he introduced Cordelia, Hedda, and Goodnight as explorers who had come all the way from America to learn of their ways and beliefs.

The ancianos looked unimpressed.

Goodnight leaned toward Cordelia and muttered, "You'll need more than teacups for this crew."

Gifts were indeed presented: a telescope, a photo of the U.S. Capitol, several spools of ribbon, some lavender sachets, rose-scented soap, a tin of maple candies, four china teacups, and a bottle of Goodnight's precious whiskey. The men seemed pleased with the gifts, especially when they tasted the candy and whiskey and the professor conveyed to them that Cordelia intended to make for them an important ceremonial drink called "tea."

Relations seemed to be off to a good start when a disturbance from the back of the onlookers drew attention from the proceedings. The crowd parted as people skittered out of the path of an old woman swaying forward with the help of a gnarled walking stick. She wore a red shawl over her head and as she approached, Cordelia thought she looked like one of the dried-apple people children in New England carve in autumn.

Frizzy white hair was visible beneath the shawl, and she had dark, piercing eyes. Bone bracelets clacked on each wrist and there were carved talismans on leather thongs hanging around her neck. When she approached the ancianos, Cordelia could have sworn the men blanched.

After giving the quartet of elders what appeared to be a royal dressing down, she investigated the gifts they held. Then with one eye narrowed, she lifted the apron she wore to form a sling and presented herself before each of them, allowing them to deposit the telescope, lavender, ribbons, soap, candies, and whiskey in her makeshift basket—spurning only Cordelia's teacups. When she had collected her booty, she turned to inspect the visitors, nodding to Hedda, smirking cattily at Cordelia, poking the professor's girth with a gnarled finger, and stopping before Goodnight to run her gaze up his long, muscular frame. She smiled flirtatiously, revealing that she hadn't a tooth in her head.

The crowd parted again as she left, melting out of her way as if by magic.

That, Cordelia thought to herself, was a woman with power.

"Who is she?" she asked the professor, who in turn, asked the ancianos.

"Yazkuz," the eldest anciano declared with a dark look. "*La bruja*."

The professor clapped a hand to his forehead. "Of course. She would be," he muttered in English before turning to Cordelia to explain. "Her name is Yazkuz and she is the local *bruja*. A *Bruja rojo*."

Cordelia frowned. "A bruja—that is a midwife, right?"

"Wrong." The professor sighed uneasily. "It is a witch."

She looked around her at the faces of the people.

"Please," she said, trying to keep her face neutral, "you can't possibly believe she really is a witch, that she has any real powers."

"I see many things in this world that I cannot explain," the professor said. "I cannot say for sure this woman has powers. But she has power over these people. That, my skeptical friend, is very real."

• • •

The ancianos decreed the visitors had permission to make camp at the edge of the houses, in a little-used pasture. Half of the village accompanied them to the spot and watched as they erected their tents, drew water, bartered for firewood, and released their burros for grazing.

There was plenty of daylight left, so Cordelia insisted they take a tour of the village and get a closer look at the structures they had seen that seemed to be made of reclaimed stones. Leaving the Platanos to secure the camp, they strolled down a winding concourse between huts and houses, trailing onlookers and village children. Beneath their feet were paving stones that had been worn by centuries of foot traffic into distinct lanes.

"This place looks like it's been here for centuries." She paused to nudge a stone with the toe of her boot. "Do you think it was part of an earlier village?"

"It is likely," the professor said, nodding to some brightly clad women watching them from a nearby doorway. "Where there are resources, people gather. They return and build in the same places again and again."

When they reached one of the buildings made of stone, Cordelia spotted some carvings on a corner block that seemed to be an upside-down face glyph. She tilted her head to make certain and smiled.

"They not only come back to the same place, they use the same materials. I wonder where these blocks came from. Could you ask someone?"

The professor obligingly approached the door of the stone house and discovered it belonged to one of the four ancianos. At their request, the elder led them through the village to a large paved area in which stone blocks of various sizes were stacked. Around the old plaza—for that was what it surely had been at one time—were the foundations of long-forgotten buildings. Only two structures now stood on those old foundations, clearly remade according to the edict requiring that old carvings be hidden. One bore a cross over the open door; a church. The other, much larger structure had many openings in the walls and a lattice for a roof, like a pavilion or summer house. As they neared, they could see long wooden benches inside and a few large tables. It was a meeting place, a market, a place for feasts and celebrations, a venue for conducting court and deciding village affairs.

"A municipal building," Cordelia said, running her hand over the cleanly cut stone. "But are there no original walls and carvings left intact?"

Her question, translated, caused the anciano to glance instinctively at a large stack of stones that backed against the sheered hill behind them.

"There are no walls of the old gods here now," the anciano declared firmly. "Come, my wife makes *kakaw* for us."

Kakaw turned out to be chocolate, but a version of it that drew the jaws, burned the throat, and caused the eyes to water. The ground cocoa beans, mixed with chilies and water and poured back and forth from cup to cup until foamy, were a revelation.

"Who knew," Hedda said later, quite disillusioned, "that chocolate could be made to taste so horrible?"

"My mouth is on fire," Goodnight declared grimly.

"Did you notice the way he looked at those stones by the cut in the hill?" Cordelia said as they returned to their camp. She looked to the professor. "We should take a closer look at what is over there, tonight, after everyone is asleep."

Later, guided by moonlight, they located the plaza and moved quickly to the stacks of stones that seemed to form a pocket against the sheered side of the hill. They had to climb the stones to see what was beyond and discovered a paved area around several derelict stone pillars that marked an entrance to a hole in the side of the hill.

Cordelia grinned. "The stones *are* hiding something."

One by one, they dropped into that narrow well and began to inspect the pillars. Shielded from the village by the stacks of stone blocks, they lit their lanterns and illuminated the half-boarded-up entrance to—a cave? Passage? Underground temple?

It wasn't difficult to pull away the two aged boards that blocked the entrance. The rough stone of the opening looked as if it had once been faced with something more refined, something that had been chiseled away. The professor ran his hand over the gouges in the rock and cursed quietly.

The farther they moved into the cave the more regular the walls became, and not far inside they became highly decorated with traditional Mayan motifs.

"I knew it!" Cordelia gleefully hugged Hedda, then the professor, and came to a stop before Goodnight and quickly dropped her arms to her sides. "Can you tell what it is, Professor?"

The professor moved along the passage, describing the usual decorative motifs, the stepped fret, the flowing serpent, the cocoa trees and beans, flowers. Then he came to very unusual images that he was at a loss to explain: worms that were clearly worms, not snakes, oval shapes that recalled the design of Egyptian scarabs, stylized butterflies—bright golden creatures that became more prevalent as they moved along. But they could all see there were no glyphs to explain the history or function of this carefully crafted complex.

After encountering several chambers devoid of decoration—blank canvases on which nothing was ever written, or frames stripped of their precious canvases—they came to a chamber that made up for all the previous blankness.

It was an explosion of color and shape and highly developed nature-consciousness, painted beasts and creatures and trees and flowers of every kind—a visual Noah's Ark. At the center of the longest wall was a jaguar, regal and remarkably lifelike. From that figure radiated sun-like rays that connected the Jaguar Spirit to all the creatures represented around the room.

Interestingly, there were the little human figures that

formed a border at the feet of the jaguar, carrying items, bringing offerings.

Just as Hedda was settling cross-legged on the floor to begin sketching, strange laughter burst into the chamber, causing the hair on their necks to prickle. The old woman, Yazkuz, was standing in the door opening, her face shadowed by her red shawl and her gnarled finger pointing at them.

Cordelia nearly jumped out of her skin when the old woman spoke. Her voice sounded like something straight out of Hans Christian Andersen.

"She says we waste no time in finding this," the professor translated.

"Tell her we mean no disrespect to this place or to the Jaguar Spirit."

"I know what you want. I saw you coming," she said with a wicked lilt, hobbling into the room and pausing before Goodnight to feel her way up his arm. "I have what you need, too, Tall One." He reddened, speechless.

Cordelia fought the urge the smack the old girl's hands while trying to decide whether to reveal their true goal to the old woman.

"We have come to find stones," she said, and the professor translated.

The old woman cackled. There was no other word for it.

"Stones? No, Fire-hair, you have come to learn my secrets." Yazkuz swayed over to her. "For those you must pay. And pay well."

"What secrets do you have to sell, Madam Yazkuz?"

The old woman laughed and held out her arms to indicate the paintings.

"The secrets of the forest. The secrets of magic." She looked pointedly at Goodnight. "And healing." She chuckled at his surprise. "Oh, I know you, Tall One. You want my secrets, too." She winked coquettishly. "And I may give them to you." She moved on to the professor, stared into his eyes, then drew back and made a quick sign with her fingers that said she didn't like what she saw. What she said to him, he did not bother to translate.

"How much you give me for the first secret?" she demanded, propping her hands on her walking stick.

"That depends on what kind of secret it is," Cordelia said, thinking that if there were a female version of her grandfather, Yazkuz would be it. They were both obsessed with profit and making deals.

"You seek the secret of this place. I can tell you." She held out her hand.

Cordelia thought for a minute, then looked to Goodnight. "I think a silver dime ought to establish a fair rate of exchange." He reluctantly handed it over.

The old woman looked at it and curled her nose. "Got anything bigger?"

A quarter sealed the deal.

"This place, this village, served the Jaguar Spirit."

"Well, that's bloody obvious," Goodnight said, crossing his arms. "Make her give you your money back." When the professor translated, Yazkuz looked at Goodnight in annoyance.

"And it still serves the Jaguar Spirit through me." She looked from one face to another, then another, unsettled by what she saw. She clearly was not accustomed to skepticism from the people she dealt with. She motioned impatiently for Hedda to stop sketching and pack it up.

"You come with me!"

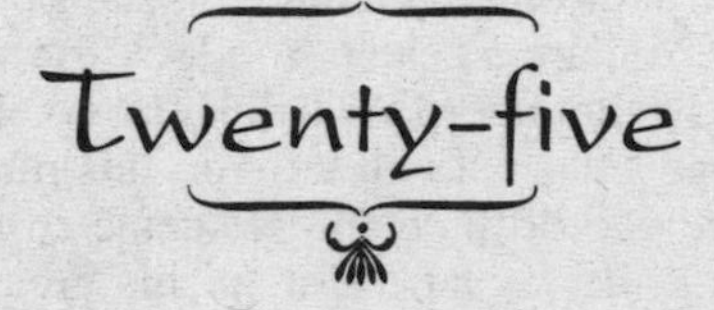

Warily, they followed her through a maze of similar, if less decorative, passages and emerged in a dark, cluttered house on the far side of the village.

Their lanterns combined to reveal more of the place than was comfortable. Jars, crocks, bottles, vats, and oiled animal skins full of heaven-knew-what lined the shelves that covered every available inch of wall space. Hanging from the low rafters were bunches of herbs, weeds, plants, and the occasional dried reptile or amphibian body. There were baskets of various vegetable matter on the way to becoming something else. There were cages of live lizards, glass jars of beetles and insects, and even a couple of dainty but deadly coral snakes. Over the hearth hung that most indispensable witching apparatus—a big black cauldron.

"I am true bruja. Of real power," she said to them. "The whole forest is my garden. The whole world is my book of knowledge. I prove it." She lighted a bundle of twigs, waved the smoke around, and after a moment with her eyes closed, went straight to Cordelia and looked her in the eyes.

"You tasted the plant called dumb cane," she said.

"Your voice still suffers." Then she went to Goodnight and looked into his eyes. With a start, she pulled down his lower eyelids and searched them. Then she went back to Cordelia and did the same to her, looking deeply into her eyes as well. Returning to Goodnight, she said with a hint of irritation, "You are a healer. You look for a great cure." She grudgingly announced: "I will show you things."

"The rest of you . . . I will tell you this much. Our village was once one of three. People came from the whole world to thank the Jaguar Spirit for his great generosity. And our villages served as their gateway. Now you have come to learn about the stones the Jaguar Spirit left behind. But the Jaguar keeps his secrets. Only He knows if you are worthy of such knowledge."

Cordelia was so busy trying to discern if there was any real news in that revelation, that she didn't protest at first when the old witch pushed all of them but Goodnight out of her hovel and told them to come back tomorrow.

"Wait," she heard him say with an edge of anxiety. "Anything you have to say or do to me, you can say or do in front of her!"

Cordelia watched the door slam behind her and was torn between outrage and amusement that the old woman had taken such a fancy to Goodnight. Pacing impotently for a few minutes, she finally sat down on a bench outside the hovel to wait for him. The amusement quickly faded. By the time he exited the cottage more than an hour later, she was roundly furious with both the old girl and him.

"What did she do to you?" she asked, springing to her feet and looking him over. He had a strange grin on his face.

"We just had a cup of tea and exchanged recipe–e–es."

She sniffed him.

"You're drunk."

"Am most certainly not. Only had a drop of whiskey in my tea. Least, I think that's what it was."

"Sounds disgusting." She headed off along the path toward the main part of the village, then went back to grab him by the arm and pull him along. "What did you do with her? You don't even speak the same language."

"What kind of criterion is that?" he said in a scholarly tone. "*We* speak the same language and we can't seem to do anything together."

"That's not true."

"Yeah? What have we ever done together? Voluntarily."

"You really want to know?" It was partly the moonlight. It had to be. Or maybe it was the old woman's blatant yen for him. Something about the place or the moment or the tension of the last hour caused her to step straight into him, lock her hands around his neck, and reel him down for a blistering kiss.

"Yeah," he said against her lips when he surfaced, "we've done that. And this." He wrapped both arms tight around her, lowered his head. "Hardacre had nothing to do with this."

And he pushed her right off the very edge of the world.

She fell . . . slowly . . . sinking . . . through an ocean of voluptuous swirling sensations that blotted out everything else. His heat, his hardness all around her. Him. This was him. This taste, these sleek supple lips, this velvety tongue—it was her Goodnight, the man to whom her desire was irrevocably binding her.

This feeling of connectedness, this joining was what she had longed for without knowing she longed. It was unlike anything she had ever imagined. This was the love she had feared, dreaded, and avoided. Just as he had.

In that moment, she understood with surprising clarity what was happening between them. The fear, the defensiveness, the fascination, the temptation—they weren't just hers, they were his as well. This force drawing them together was overwhelming and terrifying for them both. But at least they were *together* in that fear—sharing it, exploring it, sometimes defying it. Like now.

This was the passion, the need, the completion that had drawn her parents to defy father and society. This was the wanting that made them abandon their secure and predictable lives and commit to a new, unknown, and risky life with only each other, holding nothing back. It was this sense of companionship, of having a mate or partner, someone to *rely* on, that had sustained them.

She was in love with Hartford Goodnight.

And she would never be the same.

She broke away from him with tears in her eyes and headed for her tent.

He caught up with her and made her look up at him. She could hardly see him through that haze of collected moisture.

"Don't run," he said. Two words that were instantly branded on her heart.

"I can't do this."

"How can we *not* do this?" he asked, pain in his voice.

"No." Her voice was a taut whisper. "I can't—I already—" She bit her lip and blinked to release the tears. "You and I, we're headed different places. You have medicines to make and I have . . . treasures to find . . . and . . ."

His eyes seemed to have a rim of moisture growing in them.

"Now is not enough?" he said in a whisper so soft, its anguished timbre was like a caress.

Newly awakened emotions pressed hard for release, but the habit of a lifetime remained unshakable and her dependable sense of reason had its way.

"No."

She turned away and a moment later looked back to find him standing on the path, his arms at his sides, looking oddly fragile and alone.

Just as she was.

February 10, Day 21

Bruja's secrets: $0.35 (No bargain.)

Arrived in foothills at village called Tierra Rica. Old men. Old ruins. Another jaguar mural. Worst chocolate in the whole history of taste. Old bruja

(Mexican version of witch) here claims to know all manner of herbal cures. Seems to fancy me. Also fancies whiskey. Can't hold her liquor—thank God—or I'd have been ravished within an inch of my life.

Escaped the old witch's clutches only to walk straight into O'Keefe's.

Can't take much more of this.

In way over my head. Gut in knots. Whole body on fire, quivering with heat, and not a cold shower in sight. Tonight she made it clear—she's got better things to do than dally with a failed chemist/butler with no future. Dammit. When this is over—who am I kidding—it will never be over for me. I'm going to have to carry this...this wanting with me for the rest of my miserable—

Still. Got to admire the way she never takes her eye off the prize. Not for a bloody second.

Not even for a single, sweet instant of might-have-been.

The next morning, she awakened to find Hedda dressed and already heading out into the gray mist that seeped from the hills themselves each night.

"Where are you going?" she asked, sitting up and rubbing her face.

"You're awake. I was going to leave you a note. Itza made that wonderful chicken with peppers and eggs in tortillas again. And Arturo and I are going to interview some of the ancianos and the older women, to see if we can collect some of their stories," Hedda said brightly. Too brightly for this early hour of the morning.

"Stories?" She swung her legs over the side of the cot,

hoping feet on the ground would anchor her better. "You mean about the things we saw last night? I thought we agreed to keep that quiet so—"

"No, actually." Hedda pressed her sketch pad and a smaller bound notebook against her with crossed arms. "We were talking last night and realized there are probably lots of legends and stories here, ones that may be totally lost if not recorded soon. We thought it would make a wonderful project for us."

"We already *have* a project." She stood up and scratched to get the blood flowing. "We have to find the Gift of the Jaguar."

Hedda tucked her chin and settled a look on her. "I meant a little idea for Aurturo and me. You have your project. So, I thought—"

"My project? It's *our* project. We have always traveled together, worked together, decided things *together*." But not any longer?

"Oh, I didn't mean we wouldn't continue helping you search for the Jaguar stones. It's just that we thought it would be fun for us to do a little something on our own. Together." Hedda looked as if she were bracing, though she smiled. "Just a little something extra. It won't take up much time. Besides, you've been helping Hartford with his 'medicinal plant' business."

"Hartford?" It was Goodnight's given name she realized, but just then it sounded about as familiar as Kubulai Khan. Good Lord. She was thinking "undying love" and she scarcely knew his first name? And what was that about—Hedda honestly thought she was helping Goodnight with his plant search? "Wait!" she said, but her aunt was already ducking through the tent flap with a wave. Following, she stuck her head outside and saw her aunt put her arm through the professor's. They walked off together, their eyes bright and heads inclined toward some mystical plane of communion.

How could that have happened? When did "I" and "he" become a "we"? She had seen the glances, the smiles, registered some of the admiration and compliments Valiente had strewn in Hedda's way. She assumed that her aunt had more sense than to let such things influence her. After all, what did they know about the man? He could have a wife and ten children back in Mexico City, for all they knew!

But . . . if he didn't?

She had never felt so desolate. Here she was, determined to retreat into the sensible and dependable, and the sensible and dependable seemed to be evaporating around her! Her beloved aunt, her companion and confidante, her anchor in the world, was striking out on her own, reaching for something beyond their comfortable bond of kin and companionship.

Hedda was declaring that she belonged to Hedda.

Yazkuz turned out to be not only a top-notch intimidator, but also a knowledgeable herbalist, a wry observer of the human condition, and an unexpected student of English. She had acquired, through her little extortions and nefarious trading practices, three books published in English and had with patience and cunning sat down to decipher some of that foreign script.

Cordelia arrived at the woman's hut just as Yazkuz and Goodnight were leaving for the nearby forest to gather materials for herbal medicines. The sight of him filled her with dread, confusion, and worst of all, longing. Plowing determinedly through that slurry of emotion, Cordelia insisted on accompanying them, telling herself she had to pry some answers from old Yazkuz.

Instead, as they hiked into the forest she found her own brain being picked to correct Yazkuz's English. The result was an improvement in the old witch's ability to communicate with the "handsome one" and an increasing buildup of steam in her own veins.

It was a simmering, low-grade agony to have to tromp through the woods with him after what had passed between them the night before, even more so after Hedda's revelation this morning. But she was determined not to show how much it affected her. Heaven knew, he didn't seem to be suffering any ill effects. He seemed at the top of his game: full of questions, endlessly curious and focused, all while effectively fending off the old girl's advances. The one thing he didn't manage to do was look at Cordelia, except in unavoidable situations such as when she suggested that he apply some of his "tall, handsome" influence to get Yazkuz to look at their rubbings and tell them what she knew about the nearby mountains. He merely gave her a long, unreadable look and went back to examining his latest specimen, too wrapped up in his precious plants and pursing his own private mission to help her.

She realized, there and then, that one by one her party was deserting her. Goodnight . . . Hedda . . . the professor . . . even the Platanos, who were preoccupied with their "burro stud" business. The expedition's discipline was breaking down. She was losing control or had already lost it. How could this happen after they had come so far and were so close? She could almost *feel* the presence of those blasted stones.

Yazkuz ignored both her presence and her repeated requests, preferring to concentrate on collecting herbs and botanicals and admiring Goodnight's anatomy. Shortly, however, the old girl made a sharp "accidental" movement with her walking stick that jabbed Cordelia in the leg. Minutes later she tromped heavily on Cordelia's foot and then pretended not to see her standing in the way when she spit out a wad of cocoa leaves she had chewed all morning.

Cordelia had had enough.

Angered and feeling stretched and edgy, on the brink of an explosion that she could ill afford, she shook the gooey mass off her boot, turned on her heel, and left Goodnight in the old girl's clutches. Her thoughts, emotions, and frustrations were a roiling mass in the middle of her stomach as she headed back to the village. Then as she crested a small, treeless rise, over which the very top of the village was visible, she slowed and felt a strange tingle of premonition that alerted her to her surroundings.

Something was moving through the grass ahead of her and slightly to the left. A blur of gold and brown gradually became visible, and she knew without understanding how she knew, that it was a jaguar.

She stopped dead, watching as it emerged onto the well-traveled path and paused, a familiar but no less fearsome figure.

The gold of the big cat's coat shone like satin in the bright sun. Its stance was relaxed but its ears were forward, alert, and its eyes left no doubt that it was aware of every element in its immediate environment, including her. As the jaguar continued to stand there, watching something in the distance, but keeping her within sight as well, Cordelia noted in some not yet frozen part of her brain a slight reddish stain around its mouth and on the front paws. It was confirmation of what she already knew in the marrow of her bones: this was the same jaguar.

It truly was following them.

"It follows her," Goodnight said through the hold fear had on his throat, speaking as much to himself as to the old woman. He pointed to the path some distance ahead, where O'Keefe had stopped. Yazkuz gasped and grabbed his arm tightly, holding him as if afraid he might charge in to do battle with the beast. Her hooded eyes narrowed as she watched O'Keefe's erect posture and surprising calm before the great cat.

"It is the same jaguar that came before. Three times now it has searched her out." He held up three fingers and pointed between the woman and the jaguar. Yazkuz nodded gravely, intent on watching what would happen.

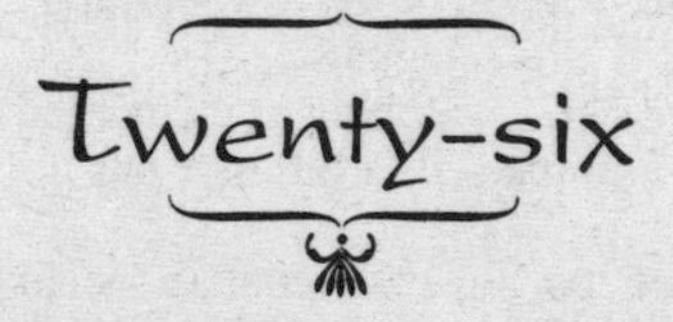

Seconds stretched into a full minute. Goodnight's lungs began to ache for air as the cat started to move toward O'Keefe. His stomach sank and opened a huge, frightening hole in him as she held her ground and watched it come.

It didn't seem like an attack, but big cats were unpredictable. It could spot the tiniest unconscious movement, hear the thudding of a frantic heart, or catch a strange scent that alarmed it—and go from serene to savage in an instant.

If anything happened to her . . .

But as the beast passed by her—so near she could have reached out a hand and petted it—she remained as still as a marble statue and the cat showed no inclination to attack.

"Jaguar Spirit tests your woman," Yazkuz said in hushed tones, a miraculous improvement over her previous attempts at English. She tapped her own chest. "Jaguar looks into heart."

The foot between cat and woman became a yard, then two. The beast moved away, back into the brush on the other side of the footpath. A moment later she was alone on the path, and in the dappled sunlight it was difficult to believe that anything out of the ordinary had occurred.

He gulped breaths. His heart was pounding as he broke free of the old woman's grasp and began to run.

Before he closed the distance between them, she had started to run herself and he had to put on a burst of speed to catch her. By the time he reached her elbow, she had heard him coming and looked over her shoulder. Her toe caught on some grass and she stumbled, allowing him to seize her arm and both pull her to a halt and keep her from falling.

"D–did—did you see it?" she said, panting.

"I saw."

"I–It's the same one . . . it really is."

Her amber eyes were huge and dark-centered as she looked up. He could feel her trembling and transferred his grip to her shoulders just as her knees buckled. The only way he could keep her from hitting the ground was to throw his arms around her, grab her against him, and hold her there. Which, in fact, was exactly what he'd wanted to do all morning—when he allowed himself to think about what he wanted instead of what he had to do.

Moments later he opened his eyes and realized he was murmuring "It's all right—you're all right" over and over again. And that Yazkuz was hauling herself up beside them, breathing heavily, looking fierce and resolved.

"You." She poked O'Keefe with a finger and after a moment O'Keefe turned her head to look at the old woman. "Bring picture to me," she said, having to search for every word. "I look." She pointed from her eyes with two fingers. "I see." Then she, too, faded off through the trees, leaving them alone on the path.

He set O'Keefe back a few inches and asked if she could walk. She took a deep, shuddering breath and nodded. He put an arm around her waist to steady her and without speaking, they walked back to the village together.

February 11, Day 22

another visit from that damnable jaguar. This cat-and-mouse thing *really wears on the nerves. Especially when O'Keefe's the mouse. Bloody thing just strolled right up to her. Rubbed against her legs like a parlor cat!*

Sure got old Yazkuz's attention. She said, "Jaguar looks into heart," or some such. That jaguar as judge and jury nonsense. Apparently Yazkuz thinks the beast approves, because she agreed to look at the rubbings. Made all kinds of magical signs when the scrolls were rolled out and said she'd take O'Keefe and me to see the stones. Just the two of us. Valiente was furious. Had a fit. Old woman wouldn't budge. Probably the first time his oily charm failed him.

Interesting: Yazkuz under misapprehension that O'Keefe is my woman.

Hell. The only place she's mine is in my dreams.

There was a strained silence in the sun-warmed tent as Hedda helped Cordelia roll and pack a spare shirt, camisole, clean socks and knickers, and a brush and some bandanas into a rucksack with canvas-cord straps.

"You shouldn't have to carry everything on your backs," Hedda said, checking the other compartment in the canvas pack, which contained a variety of cooking and camping gear, including a portable tin kettle. Beside the rucksack lay a large canteen and strapped to its top were two blankets in a tight roll.

"Yazkuz said the country is too rough for burros. And we will have to climb." She looked up to find Hedda's eyes filled with tears.

"You've never gone off alone like this."

The irony of it stuck in Cordelia's throat and she had to clear it to speak.

"I won't be alone. I'll be with Goodnight. And Yazkuz. I wish I knew why she insists on taking only the two of us. The professor was beside himself."

"That crazy old woman. Who knows what's in her head?" Hedda grabbed her hands as she reached for a bandana for her neck. "Promise me that if she tries anything funny you'll come straight back to the village."

Cordelia smiled, feeling the pull of Hedda's anxiety but telling herself she could handle anything old Yazkuz dished out. The old woman's attitude toward her had changed since the jaguar's visit.

Goodnight, however, was another story. The thought of spending days out in the wilderness with him, depending on him, was more than a little unsettling. When she emerged from the tent with her things and saw him dressed in goatskin breeches and wearing a pack that was even bigger than hers, it was little comfort that he looked just as conflicted about the trip as she was.

They collected a sizeable farewell party as they moved through the village with Hedda and the professor. As they started into the dense forest to the south and west, the well-wishers straggled back to their homes, all but Hedda and the professor. Cordelia turned back at the top of what would be the last visible rise, saw her aunt wave, and remembered the hostile look on the professor's face. She waved back with a strange emptiness in her chest, then she turned and set her face toward the frosty peaks looming in the distance.

They did indeed have to climb, but neither she nor Goodnight had counted on all of the vegetation-chopping and stream-fording and rock-face-scaling the first leg of the trip required. It was exhausting, especially since they had to help old Yazkuz every step along the way. The old girl had brought nothing but her shawl, guile, and walking stick—none of which was any help in scaling seven-foot cliffs, descending a vertical hillside, or crossing a churning mountain river.

They did encounter a few visual wonders along the way: an isolated coffee grove tucked beneath soaring hardwoods and laden with bright red coffee "cherries," a cache of brightly colored parrots collected beneath the canopy, and orchids of such rare and beautiful purple that they seemed almost unnatural.

By the first night, Cordelia had been introduced to muscles she hadn't known she had and felt a bit out of socket all over. She watched Goodnight collect wood and build a fire with almost effortless precision and found herself admiring his endurance. Looking at him now—with his tanned face, longish hair, visible muscles, and well-used boots—it was hard to believe that just a month ago he was pressing handkerchiefs and carrying nothing heavier than a breakfast tray. She made herself look away.

Yazkuz pulled out the second half of the tortillas, beans, and rice that Itza had prepared for them, and she made coffee from water seeping from a nearby rock spring. They ate in exhausted silence and washed in the spring water, then curled up in their blankets for some sleep. Cordelia was nodding drowsily when she saw Goodnight pull out his journal and settle himself by the meager firelight to write. She sat up and glared at him until he sensed her stare and looked up.

"What?" he said straightening, his pen poised over a line.

"That journal of yours. You're going to let me read it, of course, before you hand it over to Samuel P."

"Absolutely not." He went back to the line he was writing.

"Why not?" She crawled out of her blankets and leaned around the fire to see what he had written. He slammed the journal shut and glowered at her. "I have a right to see what you're writing. It concerns me and it's only fair that—"

"Fair," he said flatly, "doesn't come into it. This is my account. And no, you won't have the chance to see it before I present my report to the old man."

It felt like a poke in the eye. Unexpected and surprisingly painful.

She went back to her blankets, wrapped up, and flopped down onto the branches she'd cut for her bed. She pulled her hat down over her eyes and lay like that for two hours before she managed to fall asleep.

February 12, Day 23

Hands swollen, shoulders throbbing, legs and back hurt worse than after a rowing match on the Thames. Yazkuz weighs a bloody ton.

O'Keefe wants to see this journal after we return. Thinks she should get to edit it before her grandfather sees it. Fat chance.

Watching her in this forest—taking in the sights, reacting to the marvels here—is difficult. Every time I look at her, there's something new to want. Can only pray it's the exotic locale. Maybe back in Boston, London, or Colchester she'd be just another nose in the air.

Should concentrate on plants. Yazkuz pointed out several unique things along the way. Took seeds, noted growing conditions. There may be something in it. Hope there's something in this "jaguar stone" business for O'Keefe. For her to have come so far, worked so hard...it should be something wonderful. Something awesome. Enlightening. Profound.

Toward the end of the second day, Yazkuz began to pause periodically to stare at hillsides and squint at the rock faces they encountered. It was clear that she was looking for something, but when questioned, she rattled off something in her Mayan dialect and went back to fighting her way through the vegetation.

"Maybe we're close," Cordelia said, pulling out her machete.

"One can only hope," Goodnight replied with a sigh, tugging on his gloves and reaching for his blade.

It took an exhausting amount of additional chopping, climbing, and hiking before Yazkuz looked up through the immense tree canopy at the steep slopes of the craggy mountains and spotted something she recognized. Renewed by the sight, she slid down a moss-slippery hillside, then scrambled to her feet and charged toward an opening she had spied in the high mountain bluffs. After pausing to look up at the tall, sheer rock faces on either side of what seemed to be a cut in the mountain, she aimed between them and slogged into whatever lay beyond by splashing her way up a rocky stream that poured from the opening.

Cordelia and Goodnight paused where she had, trying to make out what she had seen. Massive dark rock faces soared on either side, looking like they had been split by a butcher's cleaver and pushed apart to make an opening of about fifty yards. No wonder the old girl had difficulty finding the place; it was mostly hidden from below by the thick tree canopy that had grown up in front of it. Exchanging questioning looks but saving their breath for their exertions, they braced their aching shoulders and headed after the old girl, up the stream that flowed between those great forbidding walls.

The canyon broadened, beyond the entrance, to a small, flat valley filled with lush vegetation and the sweet rushing sound of water falling over rocks. Yazkuz stopped several times, surveying the strange columnar rock faces above their heads. Then as she approached what had to be near the end of the canyon, she suddenly rushed to an outcropping covered with dense vegetation and thrust out her arms with a cackle of triumph. She had found it!

Cordelia looked at the tangle of vines and vegetation in dismay. *What* had she found?

The old woman fell on the heavy vines, pulling, ripping, muttering at whatever was responsible for "vegetation" in her pantheon of spirits. Cordelia and Goodnight exchanged puzzled looks, then began to help her. Minutes later, Goodnight yelped "hey!" drawing both women to where he was working.

"There's something underneath these vines—a carved block. See that?"

Did she ever! Cordelia scrambled to pull away more of the leaves and vines and discovered another block on top of it. Hours of studying the rubbings in her rucksack finally paid off—she recognized the carving.

"That's one of the blocks—two of them! This is it! We've found it!"

Twenty-seven

Aches and fatigue completely forgotten, they shed their packs and fell to work with machetes and raw muscle. After an hour of intense labor, they had the bulk of the blocks uncovered.

Out of breath, her fingers swollen and aching, Cordelia stumbled back to get some perspective and fell to her knees, staring at it in wonder.

It *was* an arch, just as she'd thought. It was squared slightly and the carved portion of the blocks was surrounded by smooth, plain stone that caused the carvings to stand out in relief. She struggled to her feet, staggered forward, and ripped off her gloves to join Yazkuz in exploring—adoring—the stones with her bare fingers.

"Look!" she called to Goodnight, glancing over her shoulder. He stood with his hands propped on his waist, grinning, just as pleased and awed as she was. "Here is the jaguar—and the trees—the flames shooting everywhere. And here is the great snake! Here are the birds and the animals—look—the crocodiles and monkeys!" She laughed, going over each block with her hands, at least as many as she could reach. "And the mountains on fire!"

Above that she had to just look in wonder, until she came to what should have been the keystone, the great, lifelike head of the jaguar. There, at the crown of the arch was an empty space where the cat guise of the Lord of Creation should have been. It was a terrible disappointment. She looked at the ground and all around, trying to see if it had fallen, but there was nothing around the entrance but a mound of small rubble and dirt that had become home to successive generations of plants and formed a hump at the entrance.

"The jaguar head isn't here," she said, stepping back, to stand by Goodnight, "but the rest is, and it's wonderful!" When she looked up, he was staring at her with a strange expression.

"Damn straight it *is* wonderful," he said, as he transferred his gaze to the arch. "You found it, O'Keefe. You found the bloody stones. Now you just have to figure out what they're doing here."

Yazkuz came back to stand with them and look at the arch. Her usually piercing eyes were misted and her mood could only be called melancholy.

"Yazkuz . . . girl . . . in old time." She pointed at herself, then at the arch and pointed from her eyes. "See this place. Old bruja take here." She struggled to find words. "To teach." Her revelations dissolved into Spanish and Mayan, and they had the feeling it was best to give her a moment.

Cordelia studied the stone arch, then turned and looked at him.

"It's an entrance." She took a deep breath. "I think it's time we found out where it leads."

They lighted a lantern, stepped over the dirt mounded in the entrance, and entered the darkness beyond. The walls on either side of the entrance broadened quickly into a rough, irregularly shaped chamber. Other than a maze of spiderwebs, a couple of abandoned nests, and a few scattered animal bones, the place was empty. The main chamber branched into what seemed to be passages, but on further examination, they turned out to be dead ends. At its farthest point, the cave was littered with rocks that had rolled from a ceiling-to-floor pile against the back wall. It looked like the roof of the place had partially collapsed. It would take a crew of men hours—days—to remove the debris. And even then, they might find only another dead end.

"So what was this? A storehouse? Did they bring treasure here?" Cordelia looked to Goodnight, then Yazkuz. "Surely there was more here at one time."

"When you were here as a girl . . . when the old bruja brought you here," Goodnight asked the old woman, "what was here?" He repeated it, gesturing around them, but it was clear to them that Yazkuz was as bewildered as they were.

"Do you think she doesn't remember? Or was she not allowed to see?"

He studied old Yazkuz, then shrugged.

"I have no idea."

The old woman looked around her, rubbed her chin, and made a magic sign, before barreling past them and climbing out into the canyon again. When they reached the outside, she was forging into the deepening gloom of the canyon floor, searching through the vegetation for something.

"What is she doing?" Cordelia asked.

"No bloody clue," he muttered. Then he looked up at the darkening sky overhead. "But I think it's time we decided on a place to camp."

That same evening, Hedda stood in the doorway of the village pavilion, watching Arturo gesturing as he delivered the final line of what seemed to be a joke. The men around him roared with laughter and refilled his glass. She clutched her notebooks tighter as he downed the native liquor with a flourish.

Valiente spotted her and his ruddy face sobered. Grabbing his hat, he bowed flamboyantly to his newfound friends and strode out the door to join her.

"I thought we were going to record stories this afternoon," she said, shading her eyes against the lowering sun.

"I was detained by those fine fellows." He forced a grin of male bravado. "They also have great stories."

"And even better liquor," she said, frowning at the smell. Since Cordie and Goodnight left without him, he had been moody and irritable, not at all the man who had charmed her into believing her heart could bloom again, at her age.

"They go together—the drink and the stories," he said, the genial threads of his persona fraying under the chafe of her disapproval.

"I thought you would remember our appointment." She collected herself, knowing what had to be said and knowing also that she took a risk in saying it. "Arturo, I know you are still angry that they would not take you."

"Angry?" He gave a bitter laugh. "To have come so far, to have given so much . . . and to be told you are not worthy to learn the secrets of this place . . . how would you feel? It is intolerable. An insult. An injustice."

Part of her heart agreed and, knowing him to be a proud and capable man, she felt outraged for him. She reached out, hesitated, and drew her hand back.

"She should never have gone without me," he ground out, starting to walk.

"She had no choice, Arturo. It was the old woman who insisted on taking just the two of them. She had to go or risk having the entire expedition fail."

"He is not an archaeologist—not even a scholar. *Madre Dios*—he is a servant! He shines shoes and presses trousers for a living!"

"What's done is done, Arturo. But all isn't lost. You may still have a chance to see and explore whatever ruins there are. The last chapter hasn't been written yet. When they return—"

An explosive crack split the air, startling them, and they both looked toward the center of the village.

"Was that a gunshot?" she said.

"I have seen no guns here." The professor was yanked from his troubled thoughts. He took her hand and ran with her toward the center of the village.

A crowd had gathered in the main square, but as they approached, the throng began to retreat in alarm, pulling back to reveal a party of eight or so men, equipped with pack burros and horses, in the middle of the square. Most wore khaki military-style clothing mixed with nonuniform hats, boots, and bandanas. But one man, the only one still astride a horse, was dressed in incongruous white and wore a pristine Panama hat.

"They must be here!" Alejandro Castille's dusky face reddened as he barked at the village elders, who had been dragged to the center of the square and were being held by men with military-style rifles. "I give you a chance to cooperate and to save yourselves much pain. I know they came this way—the yanqui woman O'Keefe and her party."

One of his men spotted the professor and Hedda and called, "There they are!" Castille turned in his saddle and his eyes narrowed as he spotted them.

"Well, well," he said with a laugh. "There you are." He urged his horse toward them, stopping a few feet away. "It took longer than we expected to get here." He took in the arm the professor had clasped around Hedda and smiled as he swung down from his horse.

"I must thank you, compadre, for leaving us so visible a trail." He tapped Valiente on the shoulder with his riding crop. "Without your help we might never have found you."

The professor reddened and glanced at Hedda, seeming at a loss.

"Arturo?" Her gaze asked him to deny Castille's implication that he had aided the Spaniard's efforts to find them. When he didn't, she was devastated.

"Goodness me." He produced a mocking pout as he

read both Hedda's unspoken question and the professor's grim lack of reply. "She did not suspect our arrangement. Poor thing. Apparently your magic actually worked on one of the O'Keefes." His voice and face hardened. "Now, where is the other one?"

"I swear to you, Hedda, I did nothing to help him find us," Arturo said.

"No notes, no handkerchiefs tied on poles, true." Castille gave an affected sniff. "Rather neglectful of you. I was starting to think you had forgotten us. Where *is* she?"

"Don Alejandro!" one of the hardbitten mercenaries with Castille came running up. "We found their camp. We're searching it now."

Hedda evaded the professor's grasp and went running toward their camp. By the time she reached it, Castille's men had already demolished one tent and were scattering their belongings from pillar to post. To one side, more men were holding Itza and Ruz, who had tried to defend the camp and bore bloodied faces to attest to the fact. She tried to go to them, but was caught and held by the burly Yago. The professor arrived then and seemed shocked by the destruction.

"Well?" Castille demanded of Yago as he strode up.

"Nothing except for a crate of guns. No trace of any scrolls." The henchman shook Hedda hard to quiet her. She bit her lip to keep from crying out and the professor roared at him to release her.

Castille stepped in front of the professor and slammed him across the face with a riding crop, drawing blood.

"I won't ask again," Castille said icily. "Where is she?"

"Gone!" The professor doubled over, holding his face and searching blindly for a handkerchief to absorb the blood. "She's gone. The old medicine woman took her and the butler to find the stones."

"Where?"

"She wouldn't say. She wouldn't take us—just O'Keefe and Goodnight."

Castille cast an eye over the wreckage of the camp.

"Take the guns," he ordered Yago. "Who are they?" He pointed his crop at them.

"Guides." The professor dabbed at his face. "From Tecolutla."

"The ones we heard about." Castille settled back into his cold, calculating mein. "If they're so good, then they should be able to help us find her quickly."

"You'll never find them," Hedda protested, and he looked at her.

"Don't be tiresome, my dear. Of course I will. And I'll claim the jaguar's great treasure. Is that not right, professor?" He watched Hedda's expression change and saw her look at Arturo in disbelief. He smirked at the professor. "You naughty boy. You didn't tell her about that either, did you? Well, no matter. You can make it up to her—if you must—with *your* share of the gold."

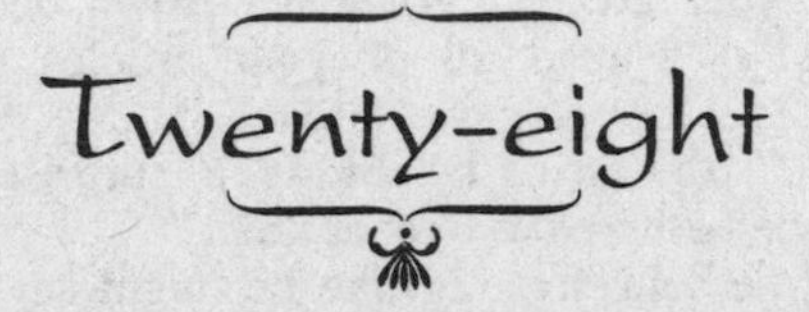

Twenty-eight

Cordelia was shaken awake the next morning by Yazkuz, who rattled on excitedly in a slurry of languages that made no sense to her or Goodnight.

They had camped in the cave last night, foregoing a fire, and when they drifted to sleep the old girl was still sitting, facing the collapsed far wall of the place, chanting and waving the smoking bundle of herbs she had collected earlier. It was a vigil of some sort, they surmised: an attempt to connect with the Jaguar Spirit for some help. And though they wanted to show respect for the old girl's efforts, they were both too exhausted to keep up with her.

They sat together earlier munching on jerky and the very last of the tortillas they had brought, sipping water from the spring outside and listening to Yazkuz's droning.

"She's in a trance of some kind," Cordelia said, glancing around the corner at the old woman's rail-straight back and uplifted face. "I've seen it before. In Morocco. They have some men there who put themselves into a state and then lie down on a bed of nails." When Goodnight looked askance at her, she raised a hand. "I swear. Saw it with my own two eyes. Ask Hedda."

"That wasn't in your article on Morocco," he said.

"They made me cut it out. 'Too disturbing for our women readers,' they said." She frowned. "How do you know what I wrote about Morocco?"

"I read your article." When her frown deepened, he looked away. "I read all of your articles from—you know—that folder you gave Hardacre."

"Really?" She raised her brows in surprise. "I didn't think anyone bothered to look at them."

"I did," he said, looking like he might say more, but then changed direction. "So, what happens if we can't find out the 'secret' to this place?"

"That will be a problem." She sighed. "I'll just have to take the news back to Samuel P. and hold his feet to the fire about my Africa funding."

"More adventuring, eh?"

"Undoubtedly."

"Is that what you truly want?" he said, his voice oddly resonant.

"Of course." She tried to stuff conviction into her voice.

"You'd never consider other options? I mean, can you imagine yourself riding camels through the Sahara at eighty? Packing gun on one hip and an ear trumpet on the other? Adding a few prunes to the couscous you cook over a dung fire?" She clamped a hand over her mouth to contain her laugh.

"You really did read the articles, didn't you."

"When you're eighty, Hedda will be a hundred and two. Think about it."

"Poor Hedda," her grin faded. "Surely she'll have better things to do."

"Maybe you will, too."

She shook her head, feeling strangely emotional, fastening her gaze on their lone lantern. "What about you? What will you do when you go back?"

"I've found a few species worth investigating. And Yazzie, there, has put me onto some things. I'll get back to working on medicines, sooner or later."

"That's what you truly want?" she asked.

"Absolutely," he said briskly. Firmly. "Nothing I want more."

Silence fell at the end of that pronouncement.

She bit her lip inside. Hard. It was a minute before she could respond.

"Then I hope you get it, Goodnight. I hope you get your true desire—your medicines and all the success and acclaim that should go with them." She drained the water in her cup, but it was a minute before she could actually swallow it. "We'd better get some sleep. I have a feeling tomorrow will come early."

She lay in her blankets, her head propped on a roll of clothes from her pack and listened for his breathing, trying to make the ache in the middle of her chest go away. And she fell asleep listening to Yazkuz's drone and Goodnight's gentle snore.

"Up! Up!" Yazkuz now ripped the blankets back and yanked both of them up to sitting positions. Then she sank to her knees by Goodnight and gave him a smack on the cheek to wake him up and get his attention. "Handsome—listen me. Jaguar Spirit . . . he speaks . . . tells me a way. Come!"

"A way where?" Cordelia rubbed her eyes and reached for her boots.

Minutes later, Cordelia and Goodnight were standing in one of the dead-end passages, staring at what looked like a wide crack in the dark stone that extended from the wall up through the side of the ceiling.

"There!" Yazkuz pointed, grinning, then mimed climbing a ladder. "Up!"

"It's a crack in the stone," Goodnight said, trying to contain his disbelief. He measured it with his hands and turned to her. "It's this big. We'll never fit."

She turned him sideways, measured with her hands and held it up to his body. There were at least two inches on either side, unless he took a deep breath. She turned to Cordelia and dragged her to the crack, pointing up.

"You." The old woman nodded fiercely and gave her a little shove. "Jaguar say . . . go here . . . this way."

Frowning, Cordelia slid sideways into the crack and looked up. It was gray and murky up there, nothing like light or an end to the opening. But then it wasn't black either, like a pure cave would be.

"Give me a boost," she said to Goodnight. "I'll take a look."

"This is the most idiotic . . ." He started to take her by the waist but she slid into the crack and asked him to stick his knee out for her to step on. He understood and gave her his knee and then helped pull her to a standing position on it, above him. She felt around on the cold smooth rock and found a small ledge—about an inch and a half wide. Using it she released Goodnight's hand and pulled herself up so that her feet left his leg.

"Hey! What are you—" She was hanging by her hands, feeling along the rockface for a place for her feet. And there it was—an inch, no more. But it was enough.

"If this continues all the way up maybe we can climb this," she called, boosting herself up with great effort to feel for another handhold. And there it was. Slightly less room this time, but still usable. She called for a lantern and as she clung to the sheer rock face, feet spread like a ballet dancer in first position on a narrow rim of stone, she told herself it would be a miracle if she could hold on even until he got back.

But she did hold on. And when he managed to pass her the lantern and she looked up, she saw that the split widened slightly above her and there seemed to be cracks and possible handholds and footholds up as far as she could see. And it was still gray in the distance.

"I think we should try it," she called. "But first, ask her what is up here. I want to know what I'm climbing toward."

There were several escalating exchanges before he got back to her.

"She says it's a throne. The Jaguar's throne," he called.

"Here—take this!" she said, sliding the lantern onto the

toe of her boot and lowering it. "Get your gloves and bring me mine—this rock is sharp. And bring all the rope we brought!"

Thus began a tedious climb that she regretted a dozen times over the next hour. As soon as she was up far enough, Goodnight entered the crack and began to climb, but his long legs and big feet weren't nearly as flexible and didn't fit the hand- and footholds she had located. He found himself spread eagle against the stone face with his legs turned to the sides. It was a hideously unnatural posture for an Englishman, he declared, and he was going to kick her posterior for hauling him into this madness—as soon as they were on something horizontal and stable and as soon as he could get his knees and feet to face the front again.

The tension and the strength required to both cling to the rock face and change positions soon had her muscles screaming and her fingers throbbing inside her gloves. She kept asking Goodnight how he was doing and his irritable snarls and complaints were her only connection with reality in that otherworldly darkness. Occasionally her hands slipped, but she was always able to catch herself by planting her feet and throwing her back against the wall behind her. That was how, in fact, she discovered a resting position that allowed her to take a break and let Goodnight catch up.

"How far do you think we've come?" she asked. His voice in the dark was comforting.

"We could calculate it. Let's see—it takes two minutes to go three feet . . . we've been doing this for twelve hours now . . . we should be halfway to China."

"Sorry," she said, "China's the other way. We're climbing *up*."

Several hundred feet? A thousand? Two thousand? How tall was the mountain above the canyon? They *couldn't* be climbing farther than that.

"I just hope when we get up there we have enough rope

to haul Yazkuz up, too," she said grimly, and heard him groan.

"She weighs a bloody ton."

"On the bright side—aren't you glad I made you bring goatskin breeches?"

"Yeah, you were spot on with that, O'Keefe. If you'd only told me to bring a goatskin *shirt* as well."

They began to climb again and conditions soon deteriorated.

"Goodnight." Her voice developed a tremor. "We've got trouble."

"What?" She could almost feel him go still beneath her.

"Water. These rocks—they're wet." She forced herself to breathe deliberately, trying to keep her heart from racing. "They're getting slippery."

"Shit."

"That's all you have to say?"

"It's a perfectly good Anglo-Saxon expletive. My *mother* said 'shit.' And there wasn't a woman born who was more proper than my mother. This is a situation that positively cries out for a good, old-fashioned—"

"Aghhhhh!" Her hand slipped, her boot slipped, and she fell back against the back wall with a scream and slid some way before she hit something solid.

It took a moment for her to reorient and realize that the thing that had stopped her fall was him. And she'd driven him against the wall like a pneumatic hammer. It was a minute before she could inhale, much less speak.

"Are you all right?" she finally managed to get out.

"Peachy. Just peachy." He was gritting his teeth. "If you'll just take your elbow out of my ribs, I might be able to breath again someday."

She was able to find footing and brace against the back wall with her legs out in front of her—sitting on air. Her muscles were on fire. Her fingers felt mushy inside her wet gloves.

"I don't know how much more of this I can do," she said quietly.

Out of the dark came a wicked chuckle.

"What's the alternative? Four hundred, six hundred feet straight down?"

"Shit," she said, squeezing her eyes shut, trying hard not to visualize that.

"Damn, O'Keefe. You're starting to sound just like dear old Mum."

Slippery rocks or not, they had to go on. She was able to right herself and find another handhold. Despite the fact that her muscles felt like jelly, she managed to climb, being more careful in her use of handholds, working to make her wet gloves grip more tightly. The water seemed to be flowing more readily down the rock, and a bit sideways, which meant, they seemed to be turning—which made no sense at all.

She started to say something about it, but the rock she'd grabbed as a handhold suddenly broke loose, she let out a cry, and a blast of rock and water came pouring down from the rock face above—all in the same moment. She heard the rock hitting the back wall and Goodnight shouting, but the roar of the water pouring down on her made it impossible to make out what he said. The water flooding down was pushing her, forcing her back and down—battering her.

She had to tuck her chin in the gravity-fed torrent to get space to breathe. Then with an instinct for survival inscribed in her very muscle and sinew, she began to pull herself up, straining, fighting for every inch of vertical gain. She groped blindly for holds, gasping for air, and just when she thought she could go no farther, her fingers touched a niche—a substantial one. Then another. And another. Step by torturous step, she hauled herself up into that raging downpour until she was even with it—and finally her head was above it. She sucked in air—real air—and felt like yelling in triumph. But there was more to go before she would be out of the water. And there was still Goodnight to get past that waterfall.

"I'm all right," she called down. "I pulled a rock loose

and there's lots of water, but if you keep your head down, there are good holds. Be careful!"

She looked up and suddenly the gray wasn't so dark.

"Hey! It's getting lighter! I think we're near the top!"

Forcing herself to be more careful, now that she was woozy with fatigue and racing toward what seemed like the finish, she found climbing holds in the last few feet and finally threw her arm over the edge of the rock face, onto a horizontal surface. She could scarcely believe it. It was a minute before she could pull herself up, swing her leg over, and roll out onto the rough rock.

Then she thought of Goodnight fighting his way through the water and flopped over onto her belly to stick her head over the edge and call encouragement to him. At first all she heard was water falling a great distance. Then she heard him coughing and muttering and closed her eyes in a prayer of thanks.

"Up here! We're here!"

"Where's here?" he called back.

She glanced around for the first time and realized she was in a cavern.

"Well, it's not exactly a throne room."

It wasn't long before he threw an arm across the edge of the rock face and dragged himself out onto the level surface. They lay for some time, half conscious, grateful just to be breathing. Then she sat up and pulled the ropes from his waist and hers and began to connect them. It looked like a pitifully short piece of rope, considering how long they'd been climbing.

They looked over the edge into the abyss and called out to Yazkuz. There was no answer. Having no idea how far they'd come, they tied the joined rope around Goodnight's waist and tossed the free end into the dark well. To their surprise, they soon felt a tug and had to brace against some rocks and fight for every inch to raise her. A small eternity later, she was climbing out onto the surface with them, perfectly dry and looking as fresh as if she'd just awakened from a nap.

"See?" She tapped her temple with a canny look. "Jaguar Spirit knows."

Cordelia looked at Goodnight, bewildered.

"Maybe she really is a witch," she muttered as they watched Yazkuz dust herself off and look around.

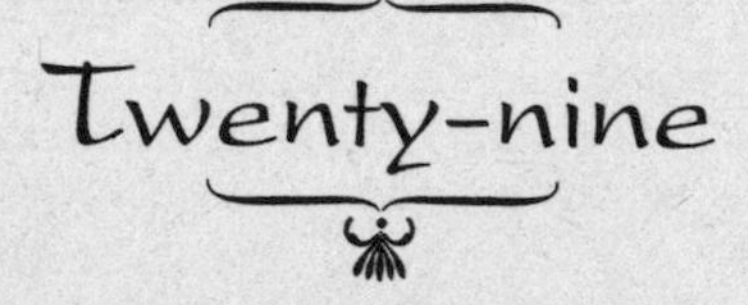

Twenty-nine

The cavern they were in contained a large depression filled by a spring, probably the source of the water they'd encountered. Yazkuz spotted a haze of light above and headed for it, beckoning them to follow. The closer they came to the opening, the brighter the light grew and the more they squinted.

They stepped out into the dazzling bright sun like unearthed moles, squinting and shielding their eyes—then disbelieving everything they saw.

They were in a massive natural bowl formation with gray stone walls that rose to blue sky with no hint of mountains or anything beyond. It was huge, a quarter of a mile across—half filled by a clear, pristine lake and half with a tropical paradise filled with lush vegetation. In the middle of that startling environment sat a radiantly white, perfectly preserved smooth-sided pyramid. An ancient Mayan pyramid.

They stumbled forward, mouths open.

"What is this place?" Cordelia asked, not really expecting a reply.

"Jaguar throne," Yazkuz declared with uncharacteristic reverence.

As they left the cavern that was part of the rim of the caldera—for that was surely what this was, she said, and Goodnight agreed, an extinct volcanic crater—they stepped from stone onto soil and into a veritable garden of paradise. All around were flowering plants like hibiscus and trumpet flower and heliotrope in full bloom, huge ferns, fruit trees, coconut palms, and tall, stately firs. The air was sweet with the fragrance of jasmine laced with a hint of cocoa. Birds were singing and there were butterflies everywhere.

As they reached the beach that divided the water half from the land half of the caldera, their attention shifted to the pearl in the center of this exotic setting, the temple. It was then they noticed: in front of the pyramid sat a large statue of a jaguar. It was astonishingly lifelike, especially its golden eyes. When Goodnight reached it, Cordelia was able to compare it to him and estimate its height at eight feet.

"It truly is the throne of the Jaguar Spirit," she said, running her hands over the statue and looking around at the remarkable environment here. She turned to Yazkuz. "Did you know this was here? Have you seen this before?"

"Only in vision," the old woman said, looking around with awe.

"This is the most amazing thing . . . I've ever . . . seen," Goodnight said, finding for once that words were inadequate to the task of expression. So he did the one thing that joy and relief had left to him—he picked Yazkuz up and whirled her around, laughing. Then he set her down and went for Cordelia, who threw her arms around him and laughed with him, savoring the hard-won triumph of their arrival and discovery.

Afterward Cordelia was dizzy and had to sit for a while. Then she realized she hadn't had food for quite a while and mentioned that fact. Old Yazkuz pointed to the forest around the temple and instructed her to go, eat. Surprised, she collected herself and did just that. Food was everywhere. Bananas, coconuts, pineapples, dates, almonds . . . she pulled off a banana leaf and filled it with fruit to carry back to the temple to share with Goodnight, who was sprawled on the steps, letting his clothes dry. It was then that she noticed the back of his shirt was almost shredded and the flesh beneath it wasn't much better. He was scratched and bleeding—the climb had been harder on him than she had realized. That, and her fall against him.

She wetted her bandana in the lake and washed his scrapes, then asked what she might find to help them. He suggested aloe vera and told her how to locate it. Yazkuz went with her to find it and soon they came back with several big, fleshy spikes to peel and rub onto his cuts. He doctored Cordelia's scrapes in turn, and they ate and rested in the shadow of the big jaguar while Yazkuz went off to explore.

Some time later, the old woman appeared at the top of the pyramid and urgently called them to come up and join her. Mounting the steps was something of an ordeal, considering their overworked muscles, but they managed to make it to the top. Yazkuz hurried them inside, beside herself with excitement, and showed them fabulous writing and murals on the walls. It was a marvelous and humbling moment as they stood in that chamber of the ancients, reading secrets from the very dawn of life. Yazkuz bowed reverently to the statue of the jaguar in the temple above, and with the Jaguar's permission, began to tell them the story recorded on those walls.

The first tableau was somewhat familiar. It contained many of the same images used on the blocks of the arch: the fire of creation, the Creator's splendid world, the development of plants and flowers and grains and fruit, then the birth of animals of every kind. Then came the great snake and the birth of humankind. But there, the story diverged. In this version, humans were much loved by the Creator, who walked with them in the guise of the jaguar. Then great trouble came into the world: an illness in the form of a dark cloud laid low humanity and nearly destroyed it.

The Creator, in his jaguar skin, brought something to humanity that caused healing, something that had to do with a series of strange little scarab-like ovals and what looked like earthworms. Suddenly there were butterflies everywhere on the walls, golden, heralding the healing that took place and would forever change the nature of humankind.

The Gift of the Jaguar, Yazkuz told them with tears welling, was *healing.*

Cordelia sat down on the polished floor of the temple with a soft thud and stared in awe at the magnificent mural spread before them, feeling there were linkages to be made, that something profound was waiting just out of mental reach. *Healing* was the Gift of the Jaguar. Healing in that specific instance or healing in general? And was it a coincidence that Goodnight—a doctor-cum-chemist seeking real and provable cures—was with her to discover this?

Humans, from that time on, have had the capacity to heal and to grow beyond their illness and distress, Yazkuz said—at least Cordelia thought it was she who said it. How the old woman found the English words for it, Cordelia had no clue, but the words were there in her head. She was suddenly aware of Goodnight sitting cross-legged on the floor beside her, and glanced over at him to find him as spellbound as she was by the sound of the old girl's voice.

"All healing comes from the Creator . . . who walks the earth as a jaguar from time to time and speaks to lowly servants who do work in his name. This is why I have brought the tall healer here to this place. The Jaguar Spirit told me of his coming long ago, in the sacred bones. So, when I saw him and learned of his interest in healing, I knew he was the one. But the jaguar himself said to bring the woman also . . . she must be here . . . she must learn of the great gift of the Jaguar Spirit, too.

"Now the tall healer must carry the remembrance of the Jaguar's gift with him back to the world."

There old Yazkuz halted and stood quietly, her hands folded, staring off across the temple and out into the paradise blue sky. They waited for her to continue, but it soon became clear that her revelations were finished.

"How?" Cordelia managed to ask. "How does he do that? Carry healing back to the people and remind them of who gave them that gift?"

Yazkuz didn't answer, or even blink. She was as still as the carved alabaster statue of the jaguar nearby. When Goodnight shook off the spell of those words, he checked the old woman and found her nearly as cold as the alabaster, too. With Cordelia's help he carried her into the sun and rubbed her hands and shoulders to restore circulation to them. Yazkuz revived but was, unfortunately, back to her monosyllabic English vocabulary, which sent a shiver through Cordelia. How was she speaking so fluently earlier?

"How? How does he take this gift of healing back to the world?" she asked again. But Yazkuz just shrugged in bewilderment.

After a few minutes in the warming sun, the old woman raised a finger, then tapped her temple with it. "I ask." She turned to Goodnight and grabbed his sleeve. "Fire." She pointed to the pit in front of the jaguar statue.

"Wood. Bring."

It wasn't long before Yazkuz had her ceremonial fire going and knelt before it, staring into the flames and chanting solemnly. She would keep a vigil there until she received an answer to Cordelia and Goodnight's question.

With nothing more to do there, the pair withdrew to look around the temple and explore it further. Because of their experience in the ruins that were hills with doors, they checked the floor for loose stones and found one. Levering it aside, they discovered a set of narrow steps that led down into the pyramid.

Wishing desperately for the lantern they had left behind, they discovered a few discarded items in a passage, one of which was a dish lamp. Another was a small store of what looked like charcoal. Hart sprinted back up the steps and came back after a time with some banana peels to rub on the pieces of charcoal. One of the few matches he had on his person in a waxed paper packet started the flame that ignited the charcoal. With their meager light, they went exploring.

The second chamber they discovered, in the heart of the pyramid, was a simple, windowless little room furnished solely with a gilded altar. Strangely, floor and altar were both littered with desiccated butterflies. They stepped carefully around the creatures to look at the figures on the walls. The same mysterious symbols appeared: the worms and scarab-like ovals they had seen in the hills-with-doors ruins, the village, and just now in the temple above.

Their light was failing when Goodnight spotted a slight variation in the drawings, something from an artist in tune with realism. Just before the charcoal fizzled to a smoking lump, he saw that the worm of the murals had both segments and antennae. Frantically, they put together another light, and sure enough, they discovered the worm was in fact, no worm at all.

"It's a caterpillar," he said, tracing the clear image on the wall. The knowledge caused a chain of linkages in his mind. "Look. The ovals—they're eggs. The worms are caterpillars and the scarab things—they're pupae. That's the four stages of the metamorphosis! It's butterflies!" He chortled and tripped like a Morris dancer through the butterfly wings all over the floor, his arms outstretched to embrace the butterflies who had ended their brief lives here. "It's so obvious now—the Gift of the Jaguar is butterflies!"

"I thought it was healing," she said, confused.

He deflated like a hot air balloon. "Well, butterflies have something to do with it—they have to." He waved a hand around him. "They're everywhere."

They rushed up the steps to the temple to consult with Yazkuz, but found her deep in meditation and, after discussing their discovery, agreed not to disturb her. Instead, they headed down the pyramid and out into the magnificent gardens surrounding the temple to look for specimens like those in the altar chamber.

The gardens were a wonderland of botanical marvels. Every vine, bush, herb, and small tree seemed to be in flower. Orchids climbed the trunks of trees and nestled in the forks of branches, in colors that existed only in the yearning minds of artists and creators. And everywhere they looked and stepped, there were butterflies—remarkably tame ones, at that. They counted at least a dozen different kinds, but the most prevalent were the great golden butterflies with the black borders.

"Monarchs." Goodnight identified them. "The ones shown in the murals."

They explored the lush gardens, watching the butterflies feeding on the flowers and then soaring in groups, shimmering and dancing on the air before swooping back to earth.

"But what does this mean?" she asked as they picked flowers and held them up, watching in wonder as the butterflies came to land on the petals and show off their exquisite wings. "I mean, do butterflies make a medicine?"

"It doesn't seem likely. Surely we would have heard about it by this time in human history. Have a headache? Take two monarchs and have a lie down."

She laughed and looked up at him in the warm, dappled light coming through the high canopy. His hair was tousled and his tanned face was relaxed and—*oh, dammit, just say it*—it was noble. And beautiful. And it tugged at her chest and made her knees go weak, because she knew, in her heart of hearts, that what you saw on the outside of Hartford Goodnight was exactly what you got on the inside. He *was* noble. And smart and handsome. Capable and reliable. Idealistic and proud. And strong—so very strong.

But most important, he made her feel alive and full of possibility and warm and feminine—like the only woman on the planet.

And she knew in that moment that he was the man she would love and carry in her heart for the rest of her life. It was a moment of sublime pleasure and deferred pain, inextricably linked.

They explored what they could reach of that crater-bound island, smelling, tasting, luxuriating in the garden's glorious echoes of Eden.

The sun was hanging on the rim of the caldera when they returned to the pyramid to check on Yazkuz. They took her some wood, tended her fire, and set a banana leaf piled with fruit beside her. Withdrawing, they stood on the top steps of the pyramid to survey the area and absorb the sight into their hearts. Cordelia focused on the lake and began to descend the long flight of steps, feeling drawn to an awareness, an insight that she couldn't yet put into words. Something about the lake puzzled her. By the time she reached the statue of the great jaguar, she had figured it out.

"What does that look like to you?" she asked Goodnight when he reached the bottom. She pointed to a wide stone platform that had been built out ten feet into the lake, directly in front of the jaguar. "Does that look like a dock?" She studied it, even as he did, tilting her head. "Why would they have a dock when there are no boats here? I can't imagine they hauled boats in for ceremonial purposes, then carried them out again. Why is it here?"

He agreed it was a good question and together they walked out onto the dock-like platform, staring down into the exceptionally clear water. Illuminated by the lowering sun, something on the bottom glinted, drawing Goodnight's attention.

"There's something—there—reflecting light. Do you see it?" He pointed and she looked and nodded. It only took a moment for him to decide to investigate and begin stripping off his shirt.

"What are you doing? You can't go in there," she said. "You hate water."

"I don't hate *water*, I hate boats. More accurately, seasickness. You'll recall, I can swim when I have to."

"You've got a snakebite sore on your arm and a back that looks like raw tenderloin. Let me do it," she said unbuttoning her shirt. "I'm a great swimmer."

"Really, O'Keefe." He watched her sit down and pull

off her boots, and his eyes popped when she stood up and unbuttoned her goatskin pants. "Honest to God—do you have a single drop of modesty in your body?"

"Don't be such an old woman, Goodnight," she chided. "Turn your back if you can't bear to see a few inches of naked skin."

Her shirt joined her breeches and boots on the quay. She poised at the edge, in her knickers and camisole, noting that he hadn't turned away. "Bet it's beastly cold." She took a deep breath, raised her arms, and sprang for the water, just as he complained.

"You just had to say the word 'naked' didn't you?"

Thirty

Down she sank, pulling herself steadily deeper in the cool water, surprised by the depth . . . a dozen feet . . . fifteen . . . at least twenty before she reached the silty bottom. She caught the fading glint and reached for the object, not really surprised to feel cool metal in her hand as she headed for the surface. She deposited the thing on the quay. It looked like a bracelet or cuff of some kind—made of *gold*.

She gasped, wiping water from her eyes.

"Is this what I think it is?"

"Ye gods." He sank to his knees and reached for the bracelet, turning it over in his hands, then giving it a test with his teeth. "It is gold." He looked past her toward the lake. "Is there more down there?"

A second later, she took a huge breath, executed a surface dive, and headed for the bottom again. This time she felt around and came up with three things that felt metallic before swimming back to the surface. She plopped them on the stone pier, then dipped her head back to clear her hair from her face and wiped her eyes before looking to see what she'd retrieved.

Goodnight was holding a cup and what seemed to be a circlet meant to be worn on the head or around the neck. Beside him on the quay was a flat disk decorated with a rendering of the sun.

"O'Keefe." He sounded a little strained. "I'm developing a theory."

"They're gold, too?" But she could see they were, despite some crusting and a bit of tarnish.

"I think this may be where they made their gifts to the Jaguar Spirit."

"Wait," she said, taking a breath and diving down to the bottom for a third time. Her two previous trips had stirred up silt that hadn't yet settled, and it wasn't as easy to find the bottom through that murkiness. Collecting what she could by touch, she shot to the surface with an armful of artifacts.

"These are—they're magnificent!" He laughed and held them up to the light. "Do you have any idea how long these must have lain there? Centuries at least—maybe millennia." Then he looked at her and realized she was pale and starting to shiver. "Okay, O'Keefe. Out of the water."

He reached her a hand and the moment she cleared the water and boosted herself onto the dock, he wished he'd left well enough alone. Her thin cotton was plastered to her body in ways that made her seem more naked than if she were naked. He reddened and shot to his feet.

"Gold!" she said, grinning broadly and glancing out over the lake. "There must be a ton of it down there, jewelry and gold plate, ornaments of all kinds." She scrambled to her feet beside him, trying on the cuff and reaching up to plop the coronet on his head. The startled look on his face caused her to laugh.

"A treasure! We found a real treasure!" Laughing, she threw both arms around him and bounced up and down.

He groaned the way he had when she and Yazkuz put aloe on his back.

"Ohhh!" Appalled by the pain her enthusiasm inflicted, she pulled back. "I'm so sorry. Did I hurt you?"

She took a step back, felt the air on her wet body, and shivered. Massively. Gooseflesh appeared on her arms, and her nipples drew taut and tingled, reminding her they were exposed and very, very sensitive.

Every nerve in her body suddenly came alive. Every desire in her body and mind and heart rushed to seize the moment.

She looked up into his gaze, knowing he wasn't immune to the sight of her, remembering the heat of his kiss and needing that warmth just now.

She took back the step she had put between.

"I'm freezing." Her voice was husky with need and promise. "Warm me."

There it was. As simple and eloquent a plea as had ever been spoken. Warmth. What she had wanted and needed all her life.

With a sound that was part groan and part laughter, he wrapped his arms around her cool, damp body and pulled her hard against him. She rocked up onto her toes to meet his kiss and felt as if she were soaring.

An explosion of warmth sent sparks all through her, igniting fires.

When he paused to cup her face between his hands and kiss her eyelids, nose, and mouth, she took his arms and wrapped them back around her.

"Here," she said against his lips.

"Here?"

"Now."

"Now? B-but—"

"Don't make me have to think, Goodbody," she said with a moan.

He seemed to get it.

"Oh. Right. No thinking. Good idea. Brains in the way and all tha—"

She absorbed the rest with her kiss and molded herself to him like a second skin. She wanted every part of her in contact with every part of him. Because he was suddenly the source of all heat in the known universe. And light. And breath.

He covered her with his hands, rubbing, stroking, and warming. Then he began to move with her . . . back . . . around . . . down. She was against something hard and oddly neither horizontal or vertical. It was, in fact, a perfect forty-five degrees. She knew before she opened her eyes she was lying on the sun-warmed stone of the temple itself, her bare feet in the warm sand, being covered by his big warm body. Steam escaped her. A sigh of satisfaction. Warm at last.

His kisses drew her deeper and deeper into her own unexplored desires. By the time he drew back to remove his shirt she was beyond every limit she had ever observed in this part of her life and began to shed her own damp garments. With trembling hands she removed those last barriers and sought his touch to replace them.

Kisses, more kisses . . . long, open, wine-sweet explorations . . . her whole body responded, tightening, preparing. She parted her thighs and welcomed the pressure and heat of him against her, wanting whatever would come, laughing with delight as his explorations drifted to her breasts and pleasure vibrated through her very sinews, arousing and tantalizing her, revealing connections she had never known existed within her.

Then he kissed and nibbled his way across her shoulders, up her throat, and by the time he reached her mouth, she was open to him, completely, nothing held back. He began to join their bodies and groaned as she accepted him inch by delicious inch. When they were completely joined she felt him lift his weight from her and opened her eyes.

He was braced above her, his arms flexed, his face bronzed and eyes hot.

He was beautiful. Like a big jungle cat. Primal. Male.

She saw and felt him move inside her and made a sound she hadn't known herself capable of—somewhere between a sigh and a growl—then responded with a movement of her own that wrenched a similar sound from him. He slid out and thrust slowly forward again. She sucked a breath. He did it again, never taking his eyes from hers. She met his movement the third time and every time thereafter, riding escalating waves of pleasure that supplanted everything else in her consciousness.

This, this need . . . this pleasure . . . this was what she wanted . . . now . . . now . . .

"Now." She groaned as she surged through a barrier of sensation that shattered around and within her in the same instant, launching her into a wild, free fall of release. His arms were suddenly around her, his weight was driving her, causing her to crest that wave again and again before he joined her in that final surge of passion.

He held her against him afterward for a time, then slid to the side of her, resting back against the smooth white stone. Their location, their activity, and the possible consequences of same caused him to close his eyes for a moment.

"I hope the Jaguar Spirit has a sense of humor about these things," he said. "After all, it's his . . . place." He couldn't bring himself to use the word temple, not after what he'd just done, practically on the steps of it.

"I don't know," she said propping her head up and nestling her legs against his. "I think it's kind of appropriate. Kind of like a church wedding." She glanced down at herself. "Except I didn't get to wear white." She giggled. "I didn't wear anything."

He looked at her in amazement. His eyes widened.

"Don't tell me that was . . . you know . . . your . . . your *first*."

"Well, yes. It was, actually."

He looked incredulous. "But you're . . . you're so . . ."

"What? Nonretiring? Nonsqueamish? Nonspinsterish? For heaven's sake, Goodbody, they don't make you check your virginity at the door just because you travel a bit and boss men around effectively."

"I–I just assumed . . ." He shut his mouth before any of the thousand inappropriate things he was thinking made it out.

With her lips kiss-swollen, her chestnut hair tangled

around her, and her breasts soft and mounded just so, she was the most beautiful thing he was ever likely to see. He couldn't believe he'd just made wild, passionate love to her on the side of a pagan temple in the middle of an extinct volcano and she was smiling at him. Suddenly he came up with the perfect thing to say, something straight from his heart.

"Are you all right?"

"I believe I'm better than all right, Goodbody."

He laughed at the sly hint of pride in her expression. "That you are, O'Keefe. Much better."

She grinned, took him by the hand, and pulled him toward the water. It was beastly cold and she could only entice him in by the promise of plentiful heat afterward. They dried with their clothes, dressed, and looked for a place to sleep. The gardens were filled with soft golden light and the fragrance of night-blooming jasmine.

He found a soft, moss-covered spot and cut long, smooth palm branches to cover it, softening the layers with ferns.

"You're good at this, Goodnight. Where did you learn vegative bed building? Not from *her*, I take it."

"Who?" He looked up as he plumped and tested his construction.

"She who taught you that women are unreliable. Who was she? A fair weather friend? Fickle flirtation? Faithless fiancée?"

He paused for a moment, looked down, and she bit her lip. What made her bring that up now?

"Fiancée," he said, looking up at her with no defensiveness.

"What happened to her?"

"She married my brother."

"I'm sorry," she said and truly meant it, thinking of the hurt he'd endured.

"Interesting." He frowned. "I'm not. Not anymore. I haven't thought of her in ages."

"What happened?"

"It was a matter of chemistry, actually." He chuckled at his own double meaning. "She had it with my brother and not me. And when she learned I intended to spend my life and fortune pursuing tawdry 'industrial' ambitions, she chose to hold out for a different bond." He grinned, looking quite pleased with his turn of phrase.

She shook her head, not certain what to make of his mood.

"Should I be weaving placemats or making grass curtains or something?"

"Deflowered ten minutes and already she's got nesting instincts," he complained to a bug before he brushed it off a fern frond he was stuffing into a makeshift pillow. "We're going to sleep," he said to her, "not setting up housekeeping."

"We're really going to sleep?" she said looking wounded.

For her contribution to their bower, she gathered fragrant flowers and strew them on the bed. Then before his widening eyes, she put one in her hair and rubbed others into her skin, bathing in their nectar and his attention. When he joined her on their bed and began to kiss her from head to toe, she shivered and admitted she was ticklish sometimes, some places. Diligent to the core, he felt obliged to catalog every one of them, ending with her laughing and blushing and melting so that she could no longer tell what was her body, her sensation, and what was his.

Pleasing him seemed as natural as breathing. And when she found that sweet combination of position and pressure that drove her passion to completion, he held her as she found full pleasure, then joined her beyond the very bounds of sensation.

Later, they lay looking up at the stars, identifying constellations, arguing over which was the real Archer and getting distracted by a shooting star that she insisted they wish on. He wished aloud, which according to her defeated the purpose.

"Which is?" he said, now roundly confused.

"Mystery, of course," she said snuggling against his chest, wriggling her toes with satisfaction.

"Oh, well. That explains it. Don't need any more mystery, thank you. I'm a man living on a planet populated 50 percent by women. That's mystery enough for any sane man."

"Nobody will ever accuse you of being sane, Goodnight."

"Not after today, they won't. And it's Hart."

"What?"

"My name. After what we've just accomplished together, I think it appropriate you call me by my first name."

"Okay, Hart." It felt so strange she had to make a joke. "You can call me anything—as long as you call me yours."

Thirty-one

Hart awakened at daybreak in their leafy bower and found her gone. The pleasurable aches in his body were a testament to how they'd spent the night; he could only imagine how she must be feeling after such . . . exertions.

Rising and pulling on his breeches and boots, he strolled through the gardens looking for her, picking a perfect sprig of jasmine to put in her hair when he found her. The light was tinged with rose gold and as he emerged from the trees and felt the sun strike his body, his mood expanded. He felt wonderful, alive in a way he couldn't recall ever feeling. And he knew just who to blame.

As he came around the far side of the pyramid, headed for the dock and the front of the temple, he stopped dead, astonished by what he saw. Cordelia stood naked on the stone quay, her clothes in discarded pools by her feet, and circling around and above her were golden butterflies. Hundreds of them. No, *thousands.* Her expression was one of pleasure as she slowly raised her arms and turned, offering herself to them, inviting them—and they accepted. Slowly they began to light on her, beginning with her hair and settling slowly on her shoulders and down her arms, then wrapping gently down her body like a garment of fluttering gossamer. She stood perfectly still as they covered the rest of her—every square inch of her except, oddly enough, her face. She was for that moment, the most exquisitely dressed woman in all of history. Clothed by nature in that most rare and ephemeral of garments. She made a small noise and he realized it was a laugh. He made himself move, treading softly, so that he could glimpse her face.

It was glowing.

"You're all so beautiful," she murmured to the butterflies, bringing her arms forward so she could see them. Then she caught his movement and turned her head enough to smile at him. Her amber eyes shone like iridescent wings.

"They tickle," she said, biting her lip. "Their little feet and fluttery wings—they're tickling me."

He approached slowly, quietly, and whispered, "How did this happen?"

"I don't know. I just came down to bathe and they collected around me and started to—remember last night? I rubbed those flowers on my skin. Maybe they're drawn to the nectar."

He stood a few feet from her, his eyes suddenly misting, his insides melting, his chest aching in a way that felt frightening and pleasurable all at once.

"No," he said, barely able to get the words out, "it's you. They're drawn to you." He took a step closer. Then another, slowly, not wanting to frighten her living cloak. "And I know just how they feel."

She opened her hands to him and moved them to get the creatures to fly. Only those on her hands were displaced, and when he took her hands the butterflies relanded on their joined hands. Then, before his widening eyes, more landed on his arms.

Soon he was covered to his shoulders, and others arrived to cover his hair, his back, and his torso. They stopped where his breeches began, covering only his bare skin, but covering it entirely, just as they had hers.

"This is mad," he said hoarsely, staring in wonder at his fluttering coat. "I didn't rub any flowers on me."

"No." She gave a quiet laugh. "But you just spent hours rubbing *me* on you. Some of the scent must have transferred."

It was logical, he supposed, in a clinging-to-the-brink-of-sanity sort of way. But there was something in the feel of those little creatures, in the caress of their wings, in the startling intimacy of them all over his skin that defied all rational explanations. It was too extraordinary. And it was entirely too much of a coincidence that it was happening now and in this place, and after making love with her all night.

"Isn't it wonderful?" she said sliding her feet closer to him, looking into his eyes. "It's like a blessing from Nature. A kiss from the Creator. Just for us."

He had never wanted anything quite so much as he wanted to kiss her just then. She was right. Blessings from nature . . . jaguars giving gifts . . . temples in craters . . . treasures in lakes . . . healing in butterflies . . . nothing seemed impossible to him now.

His lips touched hers and for a moment, one splendid, shining moment, they were one with each other and with everything else in creation. It was a divine dispensation that would bond them more surely than vows or ink on musty parchment ever could.

Then almost as quickly as it was woven, that miraculous garment began to unwind. Head to toe, the butterflies slowly peeled away and took flight, joining in a shimmering cloud of gold above and around them.

His feeling of loss was assuaged only by her presence, by her body pressed fully against his, by her moist eyes lifted with his to that golden cloud hovering nearby as if reluctant to leave.

Then en mass the butterflies flew toward the highest point of the gardens.

Stumbling into her camisole, knickers, and breeches, Cordie took the hand Hart held out to her and together they hurried after that golden cloud, losing sight of it as they entered the garden. They halted on the path, scouring the trees and vines and flowers for a glimpse of their destination. Just as they were about to give up, the butterflies found them, and in smaller numbers, landed on their hair and bare arms and shoulders. They stared at each other, trying to make sense of it.

"They came back for us," she said, knowing how crazy it must sound.

"That must be some potent flower you chose for a perfume," he said with a half laugh. "We ought to find out which one it was and bottle—"

He froze, staring at her, his eyes darting over some mental image as he made connections. She was busy watching the butterflies lift from her hair and shoulders and take off again as a small cloud.

"You know, this may sound crazy," she said, "but I think they want us to follow—"

"Of course they do—they're *the* butterflies!" he said grabbing her hand and charging down the path with her.

"What do you mean? You really think they're leading us somewhere?"

They tracked the golden cloud through the herbs, vines, and thick understory. He picked her up to carry her when she couldn't stand the sharp stalks and plant rubble on her bare feet.

"Ohhh." She hung onto his shoulders, trying to help him bear her weight. "I'm sorry. I wish I'd stopped to put on my—"

"Look!" He pointed as the cloud swooped up to drape itself on a tree.

Suddenly, there they were. A small grove of enormously tall, stately firs at the rear of the crater gardens was covered with their butterflies. He carried her to the closest tree and let her slide down him as they both looked up.

"The butterflies aren't the healing power," he said excitedly, "but I think they point to it. They must be the pollinators for some—look!"

He pointed to the lower branches of the tree, which were still well above their heads. There were flame-red orchids growing on them. When they looked higher, they found the same orchid all over the tree—on all of the trees where the butterflies had congregated.

"That red orchid—maybe that's it!"

Before she could say anything to temper his enthusiasm, he was climbing. Holding himself precariously on the first branch, which was well off the ground, he stretched for the first red orchid he could reach. It turned out to be a fine specimen, delicate blood-red flowers with snowy centers, thick, glossy leaves, and a host of wrinkled white roots. He dropped back to the ground examining his prize, and brought it back to share with her.

She was busy thinking of the murals they'd seen and of the way the message of a healing power seemed to have gotten so lost over the centuries.

"Why would they go to such extremes to protect a flower?" she said.

"It does give one pause," he said, thinking as he examined the petals and the long feathery stamens inside. "If it wasn't intentional, perhaps the object of the story got lost in translation along the way. If it was intentional, the ancients must have thought this was a fairly potent cure, to create such a puzzle concerning its identity and location."

"You think it's unique to this place?"

"I have no way of knowing. But I don't recall seeing—" He frowned and pulled off one of the petals and popped it into his mouth.

"Hart!" She was appalled. "You just said that might be fairly potent. And you're just sticking it in your mouth?

"Come on." She took hold of his arm. "We'll take it back to Yazkuz." She looked up in dismay. "We forgot all about her. I hope she's all right."

"She's praying. What kind of trouble could she get into praying?" he said, breaking off a piece of one of the thick, glossy leaves to look at the sap. "I think I'll wait here. I want to collect another specimen or two. She should probably see these trees." He gestured to the trees, butterflies, and orchids in natural proximity. "She may know something about them."

"All right. But no sampling until we hear what Yazkuz has to say."

"I'll be right here," he said, lifting the bandage on his arm and dabbing the broken leaf under it on his snakebite.

"Stop that." She halted several feet away, with a strange prickle creeping up her spine. "No sampling."

"Right. I heard."

She was halfway to the pyramid when she came to the bower containing their bed of last night. The palm fronds were already starting to curl and the flowers were turning brown. The path was softer from there and she broke into a run. There was brief delay when she detoured to grab her boots from the quay and drag them on. She was only starting up the steps of the pyramid when she heard "¡Hola!" and looked up to find Yazkuz trudging down the steps.

"We found something—rather Hart did. Come with me!" She grabbed the old girl's arm and bustled her along toward the fir grove where Hart waited.

They moved as fast as the old woman could go, but it still took a few minutes to tramp through the heavy vegetation in that part of the gardens. Concern started to build in her the minute she saw Hart wasn't there to meet them. Thinking, hoping he had climbed a tree for more specimens, she scanned the branches of several trees. He wasn't immediately visible . . . then she noticed. The butterflies were gone. All but a few had flown and were now visible only in the distance, like a golden kite hanging in the blue morning sky.

"They're gone." A bolt of anxiety shot through her. She ran ahead, calling, and found him lying on the ground, motionless, pale. "Hart!" She ran to him, shook him gently, listened for breath and heart sounds—both erratic—and called to him again and again.

Yazkuz knelt to feel his clammy skin and listen to his heart. She pried open his mouth and sure enough there was a piece of wrinkled white root there. She pulled it out and her leathery face went taut with worry.

"What . . . flower?" she demanded, holding up the root.

Cordelia pointed to the orchids in the tree behind them. Yazkuz shoved to her feet and shuffled to the tree, looking worried and making magic signs.

She had Cordelia harvest several, tied them up in her apron, then helped her carry and drag Hart back to the pyramid. Carrying him up the steps to the temple itself proved impossible, despite Yazkuz's insistence. They compromised and made a pallet for him in front of the statue of the great jaguar. Yazkuz insisted on building a fire by the statue to let the spirit know where they were.

As the day wore on, Yazkuz pulled herbs from her pockets and put some of them on his tongue. She sent Cordelia for water and more firewood.

They bathed his now feverish skin and prayed for help, each in her own way. Afterward Yazkuz demanded to know what happened and Cordelia told her the story of the images in the murals . . . of the chamber below with the altar and butterflies . . . and how the cloud of butterflies had led them to the orchids. The old woman seemed to follow most of it, indicating that she had seen just such things in her visions during the night.

"Old story . . . flower that heals." She wagged her head. "Strong medicine."

"Is there an antidote?" Cordelia asked, tears in her eyes. She mimed making a potion for Hart to drink. "Isn't there anything we can give him?"

The old woman looked sad and patted his cheek.

"Spirits test heart. If he live, he carry jaguar healing."

Cordelia sat by Goodnight, watching his troubled breathing, feeling her own slow instinctively to match it. Old Yazkuz sighed and reached out to her, giving her arm a squeeze.

"Time. Time say he live or he die. We wait."

Thirty-two

For two days Castille and his men had forced Itza and Ruz Platano to track Cordelia, Goodnight, and Yazkuz. At first the brothers refused and not even a beating from Castille's riding crop and his burliest thugs could make them agree. But Castille, whose refinement extended even to his cruelty, finally persuaded them by appealing to their higher natures. He dragged Hedda O'Keefe before them trembling, and it took only one slash of his crop across her upraised arms for them to scramble to do his will.

Keeping such a motivation fresh, however, meant that he had to drag Hedda O'Keefe with him on his trek through the jungle. And her presence created another set of problems: as a prisoner she had to be watched and imperiled, which took some of his men from carrying equipment and meant opposition from Arturo Valiente. The scholar, like so many of Castille's countrymen, clearly had a weakness for women—this one in particular.

For the second evening, Hedda sat with her back against a tree, hands bound, feeling footsore and weary to the bone. The terrain they had to cover was brutal—cliffs, hills, dense woods, and steep ravines—and she was forever being threatened and harangued to keep up. The trail had gotten so bad that morning that Castille, the only one of the group still mounted, had had to abandon his horse and take to foot himself. It put him in such a foul mood that even Yago and Blanc had had to keep their heads down after that.

Arturo was permitted to bring her food and water, but never lingered for fear of drawing Castille's ire. Truth be told, that was a mercy; she couldn't bear to hear his protestations of innocence and vows to protect her one more time. Yet, here he came again with a tin of half-edible food and a cup of awful water.

"Please, Hedda," he said, watching her turn her face, "you must eat to keep up strength. This is all over soon."

"You can't really believe that." She caught his gaze in hers. "You cannot believe that he will find the stones and whatever 'treasure' there may be and leave us alive to tell how he acquired it."

"I do not let anything happen to you," he declared, touching her hand.

"I believe you already have," she said tersely, averting her eyes.

"I swear to you—I do nothing to help him find us. I do not even know he is following behind us. You must believe me."

"Even if I were to believe that, Arturo, there is still the fact that you did not tell us that he asked you to do so. You did not warn us of his intentions."

"I think when the Spanish ship loses us, that is the end of it."

Truths and half-truths. She had seen how adeptly he played one side against the other: friend of the Spanish government of Cuba and friend of the revolution in equal measures. Where did his sympathies truly lie? And how would she ever know if the man she cared for was the true Arturo Valiente?

"And then there is the little business of the treasure you forgot to mention to Cordie, but remembered so clearly for your friend Castille."

Arturo's face fell. There was no defense for that and he knew it. He straightened and withdrew to return to the campfire.

It was well into the night that she felt something brush her shoulder and started awake to feel something being draped over her and a dark form moving silently away.

She looked down and her heart all but broke.

Around her shoulders lay Arturo's jacket.

They hadn't gone far the next morning when a tremor of excitement shot through the men and Castille went rushing to the front of the column to see what the guides had found. There was a disturbance in the surface of a steep hillside that fell to the bottom of a ravine. As they followed that trace, they found western heel prints and several broken branches, leading to a large split in the dark cliffs of the mountain.

Sensing their objective at hand, they followed the stream that flowed from that split and discovered a canyon beyond. It was cool and shaded and full of lush vegetation—and tracks that led them to the very end of the canyon.

And there it was: the arch of ancient stones that Castille had come halfway around the world to claim.

The Spaniard broke into a rare smile and ran to inspect the blocks and study the way they were attached to the opening. When he saw the carvings were part of much larger blocks, his excitement faded. They would take more manpower to move than he had available. Gradually his attention transferred to the opening the blocks adorned. He called for lanterns and led the others inside.

"Clearly they were here," he declared, staring at the blankets and equipment clustered in the main part of the chamber. He picked up the larger of the two packs and a leather-bound journal fell out. He flipped it open, paging through it, and saw nothing but sketches of flowers and plants. He tossed it back onto the floor and handed the professor their lantern.

"Light it," he snarled, "and help me search the cavern."

No one noticed Hedda snatch up the journal and tuck it back into the outer pocket of the rucksack. Looking around, she tucked the empty bag out of the way between some rocks in the side wall of the chamber.

Minutes later, they had probed all of the walls, the false passages, and the pile of rubble at the rear of the cavern. Frustrated at finding no indication of where the woman O'Keefe had gone, Castille grabbed Arturo and shook him.

"Where are they?" he snarled. "Where did they go?"

"I–I do not know. I know nothing more than you about this place."

"Is that so?" Castille's basilisk eyes narrowed. He dragged the professor outside again and shoved him against the stones of the arch. "Show me where it speaks of *treasure*."

"I cannot—the arch is not complete." The professor pointed to the missing keystone. "There was a magnificent block there . . . a carving of the jaguar."

"What difference does that make?" Castille said, eyeing him.

"On either side of the jaguar's head were stacks of figures that indicate wealth, riches, offerings," Arturo said. "Without it I cannot read of a treasure."

"As it happens," Castille said with a smirk, "we aren't without it." He ordered Yago to bring up one of the rectangular wooden crates his men had been lugging through the jungle. The bodyguard used a machete to pry off the lid and inside lay a stone carving. When they lifted it out, Arturo's gasp was echoed by Hedda's. It was the head of the jaguar that was missing from the top of the arch.

"Where do you—how do you come by this?" Arturo rushed to examine it.

"It has been in my family vault for generations." Castille sauntered over to give the cat's head a stroke. "Our family fortunes began to rise when one of our ancestors, a penniless young officer, returned from Cortez's conquest with it. It has been our family talisman for 350 years. Everything we have started with the acquisition of this stone."

"But how did you learn of the scrolls?" Hedda asked.

"A cousin—a monk in a monastery outside Madrid—came to me with word of a discovery in the monastery library, scrolls that bore the imprint of the head of a jaguar. He knew of our family legend, it seems.

"I applied to the abbot to see the scrolls, but the idiot declared them 'pagan' and said he would see them destroyed instead." He gave a harsh laugh. "I arranged for my cousin to steal the scrolls before they could be burned." His gaze narrowed. "But my greedy cousin decided they might be worth more than he was being paid. The fool tried to ransom them to me. Failing at that, he fled with them. It took two years, but I finally tracked him to Havana."

"Where you learn O'Keefe has the scrolls." Arturo glanced at Hedda.

"Where you so helpfully told me about them and about the part of Mexico where they were most likely to be found. The rest I owe to a patriotic cartographer from Campeche—whom you also visited, I believe." Then he gave the jaguar head one final pat. "Enough. If the jaguar brought my family fortune apart from the rest of the stones, imagine what treasures lie in store when they are reunited."

He ordered his men to find a way to lift the keystone back into place. It took some doing, but they were able to string ropes and hoist it. As the ropes were removed and the stone settled into place, there were loud grinding sounds. A low, heavy rumble came from inside the cavern and dust boiled from the opening into the sunlight.

All present stared anxiously—superstitiously—at the stone arch that was complete again after more than 350 years. The jaguar's head dominated the opening, looking as if the great cat were somehow emerging from its mountain lair into the affairs of the world once more.

As the dust settled, Castille took his lanterns and men inside to see what had caused the noise. At the rear of the cavern, where the piles of rock from the cave-in had been piled, they found a huge block of stone like a door dislodged and swung partway open. It had cleared back some of the debris and created an opening that was roughly two inches wide.

"A door!" Castille crowed. "My jaguar was a keystone in more ways than one!" He ordered his men to clear more of the rubble and open the door further. Excitement was running high as they moved enough of the rock to make room for the door to slide. But when they tried to pull the stone slab out further, it would not budge. They worked for an hour before conceding that it was hopeless without proper tools and the brute force required to move it.

"Damn it! Six more inches and I could squeeze through!" He thought of the tools they did have and of what might generate the power they needed.

"We have the dynamite, yes?" he said to Yago, who held up his hands to indicate ten sticks. "More than enough, I think, to unstick a stubborn door."

But when they opened the crate containing the ammunition and dynamite, the mercenary hired for his skill with munitions turned a bit pale and backed away from the crate.

"Senor, in this heat—the dynamite, she sweats. Grows unstable." The man licked his lip. "I cannot promise to direct the blast as you wish."

"All we need you to do is put it in the crack and light the fuse. All *it* has to do is explode." Castille shoved him toward the crate and stepped back, staring up at the jaguar's head.

"Predator to predator," he said with a smirk. "You understand how it is."

Hedda watched in alarm as the fuse was strung and lighted, and Castille's men took cover outside the cavern.

Yazkuz retreated to the temple to seek guidance, leaving Cordelia to sit with Hart through the night. Hour after hour she bathed his face and body, and dribbled water between his parched lips. Toward dawn his labored breathing eased, but he was still far from stable. The veins in his arms, throat, and temples were distended, and only cool water seemed to help. In desperation, she suggested to Yazkuz that they put him in the lake to cool him.

It was something of an ordeal carrying and dragging him down the beach. Cordelia paused to remove her boots and shirt before climbing into the water to hold him. No sooner were they settled in the water than they felt a strange tremor and saw a huge ripple spread across the lake as if something had been dropped into the far side. They looked around uneasily and for the first time Yazkuz caught sight of the items lying on the edge of the dock. She rushed to investigate, made a number of magic signs, and charged down the beach to confront Cordelia.

"What you do?" She demanded furiously. "Take from Jaguar Spirit?"

"Those things on the dock? They were in the lake." She pointed to the water, her throat tightening as she thought of the tender moments surrounding their retrieval. "I brought them up."

"Bad—bad! Belong Jaguar Spirit." She flung a finger toward the great statue, then brought it back to shake at Cordelia. "No *steal!*"

"But we weren't stealing." She suddenly saw it in a different light. "I mean, we didn't realize we were stealing. We didn't mean any harm."

The old lady rushed back to the dock, crept out on it, and began to throw the items back into the lake, offering a loud chant with each one she returned.

Just as the last one sank to the bottom, there was a huge

boom that shook the earth and made it seem the entire mountain had responded to the old woman's action. Old Yazkuz froze, then backed slowly from the stone quay and threw herself on her knees before the big stone jaguar.

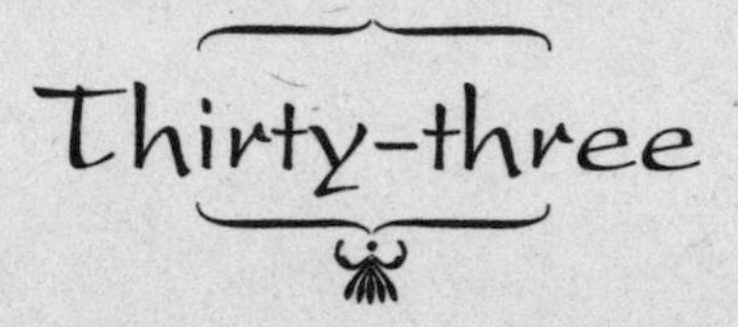

Thirty-three

The force of the dynamite blast sent dust and rubble shooting halfway across the canyon. Castille sent his munitions expert in first and the man came back to say that they had succeeded. Castille and the professor rushed inside to see for themselves and discovered the door had been blown back four feet. There was plenty of room for them to enter. They explored and found a passage that was clear for only fifteen feet. After that, more rubble blocked the way.

"Damn it! I'm sick of this!" Castille raged. He grabbed Blanc by the shirt and shoved him toward the wall of debris. "Clear it—I don't care if you have to use your hands! I want to be in that treasure chamber by this time tomorrow!"

Every man in the company was drafted to haul rocks. Castille even shoved Arturo and Hedda into the cavern to help. He stalked back and forth between the cavern and the outside where he looked up at the jaguar head, feeling now that the cat's smile had a mocking air.

"I'll have that treasure yet, you slippery bastard. You wait and see."

One of the men nearest the front noticed the water seeping through the rocks and mentioned it to Blanc, who was in no mood to deal with obstacles that would only earn him a slash with the crop his master was again carrying. He called the man a fool and told him to quit looking for excuses to stop work. By the time the professor noticed the water it was past ankle deep in the passage and seeping quickly through the wall of rock they were struggling to remove. He knew enough about rocks and caves to know this was more than just an underground spring. He looked at the wall of debris that blocked the tunnel and realized there was water—possibly a large amount of it—on the other side of that blockage. They were removing the only thing that stood between themselves and a flood.

The sight of Castille standing in the cavern entrance banging his crop against his palm sent a quiver of anxiety through the professor. He made his way to Hedda, who was wearing down under the hard physical labor.

"You must have a rest, Hedda," he said, pulling her from the line of men who grumbled that she was only slowing them down. He escorted her toward the cave entrance but Castille blocked their exit.

"Get back to work," he snarled, giving Arturo a shove.

"She is exhausted—she must rest," Arturo protested, raising an arm to ward off Castille's attack. But seconds later, Yago and another of Castille's henchmen grabbed the pair from behind and flung them back through the cavern toward the tunnel.

Just then, the wall of debris broke, pushed by a force of water they couldn't yet imagine. Shouts and confusion broke out as the men digging at the front tried to run for the opening. A moment later, the roar of water drowned the screams of the men caught in the torrent rumbling down the tunnel.

They had only a second or two to react. Arturo spotted a crevice to the side of the tunnel and shoved Hedda into it, throwing his body over hers just as a wall of rock and water burst from the tunnel with the force of naval artillery.

Hedda's scream was lost in the roar. The force of the water sucked at him, and when she realized he was being dragged away she tried desperately to save him, calling to him to hold on to her as she braced against the rock. But the force of the water pulling at him overcame what strength she had left. He was wrenched away and disappeared in a maelstrom of foam and churning water.

The high-powered flood swept everything in the cavern before it—rocks, men, tools—nothing was left by the time the water subsided. No trace remained of the human effort to penetrate the jaguar's throne and open his treasure house. Once outside, no longer constrained to a narrow channel, the water spread and slowed quickly, taking with it some vegetation and flattening a few trees with the boulders propelled by the water. The stones at the entrance had been scoured almost white by the combination of sand and water that blew past them. Above the rest, the jaguar's head looked just as fierce and enigmatic as ever.

It was some time before Castille staggered back to the entrance and saw that Yago, who had been near the entrance when the water broke through, had managed to scramble to the side before the wall of water and rock hit. The bodyguard had survived and it appeared that four other men were moving among the rubble and bodies that littered the canyon floor. Castille rallied them, setting them to look for tools and most important, guns. When Yago asked his employer in a desolate tone what they would do now, Castille looked at the bruised and weary survivors and knew he had to give them a reason to go on serving him.

"We're here for treasure," he declared, "and by God, treasure is what we'll get." He laughed at the men's stunned expressions. "Don't you see? There's fewer of you now . . . so each of you gets a bigger share of the riches!"

As fate would have it, one of the things that survived the torrent was the box of guns and ammunition they had taken from the O'Keefes' camp. After they rested and had some water, they armed themselves, found a still-functional lantern, and prepared to go up the tunnel to see where it led.

Inside, they found one more surprise: Hedda O'Keefe was slumped against the wall in the dripping cavern, soaked and shivering, numb with shock. Castille had Yago pull her to her feet.

"Bring her along," he said with a smirk at the others. "Never throw away a serviceable woman. Who knows—she may prove to be worth something."

The rumble from what sounded like a blast sent a shock through the water that caused a series of waves at the shore where Cordelia was cooling Hart in the lake. She just managed to keep his head above the crashing waves and keep them both from being dragged out into the lake. Then as abruptly as the chaos began, it ended, and all was still once more except for the lapping of the water.

She took deep breaths and realized her teeth were chattering. She had to get Hart back up onto shore and get out of this cold water. She called to the old woman, but Yazkuz was still absorbed in placating the Jaguar Spirit.

She floated Hart as far up on the beach as she could, then hurried around him to take his arms and pull him out of the water. To her surprise, the water around her feet began to disappear and his body sank slightly and was deposited on the sandy bottom. She looked up in dismay. She hadn't even started pulling him from the water yet. How could he be out of the—

The water was receding from the entire beach at a shocking rate. She released Hart's shoulders and rose, watching the water shrinking. Far out in the lake, closer to one of the stone walls than to the beach, the water was beginning to swirl. Before her eyes, a large whirlpool developed and there was a low rumbling sound that made her grab him again and pull him as far up on the beach as she could. Something was happening to the lake.

Yazkuz rushed onto the stone dock and stared at the water in horror. The lake began to separate from the walls of the caldera, then to disappear—but only around the edges. The rest of the lake stayed in place!

Cordelia ran along the beach looking at the place where the water divided. Part had run down the sloping dry lake bed and the other part remained contained. It was a wall, she realized. There was a huge stone wall—a dam of sorts—holding the lake in place! The lake was manmade!

She reversed directions and ran back down the beach to get Yazkuz. The old bruja struggled not to look at first, but when she saw the blocks of stone that formed the side of the lake, she quickly adjusted to the idea. She raised her skirts, shed her shoes, and ventured out through the muck and sand to investigate.

The stones were huge and crusted with centuries of algae and sediment. But they were ingeniously constructed and, from all appearances, were holding steady. Yazkuz ventured farther and noticed that some of the sand had been washed from the sloping floor and stone was revealed. The old bruja turned back, muttering to herself in wonder, when there was pounding like footsteps and something grabbed her from behind.

On the beach, Cordelia felt herself losing control; things were not making any sense. She knelt by Hart and tried to focus just on helping him. If only there were some sign of improvement. She laid her head on his chest to listen for his heartbeat. The strong, steady rhythm she heard caused tears to well in her eyes. She squeezed his hands, blinked, and looked around. She needed to get him back to some shade, before the sun drove his fever up again.

She was trying to lift his shoulders and thinking they should also get some water into him when the old woman let out a cry that caused the blood to stand still in her veins. Torn between tending Hart and seeing what had happened to Yazkuz, she laid him back on the sand and went to help the old woman.

But as she scanned the beach for the old woman's footprints, she saw something moving around the stone wall of the dam. She froze at the sight of Yazkuz struggling, thrashing in the grip of a man! The powerful physique, the gun strapped to his shoulder—she was stunned to recognize him. Yago.

Behind him strode Alejandro Castille, rifle in hand, and behind him came four other men bearing guns and—Hedda!

She had stumbled to a halt at the sight of Castille, but now began to run toward them again, calling to her aunt. Hedda seemed bewildered by the sound of someone calling her name and had difficulty locating her.

"Hedda! It's me!" She waved, anxiety mounting. "Look at me!"

Then Hedda seemed to understand and broke free of her captor and ran across the former lake bed to Cordelia's open arms. The minute her niece's arms closed around her, she began to sob.

"What have you done?" she demanded, looking past her aunt to Castille.

"Amazing what you can do with a little dynamite." Castille stopped a few feet away with his gun pointed at them.

She thought of the booming sound that preceded the draining of the lake.

"You caused this?" She nodded to the lake. "You blew it up?"

"How were we to know there was a whole damned lake behind that cave-in below in the cavern?" He gave a vile chuckle. "Did us a favor, however. Now the boys here only have to split their half of the treasure four ways instead of ten." He stepped closer. "Where is it?"

"Where is what?" She glared at him.

"The treasure, Senorita O'Keefe. What else?"

She shook her head, suddenly grateful for old Yazkuz's

furious disposal of the gold they had found. "The only treasure here is this remarkable place. Not your kind of riches at all. There's nothing spendable to be had."

"You don't mind if I don't take your word for it," he said, motioning his men forward and indicating with his gun that Cordelia and Hedda should go ahead of them. When they reached the pyramid, she helped Hedda to a seat on one of the steps. Castille ordered Yago to watch them while he took the rest of his men up the steps to the temple.

"I must go down the beach to bring him back to the shade," she said pointing to Hart. "He is ill . . . por favor, senor . . . please . . . help me."

He looked like he was about to refuse when Yazkuz crept toward him with one eye narrowed, making threatening magic signs in the air. Cordelia could have sworn the thug blanched. He clearly knew and feared Yazkuz's profession. He draped his rifle over his shoulder and went with her to carry Hart back up the beach and into the shade.

"What happened to him?" Hedda knelt by Cordelia after Hart was settled.

"Remember the plants? He found one that . . . This time, there may not be . . ." She couldn't finish it. After a minute she looked up. "Are you all right?"

"It was horrible. I'm still shaking. All that water just broke through and—" Tears slipped down Hedda's sunburned cheeks. "Arturo. It took him. He's gone, Cordie. Gone."

"Oh, Hedda, I'm so sorry." She held her aunt and rocked her.

Yazkuz offered Hedda a handkerchief she had stolen from one of the men.

"Men." The bruja wagged her head. "Much, much trouble."

The old woman's words were borne out a short time later when they heard a thumping on the pyramid steps and looked up to see the temple statue of the jaguar tumbling down the steps, end over end. Pieces of the stone flew off with each bang against the temple steps until the statue took a large bounce and crashed near the bottom in several large pieces.

Yazkuz was dumbstruck for a minute. Then she went roaring up the steps, moving faster than Cordelia believed was possible for a woman of her age. Hedda looked alarmed and started to rise, but Cordelia pulled her back down and held her in place by the arm. A minute later, Castille and his men came thundering down the steps with guns trained on them.

"Where is the gold?" Castille demanded. "Valiente said it was here."

"He did not," Hedda spoke up. "He said there were riches. But that could mean anything." Castille looked at her dispassionately, then smacked her across the face with the back of his hand. Cordelia lunged at him but was pushed back at gunpoint by one of the others. After a moment, Castille came to stand over Hart.

"What's wrong with him?" he said, giving Hart's inert shoulder a nudge.

"He's ill. He has a terrible fever and is probably contagious," Cordelia said. "You'd better stand back."

"And you'd better tell me the truth." Castille drew back his foot and kicked Hart in the ribs. Cordelia would have sprung for his throat—gun or no gun—but one of the men grabbed her tangled hair and held her by it. Castille gave Hart another savage kick that rolled him halfway over. But before he could deliver a third blow, he spotted something sticking out of Hart's rear pocket and bent to investigate.

He pulled out the golden cuff Cordelia had pulled up from the bottom of the lake and held it up, watching it glint in the brilliant sun. He leveled a fierce, icy stare on Cordelia as he held it up with one hand and put his gun to Hart's head with the other.

"Tell me where he got this . . . or I'll spread his brains all over the sand."

She glanced up the temple steps.

"What did you do to Yazkuz?" she demanded.

"Tell me!" he roared.

Cordelia looked at Hart and up at the temple and made her choice.

"I'll show you."

Minutes later, they were standing on the stone quay, staring down in the water, which had grown disturbed and muddy looking since the blast and subsequent rumblings. Cordelia removed all but her underclothes and slipped into the water. With a last apologetic glance at the jaguar statue, she dove to the bottom to retrieve some of the objects.

The water level had lowered markedly, and she only had to dive ten feet to feel the objects lying on the bottom. She grabbed several smooth shapes and headed for the surface. She piled them on the dock at Castille's feet and caught her breath as he and his henchmen examined them and celebrated boisterously. It came as no surprise to her when he pointed his gun at her and uttered an order.

"More."

She quietly asked Hedda to check on Yazkuz, then made half a dozen more trips, collecting quite a pile of golden objects before climbing out onto the dock. When Hedda came back it was with grim news. She hadn't been able to find the old woman anywhere. She had even checked the lower chambers.

"I did not say you could quit," Castille snarled. She was heartily sick of seeing that end of a gun.

"I have to catch my breath," she said, as Hedda put a shirt and a protective arm around her shoulders. "Nothing's stopping *you* from going in." She glanced at his men. "Or *them*. They look like they could use a wash."

Castille snatched the golden objects from the men's callused hands and ordered them into the water to speed up the retrieval. Two protested they couldn't swim, but the others were quickly stripped and pushed into the water.

"Hey—it's warm as a bath in here," the fellow declared.

Cordelia looked at Hedda, wishing she could say what she knew. Something was wrong with the lake. Earlier it had been cool and pristine. Since the blast, it had not only lowered and grown turbid, it had begun to heat at an alarming rate. She glanced at the crater walls. There was only one force in nature that could heat that much water that fast.

Thirty-four

Far below, at the mouth of the canyon, two shaggy, battered figures picked their way through the debris caused by the flash flood, checking the bodies strewn like matchsticks across the canyon floor. They found no survivors until they came to a short, stocky figure lying on his back with his arms flung out.

"The professor!" Itza said through his battered and swollen lips as he knelt to check for signs of life. He didn't expect to feel those slow but steady breaths against his cheek. "He is alive! Ruz—here—he's alive!"

The brothers Platano had been left under the watch of one of the less diligent cutthroats in Castille's band. As soon as the dynamite went off, the man abandoned them to see the results of the blast. They seized the opportunity to grab canteens and machetes and run for the mouth of the canyon. They had just climbed out of the valley when they felt the rumble and heard the water's roar.

They watched in horror as a wall of floodwater gushed from the opening and they heard rocks and boulders pounding the stone sides of the canyon. They waited for the flood to pass, then cautiously made their way back inside.

Now they had found one of their own. They checked him and found nothing broken. Carefully, they moved him outside the canyon to a spot on the far hill, where they could tend and hopefully revive him. Learning what had happened to Senorita Hedda would have to wait.

Cordelia and Hedda stood together on the dock, watching the surface of the turbid water, wondering if what appeared to be bubbles in the deepest part of the lake were indeed that. They could smell the change in the lake now; there was sulphur in the air. But Castille, obsessed with recovering as much gold from the lake bottom as possible, seemed oblivious to it. Even more alarming, the men who were bringing up the treasures seemed to ignore what was happening. Finally, one of the men came up and crawled out onto the dock.

"Hot," he declared it. "The water's just too damned hot." His beet-red skin bore him out; he was practically parboiled.

But his comrade, intoxicated by the novelty of picking golden treasures off a lake bottom, refused to give up. In fact, he was moving farther out into the lake. He waved, his red face strangely drunken in appearance, and disappeared under the water again . . . just as a low rumble shook the caldera and a geyser of steam from the lake bed sent a spray of water shooting up. Seconds later, as they watched, the man broke the surface screaming. His flesh was cooked and gray in places, peeling from his bones in others. Cordelia and Hedda looked away in horror. Yago put his gun to his shoulder and coolly shot him between the eyes.

"I ain't goin' back down there." The other diver faced Castille. "Gold ain't no good to a dead man."

The problem with gold, Castille soon realized, was that it was heavy. They had to find a way to carry large amounts of treasure out of the canyon and back down the mountains to the village. There, Castille laid out his plan to his men, they could get burros to carry the lot and a guide to take them to the coast. It seemed reasonable to men dazzled by gold's luster and entrancing color.

While Yago watched the prisoners, Castille took his remaining men and scoured the canyon for something to carry the treasure. They brought back provision bags and a strangely familiar rucksack that they found washed against the edge of the canyon. They packed as much gold as the bags would hold and stuffed their pockets and shirts with the rest. The bags were much too heavy.

Cordelia watched Castille pacing and cursing and she exchanged grim looks with Hedda. If only they could shrink back into the gardens and wait for the wretch to leave. Then his relentless eye fell on the two of them as they knelt by Hart, holding his hands.

"I said there was always a good reason to keep a woman around. You!" He stalked over and jabbed her with the muzzle of his gun. "Get up—you're coming with us." Then he prodded Hedda the same way. "You too." He gave a harsh laugh. "You're my new mules."

The men redistributed the weight of the bags of gold, stuffing some pieces into the women's clothing, and using the clothes from the dead man in the lake to make additional bags, tying up the ends of the legs and sleeves and stuffing them full. They would have to travel quickly and eat what they could gather.

When they were ready to move out, Castille came to stand over Hart with a dangerous look in his eye.

"Please let me move him," she said, trying to keep her voice steady. "This place is unstable."

"Perhaps I should just put him out of his suffering." He pointed his rifle at Hart's temple. "Might make a nice change, being a 'humanitarian.' "

"No!" Cordelia threw herself over Hart, shielding his head and chest with her own body, gambling that Castille wouldn't shoot her. Hart wasn't in pain, wasn't suffering. She couldn't bear to have her last glimpse of him be as Castille was murdering him. If there was even the smallest chance he might still live . . .

Desperately, she drew back and pressed her lips to his.

"I love you, Hart. I always will," she whispered just as Castille grabbed her arm and jerked her to her feet.

"Get moving," he snarled.

Loaded with enough gold to make her steps heavy and uncomfortable, she fell in beside Hedda in the column. As they trudged down the road that led around the lake and down to the cavern, she managed one last look back at Hart. And felt her heart break into a million pieces.

Hedda reached out for her hand and gave it a squeeze. For a minute neither of them could see through their tears, but they kept moving, kept putting one foot in front of the other at the point of Yago's gun.

Ruz reached over to shake Itza awake, motioning for silence and pointing to the party emerging from the canyon. Their eyes widened as they took in the fact that both Senorita Hedda and Senorita O'Keefe were with that devil Castille and his henchmen. They were surprised to see there were only three men besides the ever-vigilant Yago left in his group. They watched as the group laboriously climbed the rise to the trail and set off toward the village. They moved sluggishly, awkwardly, as if their packs were much too heavy. Shaking his head, Itza looked at Ruz and then at the professor, who had not yet returned to consciousness. Deciding, he pointed at Ruz and then at the professor, then connected himself with the party fading into the forest across the ravine.

Ruz understood. He nodded and made the sign of the cross on Itza, who nodded and did the same for him. Then Itza, always the better tracker, crept off down the ravine and was soon climbing the other side.

Yazkuz crept around the side of the pyramid, holding her head, cursing with the eleven torments of Hell the Spanish devil who had struck her and rolled her off the back side of the pyramid, leaving her for dead. But the old woman knew a thing or two about survival and had managed to stop herself from rolling down the steps and lie still as death until she was certain they were gone. Then she had dragged herself down into the gardens, found healing herbs to treat her cut and bruises and a little fruit to keep up her strength.

She had watched in horror as the devils packed up the offerings stolen from the Jaguar's lake and left to carry it back to their world. She had seen, even from a distance, the pain of the O'Keefe woman as she parted from Handsome One. He was still alive, still mending she hoped. Now that all was quiet, she hurried out onto the beach beside him and began to pull fruit from her pockets. He would be hungry as a hound when he awoke.

The sun was beginning to set when Hart finally opened his eyes. They felt like they were full of sand as he tried to focus. Yazkuz filled his vision and, though he should probably be pleased to see anyone at all, he couldn't help being disappointed that it wasn't Cordelia who greeted him on his return to the world.

"Ah, Handsome . . . you back." The old girl smiled with a wicked edge and stuck a banana out at him. "Eat. Go soon. Woman in trouble."

"Wh—what kind of trouble?" he rasped out. Even his voice felt rusty.

"Big trouble." She gestured broadly. "Men. Guns."

He sat up, his joints popping and creaking strangely. "Men and guns. Well, that figures."

It took a little while for him to get his feet under him and some nourishment down him. Yazkuz insisted he drink something that tasted like it was made from the lining of a dirty pocket. He shuddered at the thought, but soon felt considerably better. He rose and stretched and moved around, brushing the sand from him. There was a slight soreness to a couple of his ribs. When she brushed at his back, he realized it didn't hurt and glanced over his shoulder. From what he could see, his back was mostly healed.

He ripped off the bandage around his arm and his whip-snake bite was gone. There was only a small, pink, healthy looking scar.

"I'm well? How could I have healed so—" He remembered the red orchids, some of which lay dried and shriveled on the sand around him. "It worked! Ha-ha—it worked! It worked!" His first impulse was to grab Cordelia and—he grabbed Yazkuz by the shoulders instead. "Where is she?"

"Spanish devil take. Also gold." She made a sign. "Jaguar angry."

"He's not the only one."

The old girl handed him something from behind her back: his boots. As he pulled them on, she opened her apron, which was looped up and tucked into her waist to carry something. It was full of fresh specimens of the red orchids.

He smiled, grabbed the old girl, and swung her around once.

The minute her feet touched the ground, she pulled him down the beach toward the drying lake bed and the old road that led out of the caldera.

"Damn." He stood for a moment gaping at the changes. "What happened to the lake?"

The trip back along the cliffs and down the ravines and across the hills seemed to take forever. The women were constantly being prodded or admonished to keep up or to move faster. Cordelia didn't protest, just kept on trudging along the path, following Castille as he struggled to find his way back along the path they had taken from the village. It wasn't especially difficult; the trampled vegetation should have been a dead giveaway. But Castille was not used to the jungle and kept ignoring the signs of passage until one of his men finally pointed out the obvious and agreed to scout out the trail.

By the time they dropped their packs of gold and sank

to the ground, just after dark, no one had the energy to try to build a fire or try to find food. Cordelia knew exactly how dangerous that attitude toward the necessities was, but couldn't bring herself to care. She huddled close to Hedda for warmth in the cool air and found herself remembering the sight of Hart lying in front of the pyramid. Tears rolled down her cheeks. Hedda said nothing, only patted her.

Then later, after the others had gone to sleep—after posting a watch who soon began to doze himself—Hedda crept on all fours across the small clearing to the stack of bags of gold that Castille had insisted on mounding in the middle of them. She located the rucksack and quietly undid the buckles on the thin outer pocket. Holding her breath, she slid her hand inside and there it was. She pulled out the leather-bound journal and with painstaking care, reclosed and fastened the pockets on the pack. She retraced her path to Cordelia, who had felt her leave and sat up, watching what she was doing. When Hedda slipped back onto the trampled grass beside her and handed her the journal, she knew instantly what it was. For a moment she could scarcely breathe. Hedda put her mouth close to Cordelia's ear and whispered quietly.

"You can't go on like this, Cordie. Whatever happened to him, he would want you to survive, to live. Maybe this little piece of him will help you go on."

Tears filled Cordelia's eyes as she ran her fingers over the worn cover of the mysterious little book that had come to symbolize Hart to her—his secrets, his scholarly and insightful nature, and his stubborn pursuit of his dream.

In the moonlight she opened the book at its midpoint and was just able to make out drawings of flowers and leaves of various kinds, dotted with sections of notes written in his strong, masculine hand. She closed her eyes and ran her fingers over the pages, as if she could absorb some remnant of him from them, as if she could conjure his presence and vitality within her heart.

She closed the book and lay back, cradling it, holding it as if it were him.

"I love you, Hart. I always will," she whispered to the still night air, so softly that not even Hedda heard it. It made her ache with regret that she had never said that to him, never seen the pleasure it would create in his eyes, or the triumph. Right now she'd even settle for some gloating . . .

The next morning, she tucked the journal under her shirt and into the waist of her breeches. As they moved out she felt it there, poking her with a corner to make her keep up with the others, just as he would have done.

Later, when they stopped, Castille made them deposit their packs in one place before he would allow them to head off into the trees one at a time for relief. Cordelia waited until she was well out of sight before sitting down to pull out the journal. This time, the words, written in his impeccable hand, were perfectly clear. She started on the first page and began to read . . . his thoughts his frustrations . . . his desires . . . his fears . . . they were all there . . . the mind and heart of the man she had come to love.

And on every page. . .

Her smile . . . her legs . . . her gun . . . her kiss . . . her courage . . . her capability . . . her inner conflicts . . . his humor . . . his fascination . . . his frustration . . . his desire . . . his temptation . . .

His love.

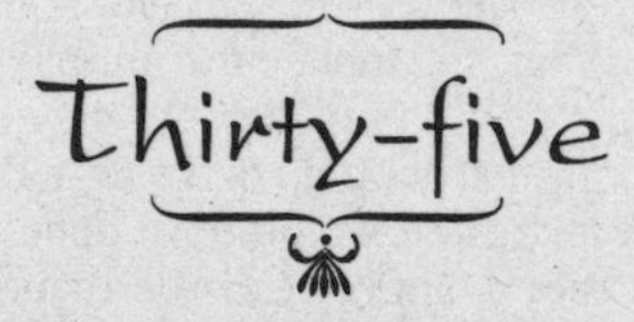

Thirty-five

Hart stood in the middle of the cavern where they had camped only two nights ago, looking back at the tunnel they had just traversed and then ahead at the arch of stones that would mark their exit. It was as if a fanatical Mother Nature had swept through in a frenzy of spring cleaning, a flash flood as mop and pail.

Yazkuz had tried to explain what had happened, but it made little sense until he saw the lake basin, the road leading down to the tunnel, and the passage through to the jaguar's cavern. The well-scoured tunnel had been abruptly and violently unblocked that morning. Further surprises awaited when they stepped out into the canyon, glimpsed the destruction caused by the water, and looked back to find the stone arch now complete. The cat's head was again in place above the rest, looking eerily lifelike and ready to pounce.

"You're right," he told old Yazkuz. "That is not a happy cat."

Yazkuz scowled and pulled him along. Whenever he spotted manmade debris and paused to investigate, she got annoyed and tried to hurry him along. But there was method in his madness. He needed a canteen, some matches . . . a shirt would be nice . . . not to mention a weapon or two.

"Why is there never a damned machete around when you want one?" he muttered, poking around through some smashed crates and finding nothing but tin cups and bags of soggy flour and beans. He was about to abandon the equipment search and go after Castille bare-handed when he spotted a relatively undamaged crate wedged between a rock and the canyon wall. It was long, narrow, and oddly familiar. He was shocked to recognize both its contents and origin before he reached it. What the devil were O'Keefe's guns doing here?

He turned and looked back at the jaguar's head, then at old Yazkuz.

"Your boss has a very odd sense of humor."

He snatched up three guns and handed one to Yazkuz, who held it out from her as if afraid it might go off at any second. He took it back and slipped the canvas sling over his shoulder with the second one before stuffing his pockets full of ammunition.

They headed out of the canyon and started to climb the side of the ravine when the sound of his name nearly dropped him in his tracks. He whirled with his rifle half aimed, and there was Ruz Platano standing on the other bank, waving frantically. Behind him, seated and looking rough, was Arturo Valiente.

It didn't take long for Hart to plow across the stream to the other side.

"You don't look so good, Valiente," Hart said, bending down to search the professor's bloodshot eyes.

"My head." The professor clapped both hands to it. "But I live. These brave young men"—he gestured to Ruz and his absent brother—"they find and save me." He glanced at the canyon. "Do you see others alive?" When Hart shook his head, Valiente sighed and pointed at the trail to the village. "Ruz and Itza . . . they see Castille take Hedda and Cordelia that way."

"How long ago?" Hart asked Ruz directly.

"Several hours," the professor translated again, looking troubled. "Itza follows. He leaves signs for us." He grabbed Hart's arm. "Once Castille reaches the village and gets to his burros and horses, he will not want anyone left to tell what he has done." He looked truly miserable as he glanced at the guns. "He is not a man to show mercy."

"Can you use one of these?" He offered the professor a rifle.

"I shoot mostly ducks," Valiente said, shrugging apologetically.

"Same principle. Aim lower." He looked at Ruz. "What about you?"

"He says he has hunted wild boar," Valiente translated.

"Same principle," Hart said, handing over the gun. "Aim higher."

As they crossed the ravine to join Yazkuz, Hart spotted something caught on one of the bushes ravaged by the floodwaters and his eyes lighted.

"Hey—isn't that a bandana?"

Every muscle in Cordelia's body was crying for relief before their first full day on the trail was half over, and she could tell from the grim faces of Castille's men that they felt the same. For the first few hours yesterday afternoon, the men had raucously traded plans for spending their newfound wealth. But by last night's camp the reality of the backbreaking work that lay ahead had become clear, and lack of proper food and sufficient water began to take its toll.

Then, this morning, they had focused on watching for springs the guides had said were safe water. By afternoon the heat and humidity had risen enough as they descended in altitude to make exertion downright miserable. They began to demand longer and more frequent stops. When Castille fumed and insisted that such delays meant another whole day on the trail, they defiantly shed their burdens and stopped to rest anyway.

Cordelia stole a few minutes at each stop to read more of Hart's journal, drawing strength from it, convincing herself she had to find the will to survive—if not for herself, for Hedda. On the trail she studied the men Castille had left and realized that of them, Yago was the most formidable. But every man had a weakness and in front of the temple yesterday morning, she had glimpsed his. He was a believer in the power of the old ways.

"You will never live to spend this gold," she said to him in front of the others, not knowing how much English they understood. "It is cursed. It was stolen from the Jaguar and he will come to reclaim it. The old bruja said so."

At the words *gold* and *bruja*, the others came alert and demanded Yago tell them what she said. He clearly tried to pass it off as the rambling of a stupid woman, but she regarded them so confidently, so knowingly that they could not dismiss her. When she said that the jaguar would be coming for his gold, they looked immediately to the forest around them. Clearly, they understood enough of what she said to make them nervous.

For the rest of the day, whenever one of the men looked at her, she narrowed her eyes and looked to the brush and grass as if telling him to beware. By the time they reached the first set of cliffs, the men were edgy enough to refuse to wait to tie their packs to a rope and lower them; they just dropped their packs over the edge before climbing down themselves. Castille was furious and struck with his crop—swerving at the last minute to slice air instead of flesh.

Complaints of hunger and a slowing pace caused Castille to send Yago out to forage for food and he came back with an armload of bananas. Cordelia had never been so happy to see food in her life. She and Hedda each ate three without stopping. Then thirst set in.

It took some time and going off the trail to find potable water. One of the men, in leaning to cup his hand under the trickle of water coming from the rocks, grabbed not a vine, but a whip snake, which did what whip snakes are wont to do. The man howled, thinking he'd been struck by a rattler. When they located the culprit, he seemed relieved.

"This is how it starts," Cordelia declared to Yago. "The Jaguar's curse. He sends his friends the snakes to punish his enemies." To the bitten man she said, "I hope your arm doesn't turn black and fall off."

Castille heard her and grabbed up his pistol and shoved it point-blank into her face. As his finger twitched over the trigger, he looked at the pack she carried and weighed her life against the trouble of having to redistribute its contents. Then from the corner of his eye he glimpsed disapproval and uncertainty in the men's faces. Lowering his gun, he began to stalk back and forth, intent on impressing the men with his bravado and refocusing their attention on his goal.

"The Jaguar will never hurt me. He has guarded the house of Castille for generations. He is my brother . . . blood of my blood . . . a part of my family."

"Your family? Then beware, for you stole his gold," Hedda said bitterly. "And how well did you treat your cousin when he stole from you?"

For her insolence, she got a slap across the face. But from the secret smile she gave Cordelia afterward, she counted that it was worth it. Castille was growing more nervous. And nervous men made mistakes.

That evening, off the trail and floundering for direction, Castille's party finally collapsed at dusk by a stream that flowed down from the mountains and provided both water and fish. They had to build a fire to roast the fish, and a fire in the dark attracts all kinds of attention.

Cordelia made a show of watching the grasses on the small clearing by the stream. But then she caught a genuine glimpse of reflected light in the grass nearby and went perfectly still. Watching for signs of movement, she caught the odd reflection twice more, circling the campsite at a distance. Her skin turned to gooseflesh; she was no longer pretending. Something was out there. When she looked back at the others, Yago was watching her. He had seen the genuineness of her reaction and held his rifle closer and began to watch, too.

Haunted by thoughts of her encounters with jaguars—for this couldn't be the same one—she had difficulty falling asleep. Through the night she kept hearing a faint panting sound that seemed to grow closer and closer.

The next morning, the men were so hungry and dispirited that Castille had difficulty making them get up and shoulder their packs and bundles. They didn't trust his leadership, and his contempt for their weakness grew more visible, only adding to their resentment. Cordelia saw Hart's journal on the ground where she had slept and registered dismay before she could check her response and retrieve it. Castille saw her reaction and rushed over to grab whatever it was she was trying to hide in the band of her trousers.

"No—it's nothing! Give it back!" She fought furiously to keep it, but he smacked her with his crop repeatedly, until she recoiled from the pain and he was able to yank the journal away. He looked it over with a snort of derision.

"What is this? A sketchbook? You are a mule now, and mules have no time for sketching." He gave her a hateful look. "Consider this a much needed lesson in the natural order of things, *puta*."

Before her aching eyes, he tossed the journal as far away as he could. Then he shoved her hard in the other direction, so that she stumbled and fell over her waiting pack.

The sympathy in Hedda's eyes made it worse, somehow. She couldn't help one last look back as they moved on. Her last link with Hart was gone. His painstaking botanical records and startlingly candid notes about his feelings for her had given her hope and served as a reminder of who she was and what she had accomplished.

And what had she accomplished in her life, besides survival? She had wanted independence and respect and someday acclaim. She had sworn to live her life outside of the limitations imposed on women and, for the most part, she had. But if she had died today—if Castille had pulled the trigger earlier—what would be the sum of her life?

There was a time when she had wanted to be a doctor like her father, to do good things for people . . .

For the rest of the day she trudged on and tried hard not to think at all.

"They were here last night," Hart whispered, stooping to feel the faint warmth of the campfire's ashes. Another part of his anxiety lifted with each small bit of evidence that they were getting closer to her.

They had caught up with Itza this morning and he had led them to this place off the trail. Then as they paused to fill their canteens, Ruz came to get him to look at some tracks.

"Jaguar." The guide pointed to a fresh set of prints in the dust around the border of the camp.

Weight descended on Hart's chest as he and Ruz followed the tracks around the camp . . . imagining the cat watching the fire-lit people from the safety of the darkness . . . imagining that Cordelia had gone to sleep never guessing she was being watched . . . fearing that this particular cat might not know that she had a safe conduct pass from the Jaguar Spirit.

"Look. Here . . ." Ruz had picked up something he spotted in the grass near the tracks. It looked like a book.

He handed it to Hart, who felt his knees go weak as he recognized the sturdy leather binding and opened it to glimpse his own handwriting and sketches. He couldn't imagine how it had gotten there—in the jungle, beside a jaguar's tracks—but he was certain it had to do with Cordelia. There was a heaviness at the bottom of his chest as he tucked it into the back of his waist and picked up his gun.

He was going to find her, he told himself furiously, and

make sure she was safe. Then he was going to strangle her for worrying him like this.

"Any word?" Hardacre Blackburn levered himself up halfway out of his chair as the pasty-faced hotel manager bustled into the parlor of his suite.

"Oh. Sorry, Mr. Blackburn." The fellow was taken aback to realize that the old tycoon thought he was there on a very different sort of errand. "No telegrams, no mail from Mexico. But I really must speak to you. The other guests have begun to vacate the hotel, sir, and—"

"The damned army's movin' in," Hardacre snapped. "Think I don't know that? Damned noisiest bunch of yay-hoos I ever heard. Can't hardly get a decent night's sleep in this place anymore."

"There is a *war* on, Mr. Blackburn." The hotel man wrung his hands.

"Well, they ain't shootin' at khaki in Tampa. When they do, I'll move."

"Really, sir. In times like these, sacrifices must be made. If you would only see fit to speak to the lieutenant in charge of billet—"

"I'm not movin' 'til I hear from my granddaughter. She'll be comin' back to Tampa and I ain't goin' anywhere 'til I see her. So I got nothin' to say to a wet-behind-the-ears *lieu*-tenant."

"However, this 'wet-behind-the-ears lieutenant' has a few things to say to you," came a clipped Back Bay Boston baritone from the door. When Hardacre looked up, a strapping, impeccably starched and pressed young man in army drab stood in the doorway with his thumbs tucked into an expensive belt. Without an invitation, he swaggered into the room and addressed its occupant.

"I'm Lieutenant Barton Montgomery, aide-de-camp to Major General William R. Shafter. The general requires the use of these rooms, Mr. Blackburn, and I'm here to see he gets it." He looked down his nose at Hardacre, clearly taking in the soup stains on the old man's smoking jacket and the frayed gout bandages on his foot. "I'm certain you would be more comfortable"—there was a suggestion of a curl to the young aristocrat's nose—"somewhere else."

Hardacre studied that splendid example of Back Bay Boston's scion breeding program . . . rubbed his chin, thinking . . . then produced a rather satisfied smile.

"Tell ye what. You tell the gen'ral that if he plays his cards right, he just might be able to strike a deal with old Hardacre. I might be persuaded to let him have my rooms—if he's willin' to help me out with a little *domestic* problem I been havin'."

Thirty-six

"I found them—the senoritas!" Itza came running back to the group that had stopped by a stream to have some food and rest. Hart was on his feet in an instant, tossing aside the coconut he'd been husking and wiping his machete on some nearby grass. They had been traveling fast, trying to make up the distance between themselves and Cordelia and Hedda. They ate while on the move and filled their canteens at every opportunity.

"Hedda? You found Hedda? She is all right?" The professor grabbed Itza. When the guide nodded and pointed, the professor rushed off in the direction Itza indicated.

"Valicnte! Professor!" Hart yelled as softly as he could, running after him. "Hot-blooded Latins," he muttered. "Professor!"

So much for the plan he had painstakingly outlined that morning, sneaking up on Castille's group once they were located, surrounding them, and calling for them to lay down their weapons. Once the guns were down, Hart, Ruz, and the professor were supposed to show themselves and collect the guns. They could do this, Hart insisted, without anyone getting hurt.

Now the professor was charging through the forest like an enraged boar, and Castille would hear him coming a mile off and probably shoot him on sight.

"Castille!" The professor's roar carried through the moist, oddly still forest. It was too late to turn back now. "Castille—where are you?"

Hart groaned, stopped short, and motioned to Itza and Ruz to spread out and conceal themselves as they crept up on the others. The brothers faded expertly into the brush, leaving not a trace of their presence.

Hart crept toward the sound of Valiente's voice, straining for a glimpse of Cordelia through the undergrowth. He spotted the professor's light-colored shirt and parted the vegetation enough to see Cordelia and Hedda. The relief that sluiced through him at the sight of her was quickly replaced by fury. Both women looked exhausted and bedraggled, bent under the weight of the packs on their backs. Shockingly, their hands were tied in front of them.

Hedda turned with a look of disbelief at the sound of Valiente's voice. "Arturo?" She sank to her knees as he stepped onto the trail pointing his rifle at the column. With a choked cry, Cordelia sank to her knees beside Hedda, calling to her, unable to do much more than stroke her unresponsive face.

Yago and the three others recognized him and, sensing that his anger had little to do with them, one by one stepped out of his way.

"You!" Castille recovered enough to speak. "But you were—"

"Dead?" Valiente advanced, his face ruddy and eyes like burning coals. "Left to you, I would have been. It appears you didn't look too hard for survivors. You were too busy looting the temple and kidnaping women."

"Don't be absurd, Valiente. We looked for you—you weren't there," Castille declared, glancing at the way his men watched between them. "We merely went on to explore the temple and locate the gold—which is just what you would have done if our situations had been reversed."

"There you are wrong, Castille." Valiente drew himself up straight, using his gun to motion Castille's men to cross over to one side of the trail, leaving him a clear path to Hedda and Cordelia. "It was never my intent to plunder the jaguar's treasury, only to discover the truth about the legend and explore the site. The treasure belongs to the people of Tierra Rica. It is they who were long ago charged with its care." He paused near where Cordelia was trying to revive her aunt. At the sight of Hedda's pale skin and bruised jaw, his fury exploded anew. "Only a coward raises his hand to a woman."

"You stupid, idealistic—" Castille looked to the men clutching their gold-filled packs and fingering their guns. "Did you hear him? He wants to take away the gold you have worked so hard to get." He looked at his trusted bodyguard, then back at the professor, his eyes darker and more fathomless than ever. "We can't afford to have him running to the government. Shoot him!"

The order hung on the air for a moment. Before Yago could react, one of the three men who had just been threatened with losing their hard-won prize raised a gun to do what had made the big Spaniard hesitate. The man slammed his rifle stock to his shoulder and sighted, even as Hart did the same. The two bullets fired almost simultaneously. One went astray; the other found its target. Castille's man was jolted back with a look of surprise that he would carry with him into the next world.

Gunfire broke out as the professor dropped to the ground, and Yago and the others realized the professor wasn't alone and began to shoot wildly into the forest. Hart took aim a second time and a third, counting every bullet and praying in his heart that Cordelia would keep her head down and not try anything foolish. The professor managed to shoulder his gun and fired, hitting another of Castille's men. Then Ruz and Itza started yelling and rose up, and, without quite willing it, Hart also sprang up and charged the group, shouting and firing repeatedly.

But he had to hit the ground when bullets whined past his head, and he had the instinct to dive behind a hummock of grass and old scrub growth. From there he was able to reload and get off two more shots. There was suddenly only one shooter left—Yago. The big man had emptied his gun and as he crawled to relieve one of the dead men of theirs, Hart shoved to his feet and squeezed off a shot that hit just as Yago reached for the rifle.

Suddenly the gunfire was over and the air was heavy with the acrid smell of burned powder. Hart straightened slowly in the haze, staring at the four bodies sprawled and contracted in varying poses of surprise. Staggering, he wheeled to go to Cordelia and found her on her feet . . . with a hand twisted in her hair and a pistol pointed at her head.

"Drop the gun or I'll shoot her," Castille demanded. He had seen the turn of the gun battle and, instead of joining it, had looked for some insurance that he would be able to escape afterward. He had made his way to Cordelia, hauled her to her feet, and pulled her in front of him.

"You'll never make it out of here. You don't even know which way the village is," Hart said, holding onto his gun, using it to point in one direction and his hand to indicate another. But his focus was on Cordelia's huge, dark-centered eyes. There in a glance, he saw her longing, her pleasure at seeing him whole and well, and her anguish at the prospect of losing him yet again.

"Shoot him," she said, her voice small but firm. "Just shoot him—don't worry about me."

"Shut up, puta!" Castille shoved the gun barrel into her cheek and began backing up, pulling her with him. His cruel grip on her hair tightened.

"You won't get away wi–i—" Castille yanked her head back so that her words were choked off for a moment. The next ones came out hoarse and desperate: "Shoot him!"

Suddenly the professor was on his feet beside Hart, with

his gun pointed at Castille. Behind them Ruz and Itza stood with a third gun.

She looked straight into Hart's eyes and he braced, knowing something bad was about to—

"Pretend he has striped tail feathers," she croaked. "Shoo—"

She dropped at that moment, trusting gravity to help her clear Hart's line of shot to Castille. But the Spaniard must have sensed what she intended and reacted, firing as she went down. In the split-second of horror that froze everyone else in place, two more shots were fired, both striking Castille in the arm and spinning him around.

Clasping his wounds, the Spaniard began to run and before they could follow him, he disappeared into the trees.

Hart was at Cordelia's side before another heartbeat went by, calling her name, untying her hands, and gently lifting the monstrous pack from her. She was bleeding and he clamped his hand over her shoulder calling for help, for Yazkuz, for a bandana to press against the wound.

She looked up at him through a cotton fog and smiled as she glimpsed a swath of red around his throat.

"You're wearing one," she said with a hint of surprise before her senses went black.

When Yazkuz arrived seconds later, she knelt by Cordelia and nudged Hart's hand aside to inspect the wound. Muttering fiercely, she set about wiping the blood and checking the extent of the damage.

"Shoulder." She looked at Hart. "She live."

He made to pick her up, but the old woman shook her head. "No move."

"The bastard. I'll kill him for this." Hart started to rise, but Yazkuz grabbed his arm in a fierce grip and shook her head.

"No." She sought his gaze. "Jaguar hunts." After a moment she eased her hold on him. "Make fire. Stay here."

Hart did as he was asked and made a fire on the trail beside Cordelia. When Hedda recovered enough, she helped him and Yazkuz care for Cordelia. Ruz and Itza gathered a selection of fruit and they opened the packs to find several golden cups, which they used to drink water from a nearby spring.

As the light failed, a hush fell over the forest. Even the frogs and crickets had gone silent. Sound carried a long way under such circumstances. They heard growls in the distance and strained to hear more.

Alejandro Castille, aristocrat, banker, financial councilor to cardinals and kings, ran for his life through the darkening forest.

Earlier, he had been puzzled that they didn't try to follow him. He expected that shooting the woman might distract them long enough for him to get away, but he hadn't expected it to work so brilliantly. He wondered for a moment if he had killed her, but decided that wasn't likely. If she were already dead, the tall Brit would probably be beating every bush in Mexico to find him. No, she probably hadn't died—they were busy taking care of her.

That was when he'd heard it. The thing in the weeds and brush—moving—its course oddly parallel to his own. The light was never bright under the thick forest canopy, but at dusk the shadows lengthened and everything seemed unfamiliar and filled with menace. He told himself he was imagining things and concentrated on how he would retrieve his horses when he reached the village. But it was there again. The rustling. The panting. An animal. Eerily close. Always moving with him.

He considered dropping the heavy pack, abandoning it to just get the hell out of this damnable jungle. But he had come too far and worked too hard to just walk away. Two of the half dozen or so artifacts in his bag would fetch him a fortune. And the others—they were for his private collection.

But he didn't find the village and he was wearing down under the extra sixty pounds on his back. And he was running out of light. That was when he first spotted it, in the shadows, watching him. Something with shining golden eyes. He knew what it was. And he began to run.

Now his heart was pounding frantically, his lungs were on fire, and his legs felt weighted with fatigue. Sweat poured down his face and his blood ran down his arm inside his sleeve. He'd stopped earlier to tie a handkerchief around it, but his arm just wouldn't quit bleeding.

Winded and growing steadily more terrified, he began to call to it.

"I have a gun. I'll shoot you before you can lay a claw on me!"

Twice he stumbled to a halt and fired into the bushes moving around him. But starting to run again was pure torture and he knew if he stopped again, it would be for good.

"You know who I am?" he panted out. "Don Alejandro Castille of Madrid. Your ancestors . . . served my family . . . for centuries. Your head brought us riches . . . and influence . . . these things . . . this gold . . . it belongs to me . . . just like you belong to me . . . to my family . . . you are my family."

Then fatigue and weakness and dehydration and blood loss all came crashing down and he stumbled to a halt against a tree and clung to it to keep from falling. The urge to free himself of the dead weight on his back was suddenly overpowering. He ripped his arms from the pack and let it fall. Lightened, he turned to run but found the way blocked.

On the narrow animal trail, in a patch of moonlight, stood the jaguar, muscles taut, tail twitching, golden eyes luminous and hungry for justice.

Terror seized Castille's throat. He couldn't speak. Couldn't scream. He remembered the gun in his hand and raised it. But his hand, still curled as if it held a gun, was empty. He didn't remember dropping it. And he looked up in the moonlight as the great cat gathered itself and let out a growl that was half battle cry, half declaration of victory. Just before it leaped and tore into his throat, he saw the look in its eye and plainly heard its thoughts.

"Predator to predator. You understand how it is."

Thirty-seven

They tended the fire through the night. No one was tempted to sleep, not after what they'd heard an hour after sundown: shots fired in the distance, the growls and the battle cry of a big cat. Imbedded in that last burst of sound, they thought they heard a human scream. A profound silence followed.

"Done." Yazkuz nodded and took a deep breath.

It took a while for the normal night noise to return to the forest. Hedda sat encompassed in the professor's arms, Itza and Ruz poked anxiously at the crackling fire, and Yazkuz alternately chanted and busied herself with finding moss and other items Hart requested for cleaning and packing Cordelia's wound.

There was one who didn't join them around the fire, but sat some distance away against a tree trunk. Yago, too, had been shot but it was a clean flesh wound to the upper arm and he simply bound it with a piece of his shirt and refused to have old Yazkuz look at it. Ruz came forward to say it had been Yago that had fired one of the shots that struck Castille. Hart searched the big man's blunt-featured face and nodded, acknowledging his help but deferring any decision on his fate until another time. To his credit, the big man did not try to run; he seemed to know there were things far worse than human justice waiting in the jungle.

It was the longest night of Hart's life. As soon as the first gray fingers of dawn poked through the upper canopy, he gathered Cordelia up and carried her all the way to Yazkuz's house on the outskirts of the village, which turned out to be closer than they thought. By the light of day, Yazkuz recognized the area from her collecting trips and was able to guide them.

It wasn't long before word spread that they had returned and the villagers arrived with gifts of food and offers of help in tidying their camp, which hadn't been touched in the six days since Castille's men searched it.

By agreement, no one mentioned the packs of gold artifacts stored in Yazkuz's cellar, or said they discovered anything more than a few old ruins in a canyon. By unspoken agreement, Yago was given some supplies and his gun and was permitted to walk the trail that led back toward civilization. They owed at least something to the man, as Hart explained to Yazkuz. And he had no stomach for vengeance.

Cordelia awakened twice after she reached Yazkuz's house. Each time she saw Hart holding her hand, smiled weakly, and tried to speak. Each time he stroked her hair, told her to save her strength, and watched her sink back into oblivion, feeling his heart sinking with her.

Yazkuz used every herb in her live-in pharmacopeia to try to reduce the inflammation that had set in and start the healing. Hart racked his brain, trying to think of things he had learned that might help. By the end of the second night, he was desperate enough to try anything. When Yazkuz brought him one of the wrinkly white roots from the red orchid, he was anguished enough by the thought of losing her to accept it.

He had no idea how it worked, when it worked, or what it did to the body.

Yet it was all he had.

He crushed the root and put it on Cordelia's tongue. And he prayed.

The effects began right away—erratic heartbeat, uneven breathing, sharply rising fever. Immediately he repented the desperation that caused him to give into the temptation to use such an unknown, unproven substance on her. It was the equivalent of witch-doctoring, he thought, looking at Yazkuz, who sat with her eyes closed, in deep communion with the spirits she revered. Indeed, that was *just* what it was. And he bowed his head to pray that whatever else it was, it would be effective.

In the depths of the third night, Hart sat bathing her skin and fanning her to reduce the heat in her. In the dimness of the little house, among the bundles of dried herbs and arcane bits of healing magic, he realized that his "scientific" efforts and the old girl's superstition had more than a little in common. They just went about their search for healing in very different ways. How ironic that the life of the woman he loved would be decided by the efficacy of a healing practice he had always decried.

He stroked Cordelia's hair and her feverish face, willing, begging her to come back to him, and powerless to make it happen. Then he knelt by her head and poured his heart out in words, knowing her body was asleep but praying her spirit would hear.

"Don't leave me, Cordelia. Not just when I've found you. Not just when I've finally figured out what a heart is for. Not before I have a chance to tell you how much you mean to me . . . how the prospect of seeing you makes the sun rise each morning . . . how the pleasure of touching you explains why I was made with hands . . . how the beat of your heart sets the rhythm of time itself . . . how your movement ordains the music of the spheres . . . how your smile, your presence, is proof of good in the world. You make me want to climb mountains and swim oceans and swing from the stars. I feel like I can do anything—everything with you in my heart."

Tears filled his eyes and his voice.

"But without you, Cordelia O'Keefe Blackburn, I don't know if I could even go on living. Come back to me. Please come back to me."

He touched her lips with his and one of his tears fell onto her cheek.

"I love you."

He laid his head down on her shoulder, murmuring those words over and over, a prayer for the living, a hope for the future. And somewhere toward dawn fatigue claimed him and he slept.

Yazkuz woke him midmorning with a shriek. He started up, knocking over the stool he'd been sitting on. "Wh–what? What is it?"

"The fever—she goes!"

Frantic over the "she goes" part, he checked Cordelia and found her cool and damp—sweating—her heart beating normally, her breathing slow and regular. He picked up the old girl and whirled her around.

"She's all right!" he shouted. "She's going to be all right!"

Every hour after that brought her closer to healing and nearer consciousness. When she finally opened her eyes that evening as he tried to get some weak tea and fruit juice into her, he thought he'd never seen anything so beautiful as her amber eyes.

"Good God, O'Keefe, give me a scare, why don't you?" he uttered, his heartfelt eloquence totally fled now that she was back.

"You were really worried about me?" she rasped out, looking at the circles under his eyes and the nearly ten-day-old beard growth on his face. She grinned. "I'll live, but only if you promise to shave."

He laughed and raised his hand. "Every day for the rest of my life."

When he ducked out the door to make good his promise, she sighed.

"The rest of his life? That sounds promising."

Hedda came rushing in with the professor and hugged her and cried.

"So how does it feel to be back from the dead?" Cordelia asked Valiente.

He chuckled. "You should know. You give us very big scare, Cordelia."

"Between the two of you, I've been a nervous wreck." Hedda's eyes shone through a prism of tears. "I'm serving notice—this is my last adventure. I'm retiring. You'll just have to find someone younger and stronger to share your adventures from now on." She squeezed the professor's hand. "I have . . . other things to do."

Next the Platano brothers came in to pay their respects, beaming pleasure at seeing her so improved. They brought news that they had a booming burro business and that little Goodnight had been purchased for a record sum.

Yazkuz finally shooed them out and made her a tisane of something foul tasting and told her to rest. When she awoke later, she found Hart sitting by her bed, writing in his journal. He was bathed and shaved and dressed once again in his clean khakis. When he realized she was awake, he laid the journal on the bed beside her and leaned close.

"Good evening," he said, his voice rumbling through her, setting everything in her soul to rights—until she realized what he was doing. She lifted her head and reached for the journal.

"Where did you get this?" she demanded.

"Funny thing about that. I found it on the trail when Ruz was showing me some jaguar tracks—near where you and Castille were camped. I couldn't believe it at first, but then I realized I must have left it in my rucksack that Castille had used for carrying some of his gold."

"I . . . I . . ." She looked up, scarcely able to confess to those beautiful light gray eyes. "I realized what it was . . .

and so I . . . I kept it for you . . . until Castille saw me with it and tossed it away. So, you *found* it."

His eyes narrowed.

"You *kept* it. You didn't happen to read any of it, did you? My private, personal journal?"

She looked straight into his eyes and blinked.

"Of course not."

He smiled and gave her a kiss on the lips that pulled at least part of the truth from her.

"The truth is, having it, holding it, got me through that ordeal. I had no idea whether you were alive or dead, but when I held it, I felt you were close to me." Her heart was beating erratically again, but not from any illness. "The thing I regretted most"—she reached up with her good arm to stroke his face—"was that I hadn't told you that I love you. But I do, Hart. I love you with everything in me and I can't imagine going on in a world without you in it."

She used his shirt collar to pull him down to kiss her.

"I assure you, the feeling is mutual," he said when he could take a breath.

"Then say it," she muttered against his lips.

"I love you, Cordelia. With everything in me. Which is basically all I have in this world. Just me. No frills or accessories."

She laughed. "I think the basic model will do just fine."

Four days later, she was well enough to travel. It was nothing short of a miracle, Hart said, vowing not to use the red orchid cure again until he'd had a chance to fully investigate the plant's properties and determine appropriate dosages and control its wild effects—like the bizarre urge to say exactly what was in one's heart. Before he left, Yazkuz loaded him up with enough herbs and botanical curiosities to keep him busy in a laboratory for years. And after considerable consultation with the Jaguar Spirit, she insisted on sending three of the bags of gold back to civilization with them, to help fund Hart's healing mission. A parting "Gift of the Jaguar."

The Platanos insisted on escorting them back down the river to the coast. But because Cordelia was still regaining her strength, Hart insisted—over her objection—that she ride every step of the way.

"My feet practically drag the ground," she protested, feeling grossly oversized for poor Rita.

"A donkey was good enough for the Virgin Mary, it should be good enough for you," Hart declared, and that was the end of it. After all, who could argue with the Virgin Mary's taste in transportation?

At the coast, they waited only two days before O'Brien appeared, right on schedule. He brought news that the battleship *Maine* had been sunk in Havana Harbor and the tide of opinion in the United States was finally swinging toward helping Cuba in its war with Spain. He was steaming straight for Tampa to pick up supplies collected by the Cuban community for the freedom fighters.

It was on the third day out that Cordelia, mostly healed, invaded Hart's cabin to see if he were all right. He hadn't been troubled with seasickness nearly as much this trip, but she worried every time he disappeared for a while that it had recurred. Oddly, he wasn't in the cabin he shared with the professor. His bunk was neatly made and on it lay his journal, open to his latest entry.

Curiosity drew her to the book—just for a glimpse of his hand, she told herself—since it had meant so much to her once. In spite of a twinge of conscience, she picked it up and read an entry that caused her stomach to melt and her knees to weaken.

March 5, Day 45

Headed for Tampa on O'Brien's boat. Hard to believe it's almost over. Must confess to feeling a little chopfallen. Gotten rather used to puking over a railing, shaking boots in the morning to check for vermin, and using leaves for toilet paper. (May never be able to look a Boston fern in the eye again.) I should be relieved to be rid of the smells of mosquito balm, gun oil, and fish charred unrecognizable over an open fire. And beans. If I never eat another dried bean again it will be too soon.

Strange how the human being can adjust to and accept even the most extreme conditions over time. Being chased, shot at, and sleep deprived... terrorized by hungry panthers, bitten by snakes, kissed witless by women...all becomes quite tolerable after a while. Shocking really.

One thing I won't miss is O'Keefe. Damned impossible woman. Reckless and stubborn, ready to risk life and limb at the drop of a hat. Stalked by wild animals, blown up, shot, half drowned, nothing seems to faze her. Crack shot, though. And those legs. And delectable breasts. Biblical pomegranates suddenly make sense. Years of catechism finally validated. And those kisses. Quite intoxicating, actually. Never felt like running stark naked through Trefalgar Square before I kissed her.

Thank God she wasn't awake to hear me make a fool of myself the other night in Yazzie's hut. Blathering on about finally figuring out what a heart was for. About how *she makes the sun rise for me every morning. And that business of the pleasure of touching her explaining why I was made with hands...and how her heartbeat sets the rhythm of time itself for me...that she makes me want to climb mountains and swim oceans...*

Whew. Glad she doesn't know yet how much my world depends on her. Do, however, wish I could see the look on her face when she reads this:

Marry me, O'Keefe.

She staggered back and plopped down on a chair, staring at those words. Then she jumped up and burst from the cabin. She found him on the aft deck, looking out over the wake they were leaving and she threw her arms around him.

"Yes! Yes, yes, yes, yes, *YES!*"

Thirty-eight

The setting sun was putting on a spectacular display of golds, pinks, and reds over the Gulf as Hardacre sat dozing in a chaise on the veranda of his quaint little house on the Bayshore in Tampa. Night after night he came out here with his lap robe and his warm milk toddy to stare off into the sunset and miss the old days . . . the old ways . . . the old boys.

One boy in particular.

Dark hair and light eyes . . . sober and earnest . . . always still as a mouse beside his mother in church . . . his slightly too-large ears alert for every nuance, absorbing every grandiose admonition and heartfelt plea. But there were other times, too . . . learning to ride a pony . . . walking on stilts . . . making a metal hoop sing on the brick pavement . . . his laughter rang out sweet . . . his mischief innocent, never mean. Good hearted, he was. And generous. A little gullible. Like his poor mother, who had the misfortune to fall in love with a man whose heart would always be divided between the halls of power and the backrooms of influence—with little room left over for the claims of a wife and child.

The sound of someone coming up the brick walk toward the veranda made him open his eyes. There she was, coming toward him, a short split skirt, boots, a khaki shirt, and a Panama hat, the same chestnut hair and hot amber eyes, the same eye-popping curves. He could have sworn there was a gun belt slung across her hip. He closed his eyes for a minute, shook his head, then reopened them in time to see her step onto the veranda.

Behind her, looming like an oversized shadow was none other than his once and possibly future butler, dressed in the oddest get-up, all big boots and khaki, looking half military and half savage, his hair way too long and his skin so sun-bronzed that his light eyes stood out like Wedgewood saucers.

"You!" He sat up completely, all eyes and ears now, focused on her and the man beside her. "You're back."

"We are indeed." She set the bag she carried on the porch by her feet and looked him over. "With results."

He tossed aside his lap robe and scooted forward on the seat, trying to gain purchase to lever himself up. Both looked as if they might step in to offer help, but he puffed up his chest and glowered to keep them back, and managed to make it to his feet on his own and reach for his cane.

"Inside," he said, gesturing to the screen doors. He stood in front of them for a moment as if expecting someone to open them, then scowled at Goodnight and opened them himself.

The parlor he headed for had high white walls and ceilings, mahogany floors, and long, plantation-shuttered windows that were open to admit the breeze from the bay across the boulevard. He thumped his way over to a parlor card table with chairs and lowered himself into a seat. Then he rang a bell on the corner of the table that caused Goodnight to start and glare at the bane of his former existence.

"Sit," he ordered them, pointing at the chairs drawn up to the mahogany table. "And let's have th' story. Did ye find the stones?"

"You rang?" came a male voice from behind them. They turned to find a tall, athletic-looking young man in full military uniform standing on the parlor rug at attention. They could see his jaw tighten and his chin rise as they looked him over, and they couldn't help noticing the officer's bars on his collar.

"Montgomery, bring us some brandy and some lemonade. With ice."

"Very good, sir." The young man enunciated each word with an emphasis that relayed his contempt for the request, the requestor, and his position as requestee. He executed a full military about-face and strode out.

"Who the devil was that?" Goodnight asked.

"My new butler, leastwise for now. Got him in a little deal I cut with old Bill Shafter," he said with a sly expression. "You know, General Shafter, head of this whole 'Cuba' thing. He's settin' up his HQ in the Tampa Bay Hotel. Montgomery there was one o' his aides des camp. Took such a likin' to th' lad, I persuaded old Bill to assign him to me for a while."

"I can just imagine," Goodnight muttered, glancing over his shoulder.

"Ain't quite broke in yet, but at least he calls me *sir*," Hardacre said, giving Goodnight a pointed look before turning to Cordelia. "Now what did you learn about my rubbings?"

"Well, there is good news and bad news. Which do you want first?"

"The bad," he said, scowling, bracing with his arms out on the table.

"The bad news is: your rubbings are gone, obliterated in a flood. The good news is: they were genuine and the carvings they were made on still exist."

This was more like it. Hardacre's eyes lit with interest.

"Still around, eh? Where were they? *What* were they?"

"They were an arch of stones that led to a temple built to honor the Jaguar Spirit. It turned out, they did have to do with 'the Gift of the Jaguar.'"

He felt like a child at Christmas dinner; he hardly knew where to start.

"Did ye find 'em? See 'em yerself?"

"We tracked them to the mountains of Veracruz, in Mexico. With the help of Processor Valiente and a good mapmaker, we were able locate a river that bore an exact likeness to a shape in the stone rubbing. We hiked there—Hart and I, in the company of an old medicine woman—and saw the stones and temple. Which, by the way, was built in the crater of an extinct volcano."

"A temple *in* a volcano?" Hardacre drew his chin back at that, doubtful, then gradually more skeptical. "An' a kindly old medicine woman?"

"Kindly. Not a word I would use to describe Yazkuz," Hart observed.

"I suppose she just *gave* you this secret." Hardacre ignored him, just like old times. "Didn't try to *sell* it to you or anything?"

"She asked nothing for her services. She seemed to think it was her duty to share with us, especially Hart," Cordelia said. "Healer to healer, as it were. She was able to read some of the glyphs and murals in the temple, which said that the gift the Jaguar Spirit gave mankind was *healing*."

"Healing." Hardacre looked at Goodnight then back at her. "*Hart?*"

"Apparently humans used to be spindlier and punier than now and were prone to all kinds of diseases," she continued. "The Jaguar gave humans the gift of healing, and the rest, as they say, is history. Humans conquered the world."

Hardacre gave a huff of disgust, then turned to Goodnight.

"You agree with this nonsense, *Hart*?"

"I do."

"You were there for all of it? She didn't waylay you somewhere and leave you stranded?"

"She did not."

"Fine. Then let's hear *your* report."

"I believe you just did." Goodnight folded his surprisingly well-muscled arms.

"I mean yer full report. You were supposed to be my agent. Keep track of my money and verify th' results."

"I was, I did, and I do." He pulled out a strip of paper and flattened it in front of Hardacre so he could see the tally. "Expenses: two thousand, nine hundred, and sixty-seven dollars and fourteen cents." He pulled a stack of coins containing a ten- and a twenty-dollar gold piece and several silver dollars from his pocket. "Thirty-two dollars and eighty-six cents change. And an unused letter of credit." He tossed a rumpled envelope onto the table. "After all we went through, believe me, it would have been a bargain at twice the price." He folded his arms and leaned back in his chair.

"That's it?"

"My report? Yes."

"Well, it ain't good enough. Where's yer writin'? Where's the artifacts?"

"My job, as it was clearly outlined to me, was to verify the authenticity of Cordelia's efforts and findings. I am doing that now. My task is complete."

"That's it? That's what I get for my three thousand, four if you count the equipment I bought before the trip?"

"That is exactly what we agreed upon," she said pointedly. "Our *deal*."

He looked back and forth between them, sputtering, until he saw the quick, speaking glance Cordelia gave Hart and his blood pressure skyrocketed.

"You—you did something to him." He jabbed a finger at her. "You batted those eyes and got under his skin and convinced him to go along with whatever palaver you decided to dish out." He turned on Goodnight. "Where's your damned loyalty?"

Goodnight snapped forward so abruptly that Hardacre recoiled in shock.

"Where it belongs." He looked at Cordelia. "With my wife."

Just then Montgomery strode into the room with a tray, pitcher, and glasses, headed for the card table.

"Not now, Montgomery," Hardacre snapped.

"But—"

"Not now, dammit!"

The red-faced fellow made an about-face and strode out of the room.

"W-wife?" Hardacre nearly strangled on the word. "You married her?" Then he looked at his granddaughter and covered his shock and dismay with a forced laugh. "You married a *butler*? That's rich. You come here to swindle me out of an inheritance, and you end up tyin' the knot with my butler!"

"I didn't come to swindle you out of anything," she declared hotly. "And he's not a butler. He never was. He was a brilliant, strong, compassionate, funny, and resourceful *man*."

"Why, thank you," Goodnight put in.

"You're welcome," she said with a nod his direction. "You treated him like he was a mere servant, but he's ten times the man you are." She stopped and went to stand by Goodnight, who rose and put his arm around her. He looked large and formidable and a little forbidding. Hardacre couldn't believe *this* man had ever busied himself sorting anybody's socks.

"You haven't changed a bit, have you?" Cordelia crossed her arms. "Shades of my father and mother's troubles with you, all over again. We're married, so that means we must have somehow betrayed you—just as my parents did. Did it never occur to you that their hearts, their desires, their feelings for each other—like ours—don't have anything to do with you? That Hart and I might have just . . . jarred and jostled and jolted ourselves into love . . . all by ourselves?"

Hardacre stood silent for a moment, braced for a blast but suffering a very different kind of broadside than he expected. He stared at the pair of them, so strong and united and—*admit it, dammit*—perfectly matched. And for a moment he saw another pair of young lovers standing in their shoes, wanting his approval but touching only his wrath.

He sat down with a plop.

"I can tell you right now," Cordelia declared, "that the sight of him green-around-the-gills and hanging over the rail of a ship was more interesting to me than all of the gorgeous bachelors in Boston combined."

"Oh, thank you," Goodnight said dryly.

"You're welcome." She nodded again and went right back to it.

"Somewhere between running through the streets of Havana with half the Cuban army on our trail . . . and watching him dress like a peasant to escape on a smuggler's ship . . . and helping him deliver a baby burro . . . and having him shoot a boa constrictor that was going to drop on me . . . and seeing him climb inside a volcano's belly, having him save me from suffocating when I tasted 'dumb cane,' and rescue me when I was kidnapped . . ." She stopped for a minute to catch her breath. "Well, somewhere in the middle of all of that, I fell madly and deliriously in love with him. I can't imagine my life without him. And wonder of wonders—he seems to feel the same about me. That's fairly rare, you know, that sort of miracle. Especially for a pair as unique as we are."

Slowly the sense of what she'd said seeped through. Hardacre was taken aback, then thoroughly confused.

"What?" she asked. "Do you just not understand love at all?"

Hell no. Never understood at all the mad, sweet chemistry that draws one poor human to another in a bond that means more than life. His old heart began to swell in his chest. He'd missed all of that while he was concentrating on less important things.

He looked at Goodnight, glowering, hoping to burn away moisture in his eyes.

"You did all that?" he demanded. "What she said?"

"Absolutely." Goodnight sighed. "Do you want to hear some of her moments of captivating charm? How she bribed a customs official, smuggled guns into two countries, hired a raving maniac of a professor—"

"Who happened to know his stuff," she put in.

"Granted," he said with a gallant nod her way. "Then she went toe to toe with a nasty Spanish banker who thought your rubbings should belong to him . . . held off a regiment of Cuban regulars with a pistol so we could swim for our lives . . . hacked her way through miles of jungle . . . faced down a jaguar in the wild—not once but three times—tended me when I was unconscious . . . got kidnapped and shot . . . damned near died . . . all while managing to be so breathtakingly beautiful and courageous and infuriating . . . that I couldn't help falling in love with her."

"You did all of that?" Hardacre looked to her anxiously. "You got shot?"

"Want to see?" she said.

"Here we go," Goodnight sighed, taking a step back.

She unbuttoned her shirt and pulled it back, baring her shoulder. The reddish scar was still quite fresh. Hardacre's jaw dropped.

Montgomery started into the room with the tray of brandy and lemonade, saw her standing there with her shirt half off . . . blanched, turned, and exited.

"Well, why didn't you just say that in the first place?" Hardacre said irritably. "Just breeze in here with nary a story . . . we're back and we saw yer stones and that's that. How's a man suppose to believe a word you say?"

Cordelia looked at Hart, who closed his eyes and shook his head.

"And you—what happened to our little deal on the side?" Hardacre turned to Goodnight.

"What little deal on the side?" Cordelia asked.

"This would probably be a good time to give him his share of the treasure," Hart declared, gesturing to the satchel by the table.

"Treasure?" Hardacre was flabbergasted. "You didn't bother to mention you found a treasure until *now*?"

"Well, it wasn't relevant to the stones, per se," she said.

"Get on with it, girl," Hardacre growled. This was turning out better than he expected. There was still hope . . .

She reached into the satchel and pulled out a heavy disk of solid gold, adorned with Mayan symbols in a broad ring around the edges and set with a three-dimensional head of a jaguar in the center. Hardacre's eyes popped.

"Is that what I think it is?" He turned on her.

"I'm not sure what you think it is, but it's gold," she informed him. "And it's your share of the treasure."

"My share?" The old man ran his fingers over the lustrous surface of the medallion. "You mean there's more?"

"I told you this was a bad idea," she said to Hart. "Money is all he thinks about. All he cares about. The sight of gold will just set him off."

"I want to see the rest of it. All of it," Hardacre demanded, momentarily entranced by the object beneath his fingers.

"See?" She gave Hart a dark look, then turned back to her grandfather. "Well, I'm afraid that's not possible. You see, this is the part of your share you're not investing in Hart's pharmaceutical company," she said. "You'll have to trust me on this. It will be a marvelous investment. Hart found several very promising medicines in Mexico that will be a great help to people. They just need to be dose-tested and regularized."

"You did what? You invested my money—"

"Treasure," she corrected him.

"—my *treasure* in some nincompoop idea?"

"As your wedding gift to us. Yes."

"After all I done for you—this is what I get?" He turned on Hart. "A hunk o' gold and a fine fare-thee-well? Ye were supposed to find me a cure."

"After all you *did* for me?" Hart stiffened with indignation.

"When I took ye in, old son, you wasn't just broke, you

was brok*en*." He jabbed a finger at Hart. "An' look at ye now. Full o' piss an' vinegar. If I hadn't sent ye off with *her*, ye'd still be mewlin' around, lickin' yer wounds and sortin' socks. An' all I asked in return was one puny little medicine."

"Fine. You want a medicine? I'll make you one." Hart stalked closer to him. "I'll regularize and dose-test some cholchicine for you."

"Don't want none of that stuff—it's poison."

"So are most medicines in the wrong dosage or used for the wrong complaint," Hart said. "That's the point of the work I tried to do. That's why I borrowed money from you in the first place, to develop *real* and *safe* cures."

"And, clearly, this gout medicine will have a priority. This investment won't only make you money, it's going to help people live healthier lives." Cordelia slipped her arm into Hart's, inserting herself between him and Hardacre and pouring every ounce of charm she possessed into a dazzling smile. "You may turn out to be quite a humanitarian. A shining example for your great-grandchildren. They may even grow up loving you."

Hardacre sputtered and started to speak twice, then closed his mouth, scowling. It was blackmail. Pure and simple. She was offering something he never expected to have at this stage of his life: a second chance.

"She got the makin's of a real tycoon," he said to Goodnight.

"Drives a hard bargain, all right." Goodnight's ire was sidetracked by the change on Hardacre's face. "You should hear her wheedling down the price of donkey rentals."

Hardacre dragged a sharp breath and sat back sharply in his chair, his anger replaced by distress. The pain in his foot flared to an unbearable level.

"Ye'd better hurry with that colchey-stuff," he said, his throat constricted. "My foot's killin' me."

His granddaughter looked at her new husband with alarm in those irresistible eyes.

"He's suffering. You could try it on him. One last time. Please," she said. "You could consider it a dosage trial."

"I vowed—*swore* I wouldn't use it again until I had run a million tests on it and understood its action and potential hazards," Goodnight said. "And I intend to keep that vow."

"Use what?" Hardacre gritted his teeth and fought the pain rocketing up his leg as he watched them.

"Well, I didn't make any such vow," she declared, fishing in the pocket of her skirt for a waxed paper packet containing a small piece of what appeared to be a wrinkled white root. She emptied it onto the polished table in front of Hardacre.

"You brought it with you?" Goodnight started to retrieve it, but found his way blocked by Cordelia.

"What's this?" Hardacre leaned forward to squint at it.

"This was a part of the healing gift the jaguar gave to humans—or so old Yazkuz believed," she told him. "It's the root of a rare orchid found only deep in the Mayan jungle."

"It contains a substance of powerful potential, but erratic and dangerous side effects," Goodnight said. "I recommend that you leave it on the table and save yourself a great deal of discomfort."

"Dis-comfert? Hell's bells. Can't be worse'n the pain I got now," Hardacre snapped, looking to his granddaughter. "Whaddo ye do with it?"

She looked at Goodnight with a pleading expression that finally produced a slight but telling lowering of his shoulders.

"If the old gaffer's heart gives out," he told his wife, "it's on your head."

She turned to Hardacre with a determined light in her eyes.

"You put it under your tongue and hold it there."

Hardacre stared at it, scowling, then looked up at Goodnight.

"Think it might help?"

"Truthfully?" Goodnight sighed, bracing himself. "I

have no bloody idea. It seems to be a kill-or-cure sort of thing."

"Seen anybody die from it?" Hardacre asked.

"No," Goodnight looked grieved to admit. "Not yet."

"Good enough for me," Hardacre declared, putting the piece of root into his mouth and giving it a good chomp, then another, before wallowing it under his tongue.

"What do you feel?" Cordelia asked Hardacre. "A flush of warmth? A chill? Dizziness? Anything at all?"

He took inventory for a moment, looked uncertain, then shook his head.

"Maybe a slight tinglin' in my tongue an' throat."

"Give it time," Goodnight said, reaching for his wrist and taking out a pocketwatch to time Hardacre's pulse. For a few moments the ticking of the mantle clock was the only sound in the room. Goodnight felt his forehead and shrugged in bewilderment. "He's flushed. Starting to feel a little warm."

"Ye know, my foot's startin' to feel better." Hardacre reddened as he struggled to pull up his gouty foot and inspect it. As they watched, he broke into a sweat and began to breathe heavily.

Just then, Montgomery entered with the tray and halted halfway across the room, looking uncertain.

Goodnight caught sight of him and waved him over to the table. When Hardacre didn't object, he strode over and deposited the refreshments.

As he made to pull away, Goodnight grabbed his wrist and held it with one hand as he reached for the brandy with the other. He poured a generous draught and thrust it into the young officer's hand.

Montgomery's eyes widened, then he seemed to understand, and with a grateful look, tossed it back in one gulp.

A moment later, the old man abruptly gave several frantic gasps, sagged in his chair, and lost consciousness. Goodnight rushed to take his pulse and pry open his eyes to look at his pupils.

"His heart is racing. He's on fire." He looked up at the startled Montgomery. "Help me get him to the sofa."

Cordelia hurried ahead of them to remove some pillows to make room for them to lay him out. She asked Montgomery for some wet cloths and helped Hart remove the old man's jacket and vest and loosen his collar. He was hot to the touch, but sweating profusely.

"I don't understand." Hart listened to Hardacre's chest and frowned. "His pulse and heartbeat are fairly steady." He glanced at Cordelia. "Better than yours and—from what you said—better than mine."

"He's a tough old bird," she said, stroking the old man's head, worry for him evident in her trembling hand.

Montgomery returned shortly with some linen and a basin of cool water.

"Is he dying?" The lieutenant stretched his neck to see past Hart to the patient on the sofa.

"Don't get your hopes up." Hart took the basin from him and handed it to Cordie. "He'll probably outlive us all."

But it was a long and difficult night, and the first gray wisps of dawn were curling around the plantation shutters before there was a significant change in his condition. They had moved him upstairs to his bed, and took turns sitting by his side, bathing his face and chest and arms to keep him cool. By early dawn both Cordie and Hart had dozed off and were startled awake by the rasping sound of the old man's voice.

"So, I'm still alive?"

"Oh, yes." Cordelia lurched over the bed and grabbed his hand, searching his face, then beaming relief. "Still very much alive."

"I figured. Where th' Almighty'd send me there ain't nothin' near as pretty as you." He gave a rusty laugh.

"How do you feel?" Hart appeared beside Cordelia to check Hardacre's pulse and temperature.

"Not bad. A little weak." The old man struggled to sit up and with a little help and some cautioning, was soon upright on the side of the bed. As they watched he sat straighter and seemed to recover more of himself. "Pretty damned good, in fact." He looked down at his foot with intense concentration, clearly trying to wiggle his toes.

"Hey, the pain's gone!" He wrestled his gouty foot up onto the bed beside him and attacked the bandages. Hart lent a hand, and by the time they reached the end of the bandages Hardacre was wiggling much improved toes. "I'll be doggoned—it worked!"

"Well, I'll be—" Goodnight sank to his knees to examine Hardacre's foot. Then he looked up at Cordelia, clearly unsettled. "I have no clue what just happened." He glanced at his pocket watch. "It's only been ten hours. With us it took days."

"Maybe it's losing strength . . . as it dries up or gets older," she suggested. "Or maybe his body is tougher than most."

He looked up at Hardacre's glowing face.

"Not beyond the pale of possibility," he said, rising, scratching his head. "See, this is what I hate—not knowing—doing it witch-doctor style."

Hardacre stepped gingerly on the foot he had so many times wished he could just cut off. The pain was virtually gone. He began to walk, then to dance around the room. Soon, he stood in the middle of the floor with his arms wide open and his heart renewed.

"Montgomery," he roared. "Montgomery!" He reached for the bell pull, and in the morning quiet, they could hear the servants' bell ringing all the way up the back stairs. The young officer came lurching into the room seconds later, looking disheveled and alarmed. He'd apparently fallen asleep on the bench in the adjoining dressing room; he had a wicked sleep crease across one cheek. "Get me my left shoe, Montgomery! By damn—I'm going to wear two shoes today for the first time in years."

But before the young officer could reach the dressing room door, Hardacre was barking still more orders.

"And tell the cook we want eggs and ham and grits and

biscuits—the whole works—for breakfast. I'm so hungry, I could eat a horse. And make up the guest room. We got family comin' to stay."

He halted and turned to Cordelia with a question in his eyes.

She felt Hart come up behind her and leaned back into the shelter of his arms with a throaty laugh.

"Yes," she said, "we're definitely family. And we're here to stay."

Epilogue

Eight years later

The long, French-gabled greenhouse was humid and fragrant with the scents of damp earth, moss, and decaying wood. The shelves and tables were lined with orchids, some in pots and others seated in wooden latices that allowed their bare, wizened roots to grow free in the moist air. The place was full of showy blooms in white and yellow, delicate green and fuschia, lilac and brazen orange. But the dominant color, from the predominant species, was a magnificent ruby red.

Cordelia, busy with her shears and watering can, barely heard the crunch of little feet on the gravel path before her four-year-old son barreled into her legs, almost knocking her off her feet.

"Mommie, Mommie, we're home!"

She looked with a smile down into the glowing face of the boy wrapped around her knees, who held her captive in a dozen other ways as well.

"Max!" She set aside her shears and stooped to give him the hug he was bent on having. A second set of footfalls caused her to look up. "Olivia!" She laughed and extended an arm to draw her seven-year-old daughter against her as well. "What are my two monkeys doing out here?"

"We just got home and came to see if you're finished." Olivia looked around, her golden-hazel eyes lighting with curiosity. "Can I help?"

"I'm nearly through. How about if you water that end of the table, while I finish some trimming?" When Olivia nodded and reached for the watering can, Cordelia held up a finger to collect her's and Max's attention.

"What's our first rule of the greenhouse?" she said for the hundredth time.

"Never put anything in your mouth," Max and Olivia repeated together.

"Right." She handed over the watering can and saw her daughter frown.

"But Papa does. He puts things in his mouth all the time," Olivia said with a maturity of perception that hadn't been there last month or even last week.

"Your father has the constitution of a Clydesdale. Because he's British. You, on the other hand, are only half British. So you can't afford to go around chewing on stray plant and animal matter. Understood?"

Olivia nodded, though she didn't seem entirely satisfied with that answer. As Cordelia turned back to her work, she heard another set of footsteps. She looked up to find Hart stopped just inside the door, bending down to look beneath the plant tables.

There was a mischievous giggle from somewhere near her feet, and Hart stalked forward menacingly, still bent in half.

"Fee Fie Fo Fum . . . I smell a tasty little boy on the run."

There was more chasing and scrambling before Max was caught and dragged out from under a table and up into his father's arms.

Flushed with pleasure, Hart carried him over to Cordelia. "Hello, Gorgeous," he said dropping a kiss on her upturned lips that drew a dubious look from Max. Then he stooped to pick Olivia up in the other arm, and for a moment—his arms filled with the bounty of their love—he looked like the happiest man on earth.

"You must have had a good day," she said, searching his face.

"We isolated another compound. That makes *nine*." He turned with the children to look at one of the showy red flowers that seemed to contain a pharmacy in each plant. "Nine out of one plant. It's unprecedented. I can't wait to write this one up. I want to see your grandfather's face when he hears it."

"Grandpa's here." Olivia gave her father an adoring look. "He went into the parlor for a nap when we got back from the zoo. He's staying for supper."

Hart sighed. "I really should start work on something for indigestion."

"Grandpa says I'm gonna be a typhoon," Max said, looking very pleased.

"He did, did he?" Cordelia removed her gloves.

"He's gonna teach me." Max's pride was quickly replaced by confusion. "What's a typhoon?"

"A very large storm. Lots of excess wind. Your grandfather's a perfect example," Hart said, drawing an elbow in the ribs from Cordelia.

"I think Grandpa meant to say 'tycoon,' Max," she said. "That's someone who buys and sells lots of things and seems to have fun doing it."

"What's it called again?" Max cocked his head.

"Tycoon," she said, helping Olivia down from her father's arms and giving Hart a loving look above the children's heads as they left the greenhouse.

"Well, Grandpa says I'm going to be an adventurer," Olivia said, claiming her share of attention. "He says I'll climb volcanos and ride camels across deserts and chop my way through jungles to find treasures."

"He does, does he?" Cordelia glanced at Hart and bit her lip. He shook his head silently.

"He says he'll teach me," Olivia said. "He says he found a great treasure once in Mexico."

"*He* found a treasure?" Hart looked at Cordelia with a remnant of old outrage rising in his expression.

"Yes, well, I'm sure he had a little help," Cordelia said turning her face into the breeze as they walked across the lawn to the house.

After dessert that evening, Hardacre announced he had a little present for the children and led them into the parlor to see a battered old trunk that was oddly familiar to Hart's and Cordelia's eyes.

"This is a very special trunk," the old man said, leaning toward the children with a twinkle in his eyes.

"Is it magic?" Max asked, running to it to explore with pudgy fingers.

"*No*," and "Not exactly," came from Hart and Cordelia respectively.

"Absolutely!" Hardacre declared with a cackle. "Chock full of mysteries and adventures for the takin'. I told ye I'd show ye how to be an adventurer, Livy Girl. Well, this here"—he patted the trunk—"is the key. An' I'm givin' it to you an' Max!"

"Wow!"

"Can we open it?"

"Samuel P., don't you dare!"

"Well, dammit. Here we go again."

Author's Note

I hope you enjoyed the story of Cordelia's and Hart's True Desires half as much as I did the writing of it. The glory of love is the power it has to change our hearts and transform our lives . . . to make us whole. It is a particular joy to bring to readers two characters who have become so real and vibrant to me.

Rest assured that the details of time and place are as authentic as research can make them. The old Tampa Bay Hotel, once the winter playground of the rich and powerful, exists today as part of the University of Tampa campus and looks much the same. The Plant Steamship Line, part of the Henry B. Plant empire of railroads, ships, and real estate, was discontinued years ago. But it served Tampa and Havana with the exact ships and schedule portrayed in the book. Havana, the University of Havana, the Hotel San Miguel, and the tensions caused by "Spanish" soldiers patrolling the city are taken from archives of journalists and historians who chronicled the time leading up to what is now called the Spanish-Cuban-American War.

I was able to secure old silent film footage (from authentichistory.com) of actual battles, the capture of prisoners, naval ships, cavalry movements with Teddy Roosevelt, and stateside parades to help set the period and details. Captain John "Dynamite" O'Brien was a historical figure, a champion of the freedom of the Cuban people who repeatedly risked his life smuggling guns, ammunition, and freedom fighters into Cuba. Cubans revere him to this day. I'd like to think he would have enjoyed spiriting Cordelia and Hart away from danger and collecting a tidy little sum to help purchase weapons and supplies for his freedom loving Cuban friends.

The details of the Mexican rainforest and the area around Tecolutla in Veracruz were taken from extensive research on the ecology and culture of this remarkable part of the world. It is estimated that 10 percent of the world's biodiversity resides in the state of Veracruz, Mexico. Its unique range of climate and extraordinary topography make for an astonishing range of living organisms—including the fabulous orchids, vine/whip snakes, magnificent butterflies, and jaguars portrayed here.

Jaguars, by the way, are very curious cats. Literally. There are numerous documented cases of them following human parties for days through the jungle just to watch them. I read this before planning Cordelia and Hart's adventure and realized that some readers might think it improbable that a jaguar would follow an expedition as Cordelia and Hart's jaguar did. Once again, truth is stranger than fiction.

As to Mayan culture . . . my understanding of and respect for the Maya has changed forever the way I look at the "settling" of the New World and the flow of subsequent history. The Mayan culture was highly developed and, unlike the Aztecs and other conquered people, the Maya still exist in huge numbers and celebrate their culture. Though their written language was lost, as many as seven million still speak native Maya dialects! Mayans revere the jaguar still. There are at least two old "temples" in southern Mexico that served as centers for rites of the "knights of the jaguar," though little is known about how they were used.

And as to the ruins portrayed here, "the hills with doors" is a good description of the odd conical mounds above some of the unexplored ruins in southern Mexico. There are many areas and ruins that have yet to be explored or excavated. There truly is, as Professor Valiente says, an entire world buried beneath the sands of Mexico.

If you would like to see some of the inspirations for this book or find references for further study, I invite you to check out the "True Desires Inspiration" pages at BetinaKrahn.com.

Grace and Peace.

Betina

The Book of the Seven Delights

by

New York Times bestselling author

Betina Krahn

Abigail Merchant travels to Casablanca to search for the remnants of the Great Library of Alexandria. There, her quest becomes entangled with the fate of a handsome ex-legionnaire. Arrogant, brash Apollo Smith hardly inspires trust…but he certainly inspires unladylike thoughts. Together they search for the remnants of the great library, but a host of vengeful legionnaires and greedy bandits is soon on their trail, threatening to put an end to the sensual delights they have just begun to discover.

0-515-13972-6